Sanctuary

Sanctuary
by Allen Steele

Copyright © 2021 by Coyote Steele, LLC
Interior art Copyright © 2021 by Rob Caswell

"Prologue" (originally titled "Sanctuary") was first published on Tor.com, May 2017.
"Part One: Starship Mountain" (in slightly different form) was originally published in *Asimov's Science Fiction*, July/August 2018.
"Part Two: The Lost Testament" (in slightly different form) was originally published in *Asimov's Science Fiction*, March/April 2019.
"Part Three: Escape from Sanctuary" (in slightly different form) was originally published in *Asimov's Science Fiction*, November/December 2019.
"Part Four: The Palace of Dancing Dogs" (in slightly different form) was originally published in *Asimov's Science Fiction*, January/February 2020.

This is a work of fiction. All the characters and events portrayed in this book are either fictitious or are used fictitiously.

All rights reserved. Printed in the United States of America. No part of this publication may be reproduced, stored in a retrieval system, or transmitted in any form or by any means, digital, electronic, mechanical, photocopying, recording, or otherwise, or conveyed via the internet or a website without prior written permission of the publisher, except in the case of brief quotations embodied in critical articles and reviews.

Fantastic Books
1380 East 17 Street, Suite 2233
Brooklyn, New York 11230
www.FantasticBooks.biz

Simultaneous hardcover and trade paperback publication
Hardcover ISBN: 978-1-5154-4773-3
Trade Paperback ISBN: 978-1-5154-4774-0

First Edition

In Memory of Fallen Friends:

David Hartwell

Gardner Dozois

Susan Casper

Harlan Ellison

Susan Ellison

Jerry Pournelle

Contents

Prologue. 11
Part One: Starship Mountain. 29
Interlude. 85
Part Two: The Lost Testament. 103
Interlude. 163
Part Three: Escape from Sanctuary. 169
Interlude. 225
Part Four: The Palace of Dancing Dogs.. 237
Epilogue. 301
Acknowledgements.. 307

TAWCETY (aka "Tau Ceti e") (aka "Bakkah")

A.H. (anno humanitus) 532

- Major Settlements
- Active Volcanic Region

Map by Rob Caswell, after Adam Steece

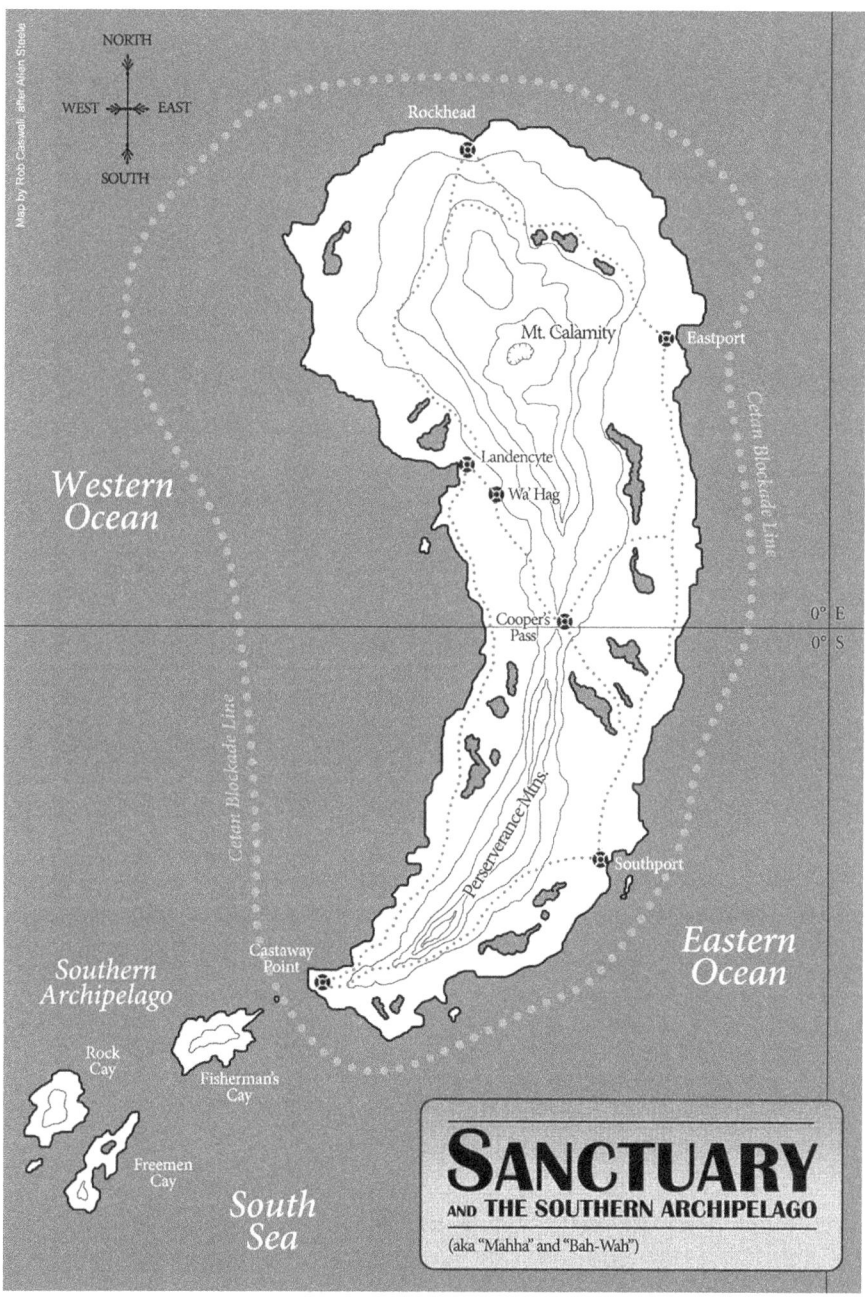

Prologue

Log Entries, EPSS *Lindbergh*

[*What follows are extracts from the remains of the logbook of the Exodus Project Starship (EPSS)* Lindbergh. *These logs are archived in the rare books collection of the Landencyte Historical Society. Some log entries are missing. Corrections and additional text in brackets where appropriate.*]

10.25.2266 rel/1232 ST/le879/Y. [Yvonne] Greer, CO
[*Third day after expedition rendezvous with Tau Ceti-e.*]
   No consensus yet from the flight crews of either ship about the naming of this world, although Capt. [Juan] Mendoza notes that majority opinion on *Santos-Dumont* favors "New Earth." Juan agrees with me that the issue is best left undecided until all the passengers on both ships are revived and a vote can be taken. He suggests a "best name" contest, but I think not. I've met some of the expedition's wittier colonists; if it were up to me, they'd remain in biostasis for a while. Kidding.
   Orbital survey complete. Results confirm—with one very notable exception!—those received from the flyby probe. Radius: 1.8 Earth (11,480 km). Mass: 4.3 Earth. Av. surface temp: 8.85°C/47.3°F. Surface gravity: 1.33g. Atmosphere: 21.2% O_2/76.8% N_2 (w/ trace amounts of CO_2, H, He, Ar, and other constituents), av. press. 926 mb. There's more (ref. Doc. LR2705) but the good news is that TC-e appears to be what the probe said it to be: a habitable planet, albeit nearly twice as large as Earth and with a slightly higher surface gravity. Although TC-e's orbit is only .54 AU from its primary, lower atmospheric pressure may account for surface temperatures that rate lower than previously estimated. Northern latitudes are quite cold, but equatorial regions are rather balmy. Whether the planet is human-habitable, though, needs to be confirmed by the landing teams.
   Which leads us to the notable exception: TC-e appears to be inhabited.
   Optical instruments on both *Lindbergh* and *Santos-Dumont* have revealed what appears to be cleared land, settlements, and connecting roads on TC-e's major land masses, mainly near coastal areas but elsewhere as well. Faint illumination has been detected from these areas at night, along with heat signatures and $CO/CO_2/CH_4$ plumes consistent with the burning of organic materials.

Absence of visible cities, electromagnetic emissions of artificial origin, or spectrographic evidence of large-scale use of fossil fuels led the probe's AI to report that TC-e has no intelligent life. This judgement now appears to be in error. Although they don't appear to possess advanced technology, nonetheless the planet is populated by an indigenous civilization.

The reason for this major omission of fact is obvious, if in hindsight. Since the Tau Ceti probe was dependent on beamsail propulsion, it wasn't designed to decelerate and go into orbit around TC-e, but instead sped through the system at .2c, never approaching TC-e closer than approx. 250,000 km. Therefore, in the few hours the probe was able to spend surveying TC-e from a distance, it was unlikely to spot the more subtle signs of habitation that only became visible after prolonged study from close orbit.

Too late to do anything about it now. Eleven and a half l.y. is a long way to come just to turn around and go home. Even if we could: the deuterium reserves of both ships are below 5 percent, with no easy means of refueling available. Drs. [Jane] Wolfe [*Lindbergh*] and [Lloyd] Kennedy [*Santos-Dumont*] have already begun preparing ASR [adaptive somatic regimen] infusion for the hibernating passengers so that they will be acclimated on arrival. However, both ships have agreed to delay resuscitation procedures until after a permanent landing site is selected.

Ground survey teams from *Lindbergh* and *Santos-Dumont* will make landfall later today. The *Lindbergh* team has selected an island, east of the central meridian and just south of the equator. In the meantime, the *Santos-Dumont* team will touch down on a highland plateau in the western hemisphere north of the equator. Both sites appear to be free of habitation, with little chance of the teams being observed by the indigents.

We will learn more once both sorties are complete and the respective teams have reported in.

[*The only surviving image of the twin starships* Lindbergh *and* Santos-Dumont *is a pencil and charcoal sketch rendered by the artist Sergei, an original Landencyte colonist. It depicts the two vessels in low orbit above Tau Ceti-e, with Sergei's ship, the* Lindbergh, *prominent in the foreground. It's an enormous craft of the Enzmann design, over six hundred meters long, its spherical deuterium fuel tank dwarfing the cylindrical habitation modules behind it. From the drum-shaped command module at the bow, a delta-winged shuttle—tiny by comparison—is departing from the hangar deck.*

[*Sergei rendered this sketch shortly after the expedition reached Tau Ceti, but it's unknown whether he drew it before or after the disaster. In his lesser-known role as Payload Specialist Turgenev, he was among the fifty members of* Lindbergh*'s flight crew to be revived shortly before the ship reached the Tau Ceti system.*

[*This sketch is the only known contemporary image of the* Lindbergh *and the* Santos-Dumont. *Because no photos or videos of either of the two vessels survive, this makes Sergei's artwork unique, priceless, and irreplaceable.*]

10.25.2266 rel/1847 ST/le881/J. [Julius] Fletcher, Senior Scientist (NOTE: log entry 880 is missing.)

Landfall successfully achieved on Landing Site 1A at 1602 hrs. ST by shuttle *Orville*.

Landing Site 1A is an open stretch of terrain on the west coast of a large equatorial island (I1) midway between Continent 3 (C3) and Continent 1 (C1) in Tau Ceti-e's eastern and western hemispheres respectively. LS1A was selected because of the availability of level ground suitable for a safe landing and also because of the apparent absence of intelligent habitation.

I1 is approximately 325 kilometers in length, 110 kilometers at its broadest point, with a tapering shape suggesting (as noted by [*Lindbergh* biologist Tonya] Van Pelt) a chili pepper. A volcanic mountain range runs lengthwise down its center, a sign that the island may be an exposed seamount created by an ancient volcanic eruption. Lack of seismic activity indicates that the three volcanoes in the range are dormant or extinct.

Tests confirm that the atmosphere is thin but breathable, with no indications of toxicity; strenuous activity should be avoided by colonists until they're thoroughly acclimated. Biochemical tests of plant samples indicate that the chirality of their amino acids is uniformly "right-handed," and therefore non-lethal to human life. No indications yet of hostile animal life, although this can only be determined by longer and more detailed surveys.

Island 1's environment is surprisingly Earth-like: trees, underbrush, lichen, and even small animal (such as birds and lizards) not dissimilar to that of our own world. The temperature at the equator is comfortably warm without being unbearable. Forests appear to cover most of the island; at least one species of tree, somewhat resembling an oak but taller, bears fruit.

Other factors are more troublesome. Higher gravity manifests itself as an increase in body weight by about 30 percent. Physical effort is therefore more difficult; even walking more than a short distance is tiresome. The three weeks the flight crew spent in microgravity following revival from biostasis doesn't help. And the lower atmospheric pressure makes things worse. At Dr. Wolfe's insistence, we took frequent breaks; future survey teams should factor in rest periods.

First sortie lasted 2 hours, 31 minutes. Survey team returned to *Orville* over objections by Van Pelt and [*Lindbergh* astrogeologist Paul] Johnson, both of whom expressed a strong desire to remain longer despite Dr. Wolfe's concerns. Efforts to avoid cross-contamination included wearing isolation suits; helmets were not removed until it was certain that the air was fit to breathe and unlikely to contain any indigenous microorganisms harmful to human life. Outer hull of the *Orville* was contaminated by soil kicked up by the VTOLs upon final descent, but it's expected that native bacteria or viruses will be eliminated by exposure to radiation and hard vacuum prior to rendezvous and docking with the *Lindbergh*.

Liftoff scheduled for 1900. All members eager to return at a later time.

Conclusion: Tau Ceti-e appears to be human-habitable, but I strongly recommend a period of physical development and ASR before the colonists are brought down. Even then, it may take a generation before humans are thoroughly acclimated to this world.

[*Log entries 882-888 lost.*]

10.26.2266 rel/0047 ST/le889/Y. Greer, CO

Orville has returned to *Lindbergh*, with Julius reporting a successful mission. I stayed up through third watch to monitor both his mission and Manny Cortez's sortie to Landing Site 6A. I read Julius's summary with no small amusement. I understand his desire to adhere to mission protocols, but I can imagine his team's frustration at landing on what appears to be an island paradise, only to have to stay in their isolation gear

—at least Julius finally let them remove their helmets!—and leave after just two and a half hours. No wonder Tonya and Paul argued with him.

Still, he managed to get his people back on the boat. Juan tells me that Manny's team has insisted on staying longer. They didn't lift off from LS6A until four hours after touchdown and still en route to *Santos-Dumont*. Wanted to stay awhile and pick mountain flowers, I guess.

Both Julius and Manny agree that it will take considerable physical effort for colonists to adapt to TC-e's higher gravity and thinner atmosphere. Fortunately, both ships can be inhabited by all 2,000 passengers for a short period of time. We can use that period—Jane recommends 30 to 60 days at least—to put everyone through an exercise regimen. It'll be difficult in zero-g, but she assures me that it can be done. Looks like the treadmills down in the rec room are about to become essential equipment.

All and all, not a bad beginning. The bottom line is that Tau Ceti-e is human-habitable; this is a relief to everyone. But we've got a long way to go before we can start ferrying down 2,000 people… and we still haven't dealt with the question of what the neighbors will think.

Something to sleep on. I'm off to bed.

[Log entries 890-893 lost.]

10.26.2266 rel/0929 ST/le894/G. [Giovanni] Patini, shuttle pilot

Second survey mission to TC-e scrubbed. *Orville* control systems not responding to preflight checks. Mechanical difficulty of unknown nature.

Santos-Dumont has scrubbed its second sortie as well. Same reason: *Wilbur* unable to launch. Spoke to Jake [Moore, *Wilbur* shuttle pilot]; says the same thing happened to him during preflight checks. Cockpit comp screens went dark, manual controls refused to budge.

Weird.

[Log entries 895-911 lost.]

10.27.2266 rel/1136 ST/le912/Y. Greer, CO

Tonya and Aaron [Willig, *Lindbergh* astrobiologist] inform me that TC-e's native civilization may be more advanced than previously believed. This could spell trouble.

Until now, it's been thought that the inhabitants are at a pre-technological stage of development, with perhaps no more than an agrarian culture. This was the opinion of our science team after studying the coastal settlements on TC-e's major continents while waiting for technicians on both ships to ascertain the causes for the shuttle breakdowns and effect repairs (ref. Doc. L2713). However, further telescopic observations confirm the existence of large ocean-sailing craft, with some appearing to be two- or three-mast catamarans. This is evidence that the "Cetans" (as Tonya calls them) have learned to harness wind power and build seafaring vessels. It is therefore possible that the Cetans may be engaged in fishing and trade, perhaps even at global distances.

One observation in particular has caused immediate concern. Julius reports that among the native vessels is a large, three-masted catamaran that was spotted off the coast of C3. This craft has steadily and consistently changed position with each orbit *Lindbergh* makes. It appears to be on an east-by-southeast heading that, in a couple of more days, will bring it to Island 1, approx. 900 km west of C3.

Since (a.) I1 is thought to be uninhabited and (b.) C3 lies on the ground track *Orville* took while making atmospheric entry, Julius believes that inhabitants may have spotted our shuttle and that this ship may be following the course it took. Certainly the stratospheric vapor trail, however short-lived, would provide a good direction-indicator. Even if the Cetans have been previously unaware of I1's existence, if their ship finds the island and its crew goes ashore to investigate, they may find evidence of the science team's visit (e.g. blast marks left behind by *Orville*'s engines, impressions of landing gear, footprints, etc.).

I will meet with Julius, Tonya, and Aaron later today, to hear their recommendations for how and when to make further sorties. I may also follow Julius's recommendation, and revive certain passengers who have psychological or sociological expertise that may be useful to us if we are indeed facing a first-contact situation.

However, given the fact that the Cetans have a considerably lower technological level than our own, I'm not greatly concerned. I'm confident that, if necessary, we can establish a colony on TC-e that is far enough out of their way that we can avoid contact with them until such a time when both of our civilizations are ready. And even if contact is unavoidable, I strongly doubt that the Cetans will pose a threat to us. Like other native inhabitants encountered by EP expeditions, this is a primitive race; I don't think we'll have much trouble with them.

However, this is not my most urgent problem just now. Crew members are reporting electronic and mechanical failures throughout the CM [Command Module]. The trouble that started yesterday aboard *Orville* seems to spreading through *Lindbergh*'s forward section, and while the breakdowns appeared at first to be random, their frequency and locations now suggest an emerging pattern.

So far, the CC [Command Center] hasn't been affected, nor have any failures been reported in the modules aft of the MFT [Main Fuel Tank]. But I've got [*Lindbergh* Chief Engineer] Kyle [Bennis] on the case, and I'm expecting a preliminary report from him shortly.

[Log entry 913 lost.]

10.27.2266 rel/1201 ST/le914/Y. Greer, CO

Addendum to le912: Juan reports nearly identical situation aboard *Santos-Dumont*. Situation there even worse; CM has begun to experience widespread failures as well.

[Log entries 915-920 lost.]

10.27.2266 rel/1704 ST/le921/Y. Greer, CO

Communications lost with *Santos-Dumont*.

During my last verbal exchange with Capt. Mendoza, he said that his ship is in serious trouble, with widespread equipment failures occurring at an increasing rate. Before contact was lost, *Lindbergh* received diagnostic telemetry indicating rapidly declining control over major systems. Then the blackout occurred.

Breakdowns now occurring aboard *Lindbergh* as well. Because the first incident was *Orville*'s failure, and the subsequent incidents appear to have begun in the shuttle bay and spread outward from there, it's believed that the survey team may have carried something up from TC-e. Since the team wore isolation gear and underwent decontamination procedures upon their return, the leading hypothesis is that the source of contamination may be the shuttle itself.

* * *

[*Log entries 922- 930 lost.*]

10.28.2266 rel/0315 ST/le931/K. Bennis, CE

Something is attacking *Lindbergh*'s control systems.

Over the past twenty-four hours, we've experienced 49 logged failures, along with countless others that crew members haven't recorded, of electronic and mechanical components. These failures are increasing at an exponential rate, and it is clear that a cascade effect has begun to take place, with even the smallest occurrences causing systemic problems that become more serious as they go down the line.

The attacks appear to be occurring at a microscopic level. Plastic and rubber components are losing their integrity. They are literally rotting away, like ripe fruit that's fallen from the tree to the ground and left to lie there. Once an object starts to lose its integrity, the rate of decay is rapid and cannot be halted.

The first indication that an object has been affected by the Rot (as crew members are calling this) are tiny holes that appear in its surface. This is a sign that the hypothetical microorganism responsible for this has found the object and begun to tunnel into it, eating its way through the object. If the object is electronic equipment, this causes failure as soon as the Rot makes its way to the insulation surrounding the wiring or printed circuits. By then, the object has become so brittle that it can be easily broken. A data pad can be snapped in half between two hands.

Everything from computer chips to ink pens to cookware is being affected. If something that has the Rot comes into direct contact with something else, the microorganism jumps from one object to another. People don't seem to be directly harmed by it (unless they're wearing dental implants that have some sort of enamel in them, such as posts or bridgework; at least three crew members have already lost teeth this way). However, any articles of clothing made of artificial fibers are likely to deteriorate as well. I've seen shirts, shoes, and trousers literally fall off the people wearing them. Funny at first, but no longer something to laugh about.

I'm recording this entry on a pad that I'm keeping in my T-shirt pocket (100% cotton) and being careful not to touch unless I've first washed my hands. However, I don't think this solution will work very much longer.

I've sent Sergei down to ship's stores to collect as many pencils and paper notepads as he can possibly find, and I'm recommending that recent log entries pertinent to this crisis be printed out ASAP while we still have the ability to do so.

[*Log entries 932-936 lost.*]

10.28.2266 rel/0755 ST/le937/Y. Greer, CO

Santos-Dumont has been destroyed.

For whatever reason—no, scratch that; we know the reason—Capt. Mendoza's crew lost control of their ship. I'm sure they must have tried to regain altitude control, but its orbit steadily decayed. As my people watched from the CC, *Santos-Dumont* entered TC-e's upper atmosphere as an immense fireball and broke apart. So far as we can tell, there were no survivors.

One thousand lives lost. No time to grieve, though. Not if we're going to save our own lives.

Santos-Dumont was in a lower orbit than *Lindbergh*. This gives us a little more time. On the assumption that Kyle's hypothesis is correct, I've ordered the CS [Core Shaft] and other access tunnels leading aft sealed in order to protect the MFT and hibernation modules. I'm also hoping that the cryogenic temperatures in the MFT will retard the Rot's spread. I don't know if these efforts to keep the Rot confined to the CM will work, though, for I have little doubt that Juan tried the same thing. However, perhaps they will buy us a little more time... or so we all hope.

[*Log entries 938-941 lost.*]

10.28.2266 rel/0921 ST/le942/Y. Greer, CO

This may be my last electronic log entry. On Kyle's advice, I've printed out as many previous entries, by myself and others, as I could. The CC printer is still operational, but only by a miracle. Once this entry is done, I'll print it out as well and add it to the stack. Further entries will be entered longhand with pencil and paper.

In short: *Lindbergh* is doomed.

Nearly all major CM control systems either fail to operate or are on the verge of total failure. This includes *Lindy*'s flight control systems as well as power and life support. Emergency batteries and a few flashlights are all that stand between us and the cold and total darkness. I'm keeping warm only because I had the foresight to bring the thick wool sweater my grandmother knitted for me many years ago. At least I'm still clothed. Our uniforms have fallen apart, and some crew members are wearing only cotton underwear or whatever they've managed to wrap around themselves.

Before they lost their lab instruments, Julius, Tonya, and Aaron were able to study the Rot enough to come up with a tentative theory. It appears to be a native microorganism that feeds on substances derived from organic petrochemicals, ethylene and polyethylene in particular. In doing so, it breaks down anything made of these kinds of plastic. Perhaps it evolved on TC-e as a natural response to the decay of organic substances, a biological alternative to the fossilization of dead organic material that eventually allowed humans to develop fossil fuels and their byproducts.

If this is indeed the case, then the Rot is in the planet's very soil, and therefore contact and transmission to *Lindbergh* and *Santos-Dumont* was unavoidable. Our expedition was doomed the moment the shuttles touched down. The Rot was probably carried back to the ships within the wheel wells of the shuttles' landing gear, which would have sheltered them from the sterilizing effects of outer space. Without the ability to study this further, though, we may never know for certain.

It's obvious that *Lindy* isn't going to be around very much longer. Since this vessel hasn't any lifeboats other than our shuttles, both of which are no longer flightworthy, then abandoning ship isn't an option.

Fortunately, we aboard the *Lindbergh* have one last chance. If we act quickly, we may be able to save our lives and those of our passengers… or at least some of them.

There is no time to explain. I'm printing out as much of the logbook as I can and taking it with me. With any luck, this will not be my final entry.

[*The remaining log entries are written in pencil on loose pages from a paper notepad whose plastic binding has long since dissolved. The dates and times are uncertain, and without an automatic numbering system their order can be determined by the events described. Underlined text in the original.*]

* * *

<u>10/28/'66 1032 Lind./YG</u>

Have transferred command to SOC [Secondary Operations Center], Deck 10, HM1 [Hibernation Module 1]. CM has been completely abandoned. All members of flight crew present and accounted for.

I ordered Core Inspection Shaft B reopened just long enough for everyone to push themselves down the tunnel through the MFT until we reached HM1, then the hatches were closed at both ends and the shaft was vented to space. I also ordered the crew to bring nothing—<u>nothing!</u>—with them except the clothes on their backs (if they still have any to wear… we're all barefoot now, and some crew members are either naked or nearly so). Most personal belongings were left behind, especially if they were made from or contained any sort of plastic materials. Only a few items were brought (Sergei insisted on his sketch pad, which I've allowed).

Hopefully, these measures will keep the Rot away from the rest of Lindbergh for the time it takes us to do what needs to be done.

Lindy doesn't have lifeboats, but its designers did not leave the ship entirely helpless. Realizing that it may be possible that the main engines could experience some kind of major C1 [Criticality 1] malfunction, they took the precaution of making it possible for the crew to jettison the MEM [Main Engine Module] and detach HM1, HM2, and HM3 together as a single unit. These three modules can then be maneuvered away from the rest of the ship via reaction-control thrusters and deorbited under control from the SOC. Once the stack aerobrakes and achieves successful atmospheric entry, it can be brought to a safe landing via retrorockets at the base of HM3 and parachutes on top of HM1.

This is all theoretical, of course. No attempt was ever made to rehearse the procedure while any of the Exodus Project ships were under construction. So no one knows if this will actually work. Nonetheless, my training included this contingency, and Kyle, Floyd [McGee, helmsman], and Susan [Kim, navigator] assure me that they practiced it as well… although Floyd admits that he and Susie rehearsed this procedure just <u>once</u> during training, and no one took it very seriously at the time. I've requested that they take it seriously now.

Tonya and Aaron are helping Dr. Wolfe prepare the biostasis cells. They will be switched to emergency power just before the MEM is jettisoned, but on Jane's advice, the passengers will remain in hibernation until after we land. To revive them now, in the midst of a crisis, would only disorient them and perhaps cause a panic. We can only pray that the Rot stays away from this end of the ship until we're on the ground. While the passengers are still in their cells, they're intubated and hooked up to IV lines and catheters, all of which need to be removed before the Rot can get to them. But not now.

I've consulted Julius about possible landing sites. He agrees with me that LS1A is our best bet: it's on the equator, isolated, and has been surveyed already. I've ordered Floyd and Susie to plot our emergency landing there.

Running as fast as we can. No sign of Rot, but that won't last long.

10/28/'66 1147 YG

MEM jettisoned. Module stack successfully detached. Deorbit burn achieved. We're on our way down.

Last look at ship. CM dark. No control possible.

Lindy will soon tumble into atmosphere. Got out of there in nick of time. Goodbye, ship.

Fingers crossed. Praying.

10/28/'66 1732 LS1A/YG

We have landed on Island 1, with our touchdown point close enough to LS1A that it's virtually the same. Commendations to Floyd and Susan for superb plotting and piloting. We all owe them for our lives.

Landing was successful, but the touchdown was very hard. The parachutes and retrorockets were just adequate enough to keep it from being a crash. Floyd tells me that, in the last seconds of descent, it felt as the planet just reached up and yanked us down. The stack remained upright and didn't fall over on its side, but there's a five-degree list to one side that suggests it won't remain vertical indefinitely. We will need to evacuate what's left of our ship as soon as we can.

No fatalities, but many injuries: broken bones, spine injuries, concussions, severe bruises, etc. Jane has drafted every able-bodied crew member to help tend to the injured. They take priority over the passengers, but Jane insists that the biostasis cells be opened as soon as possible. She continues to be concerned about how the Rot will affect the cells, and I can't blame her. The idea of a plastic breathing tube disintegrating while it's still in someone's trachea makes me shiver.

For this reason, we're leaving the hatches closed for as long as we can, so as not to expose ourselves to the native environment until all the injured have been treated and the passengers have been revived. It appears that the modules' outer hulls are Rot-resistant; thank God, no one ever figured out how to build plastic starships!

But the stack won't remain airtight for very much longer. Although Kyle was among the injured, he took it upon himself to inspect the lower decks in HM3 as soon as he was able to make it down a companionway. He confirms that the Rot has already attacked the seals on the outer airlock hatches, and he doubts that the modules will retain atmospheric integrity much longer.

Since we have only about 24 hours of air left to us anyway, this means we'll have to pop the hatches... well, sooner than we like. Once the Rot gets in, it's only a matter of time before the emergency lights start going out. Then we'll be trapped in a dark, skyscraper-size tower that's slowly falling apart from the inside out. Like it or not, we've got to leave this place, but soon.

Welcome to Tau Ceti-e. And we still haven't decided what to call this damn planet.

10/29/'66 1201 LS1A/YG

We opened the hatches earlier this morning. We had no choice. The Rot was coming in.

After Kyle and Floyd reported signs of Rot in the passageways outside the HM3 airlocks, Jane and her "nurses"—namely, anyone able to use a first-aid kit and wasn't busy doing something else—worked like madmen all through the night to unseal the biostasis cells and resuscitate the passengers. There were 16 fatalities, people who'd suffered critical injuries during landing and therefore perished in hibernation. We can only hope they died while still asleep and didn't suffer much. A number of other passengers have been less severely injured, but most of those cases were relatively minor, and they received treatment as soon as possible.

Note: Jane points that most of her medical equipment will become useless as soon as it's contaminated by the Rot. This includes not only diagnostic equipment, but also surgical supplies such as ampules, sutures, etc. We can also expect to lose some medicine as well, mainly those contained in gellcaps. She continues to treat her patients as best as she can but believes that she will soon be reduced to 19th century medical techniques.

At 1015, a couple of hours after sunrise, Julius, Tonya, Kyle, and myself went down to Deck HM3-15 and found an airlock that was already decompressed. It was unsettling to find a breeze coming in through an open porthole whose seals had failed, letting the glass fall out. Blowout training instinctively took hold, and I started to reach for an air mask, but what I pulled out of the cabinet disintegrated in my hands. This sort of thing is now happening throughout what remains of my ship.

The four of us pushed open the hatch and climbed out, and for a minute or so none of us said anything. We just stood beneath the long shadow of the module stack and looked about at our new home, a world we'll never leave again.

TC-e is beautiful: I will give it that. It ought to be. We've sacrificed much to come here.

<u>10/29/'66 1642 LS1/YG</u>

We won't be alone very much longer. The Cetans are coming.

I'd just finished rigging a canvas tarp as a temporary shelter for myself —as Captain, I rate that, at least; some of our people aren't so lucky to have even this little—when Giovanni came running back from the beach, where he and Tonya had gone to assess the likelihood of being able to do some net-fishing (for whatever passes for fish on this world). What they reported caused everyone drop whatever they were doing and run or limp down to the black-sand, boulder-strewn shore, where we gazed across the dark blue water at what they'd spotted.

Sails on the horizon. The ship we spotted from orbit a couple of days ago, all but forgotten until now.

The inhabitants of the nearest neighboring continent spotted *Orville* and sent a vessel to investigate. Now the ship is in sight of us, and while it's still hard to estimate distances on a world where the sea-level horizon is so much farther away than it is back home—damn it, <u>this</u> is home now! I must remember that!—I'm guessing it will be off the coast of our nameless little island by the end of the day.

Whoever the Cetans, whatever form they take, they'll find a shipwrecked alien crew: reduced, confused, near-naked, frightened, utterly defenseless. Explorers turned refugees, uninvited immigrants.

I've just looked at one of my earlier log entries, the one I wrote shortly after we discovered that TC-e is inhabited, and it's both embarrassing to see the arrogant contempt with which I regarded the Cetans because of their "primitive" technology. Not to mention ironic. Now we know why they don't have the things we have… and they no longer seem so primitive, do they?

All we can do now is await their arrival. I pray that they're friendly, and that they will offer us sanctuary.

Part One:
STARSHIP MOUNTAIN

I

When you're young, at some point you're bound to develop the belief that you've got the whole world figured out. This determination usually comes in stages and in different ways, but the result is always the same: *I know how everything works, and nobody can tell me anything that I don't already know. And the fact is, the world could be a much better place if everyone would only listen to* me.

Be honest: that thought has occurred to you, hasn't it?

This sort of confidence is the blessing of youth, but it comes with an equal and opposite corollary: the inevitable discovery, sooner or later, of just how wrong you are. Not only do you know nothing, but you're only *beginning* to know nothing.

With luck, you outgrow the arrogance of youth and take it upon yourself to learn the ways of the world. Because if you don't, the lessons you'll be taught will be harsh indeed.

There was someone waiting outside my flat when I returned from the swordsmith. My blades needed a good sharpening, both the saber and the short sword, and while I know how to use a whetstone as well as any other licensed sword-owner, it's good to have the professional touch. Less time-consuming, too; the neighborhood smithy had a grindwheel and I didn't, and sharpening by hand can take hours. I was between jobs just then, so I figured that it was a good time to make sure my blades had that razor-sharp quality that can make all the difference in a serious fight.

So I wasn't anticipating a visit from a prospective client. Not so soon, at least. Only last week, I'd settled a domestic-magic case in which a townswoman had hired me to investigate why her husband of twenty-plus years was no longer, shall we say, interested in her, not the way a husband should be. She believed that a neighbor's spouse, to whom her husband had been lately paying an inordinate amount of attention, had enlisted the services of a magus to cast an enchantment upon the gent.

This was her explanation for her husband's straying eye. I could have given her a much more prosaic reason, but dispensing common sense is not why people hire me. So I wasted several days questioning the mages in Landencyte who perform that kind of sexmagic—illegal, but nonetheless it's done—and when all attested that none of them had anything to do with either the accused perpetrator or the alleged victim, and a visit to the neighbor's home failed to turn up any of the talismans one would expect—a lock of the husband's hair or his fingernail cuttings—I was forced to report to my client that her husband's lack of enthusiasm might possibly have a non-supernatural explanation. The lady had just about accepted my explanation when I made the mistake of suggesting that the solution to her problem might be to pay closer attention to personal appearance and hygiene.

My clients don't usually slap me, but at least I was paid. And although the Cetan gold that I collected from her didn't make my face feel any better, at least it was sufficient to pay the rent for the rest of Wintermonth. Now all I had to do was find another job that would keep me in food and ale, and I'd be all set.

I'd just about reached the top of stairs above the vintner's shop when, by the morning light streaming in through the skylight, I perceived a pair of booted legs projecting from the wooden chair I'd placed in the hall outside my door. The boots weren't the sort that would be worn by a woman, and since most revenuers, magistrates, and jealous husbands aren't female, this meant one of three things: trouble, a job, or both.

I took a deep breath, regretted not having my blades—bad day to take them to the smithy—and climbed the rest of the way upstairs. The fourth riser from the top was a little loose; I purposely kept it that way because it creaked whenever someone set foot on it. Although I habitually avoided doing the same, my visitor heard me coming. He stood up as I reached the landing.

"Citizen Crowe? Jeremy Crowe?"

I took a second to size him up. If he was the husband of a woman I'd met in a tavern or someone who'd come to collect money, I could always tell him he had the wrong place, Citizen Crowe had moved on. Sometimes it worked. If it was someone from the magistrate's office, though, there would be no such luck; Landencyte's badges all knew who I was and where I lived, so there wouldn't be any sense pretending otherwise.

But he wasn't the law. I saw that at once. An older man about my age, dressed for cool weather in a hooded street cape, silk shirt, waistcoat, leggings, and riding boots, he didn't have a scabbard on his hip or back, and he wasn't big enough to be a goon. And the badges wouldn't ask my name; they knew that, too, even the ones who hadn't been on the force when I still wore a badge myself.

Had to be a prospective client. At least so I hoped. I could always use the money.

"That's me. And to whom do I have the honor?"

"Bolland Conklin, Steward of House Fletcher." The slightest of bows, as befitting a gentleman of Landencyte's upper class, and a Steward at that. "I understand that you're a… a…"

"A dick? Yes, I'm a dick."

He let out his breath and nodded, relieved that he'd found the right man. Not surprising. Dicks—personal affairs investigators, if you want to be formal about it—tend not to advertise, but instead let their clients find them by word of mouth. That's how I worked, too. "Good, very good. I was told you could assist me in finding—"

"Let's talk about this in private, shall we, Steward?" I didn't like discussing business in the hallway. I had neighbors, and not all of them I could trust to keep from eavesdropping.

I unlocked the door with the iron key on my belt fob and let us in. My flat had two rooms: an office up front and a small apartment off to the side, separated by a black felt curtain embroidered with a mountain squawk taking wing. It was the only thing in the place that looked pretty. I tried to keep the office neat, but the apartment couldn't help but be a wreck; I slept, ate, and changed clothes in that room, and the curtain—a housewarming gift from my ex, one of the last remnants of our marriage—barely hid my private life from my public space. It helped a little that its windows faced west; the morning sun wasn't coming in, and I decided that lighting a lamp would reveal more about myself than I wanted.

"Have a seat, please." I waved Steward Conklin to one of the two battered armchairs facing the equally beat-up desk. "May I take your cape?"

"No, thank you." He eyed the coat rack by the door as if expecting a hidden panel behind it to suddenly open and make his expensive garment disappear. He was keeping his cape on, and as he sat down, I caught a glimpse of the reason why: a small flintlock in a holster on his right, powder bag dangling beside it, and a matching dagger in a scabbard on his left.

Steward Conklin of House Fletcher obviously wasn't taking any chances while visiting the rough side of town. He knew that a rich fellow like him stuck out in the Squat, Landencyte's black market and red-light district; down here, even a member of the Council of Stewards was fair game. And the pistol showed that he must have considerable pull with the magistrates, not to mention the Guardians. Possessing and carrying firearms was against the law for Citizens and even most Stewards; guns were one thing Cetans didn't want a lot of humans to own. I had a gun, but the badges would pick me up in a heartbeat if they knew about it, and I tried to be careful about not letting Cetans see it.

"Very well. So what can I do for you, Steward?" I hung up my coat and walked around my desk. My chair groaned as I sat down; like the desk, the coat rack, and just about every other stick of furniture in the place, it was second-hand and needed to be replaced. Fat chance. I seldom made enough money to buy anything new.

Conklin glanced at the curtain as if making sure there was no one in the apartment. Last week, he would've been right to do so, but she'd decided that I wasn't really her type and had returned to her old boyfriend, or was it her husband? Satisfied that we were alone, he looked at me again.

"I want you to find someone," he said.

That wasn't a surprise. There were about a half-dozen reasons why people came to me; tracking down a missing person usually ranked second or third on the list, the first being the one thing I'd never do: kill someone. Well, *maybe* never....

"And who might that be?" I asked, as if I couldn't guess; it had to be a son, daughter, or wife.

"My daughter," he replied, and I tried not to smile. "Her name is Pilot... Pilot Fletcher, since she is still unmarried."

"Engaged?" If Pilot was old enough for her father to feel like I needed to be aware of her marital status, then she probably was. Young ladies from Sanctuary's major houses usually got hitched pretty fast, particularly if their families had money and status.

"Yes—" Conklin quickly raised a finger "—but before you ask, no, she did not elope. I've spoken with the young man in question, and I'm convinced that he's telling the truth when he says that he doesn't know where she is."

Conklin was trying to be helpful by eliminating a possible suspect, but all he did was make me want to meet the fiancé. Even if he wasn't responsible, he still might know something. "How about if we started at the beginning?" I said, making my chair protest again as I leaned back in it. "Tell me about your daughter. Who is she, and when did she go missing?"

II

Pilot Fletcher was a young lady as fresh-faced and innocent as you'd expect from a child of privilege who'd grown up in the Heights. She'd never been in trouble, her father told me, save perhaps for the usual mischief you'd expect, like dumping garbage from a rooftop on a passing Cetan or sneaking down to the Squat to try to get into the taprooms. Until lately, that kind of adolescent misbehavior had been the closest she'd come to rebellion.

But then she grew older, and all that changed. "She'd been a cheerful, obedient girl," Conklin said. "A good student in school—"

"Overlook?" I asked, and he nodded. An obvious question: Overlook Academy was a prestigious private school in the Heights, open only to the scions of Steward families and a small handful of Citizen kids who got in under patronage. "Go on."

"As I was saying, Pilot has been everything my wife and I could ask for in a daughter. A credit to the house, too. We were expecting to marry her out to another house and believed that this would happen when she met Philip Kim of House Greer."

I did my best not to visibly react. Among the houses that made up the Landencyte aristocracy, House Greer was the oldest and most prestigious. Its families had been producing Sanctuary's leader, the Cap, for so long that the position had become dynastic. In theory, the Cap was elected by the Council of Stewards, which in turn comprised the leaders of Sanctuary's eight major houses. In actual practice, though, the Caps had been coming from House Greer since anyone could remember; no one else from Landencyte or any of the other towns on the island ever won the position in those rare elections We The People get to have every now and then. So if a young lady from House Fletcher had been approached by an eligible suitor from House Greer, it meant that their parents—and their respective houses—were looking at the prospect of marrying their fortunes together. *That* would have consequences, good or bad, and even those of us who lived in the Squat would get a little bit of it.

"But over the last few months, my daughter has become increasingly… disobedient." Conklin shook his head. "No, that's not the word I'm looking for." Gazing out the window behind me, his lips pursed together. "Questioning. Free-thinking. Unwilling to accept that which she'd been taught."

Not altogether a bad thing, but I kept the thought to myself. "Do you think her relationship with Master Kim had anything to do with it?"

"No. I've spoken with Philip many times, and his views are consistent with those of his house, and mine as well." Still gazing out the window, his gaze became reflective. "No. Pilot began to withdraw from Philip as well as me. Although she still wore his engagement bangle, she began seeing less of him, and finally it became obvious that she was deliberately avoiding him. She wouldn't tell me or her mother why, and when Philip asked her about this, she claimed that she still loved him, but—"

"'Claimed'? That doesn't seem very convincing."

"It wasn't, but she still wouldn't give any reasons. And it was at that time when she began to regularly turn up missing. I'd come to see her in her room, where I thought she was reading or knitting, only to discover the balcony door open and the knotted bedsheets she'd used to climb down to the ground. At first, I thought she was just sneaking down here to the Squat—" Conklin shot me an uncertain look "—I mean, not that there's anything *wrong* about this place."

"No, of course not," I said, matching his lie with mine. Unfortunately, this was sounding like a familiar story. Pilot Fletcher wouldn't be the first kid from the Heights I'd have to bring home from the bad side of town. I just hoped I'd find her merely passed out on a tavern floor, not drugged, beaten senseless, and tied to a bed in an unlicensed brothel. Best to let him believe what he wanted, at least for a while. No sense in worrying the client with conjecture like that until… well…

Conklin reached into his cape and pulled out a scroll. He handed it to me, and I untied the ribbon and unrolled the parchment. A watercolor portrait-sketch of a young woman, curly dark hair piled up above her neck, brown eyes regarding me solemnly. As her father told me, an engagement bangle of tiny seashells laced with silver thread dangled from her left earlobe. The picture was recent; I pegged her age at thirty-six, give or take a Tawcety year or two; just old enough to marry.

I studied the portrait closely, fixing Pilot's features in my memory, then rolled up the scroll and handed it back to Conklin. It was too valuable for me to carry around, and I've got a good memory. "Nothing else? She didn't leave a note, or tell anyone where she might be going?"

"No.…"

Vague answer. He sounded like he was holding something back. "Steward Conklin," I said, "if there's anything else you think I ought to know—even if it's something you'd rather not tell me for some reason—then now's the time. I don't want to get into this only to find out later that you withheld some vital fact I should've known all along."

Conklin hesitated. Through the window, along with a cool salt breeze from the harbor, came the voices and sounds of the Squat: the cries of the fishmongers and street mages ("*Spells!* Spells for every *occ-aa-ssion!*"), the sullen *gronnnk* of a gorsch hauling a delivery cart, the mingled shouts, laughter, and arguments of Landencyte's working class. The street noise was background for me, but it made Conklin nervous. I understood. For a man like him to descend into the rough part of Landencyte, this meeting was an act of desperation.

That desperation made him admit something he probably wouldn't have revealed to a stranger. "Over the last few months," he said slowly, "Pilot has been… questioning, I suppose… certain things." He kept his voice down as he picked his words with care. "Things we've all been taught since childhood, about how people—human, that is—came to be here. On Sanctuary, I mean, but also Tawcety itself."

"She doesn't believe *The Book of Years*?"

Conklin cast a nervous glance at the door. "No," he said, almost a whisper now. "She's been lately saying that there's too many things in *The Book of Years* that don't make sense. Like why humans live on Sanctuary and nowhere else, and why we can't sail off the island. Why the Cetans are supposed to be our friends, but we're also obliged do whatever they say even though we live apart. Why *plastik* disappeared—"

"It disappeared because it was never real," I murmured.

Didn't mean to say that. Just slipped out. But Conklin's face grew hard, and he gave me an admonishing look; apparently he believed in *plastik*. Dismissively, he turned his eyes again toward the window. I kept quiet, waiting for him to continue telling me what I'd already guessed. "After she disappeared, my wife found a tract in her room, hidden in her clothes chest where she thought her mother or I wouldn't find it. My wife burned it at once. We won't allow heresy in our home, Citizen Crowe."

"Of course not, Steward Conklin. I'm sure House Fletcher always abides by Cetan Law."

He raised an eyebrow. "Then you've guessed what I found."

"*The True Origins of Landencyte*. I've seen it before. So Pilot has become an Originalist."

"She has *not*!" His eyes narrowed. "Pilot may have become curious about them, but my daughter would never… she'd never—!"

"Calm down." I raised a hand, realizing too late that I'd said the wrong thing. "You're right, she's just doing what a girl her age often does when she finds that there are… well, that there are certain things that aren't taught at Overlook, no matter how wrong they might be. My apologies for having misspoken."

Conklin held onto his anger for another moment, then slowly let out his breath. "Of course," he murmured. "Your apologies are accepted." Looking down at the floor, he shook his head. "So, will you find my daughter, Citizen Crowe?"

Naturally, I said I would. This is what I did, after all.

I told him my fee—one hundred dolas up front, with another fifty dolas per day along with expenses. I usually don't accept cheques, preferring gold coin to paper, but I decided that a note signed by a Steward was just as good, so I told Conklin he could deposit the hundred under my name at Banque Landencyte. To my surprise, though, he produced a black drawstring purse from another inside pocket of his cape. There was a satisfying clink of Cetan gold as he dropped it on my desk.

"Twenty to start, Citizen," Conklin said, pushing back his chair to stand up. "That's in addition to the hundred, which I'll deposit once I reach Merchant Street. And I expect reports by courier on a daily basis."

I refrained from picking up the purse immediately. "You'll have 'em, Steward."

He nodded, but said nothing for a moment, instead studying me speculatively. "I've been informed that you're a man who gets things done, Citizen," he said at last, looking me straight in the eye. "You'll find that I'm generous with those who serve me well—" his gaze turned cold "—and unforgiving of those who fail me."

I could have told him that I've dealt with people much more frightening than him, but I decided to let him believe that he'd intimidated me. "I'll find your daughter," I replied. "We'll discuss your generosity after you see her again."

III

The first person I wanted to talk to was the last person Pilot had probably seen, or at least besides dear ol' dad: Philip Kim. Like nearly all of the original Sanctuary families, the Kims of House Greer lived in the Heights, the seaside mesa on the north side of Landencyte.

Easy to get to, unless you're from the Squat. The average squatter, with his workingman's clothes and unsophisticated manners, stands out in the rarified society of the Heights. If you're not there on business, or forget to raise a pinky while drinking tea, you're likely to be collared by the first badge to notice that you don't fit in. If you're lucky, escorted to the top of Seaview Road, the road from the mesa to the lower part of the city. If you're not lucky, you get beat on a little, then thrown in jail until someone comes up to bribe the badges… sorry, post bail, I mean. So I'd have to fancy myself up if I didn't want to get busted for being poor.

Out of the clothes chest came my best duds, the expensive stuff I wore only on special occasions. Which is another reason why I didn't have a lot of nice things to wear; after my wife left, there weren't any special occasions. Almost everything I had was for function, not style, but I managed to find a dark purple cape and a scarlet waistcoat that didn't look bad so long as you didn't nice how old it was. My best leggings had a small hole in the butt, but my cape covered it. I'd polished my boots lately, so at least I didn't have to worry about that, and once I shaved the stubble off my face, trimmed my mustache, and knotted my hair and tucked it up under a gold-trimmed black beret I hoped was still in style, I figured I might pass for a moderately successful merchant from the Market district.

The only thing I lacked were my blades. I'd feel naked without them in the Heights, where some of the dandies like to respond to being jostled on the sidewalk by demanding a duel, but I didn't want to pick them up before they'd been sharpened; the smithy would make me pay extra. There was a cheap old saber in my closet, one I'd taken away from some guy who'd made the mistake of attacking me in my office. He'd gone to hospital and should consider himself lucky that I hadn't put him in his urn instead; I'd kept his weapon as a souvenir of our frolics. It didn't have a good balance and the blade had never been cleaned or sharpened, but it made an adequate back-up piece. I put it in a spare scabbard, slung it from my belt and covered it with the cape, and I was ready to go.

I could have walked on foot up to the Heights, but no self-respecting trader would do that. He'd take a jitney instead. So I went a few blocks, dodging the beggars, pickpockets, and drunks who made the cobblestone streets of the Squat such a charming place, and paused for a moment to buy a warm banberry bagel from a cart that looked reasonably clean. I tucked the bagel in my pocket until I reached the cab stand outside the Traveler's Rest hotel.

As I expected, a jitney was standing at the curb. The gorsch hauling it was asleep in its harness, its long neck lowered to the pavement, three eyes heavy-lidded and gazing at nothing. The Cetan drover leaned against its dark leathery flank, gnawing on a strip of bork jerky as he perused the morning *Sentinel*. He peered over the top of the broadsheet as I approached, and we recognized each other at once: me by my face, him by his pelt.

"Hello, Butch," I said, addressing him by his human name. Cetans generally don't appreciate it when our kind try to speak their language; we don't growl well enough. "How's the day?"

Butch folded the paper and took his time masticating the jerky before answering. "Well 'nuff," he drawled. "S'happenin', Crowe?" He called me by my last name because his tongue had just as much trouble with my name as mine did with his Cetan moniker; he couldn't pronounce *j*'s, and I don't growl very well.

"Need a lift up to the Heights," I replied. "Available?"

Butch didn't answer at once. Instead, he glanced back at the buckboard carriage behind the gorsch. "Emp'y," he muttered, idly scratching behind his upraised left ear. "Wan' mo' r-r-r-riders."

On one hand, I couldn't blame him. The carriage was vacant, and jitney operators preferred to carry as many passengers as possible. Fortunately, I had an answer for our problems. I produced the drawstring purse Conklin had given me, fished out a gold dola, and held it up for him to see. "That cover it?"

Butch held out his pawlike hand. I dropped the dola into it and he held it close to his muzzle, giving it a good sniff to make sure it was really Cetan gold. Some of his people brag that they're able to smell the difference between the coins they've smelted themselves and the counterfeit pyrite currency that made its way in the city from secret places elsewhere on the island. Butch was one of those guys. At least he didn't lick it, too. Satisfied, he deposited the dola in the coin purse dangling from his kilt. "R-r-r-ride back fo' *dos*," he added, getting what he wanted but trying to dicker for more.

"No." I shook my head. "Round trip, *uno*… up and back again. Paid you enough."

A low, sullen growl. He bared his fangs a little and tried to stare me down. I calmly gazed back at him and waited. A few seconds went by, then he dropped the act. "Ho'kay," he said, a smile replacing the snarl. "Good 'nuff… ge' in."

We climbed into the carriage, him up front, me in the back. He picked up the reins and shook them, saying something in his language that sounded like a yip. The gorsch woke up from its nap; raising itself upon its thick legs, it lifted its tail and dropped a fragrant load in the street, then shuffled forward, effortlessly pulling the carriage behind it. We'd already put the only hotel in the Squat behind us before the doorman appeared to start yelling at Butch about the mess his beast had left.

Once we were underway, the carriage wheels bouncing along on springs that needed to be replaced, I pulled out the bagel I'd bought and had a late breakfast as I watched the city roll by. Landencyte sprawled across Sanctuary's northwest shore like some sort of great, alien fungus… or at least I figure that's how the Cetans saw us. To my eye, this was home, in all its crowded, depraved, and sometimes awesome beauty.

In the distance, down the cobblestone streets leading to the Waterfront, I could see the tall sails of Cetan galleons anchored in the harbor, mainly trade vessels from faraway places on Tawcety few humans had ever seen. Anchored among them were the skiffs, catamarans, and sea kayaks of the local fishing fleet, the largest vessels the Guardians would permit humans to build and sail, and never more than a few miles beyond Sanctuary's coast.

Smoke rose from rooftop chimneys, carrying with it the sweet-sour scent of burning manure. Humans and Cetans alike walked the streets, neither paying that much attention to one another, avoiding casual contact unless necessary. We liked each other well enough to get along, but trust had always been in short supply. The Cetans tolerated the human presence on Sanctuary and were happy to trade with us, but they'd made it clear long ago that they preferred to keep our races apart. The Guardians saw to that, like the one the carriage rolled past. He glanced our way as we passed him, and I caught a glimpse of sharp, watchful eyes beneath the raised hood of his scarlet cape.

The Cetan enclave huddled behind a high stone wall on the southernmost edge of the city. Guardians seldom let my people past its gates, except for caravans traveling Mountain Pike on their way to the other side of the island. The Cetan name for their part of town was unpronounceable, so while it was officially known as the Native Quarter, humans privately called it Dogtown after the mythical creatures the natives were said to resemble. The Cetans considered that a dire insult, though; even calling a Cetan a dog was punishable by law. And since no human had ever seen an actual, living dog, we could only speculate why.

As the jitney moved through an intersection, I caught a glimpse of scaffolds, carpenters, and bricklayers. Another building was going up, the builders taking advantage of the cool Wintermonth days to get as much heavy work done before the warm months returned in a few weeks. Lately, the outlying parts of the Squat had become gentrified. The business class was steadily moving in from the Market at the northwest corner of the city, bringing with them jobs but also a snobbish attitude for the people who'd been living there for generations.

Landencyte has never been a pretty city, but no one could ever accuse it of being stagnant. The fungus was spreading north and south along the coast, as it had been for as long as I could remember, but there was one area that everyone avoided. On the eastern side of town, rising above the Squat without quite touching it, lay a massive hump, a long, low ridge that looked as if it had unaccountably pushed itself up from the sandy ground some ages ago.

Starship Mountain.

It was called a mountain, but actually it wasn't much more than a hill. In fact, it was no taller than the nearby mesa on which the Heights had been built. As landmarks go, though, it was the most impressive one around. About a thousand feet long and a couple of hundred feet high, its rounded flanks were covered by a layer of soil upon which trees and brush had taken root over time. The foliage gave the mountain a greenish-brown color; here and there were deep crevices, irregular and rust-red blotches were visible, as something beneath the ground was stubbornly resisting the accumulation of dirt and vegetation.

Starship Mountain had been there for as long as anyone could remember, but somehow it didn't look like a natural feature. Some said that it looked like an immense grave; others considered it to be nothing more than an eyesore. The superstitious believed it was evil, with mages in particular claiming that it was cursed. Everyone avoided it. Long ago, by unanimous agreement of both the Council of Stewards and the Guardians, a high wooden wall had been built entirely around the mountain, surrounding it on all four sides to prohibit anyone from coming close. The Squat came to an abrupt stop in the warehouse district just outside the palisades, and badges and Guardians made sure no one crossed the line.

The reason why it was called Starship Mountain was that—according to the Cetans, historians, and most schoolteachers—a magic vessel lay beneath it, a great craft that had carried humans across the stars from another world. It came to Tawcety long ago, when the mythical substance *plastik* still existed. *Plastik* vanished, and so the ship never moved again. It rested beneath the mountain, forbidden to all.

Or so the story goes. Maybe that was true, or maybe it wasn't. Like a lot of people, I just didn't care very much. I didn't believe in magic, and so neither did I believe in magic ships. The starship of Starship Mountain wasn't real.

It was just a myth, that's all. And besides, I had the world all figured out.

IV

The Kim manor was inside the walls of House Greer estate on the southeast side of the Heights. Like all the major houses, House Greer was situated within an enclosed compound protected by a high stone wall, save for the side facing the sheer granite bluff of the mesa's northeast side. Like a citadel, House Greer could be seen from lower Landencyte. It gave the rest of us something to look up to … or resent, if you were so inclined.

Once Butch's jitney climbed the steep road that had been carved long ago up the side of the mesa, he dropped me off at House Greer's main gate. I watched as he parked the carriage just down the street; the gold coin had paid for a round trip, so he'd wait for me to return from my visit. Which could last a few hours or just a few minutes, depending on what happened next.

A sentry in brass and gorsch-leather armor stood within the entry arch. He eyed me as I sauntered past the high stone wall separating the estate from the Heights, Landencyte, Sanctuary, and pretty much the rest of Tawcety. I was ready for him with a smile and my card—*Ct. Jeremy Crowe, Private Affairs Investigation*—which I handed to him through the wrought iron bars.

"Citizen Crowe to see Master Philip Kim of House Greer."

The guard didn't return the smile and he barely glanced at the card. "The Master is indisposed. Write a letter to the House Secretary and ask for an appointment."

He was just doing his job, but I didn't have time for this. "Master Philip will want to talk to me," I said. "It concerns the matter of his fiancée. I've been retained by Steward Conklin of House Fletcher to find her."

Perhaps he was just the lowly gatekeeper, but I knew from experience that a House's staff and servants had a wuwu-vine of their own. In the privacy of the pantries and sculleries and foyers, there was endless gossip about the affairs of the aristocrats they served. By now, even the house geek would have heard the rumor about Master Philip's fiancée going missing. So this fellow knew what I was talking about.

He turned my card over in his gloved hand for a couple of moments, then without letting his eyes leave me he let out a sharp whistle. On the other side of the wall, a young boy in the checkered tunic of a herald came running. The guard handed my card to the lad and said something to him in House Greer's pidgin-talk that no one who hadn't been raised in the house would understand. The kid scrutinized me for a couple of seconds, as if memorizing every detail of my appearance, then turned and dashed off across the courtyard. If he was good at what he was trained to do, he'd be able to describe me accurately to whomever he was reporting, even sketch my face if necessary.

I thought I was going to have to wait awhile. Much to my surprise, only a few minutes went by before a squat, middle-aged woman in the black frock of the house matron emerged from a side door and marched to the gate. The sentry stepped aside for her, and she regarded me through the gate with cool, appraising eyes.

"You wish to meet Master Philip, I'm told."

"I do. I've been retained by—"

"I'm not deaf, Citizen Crowe, and the boy isn't mute. Come with me."

The sentry pushed aside the crossbar and opened the gate. I gave him a respectful bow as I walked past and caught the faintest hint of a smile in response. Maybe I was all cleaned up and dandy, but this fellow hadn't been born on the Heights; he knew a fellow squatter when he saw him, and so he'd cut me a break. One day, I'd have to find him again and buy him a drink.

The house matron was less hospitable. My appearance didn't fool her a bit. I was from the wrong side of town, and it was her job—as it had probably been her mother's and grandmother's and maybe even great-grandmother's before that—to keep callous men like me on the other side of the wall, unless we were there to make a delivery or fix something. But she listened to the wuwu-vine, too, and she knew that if she kept someone who'd been hired by a Steward from another house to investigate the private affairs of a family member... well, even hereditary jobs can come to an end. She might not like me or trust me but telling me to go away was probably a bad idea.

House Greer wasn't the largest stewardship, but it was the most prominent. Its status showed in the collection of residences clustered within the compound wall. Standing in a quadrangle were several manor houses, connected to one another by sheltered walkways. The manors had red brick walls covered by broadleaf, mullioned windows, and gabled roofs; watchful gargoyles crouched upon the eaves. The interior of the compound wall was lined with deep, square niches, each holding a funerary urn containing the ashes of a deceased member of the house. Some were centuries old. A bell tower rose above the courtyard center, and on the first day of each month, someone climbed up there to give the bell rope a good, hard yank that could be heard all the way to the Waterfront, a tradition still being kept long after the reason was forgotten.

House Greer reeked of power, wealth, and heritage. It was also cold, silent, and joyless. Empty windows with black panes studied me as I was led across the courtyard, passing gardens colorless and barren with Wintermonth. This was the first time I'd ever been there, and already I hated the place.

The Kim residence was the smallest manor in the compound. It was at the far end of the courtyard next to the gorsch barn, and as quiet as the rest of the compound. I thought we were going to enter through the front door, passing beneath the Greer sigil, but instead the matron brought me in through the servants' door on the side. I wondered whether she was deliberately trying to insult me or if condescension was something that just came naturally. Either way, I contemplated stealing an engraved wine goblet on the way out, if only as cheap comeuppance.

We passed through a kitchen into a maze of narrow hallways connecting rooms whose wood-paneled walls were hung with portraits and rorf-hunting scenes. I was just beginning to get lost when the matron stopped at a door. A glance through a peephole, then she looked over her shoulder at me.

"Shh," she whispered. "Not a word until Master Philip speaks to you." I nodded, and ever so quietly she turned the knob and eased the door open.

Here was the library, a large, handsome room warmed by a gentle fire in the marble hearth and lighted by the midday sun streaming in through stained-glass windows. Beneath a high bowstring ceiling were two floors of bookcases, a spiral staircase leading to the upper gallery. Thousands of books on the shelves, more than I'd ever seen before, and yet nobody was reading. Not books, anyway.

There was a large fauxoak study table in the center of the room. Several figures stood around it, their attention fixed upon something on its polished surface. As I slowly walked closer, I saw that the person standing a little apart from the others wore the hooded black robe of a magus. An older man, he had the obligatory long white beard that everyone in his profession seemed to have; I often wondered if long white beards were mandated by the Mystics Guild, for every magus I'd ever met had facial hair, even some of the women. Eyes tightly closed, this particular spellhack stood with his arms outthrust, his hands slowly, slowly moving across an enormous wall map of Sanctuary. A bare spot between two nearby bookcases showed where the map had been taken down and spread out across the table.

A far-seer. I almost groaned. Philip Kim, or someone else in his family, had hired a far-seer, a mage practiced in the so-called art of remote viewing. Supposedly, an individual possessing this talent had the ability to locate a missing person by passing their hands across a map of the area in which the lost person was believed to be.

How? Ask a magus and they'd tell you that it had to do with the harmonics of the soul or something like that.

I'd never seen a far-seer who'd located someone in a way that couldn't be explained by coincidence. If I point to a closed door and say that someone is standing behind it, the fact that he or she *might* be on the other side doesn't prove that I possess any metaphysical insights. However, if I could *make* you believe that I did, then I was a good con man, and I've never met a magus who wasn't.

Standing closest to the seer was a young man who watched his movements with interest. Sallow and thin, with a bowl haircut and a lantern jaw, he wore a rorf-fur robe over a mandarin-collar shirt, drawstring trousers, and mocs; it wasn't hard to guess that he was Master Philip. The two other young squires standing beside him were about his age, and it was a good guess that they probably belonged to other families of House Greer. But then the figure directly across from the magus turned his face toward me, and I realized that not everyone in the room was human.

The Guardian present for the remote viewing session was a Cetan who went by the name of Bart; as usual, his real name couldn't be pronounced by our people. Beneath his scarlet cape was black fur with white streaks around a blunt snout and eyes that were dark brown and capable of quick anger.

I knew that anger well. Bart and I had squared off a couple of times back when I was a badge and was the local Guardian who'd show up for crime scenes in the Squat. He was infamous for coming down hard on humans who broke Cetan law even by accident, while I'd been known for being a badge who generally sided with humans over Guardians. Guess which of us was more popular in town.

And there was something else, too. Something I didn't like to talk about.

Bart recognized me immediately. His upper lip curled above his fangs before he got control of himself and went back to watching the magus do his bit. I hadn't seen much of him after I left the force and he'd moved up to the Heights, but there was no love lost between us. I chose to ignore him and went back to watching the magus do his stuff.

I'll say this for the old fraud: he certainly had his schtick down. Inch by inch, he slowly moved his hands across the map, keeping his palms just an inch or so above the heavy, hand-illuminated parchment A little melodrama goes a long way when you're practicing the mystical arts.

The charlatan made small, careful motions, pausing for a moment or two every now and then to make it seem as if he was actually searching for something. I've seen second-rate mages mutter mumbo-jumbo under their breaths while they worked, but he was better than that; he worked quietly, maintaining an air of concentration.

Who knows? Maybe he really did believe that he knew how to work magic. If he did, though, he wasn't above having a little help. Bart stood directly across the table from him, his hands resting softly upon the table's edge. As the magus let his hands float over the shoreline and out into the harbor, Bart waited until they reached the line of marker buoys designating the farthest extent to which the guardians allowed humans to travel out into the ocean from Sanctuary. Then the talon of his right forefinger tapped softly against the table. The boys didn't notice this, but magus had apparently been listening for the sound, for his hands immediately moved back toward land again.

It took a lot of self-control not to laugh. Guardians like Bart were always supposed to be present when licensed mages were conducting high magic like remote viewing, to make sure humans weren't indulging in any practices proscribed under Cetan law. Thus it wasn't unusual for Bart to be there, and apparently he'd taken advantage of the legal requirement to make some sort of deal with the magus. Which made sense. Both of them were working the Heights, after all, and there's no fool so gullible as a rich man who wants to believe in the impossible.

I stood by quietly and watched as the magus went about his act. With Bart's subtle assistance, his blind search brought him back to Landencyte. Bart softly tapped the table's edge again as the magus's hands glided over the Heights; the magus carefully moved them a little to the right, and when his palms were above the Squat, Bart quietly cleared his throat.

The magus stopped. His hands shook, a spasmodic tremor that ran up his wrists to his forearms, biceps, and shoulders, then he took a deep, shuddering breath. "She… is here," he murmured. Then, more dramatically, he cried out, "*She is here!*"

He let his hands fall flat upon the map, and everyone gathered around the table moved in to get a closer look at the place the magus had designated. "Where?" Philip inquired, bending over to see which part of the city his fiancée was in. "Which street? What's the address?"

"I… cannot be exact, young Master Philip." The magus let out his breath, opened his eyes, and stood up straight. "The girl is somewhere in this quarter—" he lifted his hands from the map and let them circle the Squat like a pair of bony white birds "—of this, I'm certain. But I'm sorry, my vision doesn't allow me to be more specific."

Oh, I bet it didn't. The Squat encompassed fifteen square blocks of Landencyte, from the Market to the Waterfront, from the Heights to the foot of Starship Mountain. It was the most densely populated area of the city; nearly a million people lived there. You could hide a small army within its tenements, shops, taverns, and livestock sheds. Be specific? Right.

"At least we know where she's gone," said one of Philip's companions, a young fellow with an elegantly dyed and coiffed beard. "The Squat's not *that* big." I wondered how much time he's actually spent there, or if he'd ever been anywhere other than one of its few tame streets.

"Sure. Pilot is hard to miss; there's not many girls like her." Philip's other friend was a skinny lad who looked like he hadn't met a girl until just last week, and then only because she was emptying the chamber pot in his room. "Maybe if we all went down there and searched…"

My cue. I politely coughed in my fist and cast a sidelong look at the matron. She gave me a brief nod in return; for the first time, she seemed to acknowledge that I was there for legitimate reasons. "Master Philip," she said, raising her voice, "begging your pardon, sir, but you have a visitor: Citizen Jeremy Crowe, an investigator of private affairs."

She added the last much as if she was announcing the arrival of a borkcatcher. Philip hadn't noticed me until then. Turning away from the table, he took a moment to size me up. I knew that I was expected to bow, but I don't do that; a polite nod was the best he got from me.

To his credit, Philip didn't seem to notice or care. "You're the dick Steward Conklin said he was going to hire."

"He came to see me this morning," I replied. "Once he explained the situation, I let him retain my services. You're my first stop."

As I spoke, I took stock of young Master Philip of Family Kim, House Greer. Perhaps I was expecting something different, a personality more in line with the sort of individual I've encountered before in my dealings with Landencyte's privileged class: arrogance, hauteur, the kind of stupidity that proudly flouts its own ignorance. But I wasn't getting any of that from him. From his friends, yes—the two of them regarded me as if I was a beggar someone had caught rooting through the scullery garbage —but he seemed to be better than that. Or at least that was the impression I was getting.

"You witnessed the séance just now?" He walked around the table toward me, his pals stepping out of the way. I nodded. "What do you think? Is Magus Woodstock correct?"

The magus was staring at me from beneath lowered brows, hands no longer hovering above the map but folded together within his robe's bell sleeves. There was a menacing gleam in Bart's eyes. He knew that I had no respect for magicians, and he knew why.

"If he is, then it'll be by chance and nothing more." I looked straight at Magus Woodstock, meeting his gaze squarely. "I have as much chance of finding your fiancée that way as he does, and I don't belong to his guild." I let myself relish his rising and barely-concealed anger, then added, "I hate to tell you this, Master Philip, but you're wasting your time. This man is nothing but a spellhack."

Magus Woodstock's face turned as white as his beard. He involuntarily took a step back from the table; it was clear that he'd seldom been called a fraud, and never in the presence of wealthy patrons. Philip's friends couldn't believe it. They stared at me, aghast at my effrontery.

Philip said nothing. His expression remained stolid, and he didn't appear to be scandalized or even very much surprised. I was wondering why when a low growl began to rise from Bart's throat. He didn't like what I'd said either, but before he could do anything, the boy with the pretty beard stepped forward.

"How *dare* you, sir?" His blue eyes blazed at me, but I was noticing his eyebrows; they were so immaculate, with tiny beads woven into their corners, that I was willing to bet that a stylist probably groomed them every morning. "Magus Woodstock has served House Greer for two generations! His credentials as a practitioner of the mystic arts are beyond question!"

"Really?" Keeping an eye on the kid. I gave the magus a sidelong look. "Nice work, Woody. It's a real achievement for a gorschshit artist like you to keep a steady job for so long."

Magus Woodstock's face changed hue so fast, a chameleon bird couldn't have done better. Pretty Boy sprang to his defense. "Sir, you besmirch the honor of this house!" He wrapped his hand around the rapier buckled to his left side, and there was soft whisk of steel against leather as he drew it from its sheath. "Apologize at once!"

I finally decided to pay attention to him. It seemed to be what he wanted. That and impressing his friends. His rapier was a fencing weapon, though, long and sleek and wicked-looking, but no sharper than a letter-opener. He'd probably be a worthy opponent in an afternoon duel out in the courtyard, but against someone who wasn't playing games…

I was tempted to give him a lesson in reality, but that would've been bad for business. I opted for another tactic instead. "That's a sweet sword," I said, adopting a casual tone like we were discussing badminton racquets. "It's got a nice shine to it… polish it often?"

Pretty Boy didn't say anything, but there was an uncertain look on his face. It occurred to him that I wasn't at all scared of him. Perhaps he was even wondering if drawing his blade on me might not have been a good idea. He hadn't formally challenged me yet, and we couldn't face off in a legal duel unless he did so and I accepted. But his pals were watching, and he'd already unsheathed his rapier, so it was going to be hard for him to back down without losing face.

"I demand an apology!" he snapped, trying to bluster his way out. Which was making this even more fun.

"How about a little advice instead?" I said. "It's good to keep the blade clean, but you really need to be careful about polishing it. Too much and the metal loses its temper. Here, let me show you…"

My saber was out of its sheath so fast, you could practically hear the high, wicked song the blade made as it cut through the air. I was careful to draw my weapon so that it wasn't in Pretty Boy's direction; this way, none of the witnesses in the room could truthfully say that I'd raised my sword against the little fop. Instead, I rotated my wrist so that the blunt side of the blade was turned toward him.

"See this?" I asked. "The bloodstains here and here? When you're through using a sword, you should never do more than wipe off the excess on, say, your opponent's clothes. The blood stays on the blade. It doesn't come off. You understand?"

Truth was, I'd never killed anyone with this particular weapon. As I said, I'd taken it from someone who tried to murder me. But the stains were real and that meant it had probably been used to spill someone's guts, so the lesson was the same.

As was the point I was trying to make. Pretty Boy saw the old, faded stains on the blade, and realized that he was outmatched. So did Philip. "Eric? Enough. I have business with him." Philip laid a hand on his friend's shoulder, then looked at the others. "Leave us, please. I'd like to discuss matters alone with my guest."

Red-faced and humiliated, Eric shoved his toy back in its sheath and marched out of the library. The other boy was afraid to look at me as they followed him. Magus Woodstock probably wished he did indeed know some spell that would cause me to drop dead on the spot, but he didn't, so all he could do was storm out of the room. The matron held the door open for them, then closed it behind her as she too made her exit.

This left only Bart. He never moved from the spot where he'd been observing the séance. A cloud must have passed above the Heights at that moment, for the sun faded from the library's stained-glass windows. Just for a second, the only light in the room came from the fireplace and the sinister glow it made in the reflective pupils of his canine eyes.

"S'ay-y-y'ing," he rumbled, the first time he'd spoken aloud since I'd come in. "My r-r-righ' hear."

Bart was correct. As a Guardian, he had the right under Cetan law to be present when matters of public safety were being discussed. This would include the disappearance of the children of Stewards. I didn't like it, and judging from the expression on Master Philip's face, I don't think he did either, but there was nothing we could do about it.

"All right, then," I said, "then let's try to figure out where Pilot Conklin has gone." I turned to Philip. "Any ideas that don't involve gorschshit like what your house magus was peddling?"

"Yes, sir, I do." Master Philip was calm; it was easy to see that he was more mature than his friends. "I think Magus Woodstock was right about one thing. Pilot went down to the Squat… and I believe I know where, and who she's with."

V

It was siesta when I walked through House Greer's front gates again. The streets were quiet, the shops and businesses closed for the midday hour; only a few cafes were open, for those who wanted a bite to eat before their noon nap. But some of us work through siesta—particularly in Wintermonth, when it's cool enough to stay awake and active through the middle of the day—so I declined Master Philip's offer of wine, scones, and a couch, and instead decided to pursue the lead he'd just given me.

Unexpectedly, Philip came with me. I didn't want to bring him along. It never makes sense for a freelancer to let a client join the investigation. But he was adamant. He wanted to find Pilot, and although the lead he'd given me appeared to be solid, he purposely withheld one vital nugget.

"Sure, I know his name," Philip had said in the library. "I even know what he looks like. And I'll pick him out for you as soon as I see him… and that's going to be when I take you where I know he'll be this afternoon."

"If you do," I asked, "then why call in a magus?"

"It wasn't my idea. My family insisted, and since I didn't—" He abruptly stopped himself. A wary glance at Bart, standing quietly nearby, arms crossed and ears upright, then he looked at me again. "It's complicated."

He didn't have to explain; I was figuring out the rest all by myself. Master Phillip not only knew who Pilot was with, it was also a good bet that he knew where she was, too. For some reason, though, he didn't want anyone in either House Greer or House Fletcher to know this, so he'd gone along with the pretense of enlisting a far-seer. No wonder he'd been unmoved by Magus Woodstock's pronouncement that he'd located his fiancée. The spellhack couldn't tell Master Phillip anything that he didn't already know.

This didn't make me any less impatient, though. "Look," I said, "I'm not playing here. The sooner you tell me who this guy is, the sooner I can shake him down." I was fed up with the sham politeness of Heights society. Philip's pal Eric had already shown me what to expect from the young aristocrats of House Greer.

"You won't be able to 'shake him down,'" Philip replied. "He won't talk if you come to him by yourself." He looked at Bart again. "And he won't talk to you either," he added. "A Guardian is the last person he'll want to see. Either way, he'll vanish if I'm not with you."

Bart's ears flattened and his upper lip curled back, but he didn't say anything. At least, not just then. But when Philip left the room to get his cape and hat, he had words for me.

"Is Guardian busi-nezzz," Bart growled softly. "Z-z-z-stay ou'."

"I'll stay in if that's what my client wants." I stared him straight in the eye, the way you should when you're having a disagreement with a Cetan and want to win. "I'm a licensed investigator, and the law gives me the right to intercede in the affairs of fellow humans if they or their relatives or friends hire me to do so. You want to complain, take it up with Steward Conklin… or Steward Greer, if you got the balls."

Bart's arms dangled at his sides; I didn't have to look down at his hands to know that his talons were unsheathed. But I refused to look away, and after a moment his teeth disappeared and his ears slowly raised from the back of his head.

"R-r-r-repor' wha' you know," he rumbled. "Don' hide wha'ever-r-r you fin' 'oo the badges." And then he turned and left.

Phillip nearly collided with him at the door. The kid had put on his cape and boots and came in buckling a sheathed rapier that looked about as intimidating as a knitting needle in the hands of a child. The Guardian growled a little as he shouldered past him. The scion of House Greer turned to watch Bart stomp down the hall, then looked at me with questions in his eyes. I shook my head. "Later, maybe. Let's just get out of here."

Philip didn't say much until we were through the gate and walking back to where the jitney was parked. "What's between you and Guardian Bart?" he asked at last.

"Nothing. We're bosom buddies, best friends."

"Didn't look that way," he murmured. I pretended not to hear.

Butch was napping on the sidewalk beside his jitney, back against the estate wall, shoulders loosely wrapped in a serape. He panted in his sleep, tongue lolling from the side of his mouth. I gently prodded his ankle with the toe of my boot and he woke up at once, jerking out of sleep with a startled grunt. "Let's go," I said. "Back to the Squat. I'll give you the address on the way."

Yawning expansively, cranky at being awoken before the end of siesta, Butch picked himself off the sidewalk and lurched to the jitney, where the gorsch was slumbering as well. Philip and I climbed in while Butch was shaking the big lizard awake; before we pulled away from the curb, I unfolded the carriage bonnet and raised it over the back seat.

"Sun's not out," Philip said as he watched me swing the bonnet in place. The kid had a knack for stating the obvious.

"Not putting this up for shade." I leaned across him to snap the fasteners. "I'm putting it up so we can't be seen... wanna help?"

"Help?" He had a blank look that reminded me of a bork with torchlight in its eyes, confused by the ordinary. "Help do what?"

I paused what I was doing, just stared at him. It took him another second before he seemed to suddenly remember that I wasn't one of his servants and we were no longer inside House Greer. "Oh... oh yeah, sure." He hastily leaned over the side of the carriage where I had just snapped the fasteners in place. "What do you want me to do?"

I'd already finished. Butch was half-turned in his seat, keeping the jitney still until he saw that I was done. I gave him a nod as I sat down again, and he shook the reins to get the gorsch moving, "Nothing except talk. Tell me what you know."

"I... I'm not sure where to begin." Phillip became wary again. "I mean, I know what I told you back there, but now I... I don't..."

The kid was beginning to annoy me, seriously. I reached out to pull the privacy curtain between us and Butch, then turned to the boy again.

"Now, see here—" I began mildly, as if this was nothing more than a disagreement about street directions. Then, with the back of my arm, I slammed him up against the seat. "All right, enough screwing around." I didn't raise my voice, but I put an edge in it. "Tell me everything you know, or I'm throwing you out as soon as we reach the bluffs."

Philip went pale. His eyes widened and his mouth fell open, and the way he stared at me suggested that he'd seldom been treated roughly in his life. "C-c-citizen Crowe—!"

"I know what my name is." As I tightened my chokehold, I made a fist out of my right hand and let him get a close look at it. "No more games. The next words out of your mouth better be the name of the guy we're supposed to find and where we're going to find him."

I really shouldn't have done that. When I come down hard on someone, they usually deserve it, and all Philip had done was to be overcautious and naïve. So, yeah, I'll fess up: I was trying to scare him. But it galled me to have a sword pulled on me for no reason, so I was also taking it out on Master Philip for having stupid friends.

Either way, it had the desired effect. "Okay, okay, okay!" he stammered, fear flattening him against the seat. "The guy you're looking for is Michael Gillespie, Mike Gillespie. He's a regular at the Harbor Lady's Parlor... you can find him there!"

"Who's Gillespie? What's he got to do with this?"

"He's... he's..."

He hesitated, and then, if only for a moment, there was a flash of defiance in his eyes. Kid had more spine than I thought. I raised the ante. With my free hand, I yanked back the curtain. "Hey, Butch, when you get to the top of Seaview Road, pull over. You've got some trash back here I want to throw off the bluff."

Butch made the sort of nasty snort that Cetans do when they're amused by humans. He'd heard everything, of course. For a Cetan, I kind of liked him. I just hoped that he wasn't an informant for the Guardians; I didn't want this getting back to Bart.

"He's an Originalist!" Philip blurted out. "He heads a study group that Pilot joined!"

"Study group?" That was a new one on me. "Is that what they're calling heretics these days?"

Anger flashed in Philip's eyes. "She's not a heretic," he snapped, then shoved my arm away. "And I know damn well you're not going to throw me off the bluffs, so cut it out."

I suppose I could've drawn my blade to see if that would restore some respect, but something about the kid was beginning to make me like him. Unlike his pretty-boy pals, he seemed to actually have some guts. I let him go and settled back in my seat. "All right, so why didn't you tell me any of this back at the house? Now I can find him on my own... I don't need your help."

"Because I didn't want Bart to know." Mindful of the Cetan just a few feet away, Philip dropped his voice. "If the Guardians hear that a group of Originalists meets at the Harbor Lady's Parlor," he whispered, "they'll order the badges to raid the place. And if Pilot's there—"

"*If* Pilot's there? Then you *do* know where she is, don't you?" When he didn't answer, I leaned in on him again. "Kid, I swear to you, if you're feeding me some gorschshit—"

"I'm not! She's there. They both are!" The kid knew that he'd slipped up; his face became red, and his eyes squeezed shut in self-loathing as he shook his head. "Damn it!" he hissed, and I could practically hear him kicking himself. "I didn't mean to—"

Ignoring him, I yanked back the curtain. "Butch? Waterfront... the Harbor Lady's Parlor. Know where it is?" The drover nodded his shaggy head. "Take us there... no, wait, cancel that. Drop us at my swordsmith, Harry & Sons, corner of Mill and Water. We'll walk from there. I got things to discuss with Master Philip."

"You don't have to call me that." Philip looked down, embarrassed.

"You don't like being called Master?"

"No. Not where we're going."

He had a point there. The Harbor Lady's Parlor was no place for a young squire from the Heights, and if he'd been tutored by the same swordmaster as Pretty Boy Eric, he probably couldn't hold his own in a bar fight. But I had to give him credit: he was willing to walk into such a bork pen if it meant protecting the girl he loved. In my book, loyalty like that counts for a lot.

"All right," I said, "I'll make a deal with you. I won't blow your cover if you'll help me find Pilot and get her out of there. Agreed?"

I offered my hand. Philip hesitated, and then reluctantly shook it. For the time being, I had a partner. I hoped I wasn't going to regret it.

VI

Butch dropped us off at the smithy where I'd left my blades that morning. I wanted to get back my weapons if I was going to start poking around in places like the Parlor; the secondhand saber I was carrying had impressed Philip's friends, but no self-respecting swordsman would rely on a crap blade like that. To my surprise, the smithy had just finished sharpening both swords. I paid with another one of the gold pieces Steward Conklin had given me—and added it to my mental list of expenses—then carried the blades, still wrapped in denim, back to my flat a few blocks further down Water Street.

I parked Philip downstairs in the vintner's tasting room. He reluctantly let me buy him a carafe of the shop merlot—add that to expenses, too—then took a table at the window and waited while I went up to my flat. I didn't want the kid with me while I changed out of my finery back into my street clothes, not because of any modesty, but because I didn't want him to see me retrieve my pistol from its hiding place.

The gun was the only thing I kept from my old job. I reported it lost, and so long as I didn't go waving it around in public, my former colleagues were inclined to look the other way; it made me one of the few dicks in Landencyte to have one. Once I pulled it out of the concealed cubbyhole within my desk, I loaded it with wadding, gunpowder, and a ball, plugging the barrel with another wad so I could carry it without the powder and ball falling out. I half-cocked the hammer and tucked the pistol into a soft gorsch-skin holster that went under my left arm; the powder horn and a handful of lead balls went in my waistcoat pockets, and the old brown cape I normally wore covered the holster. The saber went into my belt scabbard, and the short sword over my right shoulder and across my back. On impulse, I took the precaution of slipping a stiletto into my boot.

Maybe you think this is overkill. To be honest, so did I. But they don't serve tea in the Harbor Lady's Parlor.

Master Philip was where I left him. He watched me steadily as I came back to where he was sitting but made no move to get up. I noticed that he'd barely touched the wine; the carafe was mostly full, and it looked as if he'd taken no more than a sip from the glass he'd poured. Waste of money, something the rich don't have to worry about.

"Saving yourself for the bar?" I asked.

"Staying sober, thank you. Hope you'll do the same."

Looked like the kid had taken the time I'd been away from him to man up. He was no longer scared of me; I could see it in his eyes and hear it in his voice. Unless I wanted to try intimidating him again—which I didn't, not if it wasn't necessary—it was best to make peace.

"I agree, but there's no sense in letting good wine go to waste. And I'm thirsty." Sitting down across from him, I raised a hand and signaled the barmaid for a second goblet. "Don't worry… it's still early. I bet this guy isn't even there yet."

Philip gave an irritated sigh. "We're wasting time."

"Kiddo, I haven't even had lunch. A bagel was all I had for breakfast. If I have to take my nourishment in liquid form—"

"All right, all right. I'm sorry." Sulking, he crossed his arms, slouched in his chair, and let his off-balance left knee tremble with impatience as he glared out the window at the gigolo leaning across a lamppost across the street who'd been trying to catch his eye.

I let him stew. The barmaid brought the second glass and poured for me the drink I didn't really want but said I did. "Let me ask you something," I said once she walked away. "If you've known all along where Pilot is—"

"I don't. Not specifically, I mean. I only know someone who does… or would, I think."

"This Mike Gillespie?" I asked, and he nodded. He didn't look happy about admitting this. "Okay, that's better than knowing nothing at all. And I suppose that's why you let the magus do his song and dance, to keep everyone in the house from guessing that you knew the truth. Right?"

Philip nodded again. "Can I ask you something?"

"Sure." I took a sip of wine, decided that it really ought to age a little longer, and made a mental note to say something to the wine master the next time I came down to pay rent.

"What was going on with you and Bart? It's pretty clear that you two know each other, and something happened that—"

"We do, there is, and I don't wanna talk about it." I wasn't about to open that door to the kid, especially not in a public house downstairs from my own flat. Bad for business, and bad for me, too.

I pulled out my pocket watch, clicked it open. Nearly five o'clock. The winter shadows were lengthening upon the streets, and the breeze off the harbor was snatching at the hats and hoods of people walking along the sidewalk outside. The gigolo had vanished; either he'd lost interest in Philip or had found another handsome fellow to entertain this evening. And I no longer wanted the wine.

"C'mon, let's get out of here." I'd already put the carafe on my tab, so I dropped a couple of dymes on the table as a tip and stood up. "The sooner you show me this Mike Gillespie and I can talk to him, the sooner we'll find your girl."

VII

The Harbor Lady's Parlor was run-down, sleazy, and enjoyed the dubious rep of being the most dangerous tavern in town. It was also one of the oldest, dating back to the founding of Landencyte, 550 Tawcety years ago. There's a number of stories about how the place got its name. The one most often told was that the harbor master's wife, upset by the boozing and whoring going on in Waterfront bars, tried to provide an alternative with a harbor saloon where gentlemen and ladies could drink tea and partake of finger sandwiches while chatting about the issues of the day. This probably lasted until a fishing schooner returned from a trip around the island and its thirsty crew descended upon the parlor in search of grog and girls. At any rate, the only thing that survives of the old days is the sign above the door, which has been left untouched either because of its misleading humor or because no one's been sober enough to climb up there and change it.

The Parlor was about eight blocks from my flat, in the neighborhood where the Squat merges into the waterfront district. We walked there, pausing at a vendor's cart to scarf down a couple of pickled sausages as a poor substitute for dinner. I could have found Butch at the hotel again, but arriving in a jitney might have attracted attention, and I wanted to come in unnoticed. Not that it would've have mattered. Philip and I could have ridden in on a pair of wild lopers like we were in Guido's Raiders and no one would've cared. They had something more interesting to see.

We were almost at the door when two large gents, fishermen by the looks of them, came tumbling through the double-doors, hands around each other's throats, their battle followed by whooping laughter from within. Philip and I made way for them to fall into the street together; we immediately lost sight of the combatants in the mob of pedestrians and bar patrons who gathered about to watch.

Philip's eyes were wide. He'd probably never before seen a real, honest-to-the-gods bar brawl; the public houses in the Heights were much too genteel for that. His reaction, though, told me something: he'd heard of the Parlor, all right, but this was going to be the first time he'd actually set foot through the door.

As we came in, a bar maid was taking advantage of the distraction outside to make her way through the saloon, using a taper to light the wall lamps for the evening. The flickering glow illuminated tables littered with steins and bottles and ashtrays heaped with cigar butts. A few afternoon drunks were guarding their barstools, and over in a corner a poker game was continuing with unperturbed dedication; otherwise the place was quiet, except for the brawl outside.

Quiet, but not empty. Not everyone had stepped out for the fight. We were about halfway to the bar when Phillip touched my elbow. "He's here."

I gazed in the direction he was looking, saw three men sitting around a table near the poker game. They'd turned to watch the fight tumble out into the street but hadn't moved to follow it. They were young, a little older than Philip but not much, and wore the jackets, capes, and boots of working men. But I could tell by their smooth hands and unlined faces that they were in this part of town by choice, not because they'd been born and raised here. Rich kids slumming as Squatters. Or so I assumed.

"Which one?" I asked.

"The one in the middle, that's Mike. Don't know the other two."

Michael Gillespie was tall and dark, his head shaved save a long, narrow strip of black hair leading across his skull from his forehead back to his neck. And he'd seen us. Our eyes met, and I knew at once that he'd figured out that Philip and I were talking about him.

"Let's go introduce ourselves," I said.

Michael and his pals didn't get up as we approached their table. Getting closer, I noticed that each of them were carrying sabers. No pretty dueling rapiers for these guys; they knew where they were. Nobody laid a finger on their blades, though. They were more curious about us than cautious.

"May I help—?" Mike started to say, then he peered past me. "Why, if it isn't Philip Kim! What brings you here, Phil?"

No doubt Michael was genuinely surprised, but there was something forced about his enthusiasm. Philip didn't go along with the pretense. "Hello, Mike," he said, his voice as even as his gaze. "Seen my fiancée lately?"

"Your—?" Michael stared at him "—*what?*" Incredulity, bafflement, and an urge to burst out laughing wrestled for control; laughter won. "Are you kidding me? You still think Pilot is... that she wants to be your—?"

"*Where is she?*"

Okay, so Phillip really didn't know where Pilot was, not exactly; he'd told the truth about that. But he knew who did, and that was the guy who'd stolen her from him. That was what he'd been trying to keep from everyone. That's what it sounded like to me, and that was confirmed when Mike's flinty gaze swung toward me again.

"Who's this?" he asked Philip without look at him. "A bodyguard you hired to protect you in the bad ol' Squat?"

Mean laughter from the other guys; it wasn't hard to guess that they knew Philip, too, and shared Mike's obvious contempt for him. "He didn't hire me," I said. "I'm searching for Pilot Fletcher. Where is she?"

I reached in my waistcoat pocket, fished out a business card, and tossed it on the table in front of Mike. He picked it up and read it, and I had the pleasure of watching his grin disappear. It probably occurred to him that I might not be a good person to mess with, no matter what he thought of Philip, because he seemed to think it over a second, then turned to his friends. "You guys want to give me a minute? I want to talk this over with Citizen Crowe."

His friends stopped laughing. They traded a look I couldn't read, then without another word they pushed back their chairs, stood up, and ambled away. They didn't find another table, though, but after a moment of whispered conversation they headed for the door. I figured they were off to find another watering hole, and that they'd catch up with Mike sometime later. Once they were gone, Michael waved us to the seats they'd vacated.

"C'mon, sit," he said amiably, his arrogance replaced by an effort to exude hospitality. "Want a drink? First round's on me."

He started to flag down a waitress, but I shook my head. "Not here to drink. Just to find Pilot." I cocked my head toward Philip. "He told me you'd know where, and it sounds like you do. So look here, son… House Fletcher has hired me to find her and bring her home, and I'm not leaving until you help me do just that."

"What makes you think she wants to go home?" Sitting back in his chair, Mike crossed his arms. "Everything she's said to me lately tells me that she's done with the Heights. No one has kidnapped her. She came down here of her own free will."

His gaze travelled to Philip. "And I'll tell you something else," he added, speaking to him. "She's got something else going on now, and it doesn't include you."

"We're engaged, you gorsch's ass." Philip's face was livid, his hand hovering inches from his rapier.

Mike noticed that Philip was on the verge of drawing his blade. "Don't do it, Phil," he murmured as his own hand fell to the guard of his saber. "I'm the best swordsman in my house. Four duels, none lost, and two were to the death. That's fair warning."

"You guys want to duel, that's up to you," I said before Philip could respond, "but I'm not going anywhere until I find the girl." I met Mike's gaze. "And while we're giving each other fair warnings, friend… you might be hot stuff in the Heights, but you're downtown now, and I've put enough guys in their urns to fill a wall."

Mike seemed to think it over, which was what I wanted him to do, then he carefully removed his hand from his sword. "She's not here. She's somewhere else, along with the rest of our study group."

"So she *has* become an Originalist," Philip said.

Mike lifted a querulous eyebrow. "You make it sound like she's committing a mortal sin. All she's doing—all we're doing—is questioning the myth the Cetans would have us believe, that humans came to Tawcety on a magic ship from the sky and were never meant to live anywhere but Sanctuary. Pilot knows better now, and she's committed her life to discovering the truth."

"Then let me talk to her." Philip's tone changed subtly from demanding to pleading. "I'll accept that if I can just speak with her myself."

"Steward Conklin of House Fletcher hired me to find her," I said. "If she tells me herself that she has no desire to return, then I'll take that back to the steward and let him decide what he wants to do about his daughter." I shrugged. "That's all I've been hired to do, gents. Couples counseling isn't my job."

Michael didn't say anything for a moment. He absently chewed on his lower lip as his eyes shifted back and forth between Phillip and me. "All right, okay. If that's what you want, then—" he pushed back his chair and rose to his feet "—let's get going."

He left a silver half-dola on the table for the unfinished drinks, then led the way to the door. The brawl was over by then, and the patrons who'd gone out to watch were filtering back in. We made our way through the crowd; outside the Parlor, Mike waited for Philip and me to catch up. Instead of heading back up the street in a direction that would have taken us away from the waterfront, though, he turned into an alley between the tavern and the tackle shop next door.

"Shortcut," he said over his shoulder, and it had just occurred to me that he might be lying when my suspicions were proven correct.

Mike's friends hadn't gone far at all.

VIII

By some prearranged plan Mike had apparently worked out with his companions, after they left the Lady they hid in the alley outside, mouths shut and swords drawn, and waited for Mike to bring us to them. An ambush, plain and simple.

I didn't get through twenty years as a badge, though, without developing good instincts. I knew Mike's cronies were there a second before they emerged from the long shadows of evening. My saber was already in my hand when the guy on the right came at me; our steel clashed midway between us, and the fight was on.

Two against three are bad odds. Anyone who says otherwise, like the guys who tell bar stories about taking on three swordsmen singlehandedly, are either fools or liars. And it's never advisable to have a sword fight in a narrow alley. But it does mitigate things a bit if you've got a good sword arm of your own and another one at your side.

Unexpectedly, Philip Kim turned out to be just that.

He handled his rapier with the ease that only a lot of practice can give you; maybe his friend Eric had slept through his tutelage, but he hadn't. From the corner of my eye, I saw him parry the roundhouse swing made by his attacker, then move in with a sudden, fast thrust that neatly inserted the tip of his blade into the right side of his foe's ribs. He howled and fell back, dropping his weapon, blood spurting from a punctured lung. Philip let him go and whirled on Michael, who'd jumped in as soon as his buddies made their appearance.

Until then, I'd never thought a rapier was suitable for down-and-dirty street combat, but it only goes to prove that… well, remember what I said about what happens when you think you've got the world figured out?

I couldn't pay attention to Philip, though. I had problems of my own. The guy coming at me was strong and fast, and the only advantage I had was that he hadn't taken me by surprise. But he was also reckless, the sort of fighter who handles a saber like a machete and tries to slash 'n hack his opponent to death. I managed to fend off his wild blows until I saw an opening, then I whipped my sword around in a backhand swipe at his face.

What did I say about sharp blades? The edge of my sword cut open the bridge of his nose. He bellowed an obscenity and clutched at his schnoz with his free hand, and only succeeded in getting blood in his eyes. He defended himself as best as he could by throwing up his sword, but nonetheless his feet carried him back, his attack broken.

I could have killed him just then, but I didn't. Too much hassle; I'd just have to explain things to the badges. So I switched my blade to my left hand, yanked the flintlock from its holster beneath my cape, and pointed it straight at him.

"Drop it!"

If he'd been inclined to come at me again, the sight of my pistol, the loud click its hammer made when I cocked it back all the way, gave him pause. He stared down the barrel and froze; at this range, he knew that I could blow his face off. He dropped his sword. Good boy.

The guy whom Philip had stuck like a bork was holding his bleeding ribs with one hand while pulling out a dagger to come at him again. He saw the gun and stopped. Mike's gaze darted in my direction; he spotted the gun, realized that, yes, I meant him, too, and let his sword fall. Philip immediately ceased his attack, although he kept his blade up.

"Where's Pilot?" he asked, his voice soft yet menacing. No tough-guy act; he had one thing on his mind and putting his rival in his place wasn't a priority. Yeah, I was impressed.

Mike looked at him, then at me. I turned the gun toward him, let him get a good look down the barrel. I didn't have to worry about the other two guys anymore; clutching the bleeding parts of their bodies, they were already lurching down the alley, dragging their swords and crushed egos behind them. I figured they soon be back in the Heights, getting their wounds stitched and telling the house physician how they'd been beset by a gang of ruffians down in the Squat. There were at least four guys, maybe five.

"Where's Pilot Fletcher?" I said, reiterating Philip's demand. "C'mon, spit it out."

Mike hesitated another moment, then let out his breath and sheathed his sword. "Starship Mountain," he said quietly. "She's in Starship Mountain."

"*In* Starship Mountain? You mean she's gone up it."

"No. She's inside the mountain, not on it. And I know right where she is, too."

I glanced at Philip; he met my eye and nodded quietly, and I looked at Mike again.

"Okay," I said, "take us there."

IX

It was dark by the time we reached the palisades surrounding Starship Mountain. We stuck close to the shadows, avoiding the light of Tawcety's moons, both of which had risen by then. There were few streetlamps in this part of the Squat, but nonetheless we approached the high wooden fence with caution, taking care to make sure that we weren't spotted by sentries on fence patrol.

We needn't have been concerned. The night was chilly, so the badges were less inclined to stroll along the palisades. There was a small guardhouse about halfway down the fence's western side; the three of us crouched behind the corner of a nearby carriage house and watched through the window as the three men inside passed a bottle around. Obviously they weren't taking their job seriously tonight.

On the other hand, if there were Guardians afoot, we might have some trouble. Their vision was superb in the moonlight, their hearing was better than a human's, and if the wind was coming from the wrong direction they'd be able to smell our presence. Fortunately, tonight's guard duty did not seem to include any Cetans, a fact that didn't surprise Michael.

"We know which days they've got Guardians patrolling the fence," Mike whispered as he led Phillip and me away from the guardhouse. "That's when we sneak in and out."

"Where?" Philip was right behind him. Like me, he hadn't put away his sword. Neither of us trusted Mike.

"This way." Mike placed a finger to his lips: no more questions.

We followed him along the fence, doing our best to remain in its shadow. The palisades had been there for many, many years, allegedly all the way back to the tenure of Cap Greer, Landencyte's first cap. Immense fauxoak logs had been harvested from Sanctuary's inland rain forests and hauled by gorsch-teams across the island to the coast, where they'd been stripped of bark, coated with fish-oil preservative, stood erect, and lashed together to form a solid barrier eight feet tall.

When I was a kid, my friends and I used to poke around the fence, always trying to find cracks or knotholes through which we could peep and see what mysteries lay on the other side. We never did; the fence was solid. There was no place to wiggle through and climbing over without being spotted was damn near impossible.

But there was another way.

Mike led us to a commercial warehouse that looked just like any other. He pulled out a key and used it to unlock the side door. Moonlight revealed fireplace-size cordwood, cut lengthwise in half and stacked in neat rows, ready to be sold wholesale to retailers. It smelled pleasantly of sawdust. There was a narrow space between the stacks, just wide enough for someone to squeeze though sideways. Turning about, Mike began to shuffle shoulder-first through the space. It was dark inside the warehouse; I had no choice but to hope that we weren't following Mike into another trap.

The narrow passage led to a small open space well back from the door; the logs served as camouflage. As I was still groping my way through, with Philip beside me, I heard a soft jiggling sound from just ahead. A mellow amber light, flickering ever so slightly, filled the hidden room: Michael had found a glass jar filled with Harlan's glowworms and shaken it. Writhing in their little lantern of sand and saltwater, the worms' luminescence exposed the wooden trap door in the shed floor.

"We dug this a couple of years ago," Michael quietly explained, kneeling as he handed the lantern to me, then bent down and opened the door on its hinge. A dark pit lay below; when I moved the jar closer, a wooden ladder came into sight. "We were climbing over the fence before then, but that's hard to do without getting busted. So we bought this place and used it for cover while we excavated the tunnel."

"And the tunnel takes us to the bottom of the mountain?" Philip asked.

Mike smiled. "You'll see."

The hole was no more than six feet deep. Without another word, Mike climbed down the ladder. I passed the lantern to Philip and followed him; Philip came down last, after carefully handing the jar to me. We needn't have protected the lantern so much; the tunnel was braced by post and beam construction, with fresh wood planks forming narrow walls and a low ceiling, and every ten feet or so another jar of glowworms hung from a wire bracket, ready to be tapped or shaken awake.

Someone had taken a lot of time and effort to construct this tunnel. To successfully do so in secret, without raising the attention of the badges or the Overseers, had taken dedication and ingenuity. I knew at once that whatever lay at the end must be important enough to justify it.

There was a long cord running through hooks along the left side of the ceiling. Five feet from the bottom of the ladder, it ended with small chamber bell dangling from a hook. Mike pulled the cord a few times, causing the bell to jangle. "Letting them know we're coming," he said. We waited a few minutes, then the cord vibrated and the bell rang again. "Okay, we can go now," Mike said, then continued down the tunnel.

We had to duck low, but Philip and I had no trouble following him. It was hard to tell just how far we went, though. The tunnel took two bends along the way that threw off my sense of direction. It was close, but not stuffy; after a minute or so, I realized that I was feeling a slight breeze against my face. It wasn't a hallucination; someone up ahead was pumping fresh air into the tunnel.

My back and neck were beginning to ache when we reached the tunnel's end. This time, there was a metal ventilation tube running alongside the ladder; it was from here that fresh air from above was being pumped down. I noticed that the tube was old and appeared to have been salvaged from some piece of ancient machinery. But I didn't get more than a quick look; Mike was already climbing up the ladder, and when I stepped beneath him, I saw that the hatch above us was being held open by someone.

I emerged through another trapdoor into a room that baffled me as soon as I saw it. Illuminated by the dim light of more glowworm lanterns, the hatch was wooden, but the floor wasn't. Some sort of rotting, fibrous material covered what was apparently a metal deck, its once-sleek surface dark red and grainy with rust, riveted seams visible here and there through the tattered material. The floor wasn't flat, either, but instead curved upward on either side, ending at metal walls that bent slightly over us. The ceiling was smaller than the floor; the room was wedge-shaped, tapering upward on a vertical axis. Looking up, I saw a weird thing—a door in the ceiling, hanging ajar as if someone had just walked through it in a gravity-defying direction.

The room was large, and the wan light cast by the lanterns scattered around the upward-curved floor did weird tricks. There was a lot of junk scattered about, mostly small, rusting metal objects that were unfamiliar to me. Near the hatch we'd just come through was a handmade bellows like that in a blacksmith shop; this was apparently what had been used to pump fresh air into the tunnel.

There were two people in the room, a young woman and an older man. I couldn't see them clearly. "Where are we?" I asked, looking at both them and Mike. "Where have you brought us?"

"Don't you know?" Some of Mike's old arrogance returned. "Figure it out… you're inside the mountain."

"Starship Mountain." The women stepped forward into the light, and I recognized her at once from her portrait-sketch: Pilot Fletcher. "Or as we know it, the Earth starship *Lindbergh*."

X

"Pilot, what are you doing here?"

Philip had come up through the trapdoor. He stood beside me, staring at the fiancée he hadn't seen in weeks. And he wasn't the only one surprised. Pilot's mouth fell open when she saw him come up the ladder, and for a moment she could only stare at him.

"Phil," she said at last, "what are *you* doing here?"

I decided to save everyone the hassle of long explanations. "Your father hired me to find you, Madame Fletcher. I went to Master Philip hoping that he'd know where you went. He introduced me to Master Gillespie, who in turn was kind enough to bring us here."

"Not my choice," Mike hastily added as the others turned accusing eyes toward him. "Neil and Arne tried to stop him, but…" His shoulders slumped. "Look, he stuck a gun in my face."

"Mike, you idiot." The older man, whose greying beard nearly reached his chest, glared at him. "He wasn't going to shoot anyone." He turned to me. "Who are you, fella? I think I've seen you around."

"Jeremy Crowe. I'm a dick."

"Uh-huh. And before that, you were a badge, weren't you?" I nodded. "Thought I recognized you. You're the badge who made such a stink after that poor kid walked off the roof, aren't you?"

This was the thing I didn't like to discuss; it's why I went into business for myself. "Look, there's just one reason I'm here," I said, changing the subject. "Steward Conklin and House Fletcher wants me to find her and bring her home. Whatever else you've got going on here is none of my concern."

"Then I'm going to have to disappoint you and my father, because I'm not coming home." Pilot folded her arms across the front of the dirt-smudged smock she wore; she was the kind of girl who looked good even in filthy work clothes. "My place is here, doing important work."

"What's so damned important about this?" Philip waved aimlessly at the strange room around us. "I don't even know where we are."

"You haven't guessed?" Pilot regarded her fiancé with condescending eyes. "You're deep within the mountain, only it's not a mountain, not really. It's actually a vessel that came here long ago from another world."

"The EPSS *Lindbergh*: EPSS short for 'Exodus Project Starship.'" This from the gent who'd spoken earlier. He wasn't much older than I was; no wonder he remembered me from when I walked a beat in the Squat. "We don't know what all that means—'exodus' is an Oldeng word we haven't been able to define—but we do know that it came here centuries ago from a world called Earth."

"Uh-huh, right," I said. "This is the magic ship that brought our ancestors to Tawcety in the beginning. It was carried through space by *plastik*, the wondrous substance that vanished as soon as the starship arrived because it couldn't exist in this world. I've read *The Book of Years*, y'know, and sorry, but I don't believe in magic."

"That's good, because neither do we. This ship isn't magical, Citizen Crowe, but it did come from another world. And *plastik* was real, too, although it was once called something else: polyethylene. It doesn't exist on Tawcety because… well, that's something hard to explain. We don't think we completely understand it ourselves."

"But we do know some things," Pilot said. "The very name of this world, Tawcety, it was originally Tau Ceti-e—" she took a moment to spell it out "—and it's the fifth world orbiting a star that was originally known as Tau Ceti, not just 'the Sun' as we've always called it."

"Where do you get that?" Philip demanded. "*The True Origins*? You don't really believe that… that squawk guano, do you?"

I almost laughed. Squawk guano. Master Philip obviously wasn't accustomed to cussing. "I believe it because it's true," Pilot said, "and I didn't 'get it' from a book either." A reflective pause. "No, that's not entirely true," she added. "You're right, when I found *The True Origins of Landencyte* in my house's library, that got me to wondering about certain things. Where we came from, whether or not we've been told the truth—"

"And you went looking for that in the Squat?"

"She heard about us," the older man said, "and when she came looking, she found Michael."

"And who are you?" I asked.

He contemplated the question for a moment. "My name's irrelevant," he said at last, "but if you need to call me something, I'll settle for

Galileo." He smiled at my unspoken question. "Someone forgotten whom I happen to admire."

"She found me," Mike said, "and once I determined that she could be trusted, I introduced her to the rest of the study group. We've been together since."

There was a smug look on his face; the innuendo was clear. I couldn't help but notice, though, the angry glare Pilot gave him. She'd caught it, too, and didn't like it.

For his part, Philip was doing his best to keep his temper in check. Ignoring Mike, he turned to his fiancée. "Is this true?"

"I came down here to look for answers," she replied, "not him." The smirk vanished from Mike's face. "I didn't tell you or anyone else where I went because I didn't want anyone accusing me of heresy. And don't tell me that wouldn't have happened. Your house and mine would've reconsidered sanctioning our marriage if they'd known that I was consorting with Originalists."

"Then… then you're not breaking the engagement?" Amid everything else, it was obvious that this was the most important matter on Philip Kim's mind.

Pilot didn't reply at once. Her gaze travelled to Mike, and you could tell she was weighing the choice between two young men: the one she was supposed to marry, and the one with whom she'd apparently had a brief fling. Then she looked at Philip again.

"No," she said. "Sorry to disappoint you, my dear, but we're still getting married."

Coming closer to him, Pilot took his face in her hands. It was probably a great kiss, but I didn't see it; I gave them a moment for themselves by politely looking away. Mike was in my range of vision; the jealousy in his eyes was a pleasure to behold, but when his hand travelled to his sword, his ears caught the tut-tutting sound I made. Without looking at me, his hand moved away.

But he wasn't done with the happy couple yet. "Tell him the rest," Mike said. "Tell your boyfriend exactly how you managed to win our trust… you, a girl from House Fletcher, engaged to a boy from House Greer."

"Michael…" Galileo began.

"No… no, it's all right. He should know the truth." Pilot stepped back from Philip. "Love, I've done something awful, but… I needed to do it.

I wasn't trying to prove anything. It was just something that had to be done." A reluctant pause as she looked down at her boots. "I stole Cap Greer's logbook from House Greer's library."

I could tell Philip didn't understand what she'd said. His expression was blank, almost devoid of emotion. "Logbook? I don't follow you. There's a logbook that Cap Greer—?"

"Yes, just like the ones the fishing captains keep. But this one's not from a boat, but from this ship, the *Lindbergh*."

"I never... I didn't know there was a logbook like that in our library."

"That's because its very existence is a closely kept secret," Galileo said. "Only the Cap and a few Stewards know about it, and I wouldn't be sure all of them even understand or accept its meaning. *We* didn't know about it until... well, that's another story."

I bet it was. He was avoiding something he really didn't want to admit, not even here in the Originalists' hidden sanctum. It was a good guess that it had something to do with his role in all this. Whoever Galileo was, he was no Squatter. And if he was from the Heights as well, then it was possible that he was a figure of importance in one of the houses. If so, no wonder he was calling himself by another name; he had a lot to lose.

"The Guardians know, of course," he went on. "The Cetans have known the truth from the very beginning. Over the years, they've made a considerable effort to make sure that it remains forgotten... by humans, that is."

This was going over my head very quickly. "Would you mind telling me—?"

"What this is all about?" A weary smile. "That's more difficult to answer than you may think. Every time we think we're closer to learning everything we want to know, the truth seems to slip a little further away."

Galileo pointed up at the door that hung ajar in the ceiling. "See that up there? Funny place to put a door, isn't it? Except that's not a ceiling, that's a wall, just like the wall we're standing on now." He pointed to the vertical surface to my left. "*That's* the ceiling, and to your right is the floor. You came in through what was once an outside hatch."

"This room is resting on its side." Pilot stepped away from Philip to spread her arms wide. "The whole ship is this way. On the other side of that door—" she cocked her chin toward the ceiling "—are hundreds of compartments like this, scattered across maybe dozens of decks... or what used to be decks, until this thing came down on its side."

"What we think of as being a mountain was once a tower," Galileo said. "A vertical tower, like drums stacked one atop the other. The *Lindbergh* came down from space to crash-land here—"

"It's how the city got its name, y'know that?" It looked like Mike was getting over losing his girl; he was back to his old, annoying self. "Landencyte: 'landing site.' Get it?"

"Yeah, uh-huh." He wasn't telling me anything I hadn't heard before. The only revelation here was that the fabled ship beneath Starship Mountain did indeed exist, and that it wasn't the magic vessel of *plastik* that *The Book of Years* made it out to be. "Then why—?"

"You have many questions," Galileo said, "and I'd like to answer all that I can. Or even better, show them to you. Here—"

He looked up at the ceiling—or rather, the wall—pursed his lips and let out a shrill whistle. A moment passed, then we heard footsteps upon the other side. A jar of glowworms cast its shallow light through the door overhead, and a young woman's face came into view.

"Throw it down, Regina," Galileo called, and a few seconds ladder a rope ladder was pushed through the door and fell to the floor… I mean, the wall. He placed a hand on one of its wood-plank rungs, then turned to me and Philip. "If you'll come with us, we can show you a bit of what we've found." He looked at Philip, who'd been conspicuously quiet the last few minutes. "It's the best way I know to convince you, if still have any doubts. But before I do, I have something to ask of you."

"I think I can guess what it is," Philip said quietly.

XI

When Philip and I returned through the hidden tunnel leading into Starship Mountain, we brought Pilot with us.

The girl knew the way out, of course. She and her fellow Originalists had snuck through the palisades so many times, she could've made it down the tunnel blindfolded. It was almost dawn by the time we emerged from the warehouse. The first light of day was touching the tops of the trees that had grown atop the *Lindbergh* after Cap Greer—that is, Captain Yvonne Greer, the commanding officer—had ordered the shipwreck to be buried and a palisade wall built around it. Why she'd done this, and why the ship's crew and passengers—nearly a thousand, the ancestors of every human on Tawcety—had taken the time and effort to carry out her orders, was a mystery the Originalists were trying to solve.

One of many.

Standing outside the warehouse, I looked back at the so-called mountain. It was hard to believe that I'd been looking at this overgrown hulk all my life and never known what it was, what it *really* was. Once I followed Pilot and Galileo up the rope ladder that had been lowered into what I now knew to be something called an "emergency airlock," we'd spent hours roaming a dark maze of corridors and compartments, all tilted on their sides. Tree roots, moss, insects, and ground-burrowing critters had long since penetrated the *Lindbergh*'s outer hull; vines were curled around rusting ladders, and borks nested within empty lockers that had long ago been stripped of anything valuable. The ship's interior was a decaying labyrinth that smelled of mildew and rot and animal crap, but it was undeniably a human-made construct, evidence of a time when our people travelled between the stars. Not by magic, though, but by other means.

Pilot turned to me. "So… now what?"

"You know the agreement we made," I said. "You and Philip go home and tell everyone in the Heights that it was all just a quarrel between lovers. You got mad at him about something, and to get over it you ran away and hid out in the Squat for a while. He came down here with me to find you, and once we did, the two of you worked things out. Now you're going to go home, get married the way you're supposed to, and lie to everyone in your houses for the rest of your lives."

"And that's that."

"Don't I get a wedding invitation?" I asked. Master Philip grinned, but Madame Pilot glared at me. "No, I guess not. So there's just one more thing." I nodded toward the rucksack she was carrying over her shoulder. "You're going to put those logbooks back where you found 'em. With any luck, no one will have noticed that they're missing from the House Greer library. And since you already know what they say and made copies, you don't need to keep them any longer."

Philip frowned. "That's asking a lot, you know. These logs are evidence of things that have been kept secret for much too long. Without them—"

"It'll be hard to prove, sure. But someone in House Greer will eventually notice they're missing from your archives, and when they do, they'll search for the thief." I looked at Pilot. "The trail will lead straight to you, and from you to the Originalists, and that'll put all of you in jeopardy. Someone went to a lot of trouble making sure that our people forgot how and why they came to Tawcety—" I almost said *Tau Ceti-e* "—and they're not going to let you tell the truth. Not without a lot more proof than a ship's log."

As we spoke, we began walking up the side-street that lay outside the shed. We were no longer trying to break into the palisades, so there was no point in trying to hide. Everything was quiet. In an hour or so, the city would begin to wake up. For now, it was just the three of us.

"So go home," I went on. "Tell everyone that you had a spat but everything is okay now. Get hitched, settle in, lay low for a while. Become a respectable couple. And after everything dies down—"

"Hook up with the Originalists again," Pilot said, "and continue the work I've been doing,"

"The work *we'll* be doing," Philip corrected, and the smile he gave her left no question that he'd accepted the truth of what he'd seen and been told. The Originalists had just gained another believer.

"That's pretty much it, yeah." By then, we'd reached an intersection where another street cut across the one we'd been walking down. I recognized it as a way to get home myself, so I stopped there. "I'm going this way," I said, cocking a thumb in that direction. "You kids can find your way home from here, right? In that case…"

We shook on it and went our separate ways. I figured that I'd wait a day or two, then send a final invoice to Steward Conklin. He'd know by then that his niece was safe and sound, and would've heard the story about how the dick he'd hired had tracked her down. With Philip's help, of course, and that would work out in his favor, too; it's never a bad idea to do something that'll impress the in-laws. And no one would be the wiser.

Or so I thought.

The good feeling I had about how all this had worked out lasted only so long as it took for me to hike back across town. The shop keepers were putting out their wares and the ale wagons were making their morning deliveries, and shortly after I reached my flat, I found that the law was awake, too.

I'd just let myself in and was about to shrug out of my cape, filthy with the dirt and dust of Starship Mountain, when I heard through the open door a familiar, tell-tale sound: the creak of the stairs' fourth riser down. Someone was coming up to see me. I turned about and there was Bart.

"Good morning, Guardian." I pretended that getting a visit from him was the most perfectly natural thing. "Nice weather we're having."

"You'r-r-re back." He stood in the doorway, arms crossed, regarding me inquisitively. It was a good bet that he'd staked out my office from across the street, watching and waiting for my return. I bet he'd been there all night.

"Yes, I am," I said as I stepped around behind my desk. "Been waiting long?"

"Where you been?"

"None of your business." I sat down, hoping that he didn't notice that I hadn't yet removed my cape even though I was at home. The flintlock was beneath it, and that was the last thing I wanted him to see… well, almost the last.

He didn't like my answer. His eyes narrowed, and his claws unsheathed partway from his fingertips. "Business mine," he said, then pointed one of those claws at me. "Seen in Parlor last nigh'. Mas'er Philip wi' you. Figh' r-r-r-repor'ed ou'side. You pull gun on someone, and 'hen you bo'h wen' somewhere."

He must have had an informant in the Parlor. I hadn't noticed any Cetans in there last night, but there's people in the Squat who will sell out a fellow human to a Guardian if the price is right. "Maybe," I said, "but his eyes were playing tricks with him about the gun."

Bart's muzzle pulled back from his teeth and his ears cocked forward. "Don' care abou' gun. Wanna know where you wen'."

"And I said it's none of your business." I casually dropped my boots on top of the desk. "I found Pilot Fletcher and sent her home with Master Philip. That's all you need to know."

His muzzle and ears relaxed, but his eyes remained narrow. "Madame Gr-r-r-eer-r-r found? Gone back 'oo Heigh's? When?"

"Just a little while ago, and her fiancé, too. They should be there by now. You can go up there and check if you want." I smiled. "Do me a favor, will ya? If you run into Steward Conklin, please let him know that I'll be sending him a bill soon."

"Where you—?"

"Forget it, pal. Like I said, it's not your business." I shrugged. "It's nothing interesting. Bride-to-be got cold feet, decided to get out and enjoy being single for a while longer. Fooled around some, but nothing serious. Groom found her, patched things up, told the other guy to buzz off. Old story. Boring."

Of course, it was a lie. Or you could look at it another way and say that I'd told him the truth, just with a lot of things left out. But I wouldn't have told him everything I'd learned even I'd wanted to. Galileo had made Philip and me promise that we would never tell anyone what he, Pilot, and the other Originalists had discovered, what they were still trying to find. Their search wasn't finished. In fact, it had barely begun. But until the Originalists found their way through the dark, rusting maze of the *Lindbergh*, the secrets of Starship Mountain and the House Greer archives would have to remain hidden.

If only for a little while longer.

Bart stared at me for a few moments. I stared back, focusing not on his eyes but on a small white spot in the short fur of his muzzle. His people weren't good at staring contests; that's one human trick they'd never learned. He quickly looked away. Apparently realizing that he wasn't going to get anything out of me, he turned and walked out. Cetans never say goodbye, either; they just walk away. I watched as he disappeared down the steps.

Bart and I would have a showdown one day, but not this morning. I let out my breath, then stood up and shambled through the curtain my ex had given me, not long before she called me a cold bastard who cared for no one but myself. It had been a long, busy day and a long, sleepless night; I barely managed to get my gun off my person and hidden in its safe place before I collapsed face-down across the bed.

In the moments before I let sleep take me, my mind wandered across the things I'd seen and heard, the secrets and forgotten truths. I'd earned my pay, but there was still a mystery left unsolved.

This wasn't over yet.

Interlude

Excerpts from the Diary of Yvonne Greer (Commanding Officer, EPSS Lindbergh)

[Note: text has been edited to correct omissions and for clarity.]

10/29/'66

I've decided to continue the ship's logs as a personal account rather than as an official record, starting with this entry. The Lindbergh no longer exists, at least not as a viable starship, and it's all [but] certain that we'll never leave Tau Ceti-e, and there's no sense in pretending otherwise. But it's important for there to be some sort of historical record, even if it's only a handwritten journal, so I will continue recording our experiences for the sake of posterity and the edification of our descendants (if any).

Earlier today, we had our first encounter with Tau Ceti-e's native inhabitants. As first meetings go, it might have gone better, but it also could have [been] far worse. Language presents a significant barrier, of course, and I'm not sure we'll ever be able to fully understand each other. And there are already signs that our two races have cultural differences that will take time and effort to overcome. On the other hand, the Cetans are not hostile—so far, at least—and they seem to understand that, even though we're an alien race, we're here as castaways, not invaders.

The Cetan ship that sailed to this island—Kyle has proposed a name, Sanctuary; it's appropriate, and I intend to second his motion at the next senior staff meeting—is a large vessel that looks a little like a cross between a catamaran and a historical Chinese dhow: three masts rigged with triangular lateen sails, a long, shallow main hull with a double-deck aft cabin, and a smaller outrigger hull for maneuvering. Alarmingly, there appear to be gun-ports midship; they're closed, which is a bit of a relief, but Floyd thinks the ship may have cannons below the main deck. If he's right, that's not a good sign: they've developed gunpowder and they know how to use it.

The ship arrived this afternoon and dropped anchor about 300 yards offshore, in the small bay near our landing site that serves as a natural harbor. A little while later, two longboats were lowered over its port and starboard sides and made their way toward us; as they drew closer, we could see bipedal figures manning oars on each craft.

By then, the initial panic that had run through the crew and passengers had subsided, and after a hasty conference among the command team, we decided how to handle the situation. Every person present, including all colonists who'd been revived and were capable of walking on their own, came down to the beach, where they were ordered to remain quiet, keep their hands visible at all times, and make no sudden movements. The idea was, if the Cetans could see everyone, they'd know how many there are of us, and interpret our peaceful presence as an indication that we aren't hostile and have nothing to hide.

Julius, Tonya, Aaron, and I formed the "welcome committee," a lighthearted name for what's essentially the contact team. The people who planned this mission had taken such a situation into account even before Lindy left Earth, and had established protocols for first contact, so the welcome committee had already been selected. With the Lindbergh's complement at our backs, the four of us stood at the water's edge and waited for the Cetans to come ashore.

The boats, which resemble old-style Boston whalers [only] a bit larger, came right up to the beach, their wooden hulls scraping up against the sand just a few feet from where we stood. There were eight Cetan sailors in one boat and nine in the other, with their leader (captain?) being the ninth person in the latter. When they climbed out, we got our first good look at them. What we saw was astonishing. Of all the ways I've imagined extraterrestrials to be, I never expected this.

There are a lot of ways I could describe them, I suppose, but when it comes right down to it, their appearance is so strikingly familiar that everyone says the same thing: the Cetans look like dogs. They stand and walk upright on two legs, not four, and have four-fingered hands with opposable thumbs and somewhat human-like feet instead of paws, although they have four toes that are larger and spread farther apart, with big toes on either side of each foot. Yet they are distinctly canine, resembling nothing less than highly evolved dogs. Dogs of one single breed: lean, muscular bodies like Labrador retrievers; short, dappled fur like German shepherds (although a greater variety of colors, and even spots and stripes, were visible among members of the shore party); short, bearded muzzles and solemn, deep-set eyes like Scottish terriers. Large, pointed ears near the top of the skull, which has a cranium much larger than that of a dog; again, evolution apparently favored them with larger brains than most dogs. Some have mohawk-like crests of fur running along the top of their heads and some do not; it may be a matter of stylistic choice, but it could also be hereditary, gender-based, or some kind of status symbol. On average, their height is about 5'4" – 5'6", but there were a few taller ones about 5'9" and one giant whom I know for sure to be 5'11" because I could look her (or him) straight in the eye.

Individual gender is difficult to determine; like dogs, the physiological differences between males and females are not as obvious as they are with humans, since their genitals [are] well-hidden by clothing. No tails; Tonya thinks evolution took them away as the species learned how to stand and walk upright, though Julius points out we won't know for sure until "someone lifts his or her skirt for us." Females don't have obvious mammary organs or breasts, but I've noticed that some Cetans wore tunics with multiple button-flaps running in a double row down the chest; I'm guessing they're meant for breast-feeding more than one offspring at a time. Those Cetans are generally shorter but have larger and sturdier hips and legs… another clue that they're females of the race.

They wear clothes, but not much. Their fur makes garments unnecessary except for privacy; kilts, shorts, or loin cloths were worn by everyone, although hooded capes with elaborate (and very beautiful) embroidery seem to be favored. No gloves, but they wear peculiar-looking boots, tall enough to reach the tops of their long, backward-jointed ankles but open at the front to expose their splayfooted toes. Three Cetans in each boat wore leather body armor and matching helmets that, along with long, wicked-looking swords carried in back-sheaths, made them appear to be soldiers. I hope not, but reason tells me I shouldn't [have] expected otherwise; if I were them, I would've brought an armed escort, too.

They came ashore as a group, the oarsmen dragging the boats by their gunnels, and stopped before us, as silent and wary as we were. It's very hard to say which side was more nervous, us or them. First-contact situations had been discussed during mission training, but no one anticipated it occurring quite this way; I really had no idea what to do.

So I improvised. I took a couple of steps forward, raised both hands to shoulder height and held them palm-out, smiled while being careful not to show my teeth—I figured that a canine race might interpret that as a sign of hostility, as dogs do—and said, "Greetings, we're from Earth."

I knew, of course, that my words wouldn't be understood, but I hoped that my gestures would. Apparently they were, for one of the Cetans—a female, I believe, since she wore one of the buttoned tunics I described; if she's their captain, this may tell us a bit about their society—detached herself from the group to come forward. Stopping just a couple of feet from me, she took a few moments to look me over. While she didn't sniff me in a direct fashion, her head craned and her nostrils flared, and it appeared that she was catching a whiff of my body odor. I don't know how to <u>smell</u> friendly, so I did my best to think happy thoughts, and hoped they'd manifest themselves in my pheromones.

I guess it worked, for she raised her hands and imitated my gesture. She smiled, too, and it also seemed as if she was making a conscious effort not to show her teeth. But as soon as she spoke, I knew it was—well, unlikely, if not impossible—that we'd ever learn their language. I once had a dog, a golden retriever-collie mix named Zack who'd try to "talk" to me; what came from his mouth was an incoherent jumble of mumbles, grunts, whines, and staccato barks. This is much like what the Cetan language sounds like. We can only hope that they'll learn to understand and speak English instead.

Both of us were willing to make the effort to communicate, though, so there on the beach, the two of us had the first conversation between members of alien races. Generations of SETI scientists would have sold their souls for this moment... and screamed in frustration when they found themselves reduced to pantomime and drawing pictures in the sand.

Somehow, we managed to make it work. I had Tonya, Julius, and Aaron [there] to help me, and the captain—I've decided to call her Fae, from the first syllable of the long and unpronounceable utterance she made when she pointed to herself—had support from two of her crew. Both were males and judging from the number of times she consulted them (along with later observations of [their] behavior), I'm starting [to] wonder if Cetans have a gender-based civilization that's the mirror-reverse of human society: females in charge, but often deferring to males in matters such as diplomacy. But that's just a guess. Julius warns me that it may be much more complex than that, so I shouldn't assume anything.

Fae didn't seem very surprised to find that we'd come from the sky. After all, it was the shuttle's contrails that attracted her people's attention in the first place and caused them to send a ship out here to investigate. But she and the others were stunned by the Lindbergh (what's left of it). When we led them over to Lindy, they stared up at the module stack with fascinated astonishment, but also fear, I think. If that's so, it may not [be] something we want instill[ed] in them... not if we want to make friends.

(Again: it's important they don't perceive us as invaders! We need them for survival!)

The Cetan landing party stayed for a little while, about an hour and a half, then returned to their boats, cast off, and rowed back to their ship. As I write by firelight, I can see lamps glowing within the windows of its aft cabins. No doubt Fae is meeting with her officers right now, just as I've just met with mine. If anyone seriously believes that the inhabitants of Tau Ceti-e are going to prostrate themselves at our feet and worship us as sky gods, they're going to be disappointed. On the other hand, I don't think they're inclined to break out the stew-kettles either.

Both sides are being cautious, as we should be. For now, all we can do is try to build on what we've accomplished today and hope for the best.

10/30/'66

The Cetans returned this morning, this time with gifts: food, clothing, and rolls [of] sailcloth for making tents (the last they had to pantomime to make clear to us what was intended; they also brought plenty of ropes and wooden pegs). Apparently they've realized that the strangers in their midst are hungry, nearly naked, and in dire need of shelter, and decided to take care of us. As friendly gestures go, this is extremely welcome. As best I could with pantomime, hand signals, and much bowing, I let Captain Fae know that we appreciated their generosity; I think she understood, because she mimicked me.

On that basis, I believe communication and eventually friendship between Cetans and humans is possible. Because of that, I've asked Julius Fletcher to form an "interpretation committee" whose sole purpose will be to try to understand the Cetan language or, failing that, teach English to the Cetans. Julius has agreed to do this, and plans to enlist the colonists who were recruited for the mission as teachers. However, he cautions me that it may be easier for the Cetans to learn and use our language than vice-versa, and he may be right. When I thanked Captain Fae for the supplies, she surprised me by attempting to reiterate "thank you" after I voiced that expression several times, and her pronunciation was close enough—it sounded like "'hank you" because they have trouble with saying "t"—that I understood what she meant.

The food they bought us consisted mainly of fresh fish, some dried and salted, but mostly live and stored in water barrels; we assume this is what they caught on the way, and sure enough, later in that morning we spotted anglers casting lines off the ship's side. Tau Ceti-e apparently has a wide range of pelagic species, and while [some] are ugly as sin—the ones Tonya calls wallyfish (after an old boyfriend whom she claims it resembles) and septopi (which looks like an octopus except with one less tentacle) are gruesome—we've killed, cleaned, and cooked a few, and careful experiment proves they're edible and some (particularly faux-salmon) are even delicious.

The only surprise here is that the Cetans seem shocked that we don't eat them raw, let alone alive. I watched one of them demonstrate the Cetan way of consuming a wallyfish by putting his hands in a barrel, catching one, and sinking his teeth into it while it was still flopping in his hands. That was kind of hard to take, and I hope I didn't offend him by turning away while trying not to gag.

Cetans don't wear a lot of clothes, but their capes are quite comfortable. Fae gave me one herself—I took that as a personal good-will gesture, one leader to another—and I'm sure it'll keep me warm tonight after sun goes down and the wind off the ocean kicks up. I suspect this is a fashion that might catch on.

Speaking of which: one thing we've already noticed about the Cetans is their response to the midday sun and the heat it brings. It really gets hot around the middle of the day, enough to make you feel sluggish and uncomfortable. The Cetans cope with this by finding a shady place to lay down and take a nap for an hour or two: a siesta, just like the ones traditionally practiced in some Spanish-speaking countries. It might seem like a lazy thing to do, but it makes sense. And if the Cetans want to knock off in the middle of the day for lunch and a quick shut-eye, I see no reason not to follow their example.

So: we're making friends with the locals, who seem willing and able to come to the aid of marooned aliens. People's spirits are beginning to brighten, and the feeling of helplessness is no longer as acute as it's been. I'd say we're off to a good start.

11/1/'66

We had our first town meeting this afternoon after siesta; i.e. a formal get-together of everyone in the colony. We've refrained from doing this until all the colonists [have been] revived from biostasis and sufficiently recovered to participate in the proceedings. I also wanted to give the command team and the various ad hoc committees a little time to come up with a formal agenda and proposals for dealing with some of the things we need to do in order to transform our landing site into a viable community.

As Lindbergh's captain, I presided over the meeting, which followed the traditional rules of order. Over the course of the afternoon, we worked our way through the agenda. Here are some of the things that were discussed and decided upon:

We now have a formal government. Replacing the Lindbergh command hierarchy will be a Council of Stewards, whose officers will be democratically elected by the population at large. However, because we need a government in place at once—there are critical decisions to make right now, before an election [can be held]—it's been decided that the first Council will consist of the Lindbergh's command team, with myself in charge. So instead of our former ranks, we're now Stewards, a term which implies that its members are civil servants instead of officers. For the time being, though, I'm retaining the title "Captain" instead of using Mayor, Governor, President, etc., until we work out the specifics of the colony charter. Ted Gillespie has suggested (somewhat tongue-in-cheek) that I be addressed as "cap" instead of "captain." Not a bad idea; I like it.

A committee has been established, with Steward Van Pelt in charge (trying to get used to the new appellations by using them), to explore and map Sanctuary's coastline and learn from the Cetans the best ways of taking fish from its water. We're fortunate that our landing site (or simply "Landing Site," short for the old LS1, which seems to be what everyone still wants to call this place; kind of unimaginative, but at least [it's] better than "Crash Site") is next to a bay; once we've built boats of our own, it'll become our harbor. The Cetans are already using it, of course, and I hope it won't be long before we have a fishing fleet.

Other committees and teams were formed to undertake the various tasks that need to be done: locating materials suitable for constructing permanent dwellings; clearing land for farming (the meadows and hillsides between the beach and the mountains appears to have the most suitable soil, according to Steward Fletcher); exploring the nearby terrain for the purpose of identifying and cataloging useful flora and fauna (Johann Gorsch has already spotted a large, six-legged beast that the Cetans have told us is easily domesticated, and Bork—can't remember her first name—has captured a possum-like rodent that has a nasty temperament but which we've been informed is edible); salvaging equipment from Lindy's wreckage, including useable items such as furniture, removable bulkheads, unbroken glass, or anything else that wasn't destroyed by the Rot.

Lindbergh itself poses a major problem. The hibernation modules are not only uninhabitable, but actually dangerous; the Rot attacked the infrastructure so thoroughly that entire decks are on the verge of collapse. Not only that, but the stack is listing to such a degree that inevitably, sooner or later, the whole thing is going to topple over and come crashing down. So we've asked our colonists to move their tents and shacks outside a 1,000-ft. radius around the ship, and we're making Lindy off-limits except for salvage crews (all volunteers—dangerous work in there). Eventually, what remains of the ship will have to be safely lowered from vertical to horizontal position and dismantled. No one knows how to accomplish this without cranes, polymer cables, and lasers, but I got the engineering team working on the problem.

As for the Cetans, we're making progress in learning how to communicate with them, and a friendship is developing between our races. But (and I say this privately, because I didn't bring it up in the public meeting), there is still some apprehension between our peoples, and as much as I hate to say it, I think they distrust us more than we do them. Steward Fletcher tells me that, in his conversations with Captain Fae, there appear to be a number of questions about her people that she pretends not to hear or understand, no matter how often he reiterates them in sign-language and sketches.

Julius believes that Fae is keeping secrets from us. If that's true, this isn't a good omen.

* * *

[*Note: omitted journal entries from 11/2/2266 through 11/4/2266. The subjects discussed principally involve the day-to-day details of establishing the original Landencyte settlement, and therefore are not important to the subject at hand. Interested scholars should consult the Historical Society for missing text. —Eds.*]

11/5/'66

    We had an altercation with the Cetans today. To make matters worse, it wasn't the first. I just wasn't told about the earlier incident until now.

    What happened today was that a colonist, Debra Andretti, tried to pet a Cetan. That is, in a moment of affection, she laid a hand on the back of his neck and tried to stroke his fur, just as if she would pet a dog back on Earth. She meant no harm, of course. Indeed, as I told her later, there have been times when I've been tempted to do the same. The Cetans are generally friendly, if a bit reserved, and some have beautiful fur; petting them is such a natural impulse for us, and I confess I've had to restrain myself from stroking Fae between the ears. But they really don't like to be touched, not even as friendly gesture; in hindsight, I don't think I've seen them touch even one another in such a manner. They're protective of personal space even more than we are, and while they've been tolerant of our differences so far, this is one place where they draw the line.

    The Cetan, whose "human name" is Ralph, was startled and annoyed, and he immediately turned and snapped at her. Debra drew back at once, but then she reacted the wrong way and yelled, "Hey, cut it out!" Again, just as if Ralph was a dog who'd snapped at her.

    Ralph didn't understand what she said, of course, but the meaning was clear, and witnesses tell me that he bared his teeth and started to reach for his sword. Some of the Cetans still carry their weapons whenever they come ashore from their ship, but this is the first time any of them has almost pulled one from its scabbard (and a Cetan sword, called a "worka," is an evil weapon, a cutlass with deep, serrated crevices along the blade's cutting edge, capable of disemboweling a foe with one swipe). Before he did so, another Cetan nearby yelled something at him in their language, and Ralph stopped what he was doing at once and walked away (which is what they do when they finish speaking to you; polite ways of ending a conversation appear to be unknown to them).

Debra came to me immediately and told me what had happened. I decided, rather than let the incident fester, I should discuss it with Fae. She and I have developed a good relationship over the last week, as two captains should—there's a Cetan word for her position as commanding officer, but I can't pronounce it any more than I can pronounce her ship's name—and she is quickly learning the rudiments of English, which has helped us communicate with each other.

Fae apologized for her crewman's conduct, but she confirmed what I'd already guessed: Cetans do not like to be touched in such a familiar manner, except perhaps during mating (something else Cetans don't want to discuss, although I have a hunch that sex is different for them, too). So, above all, humans must avoid touching Cetans, even with the best intentions.

I agreed to let the colonists know this as soon as possible. Then Fae told me about something else that happened. Yesterday, several crewmen were clearing debris from the grasslands beside the beach, making room for the tents away from the stack. A Cetan was standing nearby, doing nothing but watching them. One of the crewman found a piece of driftwood that had probably washed ashore during a storm. He picked it up and threw it near the Cetan—not directly at him, but close enough that the Cetan couldn't miss seeing it—and yelled something at him.

I don't know exactly what it was, but judging from what Fae told me, I think I can guess: "Fetch!"

The Cetan couldn't understand exactly what he said, but he certainly comprehended the meaning. As with today's incident, his response was to turn and walk away. Fae said that all the humans standing nearby laughed at this—at least laughter is something both races share in common, even if humor isn't always the same—and it made her crewman angry and embarrassed to be treated this way.

Fae apparently decided to let the first incident slide, but this second one couldn't be ignored. Again, I apologized as profusely as possible for our rude behavior, and I think she's accepted it. I've put out the word that the Cetans are not to be touched, spoken to, or otherwise treated in any way as you would an Earth dog, not even in jest.

I'm hoping this sinks in, and although I can't expect for incidents like that to never happen again, I can do my best to make sure everyone learns to be culturally sensitive about our hosts. For that's who they are, and we can't afford to wear out our welcome; there's just no where else for us to go!

***

[Omitted journal entry: 11/6/2266]

11/7/'66

Woke up to a cold morning; saw my breath when I stepped outside. Happy for the cape Fae gave me. Only a couple of weeks ago, it felt like summer. I have to remind myself that this world has a short sidereal period because of its close proximity to Tau Ceti, and therefore its seasons are three times shorter than Earth's. Fortunately, since Tau Ceti-e occupies an elliptical orbit but doesn't also have an axial tilt, this will mean a regular (if unusually swift) change of seasons, with those seasons occurring simultaneously on both sides of the equator.

So while autumn is here and winter is on the way, in just a couple of months things will get warm again. Still, it reminds us that we need to move faster about building permanent dwellings. I don't think we'll see snow here on the equator, but I'm not looking forward to spending the next eight weeks or so huddled in a cold tent.

Fae and I spent another day "in school"—i.e., teaching each other about our worlds and cultures. Problem is, she's learning much more about Earth than I am about Bakkah (the closest phonetic spelling I can come up with for the way Cetans pronounce their name for Tau Ceti-e, which some of our people are already pronouncing and even spelling as "Tawcety"). Since Lindy's orbital surveys were stored on computers [that were] subsequently destroyed by the Rot, none of the planetary maps or photos survived the crash. As a result, we're having to depend largely upon what the Cetans tell about their world, and for some reason, Fae and her crew are reticent about revealing all but the most necessary information.

With assistance from Julius and Sergei (good to have a talented artist among us), we've been able to create a tentative map, based on our memories of the orbital survey and what Fae is willing to tell us.

Thus, Sanctuary is called Mahha by the Cetans, and it's been uninhabited until now. Although it's located between distant continents, trade on this world is largely localized and therefore the Cetans didn't consider a midocean island to be particularly useful and thus felt no need to settle Mahha. Same for the chain of small islands just below Sanctuary, which we've named the Southern Archipelago and they call Bah-Wah (an unintentional pun there!). The large continent to the west from which Fae's vessel set sail to find us is called Gruhar, and on its east coast is a major port city called Ha-Fahha. Fae says that Ha-Fahha translates as "City of Dancers" (I think I'm getting that right) but that's all she'll tell me about it. It seems to have some importance; I can only guess what it is.

Only very reluctantly has Fae helped us sketch out a rough map of the rest of the planet and identified its major land masses by name. But even though we now know, for instance, that the neighboring continents in the Eastern Hemisphere are called Gruhar, Ara, Barrac, and Rahr, with the largest continent, Horraf, straddling the meridian line of the Western Hemisphere, and the polar continents are Hak to the north and Haku-Ka to the south, we know nothing—and I mean <u>nothing</u>—about them. No geographical details, nothing about the distances from one place to another, and almost nothing about population centers other than Ha-Fahha (how <u>did</u> we manage to miss spotting them from orbit, I wonder?). Whenever Julius, Sergei, or I ask a question she doesn't want to answer, she either pretends not to understand us or simply ignores us… and when we persist, her response is to simply walk away.

Trying to pry such information from her crew members has likewise been futile. I suspect that they're under orders from Fae not to discuss their world or themselves, because whenever we've tried to ask the questions Fae has refused to answer, the other Cetans do the same thing she does: ignore us and walk away. For some reason, they don't want to tell us any more about Bakkah/Tawcety than what we absolutely, positively need to know.

At the same time, though, Fae wants to know everything she can about humans and Earth. Hoping that candor on our side will be reciprocated by more openness on their end, I've tried to answer her questions freely (with one major exception). Unfortunately, this may not have been a good idea. Fae is learning that humans are more technologically advanced—or at least our race is; because of the Rot, most of the technology that was aboard <u>Lindbergh</u> has been lost and cannot be replaced—and therefore we're capable of things they consider impossible, even magical. Mainly the latter; from what we've observed, the Cetans' technological level is no more advanced than what humans on Earth had in the 17th or early 18th century, and they continue to have strong beliefs in the paranormal and supernatural.

Fae was visibly surprised to learn that <u>Lindbergh</u> had a sister ship, the <u>Santos-Dumont,</u> that was lost in space with all lives. I think it unnerved her to know that there were more humans than just us who intended to colonize Bakka. She wanted to know all about it, and I let her know that it was very much like my own ship, but that her crew never had a chance to make a safe landing: I witnessed its destruction with my own eyes.

Fae has accepted that <u>Lindy</u> and her crew are all that's left of our mission, but whenever she stops to regard what remains of the <u>Lindbergh</u>, it's not hard to tell that it frightens her, for her ears flatten back and her fur raises ever so slightly. I think we scare her. And this is not a good thing. Eventually, she and her crew will leave Sanctuary and sail back to Gruhar, and there she will report what she discovered. Perhaps it's to our advantage (however temporary) that her people haven't developed radio or similar wireless communications, but nonetheless, I don't want them to feel threatened enough to bring an army down on top of us. We're at their mercy, and we can't afford to make enemies of them.

[*Omitted journal entries: 11/8/2266 through 11/12/2266*]

<u>11/13/'66</u>

Something very bad happened today: the Cetans learned about dogs.

I've been trying to keep this from them, and during our last town meeting I repeated my request that no one mention dogs to our hosts. But as many of the Cetans have learned to understand some English and even speak a little of it—they are very fast at absorbing new information—perhaps it was inevitable. And, damn it, some of our people do love to talk.

From what I understand, it happened when a group of colonists joined a handful of Cetans to go up into the foothills to hunt bork. A rainstorm came in, so they took shelter in a cave, and while they were waiting out the storm, a couple of our people observed the Cetans shaking off the rain much the way dogs do. When they mentioned this, the Cetans became curious, and so these idiots spent the next hour or so telling our hosts how much they remind us of the species of Earth animals whom we treat as pets.

The first I heard about this was later in the day, when Fae marched into my campsite and, without preamble, demanded to know if it was true that, on Earth, my people have enslaved her people. This was how the stories about Earth dogs was misinterpreted by her crew members: that there were people very much like Cetans on Earth, and they were forced to walk on all fours, wear collars and leashes, sleep outdoors on bare ground, and other indignities.

Naturally, she was quite upset about this.

Once I managed to get Fae to calm down a bit, I did my best to explain to her that the dogs of Earth were not very much like her people except in appearance and a few shared habits. Unfortunately, I ran into trouble when I tried to cite Julius and Tonya's theory that Cetans are a highly-evolved canine race and the sort of thing that might have occurred on Earth if dogs had climbed the evolutionary ladder that our hominid ancestors did. The Cetans have no concept of evolution. They haven't yet had a Charles Darwin to make critical observations about nature and arrive at a major scientific theory that, over time, has proven to be true. Indeed, they have their own impediment to Darwinian evolution: a religion called Dagahn (I think I'm spelling that right) which teaches, among other things, that their race was created in the image of their god, who just so happens to look exactly like a Cetan.

Fortunately, Fae isn't so—I almost wrote dogmatic!—adamant in her beliefs that she's been unwilling to accept the idea that intelligent life exists elsewhere in the universe. Indeed, Dagahn makes allowances for beings from beyond Bakkah, just not beings who don't look like Cetans. However, our arrival on Bakkah has unnerved some of her crew. They weren't inclined to trust us when we got here, and only gradually over the last few weeks have they come to accept us as shipwrecked explorers. This new revelation, and the misunderstanding that comes with it, could damage the fragile relationship both sides have managed to develop.

I tried to assure Fae that we didn't come to her world with the intent of enslaving her people and reiterated that the dogs of our world aren't slaves but loyal companions whom we love dearly (and I pray that her people never learn about the cruel and heartless things some people have done to some of them). I <u>think</u> she believes me and accepts my assurances, but I can't be sure. Like many Cetans (particularly females), she is very good at hiding her feelings, at least from humans who can't use their olfactory senses to detect emotional changes. All I can hope is that she could smell truth in me, that I wasn't lying about anything I told her.

Fae then broke some news of her own: her ship will be departing soon, sailing back to Gruhar. She didn't say so outright, but in previous conversations she has let slip that there is a leader in Ha-Fahha—perhaps a queen or an empress; Fae has sometimes referred to an unnamed leader for whom she uses the female pronoun—to whom she is ultimately responsible. If so, then I expect that she will report what she and her crew discovered on Mahha, and this leader (along with whatever government exists among the Cetans) will make some decision how to treat us.

Until now, I've had hopes for a peaceful and productive relationship. We'll never leave Tawcety, nor will we ever be rescued; the log entries I managed to transmit before <u>Lindy</u> lost its com [communications capability] should convince people back home that a rescue mission is hopeless, for any vessel that attempts to land would suffer the same fate as our shuttles, and same for their motherships, too. But the Cetans didn't trust us very much even before this happened, and now they're going to trust us even less.

I think they'll let us live. But I don't think they'll ever let us leave this island.

Part Two:
The Lost Testament

I

The world changed overnight, it's sometimes said, but change seldom happens that way. Even when some event dramatically alters the shape of the world in which we live, the full impact is usually slow in coming; we don't immediately see the full extent, for it takes time for the ripples to become waves and waves to build into tsunamis. Yes, the world changes, but sometimes with great subtlety, unnoticed before your very eyes.

So I didn't realize just how much the discovery of the *Lindbergh* logs would change our understanding of human history on Tawcety. I don't think anyone did, not even the Originalists. It was inevitable that the logbooks of the first Cap and her crew would have repercussions and some of them would be enormous; I'd figured that already. What I didn't anticipate was just how quietly the world would change... at first.

I didn't see Philip and Pilot again for quite a while. Once we emerged from Starship Mountain in the cool, dim hours of Landencyte morning, the two of them went their way and I went mine. I never really expected to lay eyes on them again, nor anyone else involved in the affair. And I didn't, not for some time. I sent my invoice via courier to Steward Conklin, and a day later a cheque, made out in my name and stamped with the red-wax seal of House Conklin's treasurer, arrived the same way. No personal note from the steward, though, nor the customary token of appreciation, an endorsement scroll to show prospective clients that I'd once been retained by a member of the Council of Stewards. Conklin was probably too embarrassed by his daughter's premarital affair to acknowledge that it had even happened, let alone that he'd hired a dick to investigate. He just quietly paid me off, and since he paid promptly and well, I was content to close the case once and for all.

What I learned that night from Pilot and her friends was astounding, but it didn't change the price of beans. Even if I'd stood upon a crate out front of City Hall and loudly held forth about the history that had been lost—or perhaps even stolen from us, but nonetheless lay in the steel catacombs within Starship Mountain—the reception would have been the same accorded to every raving fool who holds forth in a public place. No one would have paid attention, not even my fellow fools.

So I let the matter drop and did my best to forget about it.

Trouble came and trouble went. That's my business, after all, and it's not like I have to advertise to find it. People with problems arrived at my door or sent messages for me to come see them, and sometimes I found myself handling two or even three cases at once. Not for the first time, I thought about hiring a partner, or maybe just someone to come in and handle the scutwork. That would've meant having to pay someone, though, and I don't like sharing the money I work hard to make.

I wore out boot leather, and kept my blades polished and my pistol clean, and spent my days and nights out in the street, taking care of other people's problems. I shook down deadbeats for unpaid bills and skipped loans, and watched a lot of side windows and back doors, and stood in the shadows waiting for someone to come out so I could tail him or her, and had to tell some nice old folks that they shouldn't have given money to a freelance magus to do something for them because he was a con artist (as they always were, although under law I couldn't make that charge since professional mages are protected from libel and slander), and had a sword fight with a dude who tried to push his boss off a rooftop in the Squat (I won, and the other guy became the wet mess on the sidewalk he intended his former employer to be) and found a lost mimecat. The last job was the best; the little girl whose parents had hired me to get her pet back was so happy, I knocked twenty percent off my bill. Never let it be said that I lack generosity.

Autumn became winter, and winter became spring, and spring became summer again, and the weeks became months as the seasons swiftly went by. And then, one day nearly two years after I'd last seen them, I heard the loose step creak on my stairs. There was a knock on the door, and then it swung open and Philip and Pilot walked in.

II

Or rather, Citizen Exemplary Philip and Madame Pilot of House Greer, as they were now formally known. Pilot's engagement bangle was gone from her hair; instead, she now wore the tiara of a married woman, and one glance at its elegant Cetan gold filigree and emerald fore-stone—so different from the ordinary beaded headband my ex had worn; I couldn't afford better to give her better, not with my salary as a badge—affirmed that she was a lady of wealth and means. There was a matching band around Philip's left wrist, but somehow the matrimonial accoutrements looked better on her.

I hadn't been invited to the wedding, nor had I expected to be. I almost never see old clients again, unless I happen to pass them on the street or a waiter at a public house seats me at a nearby table. And although the business of the *Lindbergh* logs was intriguing, it was also old business. So I couldn't have been more surprised to see them come in.

"Well, now there's a pair," I said, grinning as I swung my feet down from the windowsill behind my desk. "Master Phillip—sorry, Citizen Philip—Madame Pilot, nice to see you again."

"And you." Philip stoically bowed his head and Pilot sketched a curtsy; stepping around the desk, I shook his hand and brushed my lips against the back of hers. More manners than my office is used to seeing, but the gentlemen and ladies of the Heights carry their customs with them.

But once formalities were observed, they were also done. "How the hell are you, kid?" I said, slapping his shoulder just hard enough. "Had any good fights lately?"

Philip winced but took the comment and shoulder-slap with a proud smile. No, he hadn't forgotten the altercation in the alley outside the Harbor Lady's Parlor. Proper young gents from steward families aren't supposed to engage in swordplay down in the Squat, though, so this was a subject he'd sooner not discuss. Me, I love to reminisce about my bar fights. Particularly the ones I win.

Before Philip could think of something to say, Pilot stepped around him. Another surprise; she briefly folded herself around me in a fond hug. The sort of thing I'd expect from a lady friend, even an old lover, but not from a former client's daughter. I was still trying to figure out what this was all about when, for a brief instant, her face came close to mine.

"It's so *good* to see you again," she breathed against my cheek. "I was worried we'd never find you."

It wasn't as if I kept secret my office location. Her father could have told her where to track me down, and besides, my address was listed in the city almanac. And I barely knew her, and Philip only slightly better. So why was she was laying it on so thick?

She wanted something from me. Both of them did.

"Didn't know I was hard to track down." I gently pried myself from her; from the corner of my eye, I saw Philip watching me the way newlywed husbands do when their wives go about hugging other men. I felt my face grow warm. Pilot was a nice girl, but she was young enough to be my daughter and lately I'd sworn off married women; she wasn't my type. "Just about anyone in the neighborhood could've told you where I live."

"I know. That's how we got your address." Philip nodded toward the open window behind me; the sounds of the street were coming in, carried by a warm Summermonth breeze. "Three people told us your office is above a wine shop. We only had to find which shop."

I shrugged. "The cheapest one in town. Hard to miss: just follow the drunks."

Not that funny, really, but they laughed anyway. They were nervous and trying to hide it, and in my line of work that generally means that someone wants something from you but they're anxious about asking for reasons as yet undetermined. No, this wasn't a social visit. They weren't here to share wedding stories with me.

I waved them to the chairs in front of my desk and offered them some wine from the vintner downstairs—the good stuff the landlord gives me when the rent is paid on time—and once everyone was comfortable and had a glass in hand, I resumed my seat, put my feet up again, and let them talk. Sometimes, the best way to get a client to tell you what they want is not to push at them, but instead relax and let them get there all by themselves.

In bits and pieces of anecdote, Philip and Pilot told me about everything they'd done since the last time I'd seen them a year and a half ago. As it turned out, they'd taken my advice seriously. Pilot told me she'd smuggled the logbooks back into the secret archives of House Greer's library, replacing them just the way she found them. No one in Philip's clan ever tumbled to the fact that the books had been absent from their shelves for a while.

Pilot then informed Galileo, the leader of the local Originalist cell and her mentor, that his "study group" wouldn't be seeing much of her for a while, for she'd decided to take seriously again her engagement to Philip, and needed time to seal their matrimony.

"I hesitate to ask," I asked, "but how did Master Gillespie take this?"

"Mike?" An indifferent shrug from Philip. "Not well, but he didn't have a say in it. Not unless he wanted to challenge me for milady's hand." With a possessive smile, he reached over to curl his hand around hers. "And as you found, swordsmanship isn't one of his talents."

"He couldn't cut butter with a breadknife," I said.

That brought another laugh, then Philip continued. Once these things were done, they went about getting married. It was what everyone in their respective houses had been expecting them to do anyway, so the only thing they had to explain was her abrupt disappearance. But Pilot told her father that it was merely a matter of cold feet, and that she'd only wanted to get away from everyone until she figured things out for herself—she hinted at the affair with Michael Gillespie without telling him everything and let him figure out the rest for himself—and the steward accepted this without question ("Well," she added, "at least none that I couldn't answer with a little bitty lie"). As they expected, Steward Conklin passed the word along to his peers and their families, and soon everyone in House Greer and House Fletcher knew the reason for the delayed marriage... or thought they did.

The wedding was beautiful, a traditional ceremony held in a gazebo in a park on Carson Bluff overlooking the Western Ocean. The groom wore black, the bride wore white; ceremonial sabers clashed above their heads as they marched together up the gazebo steps, and their families, clansmen, and friends let out a hurrah and applauded when he placed the tiara on her head and she clasped the band around his wrist. Even Michael Gillespie, who somehow found the nerve to show up.

"Nice of you to still invite him," I said.

"He'd already had received an invitation," Philip replied, not smiling, "and it would've raised questions if we'd rescinded it. So it was formal obligation for both of us. He wasn't welcome and he knew it, but he had to come just as it was… necessary… for us to invite him."

In this way, Philip and Pilot slipped into the roles their respective families and Houses expected of them: Citizen Exemplary and Madame Greer, a handsome young couple whose marriage sealed a bond between two old, influential Landencyte stewardships. They were given a suite upstairs in the west wing of the family manor, and together they made it their new home. Philip now had a job as a senior accountant in House Greer's financial service while Pilot was employed as an export manager in House Fletcher's inland mercantile trade, lucrative positions that subtly assisted each other and promised to maintain and raise the fortunes of both Houses.

No one knew, or even suspected, their connection with the Originalists. They carefully hid Pilot's copy of *The Secret Origins of Landencyte*. When Steward Conklin, shortly before the wedding, demanded that she destroy it, she burned an ordinary cookbook in its place and showed him the ashes. Since then, Philip had occasionally removed the book from its place of concealment in their parlor and, late at night, studied what his new wife already knew, the true history of the human presence on Tawcety.

"So," I said, "you've become an Originalist too."

Philip frowned. "I'm not sure I'd call myself that—" Pilot gave him a sharp look "—but I suppose so. The logbooks and the conclusions of the people who've studied them appear to be irrefutable. Humans came to this world from another planet called Earth, and they did so by unmagical means. This is what the Originalists believe, and since I've come to accept this as fact…" He shrugged.

"But it still leaves a lot of questions unanswered," Pilot said, picking up the thread. "Namely, why have generations of our people been taught otherwise? If *plastik* was real and the *Lindbergh* was destroyed because it can't exist here, why go to such great lengths to hide the fact? Our ancestors were shipwrecked. What's the point in hiding that?"

As she said this, it occurred to me that these were questions that I'd been subconsciously trying to avoid ever since the night Gillespie had led Philip and me through the underground tunnel beneath the stockade walls surrounding the wrecked starship. Maybe I'd been fooling myself into believing that nothing I'd learned from Pilot, Galileo, and the other

Originalists really made much difference, but the truth was, it did, and in a very profound and fundamental way. It's one thing to solve the mystery of a young lady's disappearance; it's another to explain the disappearance of history itself.

"Anyway, we took your advice and laid low," Pilot said. "Through Michael, I sent word to my study group, letting them know that I wouldn't be active for a while but that I'd return once Philip and I settled in and everyone in our houses forgot about how I'd gone missing." She smiled as she reached over to take her husband's hand. "I didn't mind," she added. "Marrying him was the wisest thing I've ever done. I'm sorry I ever doubted him, or—"

She stopped herself, and there was a moment of uncomfortable silence that caused them to look away from each other. Neither had forgotten the affair she'd had with Gillespie, short-lived but nonetheless passionate enough to make him think that she was ditching her fiancé for him. Pilot had eventually come back to Philip, but this wound in their marriage hadn't entirely healed; the scar tissue would be tender for some time to come.

"Anyway," Philip said, looking at me again, "that's been the way it's gone for the last seven months. We kept the Originalists at arm's length and stayed away from Starship Mountain. No one ever suspected, not even Steward Conklin—"

"Well," Pilot interjected, "my father suspected that Michael was involved somehow, and he let him know at the reception that he wasn't welcome at House Fletcher anymore." Another shrug. "Just as well. It just helped our cover story, that's all."

And besides, if you're going to dump an old boyfriend, it can't hurt to have your influential father on your side. But I said nothing except, "Go on. What happened then?"

"A few days ago," Pilot said, "I received a message via courier from Galileo. It was in code, of course—one of the first rules of the Originalists is that we seldom communicate in the clear—but the letter stated that the study group had learned something new, that they'd come across information of such importance that he wanted us—both of us—to come back as soon as possible. Philip had just joined the group when we left, but Galileo told me to bring him, too, because his assistance would be needed."

"Sounds serious."

"Oh, yes," Philip said quietly, and Pilot nodded. "We waited a few days, then one evening we slipped out of the house, caught a taxi—picking one not driven by a Cetan, of course—and went down from the Heights. If anyone had spotted us, we would've told them we were going down to the Squat to hit the bars or find a party"—*a good alibi*, I thought—"but no one did, and we had the driver drop us off at a public house near the mountain. No problem getting in."

"Galileo knew we were coming and when," Pilot said, "and so he and the rest of the group were there in the ship, waiting for us. As it turned out, we weren't the only people there who hadn't been told yet what Galileo and his people had discovered. He'd waited until he had everyone together at the same time before he revealed the big news."

"Which was…?"

Pilot hesitated, then reached into her shoulder bag and pulled out a folded square of rice paper. "Let me show you something. Have you ever seen this before?"

She unfolded the paper and held it out to me, and I saw:

"No." Taking the paper from her, I studied the drawing. To my eye, it looked somewhat like a headless man holding a stick in his left hand, a small ball just above it.

"Galileo told us that it had come in a message from another study group," Pilot said, "this one in Southport. The message said that the symbol was copied from an object found by Originalists over there, some sort of artifact that's been in House Van Pelt for generations. Legend says it's from Earth, but, y'know—" a shrug "—aren't they always?"

She was right, of course. Landencyte's street markets were full of Earth artifacts, most of them ascribed to have magical qualities of one sort or another. "Anyway," Pilot went on, "somehow or another, the Originalists found it, and that symbol is on it."

I knew a little about House Van Pelt. They were a small and relatively unimportant clan that nonetheless held the seat on the Council of Stewards representing Southport, a fishing village on Sanctuary's southeast coast, on the other side of the island. Like most other council members, Steward Van Pelt held his seat principally by right of inheritance; he had a reputation for being pleasantly inoffensive, more interested in supporting the local fishing industry and patronizing the arts than acquiring power for its own sake.

"All right, so what?" I handed the paper back to her. "It's a sketch of a man holding a stick. Maybe it belong to an old Earth baseball team." That's what it looked like to me. Baseball was the favorite sport among islanders. Humans, anyway; Cetans had little interest in our games except soccer, which they loved and adopted as their own. Except they used the decapitated heads of criminals instead of balls.

Philip laughed. "See," he said to his wife, "I'm not the only one who thinks it looks like that... a man holding a baseball bat."

"Well, it's not," Pilot said, obviously annoyed by his interpretation, "and our people in Southport wouldn't be bothering us if it was as trivial as that." The smile left Philip's face. I could tell that he was beginning to learn a lesson of marriage: that there were times when arguing with one's spouse was a bad idea. "The message said that the object is part of an important discovery: another logbook, or perhaps a diary, this one hidden within House Van Pelt's archives."

I immediately stopped thinking about baseball. "From the *Lindbergh*?"

She nodded. "A lost testament. A different book entirely, but they're pretty certain it comes from the original colonists, too."

"And you want to get yours hands on it," I said, and she nodded again. "And that's why you've come to me, you want me to do this for you."

"That's right," Philip said.

"No way." I shook my head. "I don't take jobs that call for me to do anything illegal—"

"You went through the palisades, didn't you? That's trespassing."

"You and me went into Starship Mountain because Mike led us there, and because that's where she was." I cocked a thumb toward his wife. "I didn't know where we were going until we got there, and I haven't told a soul where I went since."

"That's good," Pilot said with an approving smile. "The less people who know about the *Lindbergh*—"

"I didn't keep my trip inside the ship secret to protect your group. I kept it secret because I don't want to get arrested for criminal trespass and hauled up before the Magistrates. Cetan Law is tough when it comes to stuff like that, and if losing my license isn't bad enough, I could also get some serious prison time. So I'm not interested in anything that could earn me a breaking-and-entering charge."

"You're not going to be breaking and entering," Pilot said. "Not technically, I mean—"

"'Not technically'?" That's what people say when they're dodging the truth.

"We're all going in… by invitation from House Van Pelt itself."

"Invited as guests?" I asked, and she nodded. "I take it you know someone there."

"Katrina Johnson, a friend, an old Overlook Academy classmate. Her family belongs to House Van Pelt, and she lives in the manor. She's always been happy to let me visit, and I haven't seen her since the wedding." A mischievous grin. "Perhaps it's time to bring my new husband… and a friend of the family, too."

"Better make it manservant," I said. "A valet." Philip gave me a curious look. "Easier for me to fade into the background," I explained. "Call me a friend of the family and they'll notice me more, and I don't want that."

Oh… okay." A sheepish smile; this was something that hadn't occurred to him. "Anyway, I figure that Pilot can distract her friend while you and I locate the archives. They're usually in the House library, which won't be hard to find. The missing logs will be there. All we have to do is track down something that looks like that."

He tapped a forefinger on the scrap of rice paper and the stick-figure sketch it held. "And you want me to steal it?" I asked, and snorted when they reluctantly nodded. "C'mon, I'll take you for a walk down the street. Maybe we can find a pickpocket I know. This is more his kind of—"

"Then we won't steal the logs," Philip said. "If I can just *read* them, make notes—"

"Then why do you need my help? You can do that yourself."

"Because it's going to be quicker and less risky if two people search the library instead of one. Two people can work faster, or one person can stand watch at the door and let the other person know if someone is coming." He hesitated. "I'm also hoping that you have... well, certain skills... that could be useful."

He wasn't coming right out and saying it, but I knew what he meant. He was hoping—even assuming—those "certain skills" included lockpicking and safecracking. And he was right. I *did* know how to pick door-locks and open household safes, because these were things that badges tended to learn in the line of duty.

That didn't mean I was willing to commit crime myself... at least not without adequate compensation. "You want me to do something like that, you're going to have to pay extra," I said. "Double my usual fee."

Pilot's mouth fell open, aghast that I'd demand such a thing, but Philip shot her a look before she could protest. "I understand, and that's fine. I hope it won't come to that, and what we're looking for is going to be out in the open, but—"

"If the logbooks are that valuable, then they're going to be under lock and key." I pointed to the symbol on the rice paper. "At least we'll know what we're looking for, if they're marked by that."

"I think you misunderstood me." Pilot held up the sketch again. "The book is something else entirely. This marks an artifact that has been found with it, some other object that we're supposed to find."

I shook my head. "If it's not a logbook, then what is it?"

"I don't know," Pilot said. "But I was told that, if I find whatever it is, I'm supposed to press that symbol and..."

She stopped herself. "And what?" I asked.

"And it'll talk to me," she finished.

She didn't sound convinced herself, and I'm skeptical about anything that sounds like magic. But I wasn't being paid to be a skeptic. "Yeah, well, we'll have to see about that."

"Then you're taking the job?" Philip asked, and brightened when I quietly nodded my head. "That's great! I'm looking forward to working with you again."

I didn't say anything. I liked the kid well enough, but it's rare that a former client walks into my office again. When I close a case, it stays closed; that's how it usually goes. So I was already wondering if I should be doing this, and whether it was going to be more trouble than it was worth.

And of course it was.

III

The Greers left a few minutes later. Before they did, Philip wrote a cheque as a retainer, then reached into his waistcoat pocket and pulled out a small drawstring bag that jingled softly with the sound of Cetan gold. He handed me the bag and told me it was to cover my initial expenses; this would including hiring a cart to take us overland to Southpoint, but he also hinted that some new clothes might be called for as well.

"House Van Pelt is little more, shall we say, informal, than my house," Philip said, "but they're still going to expect guests to dress well." His gaze drifted down to my threadbare knee shorts and washed-out tunic. "You might consider using a little of that to refresh your wardrobe."

"I'll try to look like a proper manservant." What the hell; he was paying me well enough, and I could use some new clothes anyway.

I waited until they were gone, then I locked up and went down to the street. It was a warm afternoon, the kind of day that made the Squat a little more lively. Vendors hawked their wares from pushcarts, hookers offered afternoon delights from the windows of their second-story walkups, fishermen ashore for the day searched for fun ways to lose their pay. As I walked past the alley beside my building, I caught a glimpse of my landlord stepping out the back door to shove a bag of garbage into a waste can. We caught each other's eye and exchanged waves, then he told the wetbrain loitering near the door to take a hike, he wasn't throwing out any wine today.

From nearby, I heard a mechanical grinding sound that became a low rumble. It lasted only a minute or so before it suddenly quit, leaving behind a telltale aroma like fried food. I knew what it was: a vegetable-oil generator, one of the new kind, secretly installed in the woodcraft shop down the street to run its band-saw. Mechanically powered machinery like that was proscribed under Cetan law, so it had to be run covertly.

Recently, a number of these machines had been showing up in Landencyte and elsewhere on the island. No one knew who was making them or where they came from, but they were in demand, mainly from craftsmen who were willing to accept the risk of arrest. There were plenty of Cetans on the street, but the shop workers must have not spotted any

Guardians and decided that it was safe to run the generator for a minute. It was past siesta hour, so the Cetans who worked in the Squat by day were all back on their feet, no longer taking midday naps on sidewalk benches or in doorways. The guys at the shop were wrong, though. There was a Guardian in the neighborhood; I didn't notice him either, until he came up behind me like a furry shadow and tapped me on the shoulder.

"Well… good afternoon, Bart," I said once I turned to find him there. "Nice day, isn't it?"

"Wan' 'oo 'alk 'oo you," Bart said.

"Sorry? Didn't understand you." I cupped a hand against my right ear. "Try that again?"

Of course I'd understood him. You can't live in a city full of Cetans and not learn how to comprehend their mutilated efforts to pronounce human language. At least they generally fared better than humans who tried to speak the native tongue. But pretending otherwise was a game I played with Guardian Bart; it annoyed him, and anything that annoyed him made me happy.

He glared at me, black eyes narrowing above a muzzle that wrinkled and pulled back a little from his teeth. "I… s-s-said… I… wan'… 'oo… s-s-s-peak… wi'… you," Bart growled, slowly reiterating what he had said.

"You want to speak with me?" I asked, still playing dumb. "What about?"

"People you jus' s-s-s-aw. Man an' woman in your offic-c-c-e."

That could only mean one thing; he'd been hanging around outside, waiting for Philip and Pilot to leave. He'd followed them here, and that implied… well, I didn't know what it implied, but it couldn't be good.

"Yes, I had a man and a woman come visit me." I assumed an easy-going tone I didn't feel. "I get all kinds. Men. Women. Men who think they're women. Women who think they're men. Sometimes even your kind. It's a big town with a lot of people in it."

"You kno-o-w who I mean."

"Oh, you mean Citizen Exemplary Philip and Lady Pilot Greer." I snapped my fingers as if reminding myself. "Nice couple. Philip helped me find his wife when she went missing a couple of years ago, just before their wedding."

"Why di' s-s-s-she dis-s-s-appear?"

I shrugged. "Cold feet. Nervous brides sometimes get that way. You know how it is."

Bart's narrow lips peeled back from a corner of his mouth, exposing a white fang long enough to be a letter opener. No, he didn't know how it was. Cetans don't form long-term matrimonial relationships the way humans do. When a male and a female Cetan meet, if they like each other's body odor and the female is in heat, they don't fool around with time-consuming details like dates, engagements, and weddings. A quick, discrete hump in private, and that's it. Provided that all worked well and their sperm and eggs did their jobs, six months later the female drops twins, triplets, or even quadruplets. If the male even hears about this, he might send over some fresh-killed bork meat, which in Cetan culture is the proper thing to do after someone you mounted has just delivered offspring. Otherwise, his involvement as father is nonexistent; he might be nice to the kids if they ever meet, but's about all.

Cetans couldn't figure out why humans bother with marriage. Considering that I'd once been married myself and where that had gotten me, I had to agree that they might have a point.

"Wha' did 'hey 'alk abou'?" Bart's eyes never left mine.

There was a brick wall beside us; I rested my back against it. "Not that it's any of your business, but it was a social visit. They realized just a little while ago that they'd neglected to invite me to the wedding, and they felt bad about it, so they dropped in to apologize. We caught up a little—" a half-cocked ear signaled that he didn't understand that expression "—that is, we told each other what we'd been doing since the last time we met."

"When was-s-s 'ha'?"

He almost got me there. If I'd slipped and told him the truth, then all he'd have to do was recall the last he and I had seen each other to know that there was more to this story than what I'd told him. And Cetans have nearly flawless memories; details of past conversations that humans tend to forget, the average Cetan remembers with frequently irritating clarity.

"Oh, hell, how should I know?" Playing dumb was my best option; I grinned like a fool. "That was… how long? Six or seven months back, something like that. How am I supposed to recall what I was doing the year before last?"

Bart continued to regard me with black, unblinking eyes. He knew my memory was better than that. "Ar-r-e you wo-o-orking for 'hem?"

"You mean, like a job? No. Wish I could say otherwise, I need the money, but… no, they didn't come to see me about anything you'd be interested in. Just the wedding and the apology for not inviting me." I shook my head and snapped my fingers. "Oh, great… now that's means I gotta go out and get a wedding present. Any ideas? Maybe a nice vase, or some chimes… or maybe a book?" I looked him square in the eye. "How about *A Manual of Street Illusionists*?"

I don't know what prompted me to say that. It was a reference, not very subtle, to the incident many years ago that had turned us against each other. Bart got the jab and didn't like it; his eyes narrowed and his ears flattened against his head, and one hand fell to his saber's hilt. I remained calm and carefully kept my own hands away from my sword. If I moved an inch, it might give him cause to draw his weapon. I had no doubt that I could take him, but Bart was a Guardian, and in the long run this was one fight I couldn't win.

Pedestrians stepped around us on the sidewalk, either not noticing the altercation or deliberately avoiding having any part of it. Bart must have realized that he wasn't going to get any satisfaction from trying to instigate a public duel with me, because he slowly relaxed.

"Don' men'ion 'hat," he said, his voice a quietly menacing growl. I said nothing, didn't respond in any way. "An' find me if 'hey come to s-s-see you again."

"Sure thing, pal. Anything for you."

Of course, he knew that was a false promise. But there was nothing he could do, so he simply glared at me, then turned and walked off, rudely shouldering aside a young woman who had the misfortune of getting in his way. She hissed at him, but knew better than to say anything that might get her arrested. I waited until his back disappeared amid the crowd on the street, then I slowly let out my breath.

My hands were shaking. I never touched my sword, but only because I have good self-control.

I'd almost forgotten how much I despised him.

IV

But I'd never forget the reasons why.

It happened this way:

A long time ago, I was a badge. I didn't have high rank, not having yet achieved the position everyone wanted, becoming one of the senior officers who didn't have to beat the cobblestones any more but instead hung around City Hall, holding down a comfortable desk job and getting old, fat, and happy. But I'd been in the department for just a little shy of twenty years, which meant that I'd soon be eligible to take the qualifying tests to become a nark. Being a nark was like being a dick, only better; you were still technically a badge, but the pay was better, you didn't have to wear a uniform every day, and it put you in line for that desk job.

The streets of the Squat had been my beat ever since I put on a badge. For 118 months, three weeks, and seven days—just a month, a week, and a day short of twenty years—the Squat had done its best to kill, cripple, maim, injure, or humiliate me, and occasionally been successful at the last two. It eventually cost me a marriage, too, but that was later. I'd grown up in Landencyte, so the city wasn't new to me as it was for some of the rookies who'd come here from fishing villages or highland farm towns. Even so, each day had been another chapter of an ongoing ordeal I thought would never end, and while becoming a nark wouldn't mean leaving the streets totally behind—the job still demanded that I visit crime scenes—at least my chances of getting cut or killed would somewhat diminish.

Yet I didn't only need to pass the departmental exam. Rank advancement was merit-based, which meant that I'd have to prove I could handle being a nark and I wasn't just another badge good for nothing more than busting drunks. In other words, I needed a major crime to crack on my own.

One afternoon in the third week of Springmonth, a street illusionist—or rather, an illusionist and his crew, since "magic" like this requires assistants, some of them hidden—came down to South Market Street to pull a gag. In *A Manual for Street Illusionists,* the magician's guild secret handbook that's meant to be possessed and read only by members, this particular gag is known as the Skywalker's Stroll: a practitioner recites a

Sanctuary 121

secret incantation, then steps off the roof or window ledge of a tall building and, step by step, walks through thin air to the roof or window ledge of another building across the street.

As gags go, it's pretty good, but not extraordinary. If done right, you can stand directly beneath the skywalker and not see the thin but strong wallyfish-gut lines that his crew are using to suspend him above the street. The lines have been painted to match the sky behind him—one member of the crew is almost always a weatherseer who knows more than just the usual mumbo-jumbo but can actually determine in advance what the weather will probably be like the next day—and therefore become invisible from the ground. The lines form a cradle around the illusionist's body and are connected to hidden pulleys on either side of the street. All the illusionist has to do then is pretend to casually stroll across a phantom bridge while his concealed crew slowly winches him across the street. In the meantime, other assistants, usually first-year guild apprentices, work the crowd, collecting today's pay with their hats.

The illusionist behind this particular performance went by the guild name Magus Hong Kong, after the mythical Earth city of sorcerors. He and his crew had done the Skywalker's Stroll before, albeit not in the Squat; they were experienced, professional magic practitioners, and nothing that happened later was their really fault. They made one small mistake, and it had nothing to do with the gag itself.

It took me a long time to accept this. By the time I did, I was no longer a badge and I'd made an enemy: a Guardian named Barra'chachakahamph who went by the human-name Bart.

Magus Hong Kong and his crew successfully pulled off the gag. I watched the whole show from the edge of the crowd—I'd come over to look out for the dips and bag-snatchers who haunt public magic acts in the Squat—and I can tell you that no magus has pulled off the Skywalker's Stroll better than those guys. They were perfect, but...

But they failed to do one thing: they neglected to inform the crowd that this wasn't really magic, but rather a magic trick.

There's a subtle difference between the two, but nonethless one that the law requires guild illusionists to publicly state at the very beginning of their gags: *what you're about to see today, friends and fellow Citizens, isn't truly an act of the supernatural but rather an illusion conducted by practical means,* or words to that effect. This is to distinguish gags from "true magic" carried out by other guilds, performance art rather than deeds that are supposedly rooted in the supernatural.

Magus Hong Kong and his people forgot to do this. Either that, or—as I thought at the time—maybe they didn't want to ruin the effect, the usual excuse given those rare times when illusionists are brought to court. Whether it was accidental or deliberate, their negligence had an unforeseen consequence: the death of a child.

Seeming to walk between two four-story buildings on South Market street, the illusionist made the crossing from rooftop to another… a more challenging version of the Skywalker's Stroll, I'd later learn, because the assistants handling the lines and pulleys have to set themselves up behind chimneys and parapet walls instead of simply hiding behind window drapes. But the magus and his people pulled off the gag; from where I stood about fifty yards away, it looked as if Magus Hong Kong miraculously walked in midair, even pausing halfway across to casually bend down and tie a shoe.

When he was done, everyone on the street applauded and dropped coins into the hats held out to them, then slowly began to disperse. About three or four hundred people showed up for the stunt, and there were quite a few Cetans in the crowd. Magus Hong Kong performed his trick during the lunch hour just before siesta, so once it was done, everyone went off to their favorite nap places.

So I didn't see a small boy furtively enter the building Magus Hong Kong used as the stepping-off point. So far as I could determine during my subsequent investigation, no one noticed the lad as he climbed the stairs. The crew had already gathered their material and quietly exited down a rear fire ladder. The boy had come down to South Market to go shopping with his mother, and had slipped away from her during the act. He'd been standing almost directly beneath Magus Hong Kong when the Skywalker's Stroll began and clearly heard him speak the "secret incantation known only to a small handful of practioners"… and remembered every syllable.

His mother later told me that her child had a memory like a Cetan's. That was just one of many things she and her husband loved about their son.

I wasn't aware that a boy had fallen from a rooftop until I heard the screams. In that moment, my life completely changed; I just didn't know it yet.

I think I might have bumped into Bart as I pushed my way through the horrified people jammed together between me and the source of the trouble. I recall colliding with a Guardian who growled something in his language and tried to shove me back. I ignored him and kept going. It could have been Bart, who'd later attest to being there, but he'd claim to never have seen me. During our respective testimonies before the magistrates, this would be a point of contention, for according to Bart, I was nowhere around when the kid tried to imitate Magus Hong Kong's gag and only showed up later.

By then, it had become clear to me, if not to the magistrates, that Guardian Bart intended to dispute everything I'd stated in my report. Yes, what happened was a tragic accident. The boy believed he'd seen a real act of the supernatural, thought he could do it himself, and perished as a result. When I investigated, though, I discovered that Magus Hong Kong hadn't uttered the mandatory disclaimer—which was meant to prevent just this sort of thing, common Citizens trying to imitate professional illusionists—and so decided that he and his crew were culpable.

I'll admit that my interest in this case was mainly self-serving, at least at first. Sure, I was as upset as anyone about what happened, but justice for the boy wasn't my main objective. I also wanted a successful conclusion to come out of my investigation so I'd have that on my service record when I applied for promotion. The fact that I can't remember the poor kid's name should tell you the depth of my personal involvment in this. If I could get a street illusionist to have his performance license revoked, that would be worth the effort. And who knows, the boy's family might even get some solace from it, too.

But I forgot that, in legal disputes like this, Guardians almost always come down on the side of mages. As a culture, Cetans have very strong beliefs in magic, and Cetan Law makes allowances for magical deeds that go awry, even illusionist gags that don't really have a supernatural basis. So Guardian Bart, who was present on the scene and allegedly closer to the incident than I was, would claim in court that I was wrong: Magus Hong Kong had, indeed, issued a disclaimer. The acoustics of that street muffled his words, so it wasn't well-heard by those below; however, since Cetans have superior hearing, Bart clearly heard the illusionist say what he was supposed to say.

I objected, of course, although *objected* is a mild way of saying it. What really happened is that, right then and there in the hearing room before the magistrates, I blew my temper. Guardian Bart was a liar; I wanted the world to know this even if it wasn't obvious enough already. He was protecting Magus Hong Kong and his crew, and by extension their guild, and therefore his credibility was so low it was nearly non-existent.

That's sort of what I said, at least. It didn't come out that way; what I actually said was a lot stronger. In any case, it didn't change a thing. Bart was exonerated—my word against his; guess who won?—and Magus Hong Kong and his crew were acquitted of all charges. They were ordered to never perform the Skywalker's Stroll again, but they kept their licenses and guild memberships. Magus Hong Kong's only punishment was a guilty conscience, and I'm not sure he ever had one.

For my efforts, I earned a formal reprimand and a note from the Chief Magistrate himself in my folder, and when it became obvious that I'd never become a nark, I turned in my badge. But I wasn't good at much else, so a month or so later, I got my license as a dick and went into business for myself.

So, no, I hadn't forgotten Guardian Bart, and forgiveness was unlikely. He and I stood on opposite sides of a street, and there was a dead boy between us.

V

All that was in the back of my mind as I went about making preparations for the trip to Sanctuary's eastern shore. I shouldn't have been pondering these matters, but it didn't take a lot to trigger my memory of that awful day and recall everything that happened afterwards. But it had one positive effect: knowing that I was once again under Bart's scrutiny made me wary, and that's how I came to realize that I was being followed.

Before they left, Philip, Pilot, and I briefly discussed plans: namely, getting to Southport while being noticed by as few people as possible. House Greer had their own coaches and chauffeurs, of course; the three of us could ride to House Van Pelt in style, taking lunch from picnic baskets and enjoying fine wine as we watched the mountains go by. But while the masters of House Greer would doubtless be informed of Philip and Pilot's travel plans—I remembered my old friend the house matron and smiled—we didn't want to take a chance on the chauffeur learning something he or she shouldn't and reporting it back to the matron or someone else. The loyalty of House Greer's servants to the Steward was unshakable; this might be Philip's clan, but it was Cap Greer who had their allegiance, not the house's many scions.

That left public transportation. There are two ways to get to Southport from Landencyte: by sail or by road. By sail meant taking one of the coastal ferries that regularly made their circuitous way around the island, making stops at fishing villages along the way. This would mean having to stop overnight in Rockport if we took the ferry for the northern route, or Castaway Point if we picked the southern route; either way, it was a good bet that we'd be noticed.

I decided to go overland instead. There was an omnibus that travelled three times a week between Landencyte and Southport, with a brief stop midway at Cooper's Pass. But the omnibuses—big gorsch-team carriages with seats for up to sixteen people—were almost always crowded and, like staying overnight at seaside inns, that meant a taking stronger risk that Philip and Pilot might be recognized.

The alternative was hiring a private coach. I knew of a good, dependable livery over in Northgate. And by this, I mean not only that the carriages had four wheels and the drivers were sober, but also that the owner could keep his mouth shut. He was an old buddy who owed me a favor, and he was also human, so I figured I could trust him.

On my way to Northgate, I spent a little time in a clothier, using some of the money Philip had given me to buy a suitable outfit for my role as his valet. I paid the tailor to have his boy take my purchases to my office. It was as I was leaving when old instincts kicked; I felt like I was being watched, so I paused for a second to take a good look at the shop's front window, and it was in its reflective panes that I spotted the Cetan following me.

How did I know he was on my trail? Can't explain, really. When you do what I do, you just *know* these things. Eyes in the back of your head: you either grow some or you're not a dick for very long. There were probably a half-dozen or so Cetans within sight on the street at that moment, and my guts told me the big one whose reflection I glimpsed in the shop window was on my scent.

Maybe it was because, despite the handful of people on the sidewalk between us, he seemed to be looking straight at me. Or perhaps it was just his size. This was one of the biggest Cetans I'd ever seen, about as tall as I was, with long, brown-mottled black fur and massive jaws that looked like they could easily wrap themselves around my neck and throat. There was something weird about his left ear—mismatched with his right ear, it looked stunted somehow, as if badly torn in a fight sometime in the past—but I couldn't see a lot except that he wasn't wearing a Guardian uniform. That didn't mean anything, though. He could still be working for Bart. In fact, it was a good bet that he was.

Bart wasn't taking anything for granted. He'd probably put this dog on my scent the moment I left the office. And unless I wanted the Guardians to know that I was leaving town with a couple of prominent House Greer members, that meant I'd have to lose him.

To do that, I had to find some place that smelled, the stronger the better.

I chose a fish market.

The Cetans' acute olfactory sense makes them great trackers, but it can work against them, too. If they come into an environment where there's a heavy, pervasive odor, then it's like someone with good eyesight walking into a dark room and suddenly having a bright lamp thrust in their face; no matter how sharp their eyes are, they're going to be blinded, if only for a few seconds.

And if there's one thing Cetans smell better than humans, it's fish. Fish fresh-caught from the sea, particularly the way humans prepare it. Cetans aren't picky about the way they eat seafood. They'll pluck a strippe or a wallyfish right out of a net and chow down without bothering to clean it first. Or at least they did until my people came along. Humans scale, gut, behead, and usually cook what they bring out of the water, and with certain species like pseudo-salmon or bigmouth, we'll smoke the filets to accentuate the taste.

This drives Cetans crazy. They literally drool. So a Cetan in a fish market like the one on Upper Wharf Street is like an alcoholic in a public house; no matter how disciplined they may be, they're going to be distracted by their own instincts.

I was just far enough ahead of the one following me that, when I suddenly turned right off Water Street and began quickly walking down Upper Wharf, I was lost to sight for a few seconds. That wouldn't have fooled him under normal circumstances, for his nose would have located me even if his eyes couldn't. But the fish market was crowded that morning, with ordinary townspeople and restaurateurs alike strolling among the sidewalk kiosks on either side of the narrow street. And I shouldn't have to tell you what it smelled like.

I picked up the pace and put some people between him and me, then ducked behind a kiosk where fresh-caught septopi hung from shaded drizzle racks, their sopping-wet tentacles nearly touching the pavement. Septopi: the goddamn things are ugly as hell and stink the same, and I've never been able to figure out why anyone would want to eat one. But it was as if I'd stepped behind a certain. Making apologies to startled fishmongers, I moved quickly along the brick wall behind the septopi kiosk and the one beside it selling wallyfish. When I paused to look back, I spotted the big Cetan who'd been following me. He was still standing in the entrance to the market, eyes darting back and forth as his snout uncontrollably twitched and wrinkled. And yes, he was drooling, a glistening stalactite of spittle that caught the light as it spilled from his heedless mouth.

I came to an alley behind the kiosks. It led to the back door of a seafood wholesaler. Fifteen seconds later I was outside again, only this time a half-block over on East Harbor, running perpendicular to Upper Wharf. The Cetan was no longer in sight; so far as I knew, he was still in the fish market trying to figure out which mattered more, his job or his stomach.

I stuck my hands in my pockets and sauntered along, enjoying the view of the harbor from behind the masts of the schooners tied up at the wharf. Sure, it was funny, but when I started to laugh, I remembered a sobering fact: Bart hadn't put someone on me for no reason. He knew that Philip and Pilot were up to something, which was why he'd followed them to my place. And whatever he thought we might be doing, he'd decided that it was important enough to have me followed, too.

Nope. Not good at all.

VI

I made arrangements with my friend for a coach to carry me and a couple of companions to the other side of the island, and before I got back to my flat, I stopped by the nearest courier and had a runner carry a message up to the Heights, letting Philip know where and when he and Pilot were to meet me. I didn't see the goon Bart had put on my tail or Bart himself, so I had to assume that they were unaware of what I was planning.

Early the next morning, I walked back across town to the livery. I carried nothing more than a knapsack with the nice clothes I'd bought yesterday and my blades. Although I knew I'd be gone for a few days, I deliberately packed light; if Bart was still watching me, I didn't want to appear as if I was heading out of town.

I carried my saber, a short sword, and a boot dagger, but left my flintlock in its hiding place. I had to think long and hard over that one; every instinct told me that I ought to bring the pistol, too. If Bart was following me, though, a gun could bring me trouble. Cetan Law gave him the legal right to approach me at any time and perform a search of my person and belongings. Swords were legal for private citizens but guns were not, and Bart could come down hard on me if he found one. Also, since this job was against the law, having an firearm in my possession would make things worse if I was arrested. So I left the pistol behind and hoped I wouldn't regret it.

In the first daylight hours of morning, the streets of Landencyte were deserted, making it easy for me to spot anyone who might be watching my place. I saw no one except a drunk passed out in the doorway of the vintner's, and if he was an informant for the Guardians or a nark, the boozy stench around him was a damned good disguise.

The livery had assigned a young guy named Rodney to be my driver; I was assured that he was trustworthy and an expert coachman. I directed him to a small park off Hopscotch Street, a residential lane on the east side of town. Philip and Pilot were already there by the time we arrived. They'd been covertly driven down from the Heights by a house servant whom Philip could count on for discretion, following my instructions to keep out of sight within the park gazebo until I showed up. They were carrying more baggage than I was, but I figured this was normal for a wealthy young couple travelling to visit another steward. We lashed their bags to the back of the coach, then climbed into the upholstered tonneau and off we went.

There were few other vehicles on the streets at this early hour, but that changed once the coach reached Mountain Pike. The road was wide and dirt-packed, and already filled with traffic. Covered wagons laden with ice-barrels of fresh fish, wine casks, and crates of dry goods, two- and four-wheel buggies, a double-decker omnibus packed with passengers, all on their way to settlements on the other side of the island. The road sounded and smelled of the grunting, flatulent gorsches hauling the vehicles; now and then, we passed a hitchhiker trying to thumb a ride.

At the edge of town, we paused at the toll gate to pay the old gent who raised and lowered the long wooden pike that barred access to the highway. Our coach then joined the caravan making its way up the lower steppes of the Perserverance Mountains, the jagged range that ran lengthwise down the center of Sanctuary like the fossilized backbone of some great, dead beast. Dense rain forests lay before us, a thick blanket of woodlands that covered the mountainsides until they thinned out at the edge of the tree line near the range's rocky summit.

We passed the terraced farm fields on the outskirts of Landencyte, but before we left the city behind entirely, we came upon one last habitation: the Cetan village the natives called Wa'hag, but which the humans impolitely referred to as Dogtown.

The Cetans on Sanctuary lived among us, but they didn't live *with* us. Our respective races had some similarities, but there were also enough differences to make cohabitation uncomfortable at best. So the Cetans had their own settlements outside the human-occupied towns, and these villages were the places where our neighbors preferred to live when they weren't among us.

From the windows of our coach, the Greers and I watched as the caravan slowly progressed down what passed as Wa'hag's main street. I say "what passed as" because Cetan villages are chaotically arranged, if they have any arrangement at all. The street was sometimes wide enough for three coaches to drive side by side, and sometimes so narrow that the caravan was barely able to pass between two buildings. It randomly curved left and right, branching out seemingly at random, with no visible signage. Since Cetan buildings were always built low to the ground with no second floors, the traffic weaved around homes and shops and sheds seemingly situated at random, with little or no allowance for right of way. These dwellings were constructed of rough-cut logs or adobe brick and had no windows; ventilation was provided by rows of holes bored along the top of the walls just below the roof eaves, with the roofs themselves sharply slanted in one direction.

Adding to the chaos was the fact that Cetans seldom cut down a tree to make room for construction, and removed timber only when it was dead and in the way. They sometimes even built houses *around* trees, with the trunk and upper branches rising from a hole in the roof. So the road through town sometimes divided around the base of a massive fauxoak and rejoined on the other side… or maybe not, in which case it simply branched off in some random direction. Rodney followed the rest of the caravan; I hoped the driver up front knew where he was going.

No sidewalks; only dirt streets splayed out every which way. Marketplaces abutted houses built alongside public bath stalls where Cetans stood stood naked beneath showers fed by elevated cisterns. The markets sold food raw and uncooked; the carcasses of small animals and plucked game birds dangled from hooks, their flesh swarming with insects. Since the Cetans seldom cooked their food, they often ate their meals there in the market, tossing the remains in the street. Behind the adjacent houses were outdoor toilets; low walls couldn't hide squat-holes over which Cetans crouched to relieve themselves, and toilet paper was something that had never been invented in this culture.

The streets were packed with Dogtown's residents. Cetans generally rise with the sun and are busy until the middle of the day, when everything comes to a dead halt for the seista hour. So the locals were out in the streets in mobs, bumping into one another with soft growls and whimpered apologies, eating breakfast as they walked. They heedlessly stepped in front of the caravan's vehicles, expecting even omnibuses to stop for them; a couple of children ran beside our coach for a little while, yelling things in their language we couldn't understand.

Between the market, the bathhouses, and the toilets, all of which stood side by side, lingered a pervasive stench you wouldn't want me to describe even if I could. Philip, Pilot, and I covered our noses with our hands and sought to breathe through our mouths, but Pilot's eyes were watering and Philip's face had a green hue. I wondered if either of them had ever visited Wa'hag before. Probably not; Landencyte's privileged class usually traveled from one side of Sanctuary to the other by boat, leaving overland travel to commoners like me.

"Do you think you can hurry up?" Philip leaned out the window to call out to Rodney. Our driver had wrapped a silk bandana around his face; even from where I was sitting, I could smell the perfume it which it had been soaked. Smart man; obviously he made this trip often.

"Nothin' I can do 'bout it, mon," Rodney called back, voice thick with an East Side accent; apparently he'd moved to Landencyte from a community on Sanctuary's other side. "The dawgmen, they take their own time, they do."

He laughed, acknowledging the Cetan disregard for haste in anything they did, except eating. Apparently he wasn't afraid to refer to the locals by their hated human nickname. I wondered if he was fearless, rude, or just plain racist.

"I wonder how they can stand the smell." Pilot fanned her face with a hand; she'd found a handkerchief and was using it to dry her eyes.

Rodney heard that; he laughed out loud. "Stand it? Swee' heart, they *love* it!" Laughing again, this time in an ugly way, he shook his head in disgust. "Stinkin' dawgs," he added, dropping his voice just low enough not to be heard on the street.

That settled it: he was racist. On the other hand, didn't every human on Sanctuary share these thoughts, if only on occasion? I was mulling that over when I happened to glance out the window and spotted something I really didn't want to see.

The coach had just passed something you find in the heart of every Cetan settlement, the only example of clean orderliness anywhere in Wa'Hag: a Dagahn shrine, an open-air temple devoted to the Cetans' principal religion. A low, circular dais of carefully cut and placed stones, each carved with ideograms from their primary language, surrounded a life-size statue of a kneeling Cetan, snout and eyes lifted to the sky, hands resting on his haunches and raised in supplication. The Cetan prophet-savior whose name, even after all these many years, was still unknown to humans; the Cetans considered it blasphemous to speak it aloud, except in the softest of whispers when they're kneeling in prayer upon the dais, and never to humans.

Dagahn shrines are always islands of quiet and civilized meditation. Which was probably how I was able to notice one particular face among many: the big Cetan who'd followed me just yesterday.

He was standing just outside the temple, at the spot just beside the dais where passing Cetans often pause to pay their respects without being obliged to perform the rituals of their religion. I might have not seen him if he hadn't turned his face toward the coach as it moved past. He saw me the same instant I spotted him; he quickly looked away, but it was the awkward attempt to hide his face behind an upraised hand that sent a chill down my back.

I might have chalked up his presence as nothing but a coincidence—after all, this is where he lived; he had every reason to be there—if he hadn't tried to hide like that. But when he caught me looking at him, and made a stupid effort at concealment, I knew that it wasn't an accident. He'd been put there, on the mile of Mountain Pike that passes through Wa'Hag, to be on the lookout for me, and doubtless for Philip and Pilot as well.

I don't know how Bart did it. He was just as good at being a dick as I was, though, so it shouldn't have been a surprise. He'd somehow put two and two together, and decided to stake out Wa'Hag's main drag. Perhaps it was just to see if we had joined the morning caravan through Dogtown, or maybe he knew more about Philip and Pilot than I'd realized, but the result was the same.

We'd been spotted. And now we were going to be followed.

VII

The caravan left Wa'Hag and made its way up Mountain Pike into the central highlands. As the grade steepened, the road narrowed, the mountains gradually rising about us as we travelled upwards. Soon we were surrounded by dense forest, with the overhanging branches of fauxoak and blackthorn providing welcome shade from the midday sun. Haunyks soared in widening gyres above us, searching for borks and other small prey in the clearings far below, while sqauwks scolded us from the treetops.

    The caravan made good time, but even so, we were obligated to stop for seista. It was in Rodney's contract that he had an hour off at midday for lunch and a nap, and since just about every other gorsch-drover on the road belonged to the same union, the shoulder was soon lined with parked wagons and coaches. I hated losing time—if we were being followed, then this would give our shadow a chance to catch up—but there wasn't much I could do about it; Rodney didn't know what his passengers were up to, and I wasn't about to tell him that we had Guardians following us. So while Rodney napped on the buckboard, and Philip and Pilot curled up together in the tonneau, I sat on the ground behind the wagon and kept an eye on the road.

    No one suspicious came up behind us from Wa'hag, though, and an hour or so later the caravan was moving again. By mid-afternoon, we reached our stopping place for the night, the little mountain town of Cooper's Pass.

    As the name implied, Cooper's Pass was situated in the place of the same name, a ridge-top saddleback between two peaks of the Perseverance range. The only reason the town existed at all was that it was a convenient halfway point for caravans travelling between Sanctuary's west and east coasts. It had an inn and a stable and a blacksmith and a small general store and a public house offering what were claimed to be the best borkburgers on Sanctuary (no, they weren't). A couple of hundred people lived up there, all of them human—Cetans don't like to live at high altitudes—and the town's primary occupation was finding ways of separating travellers from their money. And as we rolled into Cooper's

Pass, it became apparent that someone had found a new way of making a living.

It had been a few years since the last time I'd been there, so the tower was new to me. On the eastern side of town, visible above the low rooftops, a wooden scaffold had been erected. About sixty feet tall, it rose from the steep bluffs overlooking the ridge's eastern side, and had been built as a public lookout; a sign posted at the bottom of the stairs requested an honor-payment, with a bucket below ready to accept coins dropped into it.

But that wasn't the only purpose the tower served.

A crowd had gathered when we got there, with everyone craning his or her neck to see what was going on up above. I tilted back my head and looked up. Something that resembled an immense haunyk lay upon the open platform atop the tower. Long, serrated wings, each spanning about fifteen feet, protruded at perpendicular angles from what appeared to be a narrow wooden sled. A complex arrangement of pulleys, ropes, and spars connected the wings to the sled; the wings themselves were black and appeared to be made of some lightweight fabric. It might have been a boy's kite if not for its size; whatever it was, it clearly was not anyone's plaything.

There were three men on the platform. As I watched, one of them knelt down beside the contraption. He lay face-down upon the sled, and as he gave quiet intructions to the men beside him, they used leather straps to secure his prone form. While they did so, he reached forward to grasp a pair of handles parallel to his shoulders. He experimentally pushed the handles back and forth, and the wings flexed along its pulleys, moving up and down just as a bird's would.

Now I understood what he meant to do. I was just having a hard time believing it. "You've gotta be kidding. He isn't going to—" I searched for the right word "—*fly*, is he?"

"Yes, he is." Pilot had come over with me from the coach station; Philip had gone off to the inn to get us a couple of rooms. When I looked over at her, I saw that my reaction amused her as much what was going on above us. "It's called an aeroglider, and it looks like we're about to be fortunate enough to witness a trial flight."

"You know about this?"

A nod and a smile. "Don't feel left out. Most people in Landencyte have no idea what's been going on up here. The people doing this have been trying to keep it quiet, so they conduct experiments at odd hours when there aren't likely to be any Guardians about, and not many visitors either."

I looked about. Only about a half-dozen or so people had come off the omnibus that had preceded us up the mountain, and it looked like most of the drivers had gone straight to the pub for a drink. As tourist attractions go, this one was a bust. But despite my first impression, it didn't sound like this—whatever the hell it was, this *aeroglider*—was meant for tourists. "But is this really what it looks like? A flying machine?"

"Yes, and why not?" a new voice asked. "What's so strange about the notion of having your feet leave the ground?"

The voice was just familiar enough for me to look around, but it still took a moment for me to recognize whom it belonged to: the squat, grey-bearded gent who called himself Galileo, whom I'd met months ago within the catacombs of Starship Mountain. I hadn't encountered him again since that night, nor had I expected that I ever would, so it was a surprise to find him here.

"Sure, I've seen people's feet leave the ground," I replied. "But when I have, it's always been a trick trying to pass as magic." I was thinking of the Skywalker's Stroll.

"Well, this is neither illusionism nor sham-magic; this is *science*." Galileo emphasized the last as if it had portent of its own. "More true than one, and far more real than the other." As he spoke, his gaze never left the tower. "I'm happy to see you again, Citizen Crowe, and pleased you're here to witness our experiment."

"You're involved with this?"

"Involved?' Galileo gave me a sidelong wink. "My dear sir, that's my invention!"

I was about to say more, but he abruptly reacted to something going on up above. "*No!*" he shouted. "No, no, *no!* Stop that immediately!" The men on the tower who'd been assisting the flyer had laid their hands on the wings and were apparently checking the joints along the ribs. That caused Galileo to march toward the tower. "Do not manhandle the ligature!" he yelled angrily. "It has been oiled and inspected already, thank you! You needn't do so again!"

"He's trying to invent a flying machine?" Still incredulous, I turned to Pilot again.

"He's not just trying, he's done so already. This is the third or fourth flight… maybe there's been more I don't know about." Pilot folded her arms and watched the tower in calm expectation. "He's invented a number of things, but he prefers not to let on about them. This is something people here in the Pass keep to themselves, and even most travelers who happen to catch a test don't know what they're seeing."

"What do they think they're seeing?"

"They think it's magic or some sort of trick, and that's what they tell their friends if they tell them anything at all. So if the Guardians have heard about this, they've probably thought it's just humans trying to make magic work again." She paused, then quietly added, "Which they encourage, of course, because they don't like to see us inventing stuff they can't control."

"Then why—?"

"Look, I need to talk to him, okay?" Pilot stepped away from me. "You can stay and watch… in fact, I think Galleo wants you to. But he's going to be meeting us in Southport after, y'know, we do what we're going to do, and—"

"I understand," I said quickly, hoping she'd shut up before anyone overheard us who shouldn't. We were on our way to Southport to commit a felony; the less said in public, the better. Besides, I figured that, so long as whatever she wanted to discuss with Galileo didn't affect the job she and her mate had hired me to do, she could have her secrets. "Meet up with us later at the pub, okay?"

She nodded, then turned and marched off to catch up with her mentor. Galileo was standing at the base of the tower, hands cupped around his mouth as he shouted instructions to the men above. The flyer was firmly strapped into the aeroglider; he'd pulled a visored cap down low on his forehead, and now he appeared to be waiting for the men to shove the contraption off the platform.

His wait was for naught, though. His friends were about to give him the heave-ho when one of them, a kid barely old enough to shave, apparently tripped over something up there. I couldn't see what it was, but it threw him off balance, and when he flailed about trying to keep from falling off the tower—if there were railings up there, they'd been removed to make room for a windlass and crane arm—one of his hands came down on the craft's right wingtip. A loud snap that could be heard even on the ground, then the wingtip sagged upon its fabric covering, useless.

A disappointed groan passed through the crowd, but Galileo just stared up at the platform. He didn't scream in rage or charge madly up the ladder or any of the things I might have expected him to do, but instead waited until his assistants looked down at him, then locked eyes with them and held their gaze. Silent fury is sometimes more potent than howling anger; the youngster who'd broken the wing said nothing but simply shook his head in mute apology, then shamefacedly turned to help his companion unfasten the flyer from the aeroglider.

So I didn't get to see a man fly that day, but I learned something just as important: Galileo was part of all this, too. And for some reason, he felt that it was necessary for me to witness a test of his invention, even if it was unsuccessful.

VIII

The inn was little more than a B&B and didn't have its own tavern, so guests had to go a little way down the street to the only public house in Cooper's Pass. The Angel of the Peaks wasn't the best watering hole I'd ever visited nor was it the worst. The gorschburger I ordered was so rare that I suspected it came from the same gorsch who'd hauled us up the mountains, but the beer was good and that was what counted.

Philip, Pilot, and I ate by ourselves in a curtained booth in the back and off to the side. I had the barmaid seat us there instead of at the center table she'd originally offered us; I wanted to be noticed by as few people as possible. We got there early, before most of the locals showed up for the evening. It wasn't long before the place was full, but the regulars ignored us. For them, we were just three more flatlanders; so long as we paid our bill and didn't do anything stupid, they were inclined to leave us alone. Fine by me.

Galileo showed up just as we were finishing dinner, still mad about the failure of the day's experiment. "I fired that idiot assistant just a little while ago," he grumbled as he took the vacant chair beside me. "Any jackass who doesn't know better than to leave his shoes untied when he's working on an elevated platform shouldn't be trusted with... well, never mind."

Half turning about, he raised a hand to get the barmaid's attention, and lifted a finger once she did. He was obviously a regular there, because she knew what he meant. "Coming up, Rick," she called to him.

"Rick?" I asked. "Is that your real name?"

"It is, but I prefer not to use it. Galileo is my professional name. Know who he was?" I shook my head. "Most people don't. A scientist from Earth, forgotten unless you manage to read the old books, which few people outside the House libraries can... thanks to the Guardians, that is."

"Now isn't a good time for this." Philip cast a wary eye on the crowd outside our booth.

"No, actually, I think it is." I turned to Galileo, whose name was really Rick. "Until now, no one told me you're part of this. Now that I know you are, I want to know why."

I was expecting him to hesitate, maybe even try to feed me a line, but he didn't. "All right, then," Galileo replied, "I'll tell you—" he raised a finger "—but only up to a certain point. If we get to something I don't feel safe discussing with you, then I'll let you know. I won't lie to you, I'll just tell you that I won't answer that question. All right?"

I shrugged. "I can live with that. So who are you? Rick, or Galileo?"

A wry smile. "Rick is the name I was born with, but Galileo is whom I aspire to be. Galileo, and DaVinci, and Edison, and Einstein, and Musk, and Sanchez, and… well, many other people you've never heard of. And although I dabble with inventions like my aeroglider, my interest in history comes from my chosen profession. I'm a teacher… a private tutor, to be precise."

"Let me guess: you're a tutor for the steward families, aren't you?"

"Excellent deduction, Mr. Holmes—"

"What did you just call me?"

"Never mind, but trust me, it was meant as a compliment. Yes, my clientele are almost exclusively stewards and their families. Not any particular one, but rather two or three at a time. I visit their manors on a regular basis, travelling in a circuit around the island to spend a few days at a time as their guests, teaching their children." The smile faded. "As best as I can, anyway. Because the Guardians don't want certain topics discussed, I'm not free to teach my students all I think they should know. Particularly when it comes to Sanctuary's history, or at least the parts the Cetans and their so-called Guardians have made a deliberate and concerted effort to have our people forget."

The barmaid came over with his ale. Galileo dropped a coin on her tray, took a moment to ask about her husband and if he was feeling better, then picked up the thread after she moved on. "Because I've been invited into their homes and given access to their libraries—which, naturally, is where I prefer to teach my students—I've been able to browse their bookcases, including the ones holding books so scarce that only one copy is known to exist. Those are the paperbound volumes that were aboard the *Lindbergh* when it was shipwrecked and managed to escape the subsequent destruction of nearly everything our ancestors carried with them from Earth."

"Galileo was my tutor when I was growing up," Pilot said. "I've known him my whole life, and in some ways I'm closer to him than my father. When he got to know that he could trust me to keep my mouth shut, he told me about the way things really are, or at least as much as people like him—"

"People like us," her teacher corrected.

"—people like us have been able to find out. Which is why I stole the logbook from my house's library, and why we need to take this—well, whatever that thing is, if it's not a book—from the House Van Pelt library."

It was becoming clear to me that, despite what Philip had said in my office, she and he intended not to simply read the logbook in the Van Pelt library and put it back, but to take it entirely, along with the mysterious object Galileo had found. "All right," I said, "now there's one thing I don't get." I turned to Galileo again. "If you're a tutor with access to the private libraries of these houses, and you're finding stuff in there that you and other Originalists—"

"Keep your voice down," he whispered sharply.

"Sorry." I lowered my voice, though that made it hard to be understood over the barroom noise; they had to lean closer to hear me. "Here's what I don't understand." I cocked my head toward Philip and Pilot. "They told me the thing you want was found by another of these so-called study groups, this one in Southport. But it sounds like you're the one who found it... is that right?"

Galileo traded a look with the couple. "Yes, that's correct. There's a small group in Southport, but I'm the person who located them."

"So why did they tell me something different? In fact, why aren't you just taking them yourself, instead of getting us to?"

"If anything is discovered missing, I'll be the very first person they'd suspect. The matrons of these houses *always* suspect that hired help like myself are stealing things, even if it's only a candlestick. It's a regular occurance for me to have my satchel and overnight bag searched on the way out the door after a visit. A logbook or anything else probably would've been found if I'd tried to take it, but if Philip and Pilot did this while I wasn't even in town..."

"Then you have an alibi if something turns up missing." I looked over at them. "But that immediately puts you under suspicion."

"Yes, but the matter stays in House Van Pelt and House Greer," Pilot said. "Steward families always handle minor altercations like petty theft amongst themselves, without badges or Guardians getting involved. If he's caught, though, the local constables would be called. And if the Guardians find out—"

"They confiscate the logbook and whatever that other thing is, and probably arrest him, too." I looked at Galileo again. "Clever."

"Thank you, detective. No, wait, that's probably another word you've never heard before, isn't it?" I let it pass and he went on, this time turning to speak to Pilot. "Once you've acquired the logs and the object in question, you'll meet with me. It can't be anywhere nearby, though, especially if you're being followed, as you've said he believes you are."

"Count on it," I said.

"Very well. So you'll have to travel to Castaway Point."

"Oh, now, wait a minute. That's news to me! I was hired to come to Southport and then go home." I looked at Philip and Pilot. "Look, no one said anything about—"

"Don't blame them." Galileo let out his breath as an apologetic sigh. "I'm afraid this is something I couldn't tell anyone until now." He turned to Pilot again. "That includes my closest student... sorry."

Pilot reached across the table to clasp his hand. "I understand, sensei, but why?"

From the other side of the barroom, near the windows that looked out on the street, someone loudly said, "Bow wow!"

Like many in Landencyte, this public house apparently had a lookout, and he'd just sounded the traditional warning that he'd spotted Guardians on the way. It was understood by everyone present. A moment of silence, then both locals and travelers went back to what they were doing. Galileo took precautions, though. Rising from his seat, he reached over, grasped the curtains on either side of the booth, and pulled them shut, leaving just enough of a crack for him to peer out. Customary for public houses when people want a little privacy, and perfectly acceptable... unless the Guardians whom the bar lookout had just spotted decided to make an issue of it.

Without a word, I picked up the beer I'd been drinking and, leaning away from the table, poured it just beneath the curtain's hem. It was probably a useless gesture, but there were many who believed that Cetans' olfactory senses were thrown off by alcohol. I'd never met a Guardian whose snouts were *that* sensitive, but maybe the altitude and the thin mountain air would help.

Galileo was watching the room through the opening in the curtain. A minute passed, then I heard the noise level outside our booth subside a little; it could have been my imagination, but it felt as if a cold draft passed beneath the curtain. "They're here," he murmured. "Two Guardians, and... oh, hell, I think I recognize one of them."

Sliding back my chair as quietly as I could, I stood up to join him at the curtain. Two Cetans wearing the harnesses of Guardians had entered the public house; they stood just inside the door, saying nothing as they scanned the room. "So do I," I whispered. "The smaller one is called Bart. He and I go way back. The other one, the big one, has been following me since yesterday. I spotted him again when we passed through Wa'Hag." I caught a sidelong look from Galileo and added, "Sorry... thought we shook them in Landencyte."

"Don't apologize. They probably would've followed you here anyway. Guardians are hard to shake once they get your scent." Galileo nodded toward the two Cetans. "It's the big one I'm talking about, though, not your friend Bart. He goes by the name Feng—" he pronounced it as *fang*, which was only appropriate "—and I can tell you, he's a real son-of-a-bitch. Likes to harrass humans whenever he can." A grim smile. "One good thing about him, at least: he's not very smart, and needs someone else to give him orders."

I slowly nodded. Feng was Bart's muscle. Made sense. Bart wasn't very menacing on his own, so he'd need someone to rough up people for him. "I take it Feng's been after you before."

"The Guardians know about my group, yes. They've been trying to catch us for years." Galileo glanced over his shoulder at Philip and Pilot. "Somehow, Bart knows they belong to us," he whispered, trying not to let them hear him. "Probably because of her disappearance a couple of years ago. At any rate, they've been keeping an eye on her ever since."

That would explain why, when Philip and Pilot came to see me at my office, Bart wasn't far behind. And although we'd done our best to shake Feng, it was possible that House Greer had informants among its servants who weren't averse to making a little extra money on the side by letting Bart know if the two of them did anything suspicious, like suddenly leave town to visit an old friend on the other side of the island without availing themselves of one of House Greer's coaches.

The details didn't matter. What mattered was that Bart and Feng had followed us straight to the Angel of the Mountains.

As I watched, Bart lifted his head slightly. His muzzle wrinkled as it cocked a few times; he was sniffing the air, trying to catch our scent. *My* scent; he'd know it better than Philip's, Pilot's, or Galileo's. Then he looked straight across the room at our booth.

The spilled-beer trick hadn't worked. So much for legend. I ducked away from the booth curtains before Bart spotted me, but that didn't matter either. Bart knew damn well I was there, and he could've marched straight across the bar room, yanked aside the curtains, and found all four of us.

He couldn't put us under arrest, though. Under Cetan Law, he needed justifiable cause; mere suspicion that my companions belonged to an Originalist group wasn't sufficient. So I stood there and waited, and a few seconds later I heard the tavern's front door open and shut again.

"They're gone." Galileo slowly let out his breath as he returned to his chair.

"But they're onto us," Philip said. "They know what we're doing."

"No, they don't," Pilot said. "They just know that we're on our way to Southport to visit another steward, and we're bringing along Philip's new manservant, Jeremy."

Her voice was calm, but I couldn't help but notice that her hand trembled as she picked up her ale mug. Everyone seemed to be looking at me, as if I was supposed to make up their minds for them whether to proceed with the plan. I thought it over for a second. "She may be right. You've got a good cover story, and they can't lay a finger on us... or at least not until after we've acquired the thing you're looking for. That's when we'll be in danger."

"You're very perceptive." Galileo pulled his ale mug closer, but only played with it, running a fingertip around its rim. "Which is why, once you've acquired the objects in question, I want you to proceed immediately to Castaway Point. If you do that, I can help you get away from Bart and Feng, once and for all."

"How?" Philip asked. It was the same question I had.

Galileo and Pilot exchanged a knowing glance, then her old tutor smiled. "Leave that to me."

IX

We descended from the mountains the following morning. Low-lying clouds hid the lower slopes at first, but then they gradually disappated and we caught a glimpse of the Eastern Ocean, its deep blue expanse dappled by sunlight. The forest rose about us again, though, and as the ocean disappeared, clouds of carnivore moths came down from the trees, forcing us to roll down the coach's insect nets while Rodney donned an insect-proof cap and gloves. The gorsch pulling us was miserable, though; although its thick hide provided some protection, there was nothing the poor beast could do about its eyes, ears, and snout. The rest of the caravan had the same problem, so it slowed to a crawl, and we weren't able to make up for lost time until we reached the lower slopes, and the warmer and more humid air the moths didn't like.

Periodically, I'd look back through the rear window to see if I could spot Bart and Feng, but it was impossible to tell which vehicle carried Bart and Feng. I had little doubt, though, they were somewhere back of us. Philip and Pilot knew this, too, but no one said anything, lest it be overhead by our driver.

By early afternoon, we reached Southport. Smaller than Landencyte, but large enough for several thousand people, it hugged the mountains, with white-stucco villas on either side of steep, narrow streets overlooking a shallow bay. Southport was Sanctuary's second-largest seaport, but in recent years it had also become home to the island's arts community. Instead of a Squat, its downtown district consisted of studios and galleries and craft shops, and there were sidewalk artists and street-corner poets instead of prostitutes… or at least not the kind who sold their bodies. On the whole, Southport was a kinder and more genteel town than Landencyte, which is probably why I didn't like it so much: too civilized for a guy like me.

House Van Pelt was located in one of the hillside neighborhoods populated mainly by artists and craftsmen, and it showed. Instead of the grim stone walls of the Heights' manors, Steward Van Pelt had surrounded his home with an ornate wrought-iron fence inlaid with abstract tile patterns, with more attention given to appearance than security. The house itself, built of blackthorn and marble, little resembled the stolid manors of the Heights. The gatekeeper swung open the front gate as soon as our coach approached, without bothering to quiz us about our identity. I guess the people of Southport liked their steward better than people in Landencyte like theirs.

Katrina Johnson, Pilot's old schoolmate, was already waiting for us in the courtyard; she'd spent the time putting some finishing touches on a painting she'd brought down from her studio. She was a bright and willowy girl about Pilot's age, the sort of young lady who's pleasant to look upon and pleasant to meet, but with whom you couldn't spend more than five minutes without getting bored. I stood off to the side while Katrina ("Trina" seemed to be her school nickname) and Pilot (who'd once been called "Lottie," although she scowled when Trina called her this) girl-hugged and air-kissed. Trina was all over Lottie's new husband Phillie; I was introduced as his valet, and Trina gave me a polite nod and smile and immediately forgot about Whatsisname. Which was what I wanted: to be ignored, nameless, and invisible. Besides, I didn't want to get to know her, either. I caught a glimpse of her artwork; she wasn't very talented.

Philip and Pilot were given a spacious guest room on the second floor of the manor's main house. I saw it when I carried their bags upstairs, and one thing I noted was its balcony. It had a beautiful ocean view, but what got my attention was the spiral fire ladder leading down to the ground. A good thing to have, particularly since this wasn't the part of the manor where I was staying. After I dropped off the bags—Philip didn't ask me to unpack them; he didn't dare—the house matron led me to the servants' quarters, an adjacent cottage attached to the manor by a covered walkway. I noted all the things as I took my place as a houseguest's servant, playing the role but never forgettting I was there as a thief.

I'm going to skip forward a bit, if you don't mind; there's a lot that happened over the next few days that you don't need to know about. Whatever you might imagine about the lifestyle of a steward and his extended family, know this for a fact: it is dull. Pleasant, luxurious, even a bit decadent, but also tedious. Yes, the rich are different... they're just not very interesting.

It did give me a chance, though, to memorize the manor's interior layout and learn the daily household routine. Steward Van Pelt and his clan were not as hidebound as their Landencyte peers were, and their servants weren't either. So I could walk around freely without anyone hassling me about why I was there; so long as it looked like I was performing some service for Philip and Pilot, no one questioned my presence. The only problem was that, during the day, there were scarcely five minutes when any one room was likely to be vacant for very long. Three families—the Van Pelts, the Johnsons, and the Dominicis—made up the clan; they all occupied the manor and its surrounding compound, and at night they tended to stay up late, sometimes into the small hours of morning. So while the library was never locked, getting in there to find something and steal it without anyone walking in on the act was going to be a bit of a trick.

Philip, Pilot, and I worked out a plan. It was simple. That night over dinner, Philip pretended to come down with a minor case of indigestion. Not hard to fake nor implausible; the meals were superb, but the Southport cuisine is generally richer than Landencyte's. So he excused himself from the table and returned to the guest room, while Pilot remained in the dining room with the other family members.

I was in the servants' quarters—a valet never dines with his employer, y'know—but at Philip's insistence, I was summoned to attend to him. I went over to the manor house and up to his room, where we listened at the door.

Shortly after I got there, Pilot discretely checked her pocket watch, then launched into a long, detailed, and very amusing story about something funny she and her husband did a long time ago, a tale that entertained Steward Van Pelt and everyone else enough that nobody thought about leaving the table. When Philip and I heard laughter coming from downstairs, we knew it was time to move.

The library was on the ground floor, at the opposite side of the manor from the dining room. Fortunately, a small staircase meant for servants was located at that end of the house, so we didn't have to use the master staircase, which was visible from the dining room. In any case, no one observed Philip and me as we crept down to the library and let ourselves in.

The House Van Pelt library was much like the one I'd previously visited in House Greer, except that there was more art on the walls. It had a high ceiling with a second-floor gallery; bookcases lined the walls, their shelves stuffed with books both new and old. The wall lamps were lit when we came in, and although the fireplace was cold, split wood neatly arranged within it told me that the room would be occupied once dinner was over. It wouldn't be long before a servant came in to light the fire and place a couple of bottles of wine on the sideboard. We had to work fast.

It didn't take but a minute for us to locate what we were looking for. Galileo had told us where to find it: a medium-size wall safe beneath the gallery, concealed behind a portrait of the first Steward Van Pelt. Philip swung the portrait aside on its brass hinges and there was the safe. He gazed at its formidable cast-iron door, then turned to me.

"Can you…?" he whispered.

One look, and I nodded. "Easy. Stand watch at the door. I'll let you know when I'm in."

Within my cape pocket was a small gorschskin bag that resembled a gentleman's boot kit. It didn't contain a boot polish and a brush, though, but something much less legal: lockpicker's tools. I'd acquired it some years ago when I apprehended a professional thief who'd been breaking into shops in the Squat. When I caught Gary the Gimp—that was his street name—I couldn't help but feel sorry for him. He'd been an honest fisherman until he'd mangled his left leg in an accident at sea. To get by, he'd become a safecracker for hire, stealing things for whoever hired him.

So I'd made a deal with Gary. If he found an honest trade, I wouldn't turn him over to the badges, and I'd also tell my clients, the local merchant's association, that I'd killed the thief who'd been breaking into their businesses and buried his body up in the hills. In return, he'd give me his tools and teach me how to use them. I didn't want to go into business for myself; I just figured that safecracking was a skill that might occasionally be useful in my line of work. And it was. As for Gary the Gimp, he kept his word; he taught me everything he knew about opening safes, and then he found a new job. Now he was Gary the Pimp. Well, at least it was honest work, if not legal.

I studied the keyhole for a minute or so, then spread the kit open on the floor before me, selected the stiff copper wires and flexible wallyfish cartilege I'd need, and went to work. It was a good safe, very well-made, but Gary had always told me I had a talent for this sort of thing: didn't take but two or three minutes before I heard the soft, satisfying click that told me I was in.

"Phil," I said, just loudly enough for him to hear me from the door, "get over here."

Philip's eyes widened as he glanced over his shoulder to see me standing at the opened wall safe. I guess he thought this would take a lot longer. Gary had also said, if you can't crack a safe inside of five minutes, you might as well put handcuffs on yourself, find the nearest badge, and turn yourself in. One more glance at the library door, then he was beside me.

I opened the safe door and we peered inside. Ledger books, a stack of currency in large denominations, a gun case that looked big enough to hold a pair of flintlock dueling pistols. A small book that appeared to have been recently rebound in gorsch-skin leather. And an even smaller box, wooden and no larger than my hand, that appeared to be quite old.

Reaching past my shoulder, Philip removed the smaller of the two boxes. It had a close-fitting lid that was slightly warped with humidity and age; it took a few seconds for him to pry it open. Within it, cushioned by a bed of soft blue felt, was a small rectangular object, matte black and somewhat resembling a ceramic roof slate except that it was made of something I'd never seen before: not wood, not stone, something in-between. It was as thin as a shingle, and etched in white on one side was the symbol Philip had shown me in Landencyte.

"What is that thing?" I whispered.

Curious, I started to reach for the box, but Philip pulled it away from me. "We'll look at it later," he murmured. "Right now, I want to get out of here."

He was right, of course. A muffled burst of laughter from down the hall reminded us that someone could walk in on us at any moment. Philip closed the box, then nodded toward the safe. "Pull out the little book, let's see if it's what I think it is."

I removed the small book and opened it. As I thought, it was quite old, its pages tender, brown, and foxed with age. The print was handwritten in pencil, faded yet still legible. It appeared to be a personal diary, but the date I glimpsed at the top of the first page made no sense: *10/29/2266*.

"That... that must be the other log." Philip's voice was quiet, yet trembling with barely repressed excitement. "Take it."

I put the book in my cape, then held out my hand to him. Philip was reluctant to give me the box, though; suddenly, he became distrustful, guarding the box and the secret whatever-it-was inside as if it were his own. "Give it to me," I whispered. "If we're caught, you don't want to be the one holding it."

I was right and he knew it, so he handed over the box and I tucked it into my cape beside the book. Then I quietly closed the safe door and made sure that it was locked. Another few seconds to make my safecracker's kit disappear as well, then I swung the portrait back in place. I took a few steps back and looked things over. Everything appeared to be just as we'd found it.

Without another word, we headed for the library door. Philip would've opened it at once, but I stopped him and instead planted an ear against the panel. I listened for footsteps, voices, anything that might indicate the presence of a passing house member or servant. Silence. I turned the knob, cracked open the door, took a peek, saw no one. Opening the door further, I glanced back at Philip and gave him a quick nod, and then we left.

We made our way back to his suite without anyone seeing us, but as soon as we were inside the room and the door was shut, Philip thrust out his hand. "Give me the log and the other thing," he demanded. "Right now."

"Sure," I said, not wanting to argue with him, "but are *you* sure? If I take them to my room, I can hide them better than you can here." I'd already inspected the room I'd been assigned in the servants' quarters; it was small, but there were about a half-dozen places where objects as small as these could be concealed, at least one or two well enough to elude even a determined search should the theft be detected before we left.

"No… yes, I mean." Philip stepped closer. To my astonishment, his other hand drifted to the sheathed dagger on his belt. "Give it here, Crowe, now."

"You're the boss." I forced a smile, trying to defuse the situation, and reached into my cape pocket. I made sure that my own hand stayed clear of my belt dagger as I withdrew the things we'd stolen and handed them over to Philip. If I'd really wanted to rip him off, I could've made a play for the back-up boot dagger he didn't know about. But I don't double-cross my clients, so I left it alone.

Philip stared at the book and the box in his hands. I could see that he was tempted to study them immediately, right then and there. The thing with the strange symbol was especially tantalizing. What had Pilot said about it?

I was told that, if I find whatever it is, I'm supposed to press that symbol and it'll talk to me.

"I'd put them away at once, if I were you," I said, deliberately blocking the thought. "Anyone could come through that door at any second. You don't want Steward Van Pelt catching you with it, do you?"

"No... no, you're right, I don't." Philip seemed to shake himself. He put the book and the box in his trouser pockets—I hoped he'd find a better hiding place than his pants, and expected he would after I left—and looked at me again. "All right, you'd better get out of here."

I gave him a nod and a quick, easy grin to let him know that we were still pals, then I turned and walked over to the balcony door. We'd already planned that I'd make my exit via the fire ladder; this way, no one would see me leaving my lordship's quarters and wonder why I'd been there so late in the evening. In less than a minute, I could be back in my quarters, with no one the wiser....

Or perhaps not.

I'd just opened the door, stepped out on the balcony, and was halfway to the ladder when I caught something from the corner of my right eye. Something shining in the night like a tiny pair of candles, side by side, on top of the ornate wall that enclosed the manor compound.

I stopped and looked, and just for an instant, I saw the candles clearly: two eyes, reflecting the light cast through the manor windows. Eyes framed by a dark, indistinct shape crouched upon the wall.

The eyes vanished, and a second later the shape did, too, but not before I recognized it for what it was: a Cetan, watching the manor from atop the compound wall.

I stayed out on the balcony for another few moments, casually pretending to take in the night air, then turned and sauntered back inside, shutting the door behind me. Philip was surprised to see me come back; he nearly jumped from beside the bed, where he'd been stuffing the book and the box into one of the bedpillows.

"Find a better place than that," I said.

X

I left the manor the way I'd come in earlier, through the servants' door near the kitchen. That entrance was the opposite end of the house from the place where I'd seen the Cetan. By then, dinner was over and Pilot had finished the long story she'd told over dessert. I ran into her and Katrina on my way out. Pilot's eyes widened when she saw me, but she hid her surprise well, and asked how her husband was doing. Playing the role of faithful manservant, I informed her that Master Greer was doing better now that he'd had some of the herbal medicine I'd packed for minor emergencies. Trina expressed her sympathies and offered the services of the Van Pelt family physician, but Lottie politely declined: this wasn't unusual, Phillie just had a sensitive stomach, no need to bother, thank you. She then took the opportunity to excuse herself for the evening; a significant glance in my direction—*we're in trouble, aren't we?*—then she went upstairs. A quick bow to Lady Katrina, then I went on my way.

Before I'd left the guest room, Philip and I had agreed to use his bogus stomach upset as an excuse to make an early departure from House Van Pelt, the sooner the better. If Bart's suspicions had been aroused, then it was a good idea to get out of town as soon as possible; we could always claim that we'd made a last-minute change of plans and decided to pay a little visit to Castaway Point on our way home. Rodney was staying in the servants' quarters, too; I stopped by his room and told him what we meant to do, and although he grumbled a bit, he wasn't upset about the extra pay I promised. Of course, he remained unaware of what was really going on… he just thought that he was dealing with the sudden whims of rich customers.

A dense fog had moved in from the ocean early the next morning when I carried Philip's and Pilot's bags from their room to the courtyard and strapped them to the back of the coach. I was glad to see the haze; the reduced visibilty would make it harder for Bart and his pet goon to follow us. Even if we were spotted leaving House Van Pelt, it was possible that we might be able to lose them on our way out of town, particularly if they were still making an effort to keep their distance.

The manor was quiet, with all but a handful of servants and Lady Katrina still asleep. Trina was yawning as she came downstairs in her robe to see us off. More hugs and kisses, and a kitchen maid appeared to give us a small breakfast basket of muffins, bork sausage, and fruit for the road, and then we were off. As the coach rolled through the gate, I peered through the windows to check the street. Nothing in sight except for a milk wagon, but that didn't comfort me very much. By then, I'd come to suspect that Bart was not only very good at tracking people, but capable of turning invisible as well.

Rodney wasted no time getting out of Southport. He knew the city well, and took a number of shortcuts that took us around the business district to the Coastal Loop, the highway that circles all of Sanctuary and provides a land route between its coastal settlements. I hoped that it would confuse Bart and throw him off our trail, if he was indeed following us. In any case, we were out of Southport less than ten minutes after leaving House Van Pelt, entering the stream of early morning traffic heading south toward Castaway Point.

Philip and Pilot had managed to keep up the pretense of a carefree life as they'd bade farewell to Katrina Johnson, but their smiles had disappeared the moment our coach left the manor. They said almost nothing, either to me or each other, until the coach was on the highway. Then Philip checked the little driver's window behind him to make sure it was closed, and bent forward to speak softly to me.

"Our plans have changed again," he said. "We can't return to Landencyte. Not for a while."

"You're going to stay in Castaway Point?" There wasn't much to the town, a fishing village so small it didn't have its own steward. There were a couple of inns for overnight travellers, as I recalled, but nowhere you'd want to take up residency. And most people there were poor: a wealthy young couple like these two would be noticed immediately.

"No." He hesitated, then went on. "We're leaving Sanctuary—"

"Well, one of us is, at least," Pilot added. "Probably me."

I stared at them, uncertain whether I'd heard them correctly, not believing it when I realized that I had. People don't just *leave* Sanctuary... not if they're human, at least. For as long as anyone could remember, our kind had been prohibited from sailing any farther from the island than its immediate coastal waters. Even the Southern Archipelago, its largest isle so close that it was visible from the docks of Castaway Point, had been forbidden to us for many years. The Guardians had maintained a permanent quarantine of the island, its gun-laden rafts anchored off the island's shores for generations. Tawcety was a world the human race would never see, except for this one island at its equator: this was a fundamental fact that the Cetans had established a long, long time ago and enforced ever since.

"How are you going to do that?" I asked. "Fly?"

"As a matter of fact—" Pilot began.

"Never mind." I already had an idea of how that might be accomplished. And if that were so, then this wasn't the most important question I needed to have answered. "What's going on? Why are you—?"

"After you left last night," she went on, "once we were sure we were alone and no one would disturb us, we read the logbook. We learned much from it, but more importantly, we listened to the… the other thing, whatever it's called." Pilot noticed the expression on my face. "Yes, it's true. When you press it, a voice comes from it. It's there for only a few minutes, but you can hear a man speaking." She looked at her husband. "Love, would you show him?"

Philip nodded, and dug into an inside pocket of his cape. Out came the slate-like object we'd taken from the safe. He held it up to let me see the odd design on its side. "It would've been been apparent what it was," he said, "if we'd only turned it over, like this…"

He turned it sideways, and now I saw:

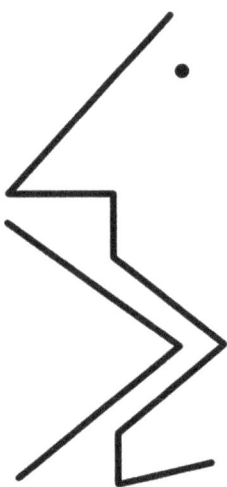

He was right. It no longer looked like a headless man holding a baseball bat. It was now a face in profile, lines depicting speech coming from its open mouth. Seeing this, I couldn't help but laugh out loud. Sometimes, a clue is so blindingly obvious, it's amazing that you missed seeing it in the first place. I was still chuckling over this when Philip laid a finger against the ideogram and gently pressed it, and from the slate, so softly I could hardly hear it, a man's voice emerged:

"*Testing, testing… this is David Chen, senior biologist, EPSS* Santos-Dumont, *reporting from Landing Site 6A, Tau Ceti-e The date is October 28, 2266, and our party has lost communications with the ship. We believe—that is, I believe, there isn't yet a conscensus for this among my teammates—that some of catastrophic accident has occurred aboard the* Santos-Dumont *and perhaps the* Lindbergh *as well, hence the loss of wireless communications with both ships and our shuttle's failure to return. If this is so, then we may be in serious trouble—"*

Philip touched the ideogram again, and the voice abruptly ceased. "There's more, much more," he said. "We listened to it twice last night, and what we learned is—"

He stopped, shook his head. "What we learned," Pilot finished, "is incredible. Originalists have always known that two ships came to Tawcety from Earth, the *Lindbergh* and the *Santos-Dumont*, but we've always believed that the *Santos-Dumont* was lost with all hands." She stopped, sighed deeply, and went on. "That doesn't seem to be the case after all. There were other survivors."

"It appears that not everyone from the *Santos-Dumont*'s landing party returned to the ship before the Rot set in," Philip said. "For whatever reason, they remained on the ground—at Landing Site 6A, wherever that is—while their shuttle went back into space. The *Lindbergh* didn't know about this because it wasn't reported to them, and that's why—"

"That's why no one on Sanctuary has never known about them!" Pilot's voice rose with excitement, words spilling from her mouth. "Do you see what this means? *We're not alone! There's another human colony on Tawcety!*"

"Keep your voice down." I shushed her, hoping that Rodney hadn't overheard us. "Are you sure about that? Even if you're right about where this came from, there's no telling how old it is. Centuries, probably. The fellow who spoke is long dead. He and the rest of his group—"

"Yes, yes, we realize that." She shook her head impatiently. "But we don't know—we *can't* know—anything from staying here on Sanctuary. And if the Cetans find this and the other logbook—which came from the *Lindbergh* and contains information we didn't know until now—then the Guardians will make them disappear."

"Besides, there's one more thing." Philip held up the slate again. "If this came from another human colony somewhere else on Tawcety… how did it get here?"

He raised an eyebrow, and a chill went down my back. He had a good point. We didn't know much about the rest of Tawcety, but we did know that it was a big planet… too big for a small, priceless object like this to get here by accident. It didn't just drift here. It was sent.

"All right, okay… I understand." I let out my breath, fell back against my seat. "I'll do my best to get you out of here."

What would happen after that, I hadn't the slightest idea.

XI

Castaway Point was much as I remembered it: not a nice place to live, nor even an interesting place to visit. The coach made its way down narrow, unpaved streets that smelled like salt and fish until it reached the waterfront district. By then, the wharf and nearby docks were vacant; the local fishermen had set sail for the day, heading out to the coastal waters where they could cast their nets and long-lines under the watchful surveillance of Cetan floating watchtowers.

There was hardly anyone around and almost no other vehicles moving on the street, which made the carriage following us all the more obvious. I'd spotted it shortly after Rodney turned off the Coastal Loop and entered town; the other coach kept its distance but nonetheless made every turn we made. It wasn't hard to figure out who was aboard.

"Bart's going to make his move soon," I said to Philip and Pilot, after pointing out the other carriage. "He'll follow us to wherever we're going, wait a few minutes, then swoop in for the bust."

"But he doesn't have any reason to—" Pilot began.

"He doesn't need one. 'Suspicion of felony in commission' is sufficient. On that alone he can put us under arrest, throw us in jail, and detain us until he comes up with formal charges." I pointed to Philip's pocket where he'd hidden both the slate and the logbook. "Once he discovers that those are stolen, he'll have us on theft. I hope House Greer has pull with the local magistrates… we're gonna need it."

"We'll be there in just a minute," Pilot said. "Galileo will be waiting for us." She looked at her husband. "Sweetheart, you know what to do."

Philip nodded, but only reluctantly. Without a word, he reached into his cape and pulled out the slate and logbook. "I'll hold them off while you get out of here," he said as he handed them to her, then he turned to me. "Jeremy, you're done. Thanks for all your help, but you better make an escape while you can."

He was right, of course, but I don't let my clients take heat from the law and it goes against my grain to back down from a fight. "Nope. Sticking with you, pal."

For a second, the kid looked like he was going to argue with me. Then he smiled. "Thank you again," he said.

"No problem. I'll add it to the bill."

A minute later, the coach arrived at the address Pilot had given Rodney. It turned out to be a large boat shed right at the wharf's edge, the sort of place used for dry-docking fishing boats for major repairs. About one-third of it was built over the water, raised on a pier to allow boats to float inside without having to be hauled ashore. There were windows along its weather-beaten walls, but I noticed that they'd been covered with paper on the inside, preventing anyone from looking in.

An odd aroma hung around the place; it took me a second to identify it. Fried food, strong and pungent, like someone had been deep-frying tuber chips and a lot of them, too. I looked around, but didn't see any dockside fish 'n chips stands. Someone around here had a vegetable-oil engine. But why?

We got out as soon as the carriage stopped. Rodney started to climb down, but Philip jogged over to the buckboard before his feet touched the ground. "Here, take this and get out of here," he said, handing him a drawstring purse that jingled with Cetan gold. "Don't worry about unloading our bags. Take them back with you, and I'll retrieve them later."

Incredulous, the driver's eyes darted from him to me. "Do as he says," I told him. "You don't want to hang around, my friend."

Rodney nodded, took the bag, tipped his cap, then resumed his seat on the buckboard and shook the gorsch-reins. The beast bid adieu by blowing a fart, then the coach trundled off down the street. I glanced back the other way. About three hundred yards back, just close enough to see between the warehouses and boat sheds, the other carriage had come to a halt. Just as I figured, the Guardians were patiently watching us. They wouldn't be patient much longer.

Galileo must have heard us coming, because he opened the sidewalk door before we reached it. He grinned as soon as he saw Philip and Pilot. "Oh, good, you made it," he said, wiping his hands on a rag; his palms looked like they were covered with cooking oil. "I thought you were coming later."

"We've run into trouble." Philip kept his voice low. "I don't know how, but the Guardians who've been following us—"

"Never mind that now." Explanations could wait; I stepped closer to Galileo. "Pilot has what you want. If you've got some way of getting her out of here, then better do it now; we've got our friends right behind us."

Galileo's face changed. He started to look past me, but stopped himself. "Right, then... I suppose I'm as ready for you as I'll ever be." He was trying to remain calm, but his voice shook a little. He reached out to take Pilot by the hand. "Milady."

"Just a moment, please." She turned away from him and fell into Philip's arms. Perhaps they'd been married only a handful of months, but just then I would've never known it. No words, just a long, silent hug beween a husband and wife who deeply loved each other and were now being forced apart.

Galileo turned about and called to someone inside the shed. I looked back up the street. Burt must have seen all this and realized that something was going on, because the carriage was in motion again, slowly moving in. "Get outta here," I whispered, putting some heat in it.

Philip tore himself away from his wife. "I'll come for you. Wait for me."

Pilot mouthed a silent *I love you*, then darted past Galileo into the shed. As she did, she almost collided with a young man, apparently the person her tutor had summoned; I recognized him as one of Galileo's tower assistants from the aeroglider test. Ironically, it was the kid he'd fired; I guess Galileo had forgiven him. Galileo had a quick, whispered conference with the boy; his assistant glanced up the street, spotted the approaching carriage, and looked back at the old man, face noticeably paler.

"You know what to do," Galileo muttered, giving his arm a fond slap. "Now run."

The kid didn't take this literally at first, but then came the crack of a carriage whip, and that was enough to get him to run.

"Go!" I yelled at Galileo. "Get outta here!"

Galileo didn't hesitate. "Good luck!" he called back over his shoulder, then the door slammed shut behind him. I heard the deadbolt snap home, and then—

"Look out!" Philip shouted.

The carriage careened to a halt in front of the boathouse, and its door crashed open and Feng leaped out to come charging straight at me. His muzzle was pulled back in a ferocious snarl, but what got my attention was the *worka* in his hands. I barely had time to draw my own sword before Feng was upon me. Steel met steel in an angry clash, and I felt the blow all the way up my arm.

Feng whirled about, brought his sword down on me again. He was graceless but strong; not much in the way of technique, but his attack was quick and brutal. If I'd been an instant slower, my head would have been rolling down the street. I dodged and parried, and was bringing my blade up for a counterthrust when Philip came to my defense. His rapier thrust forced Feng to retreat a few steps, giving me a chance to recover.

The Cetan snarled something that might have been a challenge or maybe just an obscenity. He lunged at me again, but this time he was facing two opponents instead of one. I parried as Philip went on the attack, and this time he managed to stick the tip of his blade between Feng's ribs. It wasn't a deep wound, just enough to make him back off. Only for a second, though. He was about to come at us again when Bart jumped down from the carriage.

He barked something at Feng, and when it seemed for a moment as if Feng was going to ignore him, Bart barked again, louder and longer this time. This time, Feng reluctantly obeyed; he slowly lowered his weapon.

Bart turned to Philip and me. "Drop your-r-r s-s-swords!" he demanded, pointing at us. "Pu' up your 'ands! You'r-r-re under-r-r a-r-r-r-es'."

"What the hell for?" I demanded, keeping my sword raised. "He attacked us first!"

"Drop you-r-r s-s-swor-r-rds." Reaching behind his back, Bart yanked his own *worka* from its scabbard. He hefted it menacingly, but didn't come forward. "Las-s-s' chanc-c-c-e, Cr-r-rowe!"

The odds were now even, two-on-two. And to make things worse, Philip and I had just been given an order to surrender. Bart could now add resisting arrest to the charges. Philip shot me an uncertain look; he was willing to take them on anyway. Good kid, but I wasn't willing to watch him die.

"Do as he says." I held out my sword and let it drop to the ground. Philip hesitated, then let his rapier fall from his hands.

Bart's mouth pulled back from his teeth in an ugly grin. He'd been waiting a long time for this moment. He let Feng guard us while he slid his saber back into its scabbard, then he reached to his belt and pulled out two pairs of leather manacles. "'Ur-r-rn ar-r-roun'," he demanded, "an' pu' your-r-r 'ands-s-s be'ind your-r-r—"

A loud, sudden roar from the shed behind us, like nothing I'd ever heard before. It startled all four of us, the Cetans in particular. Their ears flattened against their heads as they winced in pain; Feng nearly dropped his sword, and Bart went into a defensive crouch. I couldn't blame them; I was half-inclined to dive for cover myself.

Only Philip seemed to know what was going on. With an expectant grin, he stepped away from me and, ignoring Bart's shouted command to stop, calmly walked around to one side of the shed. I followed him; from here, we could see the water clearly.

As we watched, a weird craft emerged from the boat shed. It looked a little like the aeroglider we'd seen in the moutains, only much larger and with two wings, one above the other. It floated upon a pair of large, watertight pontoons; an engine was mounted between the two wings, driving something like a child's pinwheel, only larger and much more powerful, behind it.

Another flying machine, more sophisticated than the one I'd seen earlier. Now I understood the purpose of Galileo's experiments in Cooper's Pass; he'd been quietly developing this contraption, utilizing what he'd learned from flying the unpowered aeroglider. It was possible that this thing had never flown before; if not, he and Pilot were about to embark on its maiden flight, for as it pulled away from the shed, I caught a brief glimpse of the two of them, lying prone side-by-side between the wings.

"Did you know about this?" I asked Philip.

He didn't respond, and he never took his eyes off the craft of the air as it coasted away from shore. Once it was far enough out on the water that it was unlikely to run into any rowboats or skiffs lingering near the docks, it turned to the southeast, in the direction of the archipelago.

Something sharp prodded me in the back: the tip of Bart's sword. "You-r-r-r'e—"

"Yeah, yeah, I got that. I'm under arrest." He wanted me to put my hands behind my back so he could slip the manacles on me, so I did that. But my gaze never left the flying machine. Its engine abruptly became louder and the machine abruptly surged forward. The craft raced away, pontoons throwing up thin sheets of water, engine howling, wings bobbing back and forth a little before setting out.

The machine rose from the water. Like an immense squawk taking wing, it ascended into the air, never more than a hundred feet or so but nonetheless no longer traveling on the sea but rather in the sky above. I'm sure a lot of people in town, drawn by the noise to step out and see what was going, thought they were witnessing an act of magic.

As always, they were wrong. This wasn't magic. It was science.

Philip and I traded a look. Pilot had the lost testament, and now she and Galileo were taking it somewhere safe, wherever that may be. So far as he and I were concerned, that was worth whatever came next. So I raised my hands and turned around to face Bart.

"Okay, pal," I said, "what are you waiting for? Let's go to jail."

Interlude

Recorded Journal

[The following is a transcript from the flight recorder of the EPSS Santos-Dumont *shuttle* Brasilia. *Because large portions have been lost over time, the text is incomplete, and therefore has been edited for clarity.]*

Testing, testing… this is David Chen, senior biologist, EPSS *Santos-Dumont*, reporting from Landing Site 6A, Tau Ceti-e. The date is October 28, 2266, and our party has lost communications with the ship.

We believe… that is, I believe, [since] there isn't yet a conscensus for this among my teammates… that some sort of catastrophic accident has occurred aboard the *Santos-Dumont* and perhaps the *Lindbergh* as well, hence the loss of wireless communications with both ships. If this is so, then we may be in serious trouble.

What we know is that something from the planet's surface, we believe it to be an indigenous microorganism, is responsible for the destruction of nearly all electronic equipment aboard both ships. Before we lost contact with the *Lindbergh*, their science team had tentatively hypothesized that this microorganism, which they called the Rot, rapidly breaks down anything comprised of fossil-fuel derived materials, specifically ethylene and polyethylene plastics. If this is so—and our direct experience tends to support the hypothesis—then this so-called Rot is responsible for the destruction of nearly all of the landing party's electronic equipment. That includes the data pad I'd normally be using to make log entries.

However, when the [shuttle] *Magellan* made its final trip [to Landing Site 6A], one of the items it brought down from orbit was a portable weather station meant for gathering and reporting data about local climate conditions. The weather station itself has been rendered useless along with just about everything else. However, it contained a recorder that's impervious to the Rot because its graphene outer shell is comprised of carbon rather than plastic. I managed to detach the recorder before the Rot could infiltrate it through the serial port, and while it's now useless for its original purpose, its verbal-recording mode remains intact. I've also been assured that, because the recorder has a thorium battery that uses radioactive decay as its power source, it should remain usable almost indefinitely.

Because we have the means of making a historic record of what has happened to us, Executive Officer [Sherilyn] Kaufman has asked me to do so. I'll do as best as I can, but considering that there is much we simply do not know, my account may not be... I mean, it might be incomplete.

[*Pause. Sounds of shuffling paper and unintelligible voices in the background.*]

We've survived—that is, those few of us who managed to get off the *Santos-Dumont* before it was destroyed—only by fortuitous circumstances. In hindsight, it's lucky for us that Manny [Cortez, *Santos-Dumont* Senior Scientist] decided to disregard Julius's [Fletcher, *Lindbergh* Senior Scientist] orders to his own landing party that no one was to remain on the planet's surface until a complete biological evaluation had been completed by both ships. I was with the first landing team, and Manny agreed with my opinion that there was nothing on the surface that posed an immediate hazard to human life. He relayed this opinion to Captain [Juan] Mendoza, and the captain agreed that there was no sense in keeping everyone off a planet that seemed to be perfectly habitable. Everyone was sick and tired of the ship, and all we wanted to do was set foot on the ground.

So the decision was made to send down a second landing party, this one aboard the *Clark*, without informing the *Lindbergh* of our plans to do so. This way, neither Captain [Yvonne] Greer nor Julius would be able to formally object to what the *Santos-Dumont* crew was doing. I think Manny would've eventually told Captain Greer what he'd done... just not until after a permanent location for a colony had been settled upon and the flight crews and passengers of both ships were reunited there. What they [i.e., Greer and Fletcher] wouldn't know would never hurt them... that was the rationale.

So I stayed behind at 6A, along with most of the [*Santos-Dumont*'s first] survey team, while the [shuttle] *Lewis* returned with only its pilots aboard. By the time it returned to the ship, *Clark* was loaded and ready to go. Everyone aboard *Clark* wasn't a vital member of the flight crew, and therefore could be spared for at least a little while.

Clark departed almost as soon as *Lewis* docked with *Santos-Dumont*, and therefore escaped the Rot. To further hide what they were doing, *Lewis* made its departure when *Santos-Dumont*'s orbit—which was significantly lower than the *Lindbergh*'s and therefore faster—had carried

Sanctuary

it around the other side of the planet from *Lindbergh*. Since Landing Site 6A is located on the other side of Tau Ceti-e from the landing site selected by the *Lindbergh*, no one aboard the other ship was able to visually observe what we were doing.

So [*Lindbergh*'s crew] doesn't know what happened to us. That is, not unless Captain Cortez and Captain Greer managed to speak to each other before communications were lost, and we have no idea whether they did. Of the fifty members of the *Santos-Dumont* command team, forty-two have made it safely to the ground. The remaining eight members of the command team, including Manny Cortez, were lost with the ship and its hibernating passengers. We know for certain that *Lindbergh* was destroyed because we saw it burn up above us in an uncontrolled re-entry, and we must presume that our own ship met the same fate.

[*Pause. Static begins to erode the recording.*]

We might be considered lucky to have escaped with our lives, but it's hard to believe that just now. Most of our equipment has been lost to the Rot, much of our food has been [inaudible] by dissolved plastic packaging and therefore rendered inedible, and [inaudible] very clothes are falling off us. Forty-two survivors [inaudible] expedition that left Earth with two thousand members. I don't [inaudible] how we're—

[*End of transcript. The rest of the recording has been lost to data decay and cannot be recovered.*]

Part Three:
Escape from Sanctuary

I

Back when I was a badge, I didn't have much sympathy for the people whom I arrested. Everything was in black and white, with only the narrowest band of gray between. If I busted you, then it was because you'd broken the law. The way I saw it, if you broke the law and I caught you, then you deserved to go to jail, at least until the magistrates decided what to do with you. And if jail was unpleasant, then you had only yourself to blame. Don't do the crime if you can't do the time and all that.

So you couldn't say that I had warm and fuzzy feelings for those whom I considered to be lawbreakers. But once I gave up my badge and went into business for myself as a dick, it didn't take long for me to learn that the band of gray between black and white was much wider than I'd previously believed. And when my new line of work carried me across the line, I discovered that things are different when you're on the other side of the bars.

As jail cells go, the one Phillip Greer and I shared in Castaway Point left much to be desired.

The bunks were wooden frames bolted to the concrete walls; their mattresses were thin, yellow-stained pads that smelled of every drunken sailor who'd slept on them. The window was a narrow slot, iron-barred and without glass, with a wooden storm shutter that could only be closed from the outside. It was too high above the floor to see through, so I had no idea what the view was like; Castaway Point was a crappy little fishing town, so I probably wasn't missing much. No sink, and the toilet was a squattie, nothing more than a hole in the floor with a pile of discarded newspapers beside it. The door was solid blackthorn with a peephole in the center and the slot at the bottom for meal trays. I'll refrain from describing the food; you may have an appetite just now, and it would be rude of me to ruin it.

And it was cold. We were in there five days, long enough to feel the change of seasons as Summermonth faded into Autumnmonth. The second night, a storm came off the ocean and blew cold rain through the window. The Castaway Point badges didn't always keep someone on duty at the jailhouse, so until one of them remembered to drop by and close the storm shutters, Philip and I had to huddle together against the door, our knees against our chests and hands tucked beneath our armpits. The next morning, I cajoled the same badge into giving us some blankets. He felt guilty about his negligence, so we got the blankets without much argument, and he promised not to forget to close the window again. There was nothing to be done about the cell itself, though. It didn't have its own wood-burning potbelly, which meant that we'd be cold at night and only hope we'd be out of there before Wintermonth rolled around four weeks later.

Philip and I spent our time sleeping, playing poker—another badge loaned us the beat-up deck of cards they kept for prisoners who behaved themselves—and, when we were sure we were alone, discussing what had happened. It was pretty clear that the Cetans had figured out the reason why Philip, Pilot, and I had travelled to Southport: to steal the *Lindbergh*'s logbook and that weird slate from the House van Pelt library.

"*How* did they know we were here?" Once again, Philip raised the question that had been bugging both of us for days. "What led Bart to figure out that we'd come over from Landencyte in the first place?"

I shrugged. We were finishing breakfast and it was lovely: scrambled eggs, smoked bork, toast, and seaweed tea. No, I'm kidding; it was septopi stew, the same thing we'd been given for breakfast for the past four days. If it had only been tasteless, at least that would've been an improvement. And like the stew, Philip's question was repetitious. I'd heard it before, and my answer was the same.

"I don't know," I said.

"How could you *not* know? You're a dick, aren't you? What am I—?"

"Paying me for? Not to make guesses."

I wasn't being thick. I was just being careful not to speak aloud the major reason why he and Pilot had hired me: to crack the safe in House van Pelt's library. Although I was what Galileo called a "detective"—if I ever saw him again, I'd have to ask him exactly what that meant—burglary wasn't part of my job description. Or at least it hadn't been until now. In any case, it was always possible that someone might be eavesdropping on us from below the window, and I didn't want to say anything that might incriminate me any more than I already was.

We'd been charged with burglary, petty theft, and resisting arrest, and the local magistrate to whom we'd been taken before shortly after our arrest refused to let us post bail. Nor had he allowed Philip to send word to House Greer that we required the services of its solicitor, or even appoint a public solicitor to represent us in court. So we were in a sort of legal limbo. Neither of us could figure out why the magistrate was keeping us incommunicado or how much longer we'd be stuck in this stupid cell.

Philip was quiet for a minute. He put his bowl aside—unfinished; he didn't like the jail food any better than I did—and stared off into space. I ate quietly, telling myself that I needed to keep a full stomach, and presently he spoke again.

"Someone must have told them," he said quietly. "Someone who knew why we—"

A rasp of an iron key turning in the door at the end of the cell block, followed by the rusty squeal of hinges. I figured it was Josh, our favorite badge, returning to pick up the breakfast tray. I was only half-right. Yes, it was Josh, but that wasn't why he came to see us. He'd brought a visitor, and I recognized him as soon as I saw him.

Steward Bolland Conklin of House Fletcher. Pilot's father. And he didn't appear to be very happy with his son-in-law.

II

It was obvious that Steward Conklin's journey from Landencyte to Castaway Point had been long and unpleasant. It had rained hard last night, and from the looks of things he'd been caught in it. His gorschskin cape and slouch hat were damp, as if they'd been worn overnight and maybe even slept in, and his boots were caked with sand and mud. One look at his face and I knew this wasn't going to be a cordial visit, even for a jail.

For a few long moments, Philip and Steward Conklin regarded each other in silence. It wasn't hard to see that they were separated by more than iron bars. Deciding not to speak until I was spoken to, I sat quietly upon my bunk. Conklin barely noticed me, and it wasn't a good time to remind him of my presence.

"Bolland… good to see you again." When Philip finally spoke, it was with the first-name familiarity one becomes accustomed to using with one's in-laws. Nonetheless, there was a tinge of apprehension in his voice.

"Really? I'm surprised." The Steward's eyebrows twitched, a nervous tic that was his only outward sign of emotion. "If I was where you are now, the last person I'd want to see would be my wife's father."

"I—"

"Or were you expecting me to bail you out? If so, I'm afraid I'm going to have to disappoint you. So far as I'm concerned, you are exactly where you're supposed to be."

If Conklin had been cold before, he was positively freezing by now. Although Philip hadn't said as much while we'd been in the coop together, it was plain to me that this was exactly what he'd been anticipating: a patriarch from either House Greer or House Fletcher to come riding to the rescue, bag of Cetan gold in hand, ready to pay off badges, bondsmen, Guardians, magistrates, and whoever else needed to have their palms greased.

Philip's eyes widened. He was hiding his disappointment, but not well. "No, I… I wasn't," he stammered. "I… I'm just… I mean, I'm sorry that you had to ride all this way." He waited for Conklin to respond. When he didn't, he tried to fill the silence with good manners. "Did you have a good trip?"

It was a courtly pretense that bordered on the absurd. Nonetheless, it thawed Conklin just a bit. "I left Landencyte as soon as word reached me. That was the day before yesterday. Someone here took their time notifying your family." He didn't look at Josh, but the screw became red-faced with embarrassment; inconveniencing a Steward is not good for anyone's government career. "We came down on South Island Road and didn't think it would take so long, but the weather changed and a storm forced us to seek shelter along the highway. So, no, it was not 'a good trip'."

South Island Road was the stretch of the Island Loop that ran south-by-southwest along the coast. It was a shorter and more direct route to Castaway Point than the way we'd come, across the highlands on Mountain Pike, with stops along the way. The problem with South Island Road is that, along this particular part of the Loop, there were no settlements. The beach was too narrow for a town to take root beside the ocean's edge, and the limestone bluffs towering above the road regularly had landslides. If Steward Conklin and his party were forced to stop overnight, they'd either huddled together beneath rain-tarps or sought cover within a cave or crevice at the foot of the bluffs.

Either way, given the wind and the rain, they couldn't have been comfortable. No wonder the old man was cranky. And now I knew why Philip and I had been hung out to dry. The badges had neglected to send word of our arrest to House Greer and House Fletcher, and when a courier finally delivered the message informing them that Philip had been arrested and jailed in Castaway Point, the affair had been dropped in Steward Conklin's lap.

And he wasn't happy about it. Not at all.

Realizing that he'd said the wrong thing, Philip looked away. When he did, his eyes met mine, and I could tell he wanted me to step in and save him. But I wasn't crazy about where my adventures with him and his damn wife had brought me, and I didn't figure that I owed him any favors. So I crossed my arms, leaned back in bed, and watched him burn.

"Why did I come?" Gathering his cape around him and tilting back his hat, Conklin took a seat on a wooden stool set aside for visitors. He started to go on, then seemed to remember Josh was still there. "Sir, if you'll excuse us…?"

Josh vanished, and once the cell block door slammed shut behind him, Conklin went on. "As I said, I'm not here to post bail," he said, leaning forward and lowering his voice. "I intend to petition the local magistrate to release you into my custody, so that I may extradite you and escort you home for a hearing before the Landencyte magistrates."

Relieved, Philip let out his breath. "Thank you, Bolland. I—"

"But before I do, I want you to answer a question: where has my daughter gone?"

Philip frowned. Now he understood, as did I. Steward Conklin wasn't concerned about his well-being; all he wanted was to get Pilot back. And he figured that Philip would know where she was.

But it was clear to me that he didn't, so I knew Conklin was making the same error of judgement. "I don't know," Philip said. "Really, I don't. She doesn't tell me everything—"

"Gorschshit. You're her husband."

"I'm telling the truth."

"Really, he is." For the first time since Conklin entered the cell block, I spoke up. "Believe him when he says that Pilot doesn't always say everything she knows. That includes—"

"Was I addressing you, Citizen Crowe?" Conklin glared at me. "I paid you off months ago. So far as I'm concerned, you're not part of this. If you know what's good for you—"

"Citizen Exemplary and Lady Greer are now my clients," I said. "They're paying me for my services, which makes me involved. And since you're a former client as well, I'll let you know, in all honesty, that neither Philip nor I know where Pilot has gone. She didn't share that information with us before she escaped." I raised my right hand, palm out. "And that's the truth, Steward. I'd swear that before the maggies."

Conklin studied me for a moment, a pensive frown upon his face. I knew that look: he was trying to decide whether to trust me, and if so, what to do about it. "If you're looking for a way to get out of jail," he said at last, "then you've played a good hand. I'll include you in my petition, but only so that the magistrates can hear from you as well." A humorless smile. "If you're lying, Crowe, you may find yourself wishing I'd left you here."

He didn't explain what he meant by that. He didn't need to. If the Landencyte magistrates chose not to believe either Philip or me, they could hand us over to the badges for further questioning. As a former badge, I knew what sort of interrogation techniques they used. The one where they simulate drowning is particularly nasty; they say it's not really torture, but I knew better. I'd done it myself, and my conscience has never let me forget it.

Conklin stood up. "I'll go have a word with the local magistrate. Shouldn't take long. We'll have you out of there by noon, I expect." He raised a fist to knock on the door, then paused to look back at Philip again. "By the way, your father sends his best regards."

Philip's face lost color. "You didn't tell him…?"

"That you've been arrested?" Conklin shook his head. "No. He heard that you were in some sort of trouble, but so far as he's concerned, you've simply gotten in a little over your head in gambling debt, and I've come to your aid." His face softened. "If he doesn't need to know the truth, then I see no point in telling him."

"Thank you." Philip gave a grateful nod. "I appreciate it."

Conklin grunted noncommittally. The door opened again, and without another word he stepped through. Josh shut it behind them, and once again we were alone. Philip waited until their footsteps receded, then he lay back against his pillow. "Well, at least we're getting out of here."

"Yes," I said, "and you'll be pleased to know that jail cells in Landencyte are much nicer. The breakfast buffet is particularly delightful." Philip cast me an annoyed look but said nothing. "So, what's that about your father?" I added.

"My father isn't well." He hesitated. "I'm glad Conklin spared him this, at least. I don't think he'd understand, but if he did, it wouldn't do him any good."

Searching my memory, I remembered hearing that Steward Greer had been bedridden lately, the sort of thing that happens when you reach an advanced age and your mind is no longer as sharp as it once was. Steward Conklin's role as Philip's father-in-law was more than a traditional formality. No wonder the kid was embarrassed to be found here by him.

Yet I doubted that the Steward's concern for his daughter's husband would be extended to me as well. We were getting out of the Castaway Point jail, but that didn't mean we were getting out of trouble, too.

III

Conklin must have had a lot of pull with the Castaway Point magistrates, because Josh had just delivered the lunch tray when the word came to release us from jail. Another badge came to the cell block; a silent hand-gesture in the secret vernacular that all badges understand (fingers pinched together as if holding a key, a counter-clockwise twist of the wrist: *let 'em out*: no, I hadn't forgotten) and Josh turned to Philip and me.

"Looks like you're being let out," he said.

Philip's face brightened "You mean we're—?"

"Don't get your hopes up. It only means that you're getting out of here. You're still in custody."

The other badge, Blake, held up the two pairs of handcuffs he'd brought with him. "Don't even think about making a break for it, boys. There's a half-dozen badges waiting outside for you, and a nice paddy wagon for the ride home." There was a smirk on his face as he said this; Blake had been kind of a shit ever since Philip and I got there.

"Wouldn't dream of it." I looked down at the tray Josh had just brought us. Fried bork sandwiches; if it was anything like the rest of the meals we'd had over the last four days, the bread was stale and the meat was fatty and undercooked. "You can have our lunch, if you'd like."

Blake gave a mean little laugh; the bastard probably made sure our meals were lousy. Josh gave me an apologetic look and quietly shook his head. Sometimes lawmen will play the "good badge-bad badge" routine to elicit information from prisoners, but that wasn't what Blake and Josh were up to. Josh was civilized, but Blake really was the kind who takes sadistic pleasure from making things tough for people who wind up in jail. I privately vowed to come back one day and make him regret everything he'd done to Philip and me.

Before we left the cell, Josh had us turn around and hold our hands together behind our backs so that Blake could put on the cuffs. Only then were we allowed to leave the cell; Josh escorted Philip, and I got Blake. Before he took my arm, Blake gave my manacled wrists a good, hard yank. "Just making sure they're not loose," he said, ignoring the discomfort he'd plainly intended.

"Hey, are you married?" I asked casually. "When I come back, I think I'll look her up. Maybe she'd like to spend time with someone who acts like a man and doesn't—"

I didn't get to finish the thought before his baton slammed against the back of my thighs. He hit me just hard enough to put me on my knees, but not hard enough to break anything or leave bruises.

"Cut it out!" Josh snapped. He stepped back to grasp my elbow and help me back on my feet. "Sorry about that, Crowe. That was uncalled for."

I said nothing. Instead, I locked eyes with Blake and didn't look away. The smirk vanished, and he didn't touch me again. He was on my payback list; if he didn't know that before, he knew it now.

But he'd have to take a number and get in line. The guy at the top of my list was waiting outside.

I wasn't surprised to see Bart among the badges standing in the jail courtyard. Guardians often accompanied badges on official business like this. They'd claim that they were just there as observers, but everyone knew it was so that Cetans could keep an eye on humans and make sure that we didn't pull a fast one on them. It was a good guess that Bart was there to make sure Philip and I wouldn't be spirited away by another flying machine.

Bolland Conklin was there, too, as were four badges, each wearing the insignia of the Landencyte constabulary on their uniform berets. It was a clammy autumn morning with a cold drizzle falling from the leaden sky. Everyone was wearing hooded cloaks except for Philip and I, who hadn't been given back the cloaks we'd been wearing when we were arrested. Two gorsches stood in the courtyard as well; both had carriages hitched to them, one an enclosed wagon with barred windows used by badges to transport bad actors from one place to another, the other a much nicer vehicle with curtained windows and the Fletcher crest emblazoned on the tonneau door. It wasn't hard to guess which one would carry Philip and me back to Landencyte.

"We're here to escort you home," Conklin said, possibly the most obvious thing anyone has ever spoken to me. "It'll take us a couple of days to get there. I'm going to trust that you'll be on your best behavior till then."

I almost laughed when he said this. It sounded like he was warning us not to taunt the badges. "Thank you, Steward," Philip said, his tone cool and formal. "We'll not cause any trouble for you, I promise, and I'm sure my family will appreciate your efforts on my behalf… as will Pilot, when we see her again."

Conklin's mouth tightened. The implication was unspoken yet clear: if we behaved ourselves, we wouldn't be abused any further, but if we caused any more trouble, then House Fletcher would hear about it from House Greer. And if that wasn't threat enough, then Bolland Conklin would find himself having to explain things to his daughter, if and when he saw her again. If there is one thing the Houses dread, it's losing face because of the action of their young.

He didn't answer his son-in-law, though, but instead turned to me. "Since you're apparently part of all this, Citizen Crowe, I negotiated your release as well. Once we're back in Landencyte, though, I'm going to request that the magistrates separate your legal case from Philip's. Is that understood?"

Oh, yeah, I understood, all right. Steward Conklin would probably do his best to have the maggies dismiss the case against his son-in-law, or at least reduce his punishment as much as possible. He was the scion of Sanctuary's most influential House, after all; being brought home in a paddy wagon was probably the worst indignity he'd have to suffer. But I wasn't going to be as lucky. I had little doubt that I alone would bear the brunt of all the charges presently facing Philip.

I'd better get used to jail food. That was the only thing I was going to be eating for some time to come. It's hard to give an indifferent shrug under circumstances like that, but I managed. Never plead for mercy… you're probably not going to get it anyway.

Conklin waited a moment to see if I would beg for him to change his mind, and when I didn't, he turned to Josh and nodded. Josh touched my arm, gently prodding me toward the paddy wagon. As I turned toward the wagon, my eyes turned toward Bart. He met my gaze with one just as cold, and although he said nothing, his muzzle pulled back from his teeth. But I'd seen his fangs before and there was nothing in his canine expressions that intimidated me, so I didn't react at all and was rewarded by seeing the short fur atop his head raise a little.

But he didn't speak or even growl, and that was unlike him. I had little doubt Bart had been waiting for the day he'd see me like this: arrested, charged, handcuffed, and loaded into a paddy wagon. He should've been gloating, yet aside from that silent snarl, Bart remained where he stood, arms at his sides. He didn't even touch the hilt of the worka sheathed at his waist.

I was still puzzling over this when I came to the paddy wagon. It was a little smaller than a normal covered carriage, built of sturdy blackthorn, its dark blue paint weatherbeaten by much use. The rear door was already open, although the stepladder hadn't yet been pulled out from underneath.

Josh bent down to do so. As he straightened up to take my arm, he whispered, "Be ready."

I was so startled, I almost asked him what he meant. But he pointedly didn't look my way, and I realized at once that his words were meant for my ears alone. I pretended not to notice; from the corners of my eyes, I saw no reaction from anyone else standing nearby. If anyone overheard this, it would've been Bart, but his ears didn't perk up even in the slightest.

Something was going to happen. I had an idea what it was.

I raised my right foot and planted it on the bottom step, but just as I was about to climb aboard, Josh stopped me. He then turned to Bart. "Guardian, may I please remove the prisoners' handcuffs? The door will be securely locked once they're in, but the trip is going to be long and hard. If they ride like that, they're likely to be thrown from their seats and injured, perhaps seriously."

Bart's tawny eyes flashed as he said this; I think he would've loved nothing more than to have me arrive in Landencyte with a broken arm or hip. Before he could reply, though, Conklin spoke up. "Yes, please do. I want these men to be well-treated on their way home, Guardian. They're not to be harmed or their safety neglected."

Bart's muzzle remained stiff, as if he was consciously controlling his reaction, something Cetans have a hard time doing. He said nothing, only crossed his hands and looked down, the Cetan way of expressing compliance under protest.

Josh had me step back down and turn around. I heard the jingle of his eyes, felt him tug at my wrists. The soft snap of a hasp opening, then the cuffs came loose.

At that moment, a fat raindrop fell on my left cheek, followed a half-second later by another on the back of my head. The cold drizzle that I'd barely noticed since coming out into the courtyard was starting to become a little more serious. The driver—a heavyset young woman wearing the hooded cape of a gorsch drover—turned about in her seat upon the buckboard to look back at us. "'Ey, can ya hurry it up back there?" she said. The accent identified her as coming from Rockhead, a small fishing town on Sanctuary's northern coast. My guess was that she was a country girl who'd recently moved to the big city. "Got us some serious weather comin', you b'sure."

"Yes, we need to hurry." A final glance at Philip and me, then Steward Conklin headed for the carriage parked behind us. Josh watched him go, then he clapped a firm, authoritative hand on my shoulder.

"All right, let's go." He was back to playing tough-but-fair jailer, but obviously there was more to him than I thought I knew. And that little detail made me uneasy. I thought I'd figured out what was going on and what was about to happen, but I couldn't be sure.

I stole a glance at Philip. We caught each other's gaze, and although his face revealed nothing, I could see from the look in his eyes that he'd put things together, too. I took a chance and gave him the slight nod. He hesitated, then blinked twice, slowly. Message received and understood:

Be ready.

IV

I don't know how paddy wagons got their name. All the ones I've seen, including the one Philip and I were in, weren't padded in any way. We sat across from each other on narrow wooden benches that lacked upholstery, and the only notable thing about it were the small, barred windows on the rear door, sides, and forward wall. Nothing about the wagon was made for the comfort of its unwilling passengers. Someone once told me that, long ago, "paddy" was a derogatory name given to men of Irish descent, so maybe that's the reason… but he didn't know any better than I did who the Irish were.

Noticing the iron rungs anchored to the floor, I was just happy that Bart hadn't insisted upon having us put in leg irons. Those would have only made the ride worse; the driver wasn't making much effort to avoid potholes, and the wagon needed new springs. Every hole we hit threatened to slam Philip and me against the walls, the floor, the door, and each other; it was all we could do just to remain in our seats.

After a few minutes, I reached forward to knock on the panel covering the forward window. The badge sitting beside the driver slid back the panel; he carried a loaded wheel-lock rifle across his lap and looked like he'd love nothing more than to use me for target practice. "What d'ya want?"

"Could you be a little more careful?" I asked, addressing the driver although her back was still turned to me. "My friend and I are collecting bruises back here."

"Nothing we can do about it," the badge said. "It's not—"

"Gets better, sure 'nuff," the driver said, interrupting her companion. "Streets inna this town are f'r shit, but be bett'r once we get to th' highway. Graded last Springmonth, smooth as'a baby's ass."

She barked laughter at her own joke. Having not touched any baby asses lately, I had to take her word for it. The badge started to shut the window, but she reached over to stop him. "No, leave'r open, Cyril. Gotta long trip 'head, and de blokes need'a cross-breeze. 'Sides, dey might wanna talk… no harm in dat, is dere?"

"No... no, guess not." Cyril looked back at me again. "Okay, we'll leave it open... but you give us any trouble, we'll stop the wagon and I'll come back to straighten you out. Understand?"

"Perfectly," I said. It was an easy promise to make. If there was going to be any trouble, then it wouldn't be instigated by either Philip or me.

The driver was right. Castaway Point's streets were seriously eroded and in need of repair, but shortly after we crossed the town line and got on the southeast stretch of the Island Loop, the road surface became smoother and less bumpy. The rain lessened, although it didn't stop completely. Through the back window, I could see the carriage following us, with badges on gorschback riding alongside. But this was all standard procedure when transporting criminals from one side of the island to another. No one was expecting trouble. Swords were sheathed and pistols were holstered.

To keep from appearing nervous—there's nothing that puts a seasoned lawman on edge more than silence—I struck up a conversation with the driver. It occurred to me that I'd seen her somewhere before, and I was right. Her name was Gillian, and where I'd seen her was at the annual Landencyte Midsummer Fair, the three-day festival outside town that draws people from all over Sanctuary. The fair has plenty of games and competitions, and one of them is the axe-throw, which is exactly what it sounds like: contestants hurling axes, the sort used for chopping wood, at a painted target twenty-five feet away. Gillian was a three-time blue-ribbon winner; I'd seen her perform the second time she finished in first place, and it had astonished me that anyone could hit the bulls-eye again and again and again, missing the target only once.

"Me mate, she say I don' need no practice, but I don' t'ink she right." Once I'd gotten her talking about her favorite sport, Gillian wanted to tell me all about it. "So I buy two new axes wid' d' gold I win, nice'uns dat I ne'er use f'r anyt'ing but practice, and in da af'ernoon, af'er I get done wi'd m'udder mate, I go back'a his woodcraf' shop an'—"

"You have two mates?"

"Y'bet... Karen 'n Harry. Marry bot' at same time, I did." Gillian glanced back at me and favored me with a saucy wink. "A'ways lookin' for third... wanna meet dem sometime? Three of us, we keep you warm in Wintermonth, you b'sure."

I heard Philip snort. Looking over at him, I saw that he had a hand covering his mouth, as if stifling rude laughter. That kind of multiple-partner marriage was something the upper classes tended to look down upon; although each House had several extended families, it was expected that you married only one person at a time. I don't know which amused him more, the thought of turning a triad into a quartet, or sleeping with a woman who could probably break my back.

"Well, that's a nice invitation," I began, "but I—"

"Someone up ahead," Cyril said.

I couldn't see the road ahead very well through the forward window, but once I shifted position to peer between Gillian and Cyril, I made things out a bit better. By then, Castaway Point lay about five miles behind us; just ahead was the place where the woodlands ended and the seacoast began. And it was here that a gorsch with a single rider on its back stood in the middle of the road.

"Prolly jes' someone takin' a breather." Gillian didn't sound worried, but nevertheless her right hand travelled from the reins to her waist. She pulled back her cloak, revealing a hunting knife in a belt sheath. The knife was the size of a short sword, and I had little doubt that she'd practiced throwing it just as much as her axes.

The lone rider watched quietly as the caravan approached. When we got closer, I saw that the person seated on the gorsch was a young woman. She wore a dark grey travel cape, hood pulled up over her head. She'd turned her gorsch sideways so that the beast blocked the road, and apparently was in no hurry to get out of our way. But while she held the gorsch reins in her left hand, I noticed her right arm dangled out of sight, on the other side of the animal.

I turned my head to glance out the rear window. The carriage behind us came to a halt just as soon as the paddy wagon did. Bart was riding on the buckboard beside the driver; he turned to speak to someone inside, and the carriage door opened and a couple of badges climbed out. They didn't seem greatly concerned, though, for their swords and pistols remained untouched as they ambled forward.

"Can I help you, Citizen?" Cyril called out.

"Yes," the woman on gorschback replied, "as a matter of fact, you can." She raised her hand to stick two fingers between her lips and let out a shrill, sharp whistle.

That's when Guido's Raiders appeared.

V

When I was still a badge, Landencyte was overrun by street gangs. Most of these gangs called the Squat their home, but as they grew in both size and number, they began to spread out across the city, claiming streets and entire neighborhoods as their turf. Small gangs like the Crawp Eaters, the Water Street Champions, and the Wrong Kind of Guys had only a handful of members, while the larger ones—the Squat Kings and the Bad Mothers—claimed several dozen. And while each gang had a specialty of one sort or another—the Eaters were dope dealers, the Kings were heavily into extortion, and the Mothers ran the city's biggest prostitution ring—there wasn't a criminal offense any of them were unwilling to commit, for money if not for fun.

At first, most people didn't pay them much mind. So long as the gangs stuck to their declared territories in the Squat and kept a low profile, law-abiding Citizens were willing to look the other way. Besides, the gangs performed certain services, illegal yet nonetheless desirable. Want some good jackweed for your next party? Go down to Burroughs Street and find an Eater. Opening a new business in the waterfront district? You'll need to pay protection money to the Squat Kings to make sure that burglars won't break into your shop and steal everything you've got. The Bad Mothers can get you laid, the Water Street Champions provide excellent bodyguards, and while no one seems to know exactly what the Wrong Kind of Guys do, whatever it is, they're pretty good at it.

If you were a badge and walked a beat in a particular neighborhood, then you had a choice: you accepted bribe money from the local gang or accepted the risks that came with being an honest lawman. I'm not proud to say that I took money from the Eaters, but I'm not ashamed of it, either. They were the gang in my part of town, and so I struck a deal with their chief: so long as they didn't peddle dope to kids, I'd accept their weekly pay-off and pretend to have never heard of them. Most badges worked out similar arrangements, and those who didn't were liable to end up in the hospital… or the morgue, if the first warning didn't take.

The status quo might have stayed that way indefinitely if the gangs hadn't become too big and too greedy. As they grew, they began to intrude more regularly on neighboring turfs. This led to territorial disputes that, more often than not, were settled with bloody street battles that cost the lives of bystanders unfortunate enough to be caught in the way. And when the gangs discovered they weren't making enough money—one drawback of the dope racket is that your best customers tend have short life spans—they began to spread out of the Squat and into the more genteel parts of the city. So when the wealthy residents of the Heights began finding prostitutes on their clean and tidy streets, or looked out their windows to see smoke rising from neighborhood shops that decided not to pay protection, the crackdown was inevitable.

It wasn't easy, and it took a long time, but the gangs of Landencyte were finally brought under control. The smaller ones were broken up and the larger ones were chased back into the Squat, and eventually the gangs found their numbers diminished, their members either sent off to prison or killed. To get away from the law, many of them left town and moved up into the mountains where the badges had no jurisdiction and the Guardians were reluctant to go. There they formed a new gang, one specializing in an old profession: highway robbery, confronting travelers on the roads leading from one coastal settlement to another and fleecing them of everything they could take.

They called themselves Guido's Raiders. And it wasn't long before they learned a skill that made them the most formidable gang on Sanctuary.

They learned how to ride lopers.

VI

When the girl on gorschback whistled, I knew it was a signal and changed windows, peering out the one to the right, where I could see the woodlands. Philip crowded in beside me, and what we saw caused him to gasp in astonishment.

"Is that what I think it is?" he asked.

From the woods on either side of the road, eight men and women emerged, each riding a four-legged creature that loped along on its hind legs with long, bounding jumps. I'm told that, in Old Earth mythology, there's an animal called a jackrabbit, or a hare, that looks much like a loper. The big difference is that lopers are quite a bit bigger than rabbits—standing upright on their muscular hindquarters, a full-grown loper is about eight feet tall—but they have small ears and long tails. But it's the hind legs that count. A loper at full sprint can run sixty feet in five seconds or jump ten feet in a single bound. A gorsch is a plodding, dim-witted lug by comparison.

You can live a long time on Sanctuary and rarely see a loper, and then only if you're out in the wild, away from any settlements. They run from both humans and Cetans, and they're fast enough that there's no way to catch them on foot. Guido's Raiders were the first to do so. They used elaborate snares strung from bent saplings to snatch lopers by their hind legs and yank them off their feet so they couldn't escape. The adults were released—once they got past a certain age, they were untamable—and the young were kept. Immature lopers were more easily broken and trained, and only the gods knew how long it took to get to where the Raiders could put a saddle on them. It's probably correct to assume that quite a few bones are broken in the process.

Lopers' short, reddish-brown fur enables them to blend in with woodlands and meadows. The hooded serapes the highwaymen wore over their clothes were made from their hides. With that kind of camouflage, it was no wonder they were able to lurk along the roadside and wait for someone to come by. And if they were put off by the fact that their target was a paddy wagon escorted by a half-dozen badges and a Guardian, they didn't show it. The gang were upon us before the girl's whistle died in the air.

"Drop your weapons!" The Raider who made this demand was obviously the gang leader; it was probably a good guess that his name was Guido. Like the others, he had a bandana tied around the bottom part of his face; together with his serape's raised hood, it made an excellent disguise. He raised the flintlock in his right hand, pointed it in the general direction of the caravan. "Drop 'em now!"

Good advice, but there's always some dummy who doesn't listen. Cyril apparently believed that he could take out a Raider on loper-back, but he'd barely raised his rifle when the woman who'd stopped us brought up the crossbow she'd been holding out of sight. A soft *tung!* and a bolt was sticking out of Cyril's chest. He toppled from the buckboard without so much as a grunt. His gun hit the ground the same instant he did; it discharged loudly but harmlessly, hurting no one.

Through the forward window, I saw Gillian's right hand move toward the knife on her belt. "Don't be stupid," I said, quietly so that only she could hear. Gillian hesitated, then put her hands on the buckboard where they could be seen. Smart girl.

"Wha' izzi' you wan'?" Hearing Bart's voice, Philip and I turned to peer through the wagon's rear window. The Guardian had raised his hands, as did the badges. The Raiders were armed with flintlocks and crossbows, and each one of them were trained on the lawmen.

Up to that point, I would've been willing to bet that everyone but Philip and me believed this was just a robbery; these men were after money and valuables, which is what Guido's Raiders usually took from the caravans they ambushed. That assumption was disproven by the chieftain's next words.

"You're carrying two prisoners," Guido said. "Hand 'em over and no one else gets hurt, plain and simple."

"You're not after gold?" one of the badges asked.

"No, just the people you've got with you." With his gun, Guido gestured toward the paddy wagon. "Those two," he said, meaning Philip and me.

"You'll never away with this!" This from Steward Conklin. He was still in the carriage, but his voice carried.

Philip snorted and shook his head. I couldn't believe I'd heard that either. Some people speak in clichés without realizing it, but Conklin seemed to think that his threat was anything but empty. Several highwaymen laughed out loud; I couldn't see the steward, but I imagine he was annoyed at not being taken seriously.

"With all due respect, Your Honor," the gang chief said with mocking politesse, "but I disagree." His expression was hidden by his mask, but no doubt that he was amused as well. "Now, if you'd be so kind, please step down from the carriage. Everyone, come over here where we can keep an eye on you. Thank you."

The carriage door opened, and one of the badges who'd been riding with Steward Conklin hopped down to open the stepladder and extend it to the ground. Once this was done, he obediently stepped back and raised his hands. A moment passed, then Conklin climbed out, carefully keeping his hands at shoulder height. He was followed by the two other badges who'd been riding with him. "You, too," the chief said, beckoning to the driver and the badge sitting beside him on the buckboard. They reluctantly joined the others.

Three Raiders kicked their ankles lightly against the sides of their lopers. Or rather, two of them did. For some odd reason, one of the gang members was sharing a loper with another. The animals obediently squatted on their haunches, allowing their riders to dismount without twisting an ankle. Once they were on the ground, the two Raiders who'd been riding together wasted no time frisking everyone while the third held a cocked flintlock on them. Knives, short swords, rapiers, and guns were tossed into a pile. One of the outlaws found a miniature pistol in Conklin's waistcoat pocket; he took a second to admire the novelty weapon—which was probably harmless unless aimed and fired within arm's length—before slipping it into his own pocket. "Thanks for the toy, Your Honorfulness," he said to Conklin, who just glared at him.

One of the masked men turned to Gillian, who'd climbed down from the paddy wagon and joined the others. "Key?" he asked, and when she told him that she didn't have it, he strolled over to where Cyril lay. He knelt down beside the body; a faint jingle, then he stood up again, keychain in hand. It took only three or four tries for him to find the one that unlocked the paddy wagon. Philip and I waited until he opened the back door, then we jumped out.

I needed weapons, too, so I went over to the pile of swords and firearms the Raiders had collected from the badges and picked out a saber and a flintlock. Thrusting them in my belt along with the powder bag, I thought about apologizing to the badges for the pilferage, but the looks on their faces told me that forgiveness was out of the question. I made a mental note to myself not to show my face in these parts again for a while.

"I'm not sure I'm ready to thank you," Philip said, looking up at Guido. "I didn't ask to be rescued."

I thought the remark was rather ungrateful, but Guido didn't take offense. "You'll appreciate our efforts when you find out where we're going." He pointed to one of the lopers whose rider hadn't dismounted. "Go with him."

"You're letting me go?" I asked.

"Oh, no, Citizen Crowe. You're coming with the Citizen Exemplary whether you like it or not." A quiet laugh from behind the bandana. "Besides, it would be a shame if you stayed behind. You'd miss all the fun."

I wasn't crazy about becoming a fugitive—this job had given me enough problems already—but I didn't like being a prisoner, either. It didn't look like Guido was giving me a choice, so I walked to the loper he'd indicated. The Raider dismounted, took down a bedroll and tossed it over the loper's back behind his saddle, then showed me how to climb on. It was easier than it looked; incredibly, the loper didn't seem to mind the extra weight.

While this was going on, the other Raiders were keeping busy. At gunpoint, they made everyone who'd been in the procession sit down on the ground, legs outstretched and hands behind their backs. They then had their wrists and ankles bound. One of the badges who'd been in the carriage with the steward put up a fight, and he was doing so well that I thought for a second or two he might make a run for it. But he got knocked upside the head with an unloaded flintlock held in reverse, then two highwaymen sat on him while a third hog-tied him. Everyone else cooperated after that.

"All right, is that it?" Guido looked about, making sure nothing had been overlooked. I'll hand it to him: as plans go, this one went off without a hitch. The Raiders obviously had a lot of practice at this sort of thing. "Very well, then. Ladies and gentlemen, let's ride."

The Raiders hurried for their animals. As they did, one of the men who'd tied up the prisoners—the one who'd been sharing a loper with another—paused beside the loper carrying Philip. He silently regarded

Philip for a moment or two, and I thought that he was about to say something. Then Guido told him to hurry up, and the Raider left Philip to dash over to the loper he'd been riding earlier. I couldn't help but notice a certain clumsiness as he mounted the beast again. Obviously, he was still new at this. Well, there's a first time for everything.

Once everyone had mounted up, Guido whistled sharply. "Hold on," said the rider I was sitting behind. He shook the reins, and I had just enough time to grab hold of him before the loper launched itself.

My stomach was left about fifteen feet back.

VII

We were close to the seacoast, so there were only three directions Guido's Raiders could have taken: north, out of the forest and up along the coast toward Landencyte; east, off the road and inland toward the mountains the gang called home; or south, through the forest back to Castaway Point just a few miles away.

I would've bet good money on the second option. In the Perseverance Mountains, no one would be able to find us; Philip and I could hide out there indefinitely. But the gang surprised me: instead, they began riding south as hard as they could.

So now we were headed back to the place where Philip and I had been arrested and jailed. We didn't have much chance to protest, though. It was all we could do just to hang on and keep from being thrown to the ground. The lopers didn't get that name for no reason; urged by the Raiders, they bounded more than ran, each leap carrying them a dozen feet at a time. I didn't like hugging the Raider in front of me—not to put too fine of a point on it, but I don't swing that way—but the blanket I was using as a saddle lacked a belly strap and stirrups, so the only way to keep from being hurled off the loper's back every time it jumped was to wrap my arms around the Raider's middle and hope that he didn't get the wrong ideas about me. He didn't seem to mind, though, so I guess this was something he'd done before.

About a mile down the road, just as we reached a clearing, I glanced back to make sure Philip was still there. He was, and although it looked as if he was also hanging onto his own rider as if his life depended on it, that wasn't what caught my attention. From the distance, I heard a thin, whistling shriek as, above the trees behind us, a tiny fireball shot straight up into the overcast sky, trailing a smokey red plume behind it. The fireball exploded just before it reached the low-lying clouds, a loud bang that could be heard for miles.

Recognizing the fireball for what it had been, I prodded the Raider's shoulder. "Someone back there just fired off a flare."

The Raider looked over his shoulder just in time to spot another flare. He cursed, then stuck his fingers in his mouth and whistled, obviously the gang's preferred way of getting other riders' attention. Everyone pulled back on their reins, bringing their lopers to a halt. The Raiders had just stopped when a third flare, identical to the first two, rose from beyond the trees.

"Damn it!" Guido snapped, yanking down his bandana to reveal an older man with a blonde-turning-grey handlebar mustache. "Who didn't hear me say to look and see if the badges were carrying emergency flares?"

The Raiders glanced at one another; no one was willing to fess up. Now that we were a safe distance from the badges, everyone followed their chief's example and pulled down their bandanas. "Dey wouldn'a git loose if someone'a tied 'em up better," another gang member said, speaking in the same north coast accent Gillian had. "If'n dey couldn'a use dere hands, dey couldn'a got dere hands onna flare, you b'sure."

"So who the hell tied up those guys?" Guido looked about. "Gillespie, was it you?"

Gillespie? Did I hear that right? Not quite believing it, I followed the outlaw chief's gaze to the person he'd just addressed. It turned out to be the same person I'd noticed earlier, the one who'd paused by Philip's loper, then displayed a lack of practice in remounting his own. He'd pulled down his bandana, and yes, it was who I thought it was: Michael Gillespie.

I hadn't seen Gillespie again since that night Philip and I were taken into Starship Mountain. Although he still belonged to the Originalists, I figured that he was out of Philip and Pilot's lives for good once they were married. And yet here he was, riding to the rescue of the man who'd stolen back the young lady they both loved.

"I thought I tied them up well." Gillespie was red-faced; he couldn't seem to meet the chief's gaze. "I'm sorry. I was in a hurry, and—"

"Never mind." Guido turned to look at the others. "I doubt anyone in town will spot that flare—a little too far for that—but if the badges managed to get their hands on it, it also means that they'll be coming after us."

"We've got a head start," another gang member said, a young woman with a noticeable scar running down the lower left side of her face. "They've got gorsches and we've got lopers."

"That's a good head start, but it's not going to last. Once they reach town, they'll waste no time getting the rest of the badges to join them in a door-to-door search. We've got to be gone by then."

The others nodded. Except for Gillespie, whose embarrassment hadn't lasted very long. "I don't get it. If the badges figure we're on our way back to town, then why are we—?"

"You'll find that out once we get there." Guido pulled his bandana across his face again. "Okay, that's enough. Get going, and don't stop 'til we get there."

Get where? Like Gillespie, no one had told me anything. Not only that, but I also wanted to know how and why he'd come to be riding with the Raiders. But there was no chance to ask those questions. I barely had time to wrap my arms around my rider before the lopers launched themselves again, out of the clearing and down the road to Castaway Point.

VIII

Say what you will about the Raiders, but they knew how to make an entrance.

The gang made the trip back to Castaway Point in half the time it took the paddy wagon and its escorts to reach the place where they stopped us. Once I got used to the way the lopers travelled—lunge, land, lunge, land, repeat—I knew what to expect. Still, my heart was beating about as fast as the loper was loping, so the sight of town meant a welcome end to an hour of terror.

I thought of something just then. "Hey, where are we going?"

The Raider whose loper we were riding gave me a disdainful glance over his shoulder, as if I'd just asked the dumbest question he'd ever heard; I rephrased it. "I mean, where *in town* are you taking us? Is there a hideout you guys use?"

Still no answer. He bent forward to shake the reins and clap his ankles gently against the loper's side. The beast leaped a little farther with its next lunge; I think the damn thing was trying to fly. A lot of street mages back in Landencyte practice levitation. The lopers we were riding put them all to shame, and they weren't faking it.

The rain had slacked off by the time the Raiders passed through Castaway Point's south gate. It was early afternoon, the time of day when it's unnecessary to keep someone in the watchtower, so they charged through town before anyone had a chance to ring the tower bell. The lopers' four-toed hind feet beat against the muddy streets; the low thunder of their passing drew townspeople to their doors and windows to gape at the Raiders, while pedestrians scurried out of their way and gorsches shrank back and mewled with fear.

I expected the gang would head for the seediest part of town, the sort of neighborhood where everyone seems to go deaf and blind whenever a badge shows up. I was only half-right: the Raiders went straight for the waterfront, which was not what I was expecting, since that was where Bart cornered Philip and me.

Indeed, the next I knew, we were riding down the street alongside the municipal pier. We passed the boathouse where Galileo had kept his amphibious flying machine but didn't stop there. Instead, we rode another thirty yards or so to another boathouse. This one was larger than the first, but like that one it was built over the water, with half of the structure raised on pilings so as to allow boats—probably a small trawler, I guessed—to dock since.

There the Raiders came to a halt. The Raider who'd shared his loper with me gently nudged the animal with his boot-heels, and his steed knelt on its hinds, allowing me to slide down its furry back. I managed to dismount without making a fool of myself, but once my feet were back on the ground, I swore to myself that I'd sooner walk a hundred miles than ever hitch a ride on a loper again.

Philip was climbing down from the loper that had carried him here, as was Michael Gillespie. They'd been riding just ahead of me, and when I hadn't been struggling to keep from throwing up, down, and out, I'd watched the two of them. All the way back to town, Philip and Michael had studiously avoided any contact with each other; no talk, no gestures, no glances, and if one of them happened to catch the other's eye, they both immediately looked away. This wasn't good. I'd seen that kind of behavior before, and it was usually from people who really and truly despise one another. The last time I'd seen someone act like that, it was my ex-wife when she hauled me in front of a maggie to demand a divorce.

Philip walked over to where Guido sat upon his loper. I followed him. "Is this it?" Philip asked. "Is this how we're getting out of here?"

"Uh-huh." The gang chief nodded toward the boathouse's back door. "They're waiting for you inside. Should be ready to go, according to plan."

"Okay." Philip cocked a thumb at me. "He's coming too, right?"

"Uh-huh, and so is your other friend." He pointed toward Gillespie.

"Oh, now wait a minute!" Hearing this, Michael hurried over to us. "Look, I told you, I just wanted to come along when you rescued them. I have no intention of leaving the island."

"I agree," Philip said. "I have no use for this guy, and I doubt Pilot does either, even if he still believes otherwise." He glared at his former rival as he spoke, and Michael turned red and hastily looked away. "If you have something to do with our rescue," Philip added, directly addressing him, "then you have my gratitude. But neither my wife nor I have any need for you, and I'd take it as a favor if you'd kindly stay out of our lives."

"No." Guido shook his head. "The instructions we received from Galileo are clear. All three of you are to be taken off Sanctuary. No one is to be to be left behind except the kid." Once again, Michael started to object, but the gang leader locked eyes with him. "One exception: you're to remain here if you're killed. Would you care for me to arrange that?"

As he spoke, he pushed aside his cape to lay a hand on the hilt of a sheathed saber. Some of his men chuckled at this. It didn't appear as if the Raiders enjoyed Michael's company any more than Philip or I did. No time to ask, though. Michael blanched and looked away, and Guido turned to Philip and me again. "All right then, hurry up and get outta here. The badges are slow, but if some law-abiding individual should happen to see us…"

"Understood." Philip extended his hand. "Many thanks, sir. I'm in your debt."

"Any time, brother, any time." The gang chief solemnly shook hands with the young Citizen Exemplary. Obviously, he and Philip had met before. I couldn't think of two individuals more unalike, but apparently there was some sort of link between Guido's Raiders and the Originalist study group in Landencyte. Maybe they did bake sales together.

Another sharp whistle from Guido, and the Raiders took off down the street. As they rode away, Philip went to the boathouse and knocked three times on the back door. The Raiders had just vanished from sight when the door opened.

"Hurry, get in here!"

Standing in the doorway was someone I'd briefly met before: Galileo's assistant, the nameless kid he'd told to run for it just as Bart and the badges were swooping down on Philip, Pilot, and me. I'd already figured out that Galileo had sent the kid off with a message for the Raiders; somehow or another, Michael got mixed up in this as well. Sure, he belonged to Galileo's group, too, but still…

"C'mon, before somebody spots you." The kid darted a cautious look up and down the vacated street before stepping out of our way. Philip and I hurried inside. Gillespie hesitated, then followed us reluctantly, as if he didn't want to be there just then. I noticed this, but a second later I forgot all about it. What lay inside the boathouse was much more interesting.

By then, I was expecting to find another motorized aeroglider hidden within, just like the first one only bigger. I mean, if you're going to build one flying machine, why not two? I'd underestimated Galileo, though. He hadn't confined his imagination to inventing a craft that could take to the air; he'd been studying the sea, too.

Within the boathouse was a U-shaped slip large enough to accommodate a fishing boat. It was hard to see much at first, for the windows were painted over and the only illumination was from glowworm lanterns hanging from the rafter beams. Then my eyes adjusted to the dim light, I saw a vessel unlike any I'd ever seen before. At first I thought it was a capsized boat floating upside down, its lower hull belly-up like an immense dead fish. Then I realized that my first impression was wrong; what I was looking at was an ovoid-shaped craft, like a teardrop made of iron, with only a flat, narrow deck on top. A circular hatch lay open at the center of the topside deck; at the bow was a round turret with glass portholes on all four sides and what appeared to be a crooked pipe rising beside it. At the stern, half-hidden underwater, was something that looked a bit like a child's pinwheel, only much larger and mounted within a swivel-mounted vane that resembled a rudder of some sort. Horizontal planes, also swivel-mounted, thrust out from either side of the bow. The craft was mostly submerged, making it hard to judge its length, but it appeared to be about forty feet long.

"What the hell is this thing?" I asked.

"The boss calls it a submersible undersea vehicle," the kid said. "We call it a 'sub' for short."

"He built this?" Awestruck, Michael stared at the strange craft. "I thought he only did, y'know, those gliders of his."

"You think Galileo works on just one thing at a time?" The kid gave him an annoyed look. "Don't know him very well, do you?"

"I don't think that's called for." Michael was stung. "I got in touch with the Raiders, didn't I? I passed the message to them, not you."

The kid scowled and was about to say more when footsteps rang upon a metal ladder within the craft's open hatch. A dark-skinned, bare-chested man wearing a fisherman's cap over a shaved head climbed up from below. He regarded the four of us for a moment, then his face broke into a wry grin.

"Well, what're you waiting for, an engraved invitation?" He looked at the kid. "Marty, bring 'em aboard. We need to get underway as soon as possible."

The captain—I assumed that's who he was—disappeared back down the hatch, and Marty turned to Philip, Michael, and me. "This way," he said, then led us around the slip to the sub's port side, where a wooden gangplank rested against its metal hull. "Hurry. The skipper wants to get out of here before we lose the daylight."

Philip nodded and stepped onto the gangplank, but Michael hesitated. "Look, you don't need me any more. Why don't you let me stay behind with Marty so we can make sure you get away?"

"Did Galileo say in his message that he wanted Michael to come, too?" I asked Marty. Marty nodded. "Then I think it's better if you come with us," I said to Michael, resting a hand on his shoulder to gently but decisively push him toward the gangplank. "You don't want to be here if the badges catch up with us, do you?"

"I was wearing a mask. They're not going to know—"

"Even if you were, they might put two and two together, and figure out that you're involved."

"But—"

"Oh, no, I insist." I gave him another push, a little more firmly this time, giving him no choice but to step onto the gangplank. Philip was still topside. He silently watched as Michael walked across the plank to the sub; he and I exchanged a glance, but neither of us said anything.

Two men who'd been quietly standing inside the boathouse removed the gangplank as soon as the four of us were aboard. Philip and Michael climbed down next; I was the last man aboard, and just as soon as I'd climbed down the ladder, there was a metallic bang as one of the men closed the hatch behind me. Marty waited until I was off the ladder before climbing back up again. There was a faint squeal as he turned a lock-wheel to dog it tight, but I wasn't paying much attention to what he was doing. I was too busy marveling at the craft I'd just boarded.

The interior was cylindrical, windowless, and cramped, about six feet in diameter, with riveted seams evenly spaced among the iron plates that comprised its hull. The sub was lit by glowworm lanterns arranged along the rib-like support bulkheads. An iron axis ran down the length of the sub; spoke-like handgrips protruded at perpendicular angles from the center shaft, their purpose was made clear by the five crewmen seated on wooden benches on either side of the shaft, ready to begin turning it. In the stern, behind a chain-link divider, was a large vegetable-oil engine. At the bow, just below the turret, the captain stood before the bottom of the crooked pipe I'd noticed earlier; it had handgrips and an eyepiece of some sort, but I couldn't for the life of me figure what it was used for. Another crewman was perched on a stool in the bow; a complex system of wheels, levers, foot pedals, and glass-fronted dials were arrayed before him, and it wasn't hard to figure out their purpose as the vessel's controls.

The captain turned about to look at Philip, Mike, and me as we came down the ladder. "Welcome aboard the *Sea Witch*, gentlemen," he said. "My name is Mahmoud McKenzie, and if you haven't guessed already, I'm in command. You have any questions, feel free to bring them to me. Otherwise, if you'll take your places at the screw, we'll be underway."

"The screw?" I asked. "What's—?"

"He means this." One of the sailors patted the axis shaft with a meaty hand. Like everyone else aboard, he'd removed his shirt. "It's what we call the propeller," he explained. "We're the engine, or at least until we've crossed the blockade."

"You've got a real engine. Why not use it?" Michael was eyeing the machinery in the rear of the sub. The axis shaft ran alongside the engine; it appeared to be attached to a cog-and-gear system that could be engaged to turn the shaft without human assistance or disengaged to allow the sailors to use their muscles instead.

"Because we can't vent the fumes while we're running submerged," Captain McKenzie said. "So it's muscle power for the first couple of miles. Once we're clear of the blockade and they can't see us, we'll surface and use the engine to get us the rest of the way."

Philip and I found seats on the benches across from each other; Michael reluctantly sat down beside me. "So where are we going?" he asked.

"You'll see." McKenzie picked up a hammer from its resting place beneath the helmsman's stool. He raised it above his head and banged it three times against the ceiling. A few moments went by, then we heard three hard bangs from outside the sub. "Right, then," McKenzie said. "Charlie, take us down one fathom. Prop, stand by to engage. Dive!"

The helmsman reached over to a pump handle beside his seat and began rapidly moving it up and down. From my seat on the starboard-side bench, I heard a loud gurgle from beneath my feet as the sub's tanks were flooded.

The *Sea Witch* was going down, and we were going down with it.

IX

For as long as anyone could remember, there had been a blockade around Sanctuary.

It consisted of a ring of large rafts surrounding the island. Each raft supported a watchtower fifty feet tall, and was anchored to the sea floor about a mile offshore, the place where Sanctuary's undersea shelf ends and the deep ocean begins. The rafts were one mile apart from one another and were connected by a ring of floating buoys. Each raft was manned by two or three Guardians, and their job was to monitor the coastal waters surrounding the island to prevent human vessels from sailing any farther than the quarantine zone marked by the buoys. Fishing boats, ferries, and other small craft could sail these waters, but only with a permit from the Guardians. And since getting said permit required taking a nautical instruction class, one thing that got drilled into sailors was that failure to obey this part of Cetan Law could have lethal consequences.

If a vessel approached the quarantine zone, the Cetans on the nearest raft had a choice of actions: send out a small catamaran to intercept and board the errant vessel, or fire one of the tower's mortars in the craft's general direction as a warning. If that ship or boat didn't heave-to or turn about and go back the way it came, then the Cetans on the raft were authorized to train the mortar upon the vessel and open fire. And say what you will about the Cetans, but their aim was drop-dead accurate; nearly every ship that ever attempted to cross the quarantine zone was sunk by the Guardians, and those few that weren't sunk were never seen again.

Long ago, fishing boats were allowed to harbor overnight on Fisherman's Cay, a small isle about three miles off Sanctuary's southern coast, the nearest island of the Southern Archipelago. It even supported a small colony of its own, a fishing village. This ended when more adventurous seaman began to dare sailing farther south, exploring other isles of the group. The Guardians were steadfastly opposed to this, and the quarantine was imposed as a result.

History had forgotten the reason why the Cetans decided to isolate humans from the rest of Tawcety. Like the stockade wall surrounding

Starship Mountain, it came into existence many, many years ago, and any written record of what caused the native inhabitants to take such measures was no longer public knowledge. No child born on Sanctuary was told why he or she could never sail farther than the quarantine zone: it's simply the way things were and questioning it could get you in big trouble.

Yet the quarantine could stop only what the Cetans minding the towers were able to see.

Perhaps it was only inevitable that something like the *Sea Witch* would be built. Humans just don't like to be cooped up.

This was my train of thought as I put my back into making the sub move. It wasn't easy. Counting those who'd come aboard in Castaway Point—Philip, Michael, and myself—the four men seated on either side of the shaft provided the sub's propulsion by laboriously turning it clockwise hand over hand. It was tough work; the sub's interior was warm and humid, and it wasn't long before I peeled off my shirt as well. Only Captain McKenzie and his helmsman were spared. So there were no idle passengers aboard the *Sea Witch*; if you were there, then you pitched in and helped run the boat.

For the first ten minutes of the trip, McKenzie focused his attention on the eyepiece of the crooked pipe that came down from the ceiling. I learned that the instrument was called a periscope, and it used a system of lenses and mirrors to observe the surface while the *Witch* was submerged. Whoever invented the thing—Galileo, I assumed—had also managed to devise the means of keeping the part of the periscope that penetrated the hull watertight enough so that it didn't leak. After we cleared the boathouse and out of Castaway Point's small harbor, McKenzie ordered the helmsman to take us down to five fathoms—the sub's maximum cruise depth, I was told, about thirty feet.

"We can go deeper than that," McKenzie said, taking a moment to look back at Philip, Michael, and me, "but below thirty feet, the nitrogen in the air turns bad and we stand a chance of getting something called the bends." He pointed to a conduit running down the length of the ceiling; it led from a large tank in the bow, and air softly hissed from vents set every six feet. "We've got enough compressed air in the tanks for us to remain below for about five hours, but it shouldn't take that long to get past the blockade."

"So how… do you know… where we're going?" Philip asked. We were all breathing hard by then, with sweat dripping down our chests and backs. The metal skin of the sub's interior was sweating, too, beads of condensation dimpling its cold iron surface. "Does the… periscope… still work this… far down?"

"No. It's only good up to eight feet, then it's under water, too." McKenzie pointed to a large dial above the helm. "Once we're this far down, we can only go by what the compass tells us. But we're lucky: no reefs on the course we usually take, and even if there's another ship in our way, we'll pass below its keel. And this late in afternoon, the sun reflects off the water in such a way that no one on the rafts can see the *Witch* as we pass between them."

"How many times… have you done this?" I asked.

McKenzie didn't answer that question. Nor did he tell us why someone had gone to all the trouble of building the *Sea Witch* and using it to run the blockade. It was hard to talk anyway; turning the prop took a lot of effort, so there wasn't a lot of conversation for the next hour or so. True to her name, the *Witch* moved beneath the waves as a silent wraith, invisible to the Cetans on the raft watchtowers.

My arms were sore when McKenzie told those of us turning the propeller to take a break, then ordered the helmsman to take the sub up to one fathom. The two of them began working the pump again, this time to flood the tanks with air, causing the sub to gradually ascend. As the men seated around the shaft groaned and stretched their aching backs, the *Witch* slowly rose. McKenzie closely watched the depth indicator until the needle touched the one fathom mark, then he ordered a halt, and raised the periscope to check the surface. He slowly rotated the scope in a complete circle, then lowered it again and gave the order to ascend the rest of the way to the surface.

A few moments later, we felt the *Sea Witch* gently bobbing up and down, a sign that we'd reached the surface. One of the crewmen stood up from the bench and climbed up the ladder to turn the lockwheel. Fresh air, cool and tasting of salt, rushed through the open hatch, but not much sunlight; it was brighter inside the sub than it was outside. The crewman disappeared through the hatch, then came back down to confirm that we were beyond the quarantine zone.

"Mind if I go topside, skipper?" I asked.

McKenzie shrugged. "Sure, if you like. It's an interesting view. Not many people get to see it."

My knees cracked a little as I rose from the bench. I picked up my shirt from where I'd dropped it and put it on as I made my way to the ladder. Philip was right behind me; I stepped aside and let him go first, then climbed up the ladder behind him.

The rain had stopped and the clouds had lifted. The sun was touching the ocean off the starboard side, casting silver-orange highlights upon the dark blue water that hid everything passing below. Looking aft, I could see the quarantine as a broken line of spindly towers. The Cetans had already lighted the fish-oil lamps on their roofs, making the rafts easy to spot from the distance.

Sanctuary was a long, dark hump in the distance. Lights were already appearing along the shoreline; it was early evening in Castaway Point, and the town was preparing for the night ahead. I felt a chill run down my back. There was the place where I was born, where I'd lived my entire life. I'd never expected that I would ever leave it. Sanctuary once seemed so large, and now... now it was just an island, an incidental piece of dry land surrounded by a dark and limitless ocean. In more ways than one, I was leaving Sanctuary.

Feeling uneasy, I looked away. In the other direction, off the port bow, I saw another hump in the water: Fisherman's Cay. There were no lights there, though, no other signs of habitation. Yet it was only about a mile away. McKenzie was right. Very few people saw Sanctuary from the distance. You'd have to cross the quarantine line to get the view Philip and I had now.

"Wonder where we're going." He was standing beside me on the deck, shading the setting sun with his hand as he peered at Fisherman's Cay. "If there's anyone over there, they're keeping well-hidden."

"I don't think that's where we're headed." As I spoke, a new sound came up from below: the coughing rumble of an engine being started. A few moments later, my nose caught the aroma of frying food. The *Witch*'s veggie-oil engine was engaged with the prop; the sub surged forward, leaving behind a v-shaped wake that glistened in the setting sun.

The clang of boot soles upon the ladder. Captain McKenzie emerged through the hatch. He grinned when he saw Philip and me. "So, how do you like my little boat, gents?"

"Kind of hard on the arm and back muscles," Philip said, "but I'll consider it proper exercise."

"That's one way of thinking of it." There was a shirt tied around McKenzie's waist; he unknotted it and used it to mop the sweat from his face and chest. "Sorry to put you to work like that, but as you can see, it takes a lot of men to make the *Witch* swim."

"How long will it take for us to get there? Wherever we're headed, that is."

"We'll be reaching our destination in a couple of hours. Freeman Cay, southeast of the other side of Fisherman's Cay. You're welcome to stay up here as long as you like, but be aware that, as a rule, we don't allow more than three people topside at any one time, and the other guys might want some fresh air, too."

I nodded; I'd already figured as much. "Is my wife on Freeman Cay?" Philip asked.

"She is indeed, and so is Galileo." McKenzie laughed and shook his head. "Y'know, here I was thinking that the *Witch* was his greatest invention, and here he comes with that flying machine. If he builds something like that again, only larger, he might just chase me out of business."

"And what business is that?" I asked.

"Why, smuggling, of course. That's why the *Sea Witch* was built, to smuggle certain items to Sanctuary."

"Such as?"

"You'll see." McKenzie put on his shirt, then turned toward the ladder again. "Get some fresh air, then c'mon back down. Sorry I can't offer you anything to eat, but it looks like we're going to have a good night for sailing, so I reckon we'll make port by dinner time."

Stepping onto the ladder, the captain went back down below. Philip was next, but I didn't immediately follow them. Instead, I lingered on the deck for a few more minutes, watching the sunset and trying to put things together. As always, it seemed like every time I found an answer to something, two more questions would take its place. And while this particular question seemed trivial, it wasn't.

Galileo had designed and built first a submarine, then a flying machine, with the intention of escaping from Sanctuary. But not permanently. He and the other Originalists were searching for answers to a question of their own: what happened that caused the Cetans to despise and fear humans so much?

Once more, I gazed back at Sanctuary. I wasn't going to find the answers there. This mystery could only be solved… somewhere else.

X

I went down below for a little while, but it wasn't long before I climbed back up top. Perhaps I was overstaying my turn topsides, but the *Witch* wasn't made for comfort. Within its closed confines, the rattling chug of the engine made conversation difficult. A box of wax earplugs was passed around, but all they did was reduce the noise to a slightly less oppressive level. And although the engine was equipped with an air filtration and exhaust system, the sub reeked of vegetable oil mingling with the sour-sweet stench of man-sweat. The crew seemed to be accustomed to this, but I was deafened and nauseated. As soon as I could, I climbed back up the ladder, and no one complained that I remained there for the rest of the trip.

The *Sea Witch* sailed through sunset into night. As the last reddish-orange light of day faded on the horizon, the stars began to come out and the familiar constellations appeared: Bear, Snake, Bull, and other mythical creatures of Old Earth. I've always wondered why there were none for my misspelled namesake, but on the other hand, astrology was something I'd never really believed in. I knew enough about the stars, though, to figure out that we were on a south-by-southeast bearing.

I'd been up there for a while when Philip joined me again; the racket and the stink finally got to him, too. We sat down cross-legged on the deck and chatted quietly about nothing in particular, and not long after that we realized that the *Witch* was making a ninety-degree turn to port.

Peering in that direction, I made out an area of darkness low to the horizon where there were no stars. It was another island, yet it appeared to be uninhabited; there were no lights to be seen, and nothing from the water indicated that anyone lived there. Nonetheless, it appeared to be our destination.

Captain McKenzie came up from below. He knelt beside the hatch and reached back down to let a crewman hand him a lantern and a long wooden pole with a crook at one end. He carried both forward to the bow. There was a small hole in the hull just aft of the turret; the straight end of the pole was inserted in the hole, and the lantern was dangled from the crook.

This done, McKenzie bent down and rapped his knuckles against the top of the turret. A moment later, he was answered in kind by the helmsman. Standing straight, he turned to Philip and me. "Okay," he said, "now we'll let them know we're coming."

"Let who know?" Philip asked.

McKenzie didn't reply. Instead, he pulled a whistle from his trouser pocket, stuck it in his mouth, and blew it several times. The whistle was shrill in the quiet of the night, but I couldn't see anything ahead of us.

And then I could. As if by magic, lights abruptly appeared along the shore. It wasn't as if they were being lit, but rather like they'd always been there and had suddenly emerged from behind cover. I was still trying to figure out what was happening when McKenzie said, "Duck your heads, gents, if you want to keep 'em."

Philip and I did as we were told, and a few seconds later, by the light of the bow lantern, we saw what lay between us and the shoreline: a long rope, its ends disappearing into the darkness, suspended horizontally above the water. Hung from the rope were thick, opaque curtains made of gorsch-hide. As we watched, the *Witch* passed between the curtains, which had been parted to allow the sub to go through.

Now I understood. The curtain had been set up at the mouth of a narrow lagoon, with the rope strung between two trees on either side and its panels suspended over the water, effectively masking the lights of the island's shore. This way, the settlement on Freeman Cay couldn't be seen at night from a vessel that happened to pass by. But when the *Sea Witch* approached and a whistle was blown, people ashore would pull lines that would part the curtains and allow the sub to sail into the lagoon.

"Nice trick," I said.

"Isn't it, though?" McKenzie was justly proud of the ingenuity that had gone into it. "No one knows we're here unless we want 'em to know, and this way we stay hidden."

Now that the *Witch* had entered the lagoon, we could see the settlement clearly. It appeared to be a small village half-hidden by the forest that lay not far from the beach. "Is there a name for this place?" Philip asked.

"Yes, there is: Smuggler's Cove. " McKenzie's expression darkened. "And if either of you ever let anyone know this place exists. I swear I'll hunt you down and kill you myself."

It's possible that the captain was only joking, but I decided to let him know that I was taking him seriously. "My lips are sealed," I said.

Philip nodded quietly. He continued to gaze straight ahead, and I knew without asking that he was anxious to be reunited with his wife… that is, if Pilot was indeed here, as McKenzie said she would be.

As the *Witch* approached the shore, a pair of rowboats came out to meet us. Two men were seated fore and aft in each boat, and the sub cut its engine as they came alongside. McKenzie put Philip and me to work catching the mooring lines tossed to us from the boats; once we fastened the lines to hooks along the sub's hull, the rowboats commenced to tow us the rest of the way in.

There was a floating dock within the lagoon, illuminated by oil lanterns mounted on posts along its length. The aeroglider that Galileo and Pilot had used a few days earlier to make their escape was there, floating on its pontoons alongside several small fishing boats. The rowboats hauled the *Witch* to other side of the dock, where men were waiting to catch the mooring lines. Philip and I threw the lines to them and helped tie up the sub. We'd barely done so when a woman on shore called Philip's name, and he turned to see Pilot running down the dock toward him.

It had been only a few days since the last time Philip had seen her, but there's no telling how much longer it must have seemed to him. I watched as Philip caught his wife in his arms, then politely turned away to give them a little privacy. The gang plank had been put down by then. One by one, the crew of the *Sea Witch* emerged from the moored sub and, sweaty and exhausted, trooped off the sub. Mahmoud McKenzie came off last; he stopped for a moment to accept my thanks with a handshake and a smile, then quietly walked over to where Philip and Pilot stood.

"See?" he said, once they came up for air. "Just as I promised: safe and sound." The captain clapped a hand on Philip's shoulder. "She wouldn't let me go until I took an oath to bring you back. If my ex had treated me this way, I think I'd still be married."

Philip accepted this with an appreciative smile. "However grateful she may be," he said, shaking hands with McKenzie, "it's only half of how I feel. So thank you—" he glanced over his shoulder at me "—both of you."

"Sure, you're welcome," I said, "but you know as well as I do that I didn't get us out of there. Michael did."

Michael Gillespie was standing nearby with the *Witch*'s crew, chatting with them. His back was turned, but upon hearing his name he looked over his shoulder. Pilot hadn't noticed him till then, and her mouth fell open in astonishment. "Michael? How did *you* get here?"

Michael looked as if he wished he could disappear. "Hello, Pi," he said, forcing a smile. "It's… kind of a long story."

"Yes, I imagine it is," a familiar voice said from behind us.

We turned to see Galileo strolling down the dock. Sometime in the past few days, he'd trimmed his grey beard; otherwise, he hadn't changed a bit. Smiling, he shook hands with Phillip and me; he ignored Michael, though, even though Gillespie extended his hand as well.

"I'm sorry you were put in harm's way like that," Galileo said to Philip and me, "but you're here, safe and sound, and that's what counts."

"It was quite an unexpected journey, to put it mildly." Philip gestured to the *Sea Witch*. "That's some invention. My compliments."

"Yes, well, it does have its uses. But I imagine you're tired." Galileo turned to Pilot. "My dear, why don't you show our guests to their quarters? After that, bring them over to the dining hall. We should have some stew left over from dinner."

"Sure." Smiling, Pilot crooked her arm around Philip's elbow. He smiled at his wife and let her lead him away. Michael hesitated, then fell in behind them as they strolled down the dock. I was about to follow them down when Galileo touched my arm, a wordless gesture for me to remain.

I hung back, and once the others were out of earshot, I turned to him. "Yes?"

"I've asked Pilot to put you in a cabin with Gillespie," Galileo said, keeping his voice low.

"You want me to keep an eye on him?" I asked, and the old inventor nodded. "How come?"

"Same reason why I told Guido and Mahmoud to make sure that he got on the *Witch*. I don't trust him, and it's not wise to turn your back the people you don't trust." Galileo noticed the querying look I gave him. "I strongly believe that the badges have placed an informer among my people, and Gillespie is my chief suspect."

"But why would—?" I began, then stopped myself.

Galileo must have read my mind, because he nodded in silent agreement. "He still has a crush on Pilot," the old man said, "and jealousy can cause men to do hurtful things. So keep on a sharp eye on him, okay? I think he's up to something."

"Leave it to me," I replied.

XI

For an outlaw settlement on a small island, Smuggler's Cove was surprisingly well-established. A boardwalk had been laid from the boat dock and the beach into the adjacent woodlands, where a fairly large village had been built within a clearing. The trees provided camouflage for the log cabins and sheds clustered within the clearing; Galileo told us that several dozen men and women presently lived there, some of whom hadn't set foot on Sanctuary in years.

By Tawcety reckoning, the village itself was about thirty years old. It had originally been established by malcontents of one stripe or another who'd chafed against the Cetans and Cetan law, and who'd managed to escape from Sanctuary. The settlement had grown little by little, eventually becoming self-sufficient. The people here had adopted a communal lifestyle; they had their own rules, grew their own crops in small farms ashore and caught fish in coastal waters around the Archipelago, with everyone pitching in to handle the daily chores that needed to be done.

The largest structure in Smuggler's Cove was the dining hall. Everyone who'd come in on the *Sea Witch* were brought there for a late meal; the residents had already eaten, but there were sufficient leftovers to feed us. Fish stew, and pretty good, too. Of course, if you're hungry, anything tastes good, but even so I had as much as I could eat. Better than jail food, that was for certain. Galileo and Pilot sat with Philip, Michael, and me while we ate, and Galileo told us about the settlement. Neither Philip nor Michael had known of its existence until now, nor had Pilot until she'd arrived here. Freeman Cay was a well-kept secret. No one learned about this place until they came out here, and Galileo and Mahmoud alone decided who got aboard the *Sea Witch*, the sole access to the island.

"So what are you doing out here?" I asked. "Besides getting away from the Cetans, I mean."

"Whoever said anything about getting away from Cetans?" A sly smile crept across Galileo's face as he reached across the table to take a slice of fresh-baked bread from the basket that had been placed before us.

"We're smugglers because we've got something worth smuggling… and we're getting that from the Cetans themselves."

"You're in business with them?" I couldn't have been more astonished.

Galileo nodded. "We are, indeed. When their merchant ships come to Landencyte or Southport, some of them drop anchor here first to do a little business on the side. The Guardians don't know about this, of course, and we aim to keep it that way."

He pointedly didn't look at Michael when he said this, but his meaning was understood… by me, at least. "What are they bringing you?" Philip asked.

Galileo thought it over for a moment; he'd suddenly become reticent, and I had a sneaking suspicion why. "Maybe it's better if I show you tomorrow," he said at last. "There's a lot to tell, and… well, you really ought to see this yourself."

"He's right," Pilot agreed. "It's a little late for a tour. If you'll just be patient, we'll explain everything tomorrow."

She was right. It had been a hell of a long day, and I was dead tired. So once we'd finished up, Galileo led us from the dining hall to a couple of small cabins reserved for guests. Freeman Cay and Smuggler's Cove apparently had enough visitors that separate quarters for them were necessary. As a married couple, Philip and Pilot naturally shared one, while Michael and I were put in the other.

There were two beds in the cabin, one across from the other, with a pot-belly wood stove between them. It was a chilly evening, and the stove hadn't been lit. This gave me an excuse to keep my clothes on. Michael did the same. He was cordial enough, but he discretely watched while I removed my boots and placed them at the foot of my bed, my saber and flintlock beside them. He didn't take off his own boots, but instead lay down with them still on his feet, pulling a blanket over himself as if going to bed with your footgear on was the most natural thing to do. I pretended not to notice as I loaded the stove with firewood from the stack beside it. I got a fire going, then blew out the wick of the oil lamp hanging from the ceiling, got into bed, and went to sleep.

Or rather, I played at acting like I was going to sleep. I needed some shut-eye, but I had a gut feeling that, if my suspicions were correct, Michael would make his move soon. So I turned my back to him and lay quietly in the dark, keeping my eyes open while pretending to snore. And before long, it turned out that my guts were right again.

Michael waited a little while, maybe an hour or so, before I heard him stir. The rustle of a blanket being pushed aside, followed by the soft creak of the floorboards, told me that he was getting up. I lay still and silent, breathing in deep rhythm the way a sleeping man does, as I listened to him creeping across the cabin. He hesitated at the door, making sure that I was still out of it, then I heard the door open and shut, ever so softly.

I opened my eyes and sat up, but didn't light the lamp, instead groping in the dark for my boots and weapons. It took me just a minute to put everything on; by then, I figured that he'd had enough of a head start to reassure himself that he'd given me the slip.

Sure enough, there was no one outside. The windows of the other cabins were dark; Smuggler's Cove was fast asleep. I lingered by the door, listening to the night as I let my eyes adjust. I couldn't see Michael nor could I hear him, but I had a hunch where he was going. I took a few moments to load my pistol, then I quietly set out to follow him. I hoped that my guess was correct and that he hadn't simply stepped out to visit the outhouse.

I'm not always right, but when I am… well, whatever else you may say about me, you can't say that I'm not a pretty good dick. When I caught up with Michael again, he was where I thought I'd find him: at the dock, getting ready to steal a boat.

He was kneeling on the dock, untying the painter of a small, single-mast fishing boat. I tried to be as quiet as I could, but he must have heard me when I set foot on the dock, for he suddenly looked up in my direction. I leveled my pistol at him; the loud click it made when I cocked the trigger was sufficient to make him freeze.

"Who's there?" he called softly.

"Crowe," I replied.

He didn't move, but his mind must have been racing. "I… I… I decided to come out here and… and check to make sure the boats are secure. I mean, I looked earlier and thought… y'know, one of them looked like it wasn't tied down, so…"

"Gorschshit. You were about to make a run for it. Back to Landencyte, I assume. Or are you going to tell me that you got it in your head to go fishing in the middle of the night?"

Michael slowly rose from his crouch. "Jeremy, it's not what it looks like. I... I didn't want to come along with you and Philip, and this isn't where I belong. So I decided to sail back on my own."

"And not bother to tell anyone where you were going?" I snorted. "How considerate." Gillespie took a couple of steps towards me. "Stop right there," I added. "I don't want you to—"

Most people, when you point a gun at them, will figure out that you mean business and therefore will do whatever you tell them to do. Every so often, though, there's someone who panics and does something stupid like charge you. Which was exactly what Michael did. He let out a yell and, ducking his head and shoulders, hurled himself at me. I wasn't expecting that, and it rattled me enough to throw off my aim. I squeezed the trigger, and there was a loud bang and a dazzling flash as the flintlock discharged, but the ball must have missed him because Michael wasn't stopped. In the next instant, he was on top of me. Before I knew it, he'd knocked both of us off our feet, off the dock, and into the water.

It was fairly deep next to the dock, but not so much that we were in any real danger of drowning. My feet touched bottom, and I immediately kicked off and struggled to the surface. Michael was trying to get his hands around my neck, but I knocked them aside and managed to land a punch. His nose caught my fist and he fell back, which enabled me to swim around behind him and wrap an arm around his neck. He struggled to break free, but I tightened my hold and used it to push his head underwater. I counted to ten, then allowed him to come up for air.

Michael was gasping and coughing, and it sounded like he'd swallowed some seawater, but he continued to fight, so I dunked him again and this time counted to fifteen. His struggles became less violent, and I let him up before he drowned.

"Are you done?" I asked. He weakly nodded his head, and I let him go.

We half-swam, half-lurched ashore. I wasn't surprised to find we were no longer alone. Others had heard my gunshot and come out to see what was going on. A dozen or so people had heard the fight and run down to the dock; Galileo was among them, and so were Philip and Pilot. In the unsteady light of the lanterns several villagers had brought with them, I could see Pilot's face. Her eyes were as cold as the water dripping off Michael and me; she too had figured out Mike's intentions, and she wasn't in a forgiving mood.

I started to explain what happened, but I didn't get but a few words in before Galileo cut me off. "When did you become an informant?" he asked Michael. "For the badges, I mean."

"I'm not—"

"Detective?" Galileo didn't look at me as he spoke. "If Citizen Gillespie lies again, I want you to cut his throat."

I didn't respond except to lay a hand on my dagger. I don't know if Galileo truly meant what he said or not, but it was sufficient to persuade Michael that we were serious. "Okay, okay," he said hastily as I started to pull the dagger from its sheath. "It wasn't the badges I went to; it was Guardian Bart. I went to him as soon as I got word that they—" he meant Philip and me "—had been taken into custody, and he told me that he wanted me to set things up for him and the badges."

"Set what up?" Philip asked. "Our rescue?"

Michael was reluctant, but he nodded anyway. "Bart instructed me to follow Galileo's instructions and get in touch with the Raiders and keep him informed of what they planned to do if they decided to rescue you. When that happened, he told me to go along with them, then slip away as soon as I found out where they—and you—were hiding."

"I don't understand," I said. "How was that going to help them if—?"

"If you and Philip were taken off the island? They had no idea that's where you were going. Even with that… that flying machine, they thought everyone involved was still on Sanctuary. That underwater boat…" He shrugged, shook his head. "They had no idea it even existed."

"And since no one gave you a chance to tell them, they still don't." Galileo's eyes narrowed. "And that's why you were trying to get away just now. You meant to sail back on your own and let the Guardians know all about this place."

"Why?" Pilot stared straight at Michael. Her voice was quiet, but she could just as well have been shouting in his face. "Why did you do it?"

Michael said nothing, yet he couldn't look at her, and that told her all she needed to know. Jealousy is an emotion that can make people do stupid things, including the betrayal of the very people you thought you loved. Pilot had dumped him to marry Philip, and Gillespie had probably been wanting to get even with both of them ever since. For that, he was willing to turn on Galileo and the rest of the Originalists as well. As a rationale for treason, it was pretty pathetic, but isn't it always?

Galileo regarded him with almost as much contempt as Pilot did. "All right," he said at last to no one in particular, "take him away. Lock him up somewhere he won't cause any more trouble."

"You're not going to kill me?" Michael seemed surprised.

A derisive snort. "No. You're not worth having your death on my conscience."

Two men standing nearby came forward. Bracing Michael between them, they led him away, back toward the cabins. Pilot glared at him as he went, but he couldn't meet her gaze. I don't think any man could have without turning to stone.

Galileo turned and started to walk away, but I caught him by the arm. "You want to tell me what this is all about?" I asked. "All this, I mean. The village, the sub, the secrecy: I don't get it."

"No… no, I imagine you don't. Go get some sleep, detective. I'll tell you tomorrow, while there's still time."

"Time for what?"

An enigmatic smile. "You'll see."

XII

I slept. I ate. I went to the bathhouse and took a rainwater shower beneath a cistern heated indirectly by a wood stove, which I presumed to be another Galileo invention because I'd never before bathed standing up. I was given a change of clothes, including a loose-fitting ash-grey shirt woven from some soft, light fabric I didn't recognize. Embroidered down its bell sleeves and across the back were complex asymmetrical patterns that I recognized as Cetan handscript. The garment was too large for a Cetan to wear, but the way it bunched slightly at my shoulders and the sleeves covered my wrists all the way to my thumbs made me suspicious. It may have been a shirt meant to be worn by a human, but it seemed to have been sewn by someone who'd never worn human clothing themselves.

Aside from capes, though, the Cetans didn't make clothes for us. They just didn't, not any more than a cobbler would make boots for a gorsch. So where did this thing come from?

I'd just finished getting dressed when Pilot knocked on my door. She'd come to bring me to Galileo; he was somewhere in the village with something that he wanted me to see, and he'd sent Pilot to fetch me. I asked her to tell me what it was, but she only gave me a coy smile. "It's better if we show you," she said. "Trust me."

Right. Like trusting her had always been a wise idea.

Walking beside me, Pilot led the way across Smuggler's Cove. Until then, I hadn't seen the village in the light of day. What I saw as we walked through the tiny village was fairly impressive. As a pioneer settlement, Smuggler's Cove obviously hadn't been there for very long—all the cabins seemed recently built—nonetheless, it had grown fast enough to sustain several dozen people. But it was a well-hidden camp, all the cabins and sheds carefully scattered among the blackthorns and sprawlroots of the coastal rain forest that surrounded and concealed the inhabitants. There weren't many people, and their lives were neither simple nor luxurious, but they carried themselves in a way that made me think they'd earned the right to name their island retreat Freeman Cay.

There was a large shed on the other side of the village, away from the waterfront yet connected to it by an elevated boardwalk that looked like it'd had a lot of use. As Pilot led me onto it from the dirt path we'd followed through town, I noticed a handful of men at the other end of the walkway. It appeared that they were using a couple of two-wheel handlifts to transport a pair of large crates to the dock.

"Are those going on the *Sea Witch*?" I asked, pointing to them.

Pilot gave me another annoying smile. "Could be."

"Knock it off." I gave her the kind of look that used to scare my ex when she wasn't being straight with me, and that damn smile vanished like it had never been there. "I'm tired of having you jerk me around every time there's something I need to know that you don't think I should. You and Philip and Galileo, but mainly you, have put my ass at risk again and again since this began, and I'm—"

"Crowe."

Galileo was standing in the shed's open side door. I don't know how long he'd been there, but it was obvious that he'd heard everything. He wasn't smiling either and I don't think he ever had been. Yet he hadn't raised his voice, nor did he show any anger when he called out to me.

"I'm sorry we haven't been truthful with you at all times, Citizen," he said; for once he didn't call me *detective*. "There were things we didn't believe you needed to know, and when the time came that you should have been told, we neglected to do so."

He was trying to placate me, but I wasn't having any of it. "So what's in here?" I said, pointing past him to the shed. "Another flying machine or underwater boat?"

"Why don't you come in and find out?" Galileo stepped aside, leaving the door open behind him. "I don't have all the answers, but maybe it'll help you understand what we're doing here."

I glanced at Pilot again. No longer childishly smug, she nodded and beckoned toward the shed, silently encouraging me to accept her mentor's invitation. *This better be good*, I thought, and headed for the shed.

There was no aeroglider inside, nor another submersible. Instead, a long table ran down the center of the shed's single room, with men and woman seated on either side of it. They stopped what they were doing and quietly watched as we came in. At first I thought there was a banquet going on, but then I saw what they were doing, and it wasn't eating.

The table was littered with parts and pieces of metal, copper and steel, seemingly of every shape and size. There were small boxes of bolts and screws, and everyone had tools in hand: screwdrivers, pliers and wrenches, rulers and calipers and other means of precise measurement. Empty crates, identical to the ones I'd just seen, were stacked against the unpainted wall behind them. Tacked to it were large, complicated-looking charts showing what appeared to be a sequential series for drawings, depicting the assembly of…

Another glance at the table, more closely this time, confirmed what I thought I was seeing. Yes, these people were putting together generators, just like the ones that had been cropping up in Landencyte and other settlements on Sanctuary over the last several years. No one had ever learned where these things were coming from or who was making them. And now I knew.

"Yes, they're generators… *electrical* generators, if you're familiar with the term." Galileo had come up beside me. "We build them here, then box them up and, two at a time, put them aboard the *Witch* and smuggle them to Sanctuary."

The picture was now clear. The submersible carrying crated generators would glide undetected beneath the Cetan blockade and surface at Castaway Point, where it would dock unseen within the boathouse. Once there, the generators would be distributed to those who wanted them enough to find out who was selling them. When I said as much to Galileo, he nodded in agreement. "A little simplistic, but yes, that's what we're doing."

"And the aeroglider?" I asked. "It doesn't look big enough to carry a generator."

"It isn't. I designed and built it for the purpose it eventually served: as a means of escape." He laid a fatherly hand on Pilot's shoulder. "It's fortunate that it worked as well as it did. We didn't get a chance to test it before it had to be used."

Pilot grinned. "Next time, I want to be the one who operates the controls. Looks like fun."

"Well, that's the meaning of your name, so I suppose you're entitled. But I doubt it'll ever return to Sanctuary. Too many people saw the take-off from the harbor, and from now on the badges and Guardians will be on the lookout for it."

"Well," I said, "if you're smart enough to build an underwater boat, a craft that flies through the air, and machines that make electricity, then—"

"I didn't invent the generators."

That brought me up short. "Those aren't something else you've made?" I asked, nodding toward the machine presently being put together on the table.

"No." Galileo shook his head. "I'm smart, but I'm not *that* smart. No, these generators are coming to us in pieces, inside the very same crates we use to carry the assembled units to Sanctuary." He pointed to the charts I'd already noticed. "See those instructions? If you'll look closely, you'll see they're in two languages: Anglis and Cetan. What does that tell you?"

"That the things were made by Cetans?" I asked. Galileo nodded again, but I didn't believe him. "Oh no, really, you can't expect me to—"

"He's telling the truth." Pilot had gotten over being intimidated by me. "The generators are Cetan inventions, not his. They're shipped here in pieces and assembled before being sent on to Castaway Point." I started to say something, but she anticipated my next question. "Yes, they're sold to us by the Cetans themselves. Those crates were brought here aboard galleons from another part of Tawcety: Gruhar, we think."

Gruhar was a small continent due west of Sanctuary, about 600 miles away. Aside from the Southern Archipelago, it was the closest major land mass. Humans knew very little about it other than the fact that most of the goods imported to Sanctuary by Cetan traders came from there. Some of them, at least. "Cetan law expressively forbids humans from building or using powered machinery of any sort. Are you saying they're breaking their own laws?"

"That appears to be the case," Galileo said, "but we don't know why. The Cetans on Sanctuary aren't aware that Cetans from elsewhere are selling us disassembled electrical generators manufactured on the mainland. After they're done here, the ships then sail on to Sanctuary, where they receive their payment from us in the form of gold coin, the wholesale revenue our people get from selling the generators on the black market."

Pilot picked up the thread. "We think this is how the artifact we found in Southport—the *Santos-Dumont*'s recorder—got to Sanctuary. Some time in the past, a Cetan trader must have brought it here and sold it on the black market. It found its way to House Van Pelt, where the Steward took possession of it and locked it away."

"That's the theory, anyway," Galileo said. "Why, of course, is still an open question."

"Okay," I said, "but I still don't understand how this whole thing got started. Whose idea was it to start buying generators from the natives?"

Galileo sat down on one of the empty crates. "There's been Cetan smugglers all along. As a former badge yourself, you should already know this."

I nodded. The waterfront wasn't my beat, but I was aware that Cetan sailors often sold prohibited items, narcotics and such, to humans who'd resell them on the black market. "The first generators were smuggled in through Landencyte," Galileo went on, "but as demand rose and more were needed, it became difficult to use the harbor anymore. So the people who set up the operation decided to establish an offshore shipping port on Freeman Cay, just as they've smuggled other items in the past. But this time, instead of trying to outrun the blockade boats, they recruited me to solve the problem of getting the generators from here to Sanctuary. That's how I got involved. The *Sea Witch* was my solution."

"We've been getting the generators," Pilot said, "and now we've got the *Santos-Dumont* recorder and the second logbook from the *Lindbergh*, and all that points in the same direction: to Gruhar. We're not going to get any answers on Sanctuary or here. If we want to find out—"

"We're going to have to go to Gruhar." Even as those words left my lips, I realized that I'd made an error of judgement: I'd said *we*, not *you*. By saying this, I'd included myself in their plans. I wasn't an Originalist, though. I was just the dick they'd hired to do a job. By all rights, I should just take my pay, then wait for the next time the *Sea Witch* made the return trip—if ever—and hitch a ride back to Sanctuary.

Yeah, okay, and then what? I was now a wanted man. The minute I showed my face in Castaway Point or Landencyte or even the Squat, I'd be picked up by the badges or the Guardians. And if Bart ever got his hands on me, he'd make sure I'd never see the light of day again. Another jail cell would be my residence... or an urn.

"That's been my thinking lately, yes." Galileo crossed his arms. "Another Cetan merchant ship is set to arrive here in a few days. I'm hoping to do something no one has ever done and ask its captain if he'll carry us to Gruhar when the ship makes its return trip. And by 'us' I mean Pilot, Philip, and myself... and you as well, if I can persuade you to come."

"How about it?" Pilot asked. "I know this is more than what we asked you to do, but we could use your help."

I had little doubt that they could. So far as anyone knew, no one had ever travelled farther from Sanctuary than the spot we were standing on. I wasn't an Originalist, but where they were going, they could use another strong sword-arm. And it wasn't like I had much choice in the matter.

"Yeah… yeah, I'm in," I said, and told myself that this was just another job. But the truth of the matter was that I was in deep, and unless I intended to be on the run for the rest of my life, I needed to get to the bottom of this. I wasn't going home again until I did.

We were bound for Gruhar. I could only hope that we'd return.

Interlude

Excerpts from the Diary of Yvonne Greer (Continued)

2/14/'67

Back on Earth, it's Valentine's Day. I know we shouldn't be observing all those old holidays, just as I should be using the new calendar that's been devised for Tau Ceti-e (aka "Tawcety"—still not used to that, either!), but Valentine's is special to a lot of people here. Over the past several months, a lot of new romances and relationships have sprung up among the colonists. Even though I no longer have a ship, for many I'm still the Lindbergh's captain, and therefore entitled to officiate at marriages. I've got three to do today, and before long I'll have to find someone to do the honors for me, since Grey [*Orlando*, Lindbergh's *former navigator*] proposed to me just last night.

Didn't see that coming. Well, no, let's be honest: I had a feeling it was. Gray has been very sweet lately, even more than usual. And after all, ever since the Council of Stewards passed a resolution calling upon unattached colonists to marry and have kids (if biologically possible, that is, since artificial insemination and bioclasts are no longer available), we've been doing our best to propagate our species, since a larger population would assure our long-term survival. So last night, when he offered me a nice handmade tiara as his engagement gift (since gold is scarce, and the Cetans have yet to show us how they extract it from seawater, we've substituted tiaras and chokers for rings), I had little choice but to accept. Not that Grey isn't a good catch, but after my first marriage went belly-up, I swore I would never get hitched again. I'm the "cap" now, though, and that means I've got to set a good example. And what the hell, maybe it's time to be a mommy, too.

It would be a happy day for everyone were it not for one thing: a typhoon may be coming. Any hope we may have had for Sanctuary's equatorial location making extreme weather unlikely has been dashed by a report from our climatologist, Katie Walthers. Lacking electronic instruments, [it's] hard for her to make accurate weather forecasts; however, she has determined to her satisfaction that something is brewing to the west of us. "Red sky at morning, sailor take warning" is still an accurate mnemonic, and at daybreak earlier today, the sky over the ocean was the color of dilute blood; not a good omen.

So I've sent out messengers to the other Stewards, asking them to spread the word to their respective Houses that everyone should prepare to pack up [and] move inland, if only temporarily. The highlands east of us should provide adequate protection from high winds and storm surges, and we need to be ready for the worst. Katie thinks we have about 48 hours to get ready. I'm going to tell those couples who want to get married today that their wedding ceremonies should be short and sweet, and don't expect to be doing much on their honeymoons except heading for the hills.

I wish the Cetans were still here. When their expedition set sail a few months ago—over a year ago by the new calendar—Fae told me that she expected to return fairly soon, once she'd reached Gruhar and reported what she found to Iko (i.e., "Princess" Iko, our approximation of the formal title for the individual who's the heir apparent to the ruling monarchy). The Cetans make us nervous just as much we make <u>them</u> nervous, but it's their planet and they know its weather better than we do. I just hope that, once we see them again, they won't find a devastated colony. It's taken us a long time to get to the place we are now. A typhoon could be the worst disaster since the Rot, and I'm afraid any sort of major setback could be lethal.

That's all for now. Off to perform my first marriage for the day. Think positive.

<u>2/16/'67</u>

Disaster: the <u>Lindbergh</u> has fallen.

We've cleared everyone out of the settlement and headed up into the foothills, bringing everything we could pack onto the gorsches or carry on our backs. I ordered the evacuation yesterday morning when it became apparent that the typhoon was on its way and that we needed to get out of there fast. By then, the wind was rising and there were whitecaps in the harbor. Our fishermen pulled their boats as far ashore as they could; there [are] a couple of boats still out there, though, and because we haven't seen or heard from them, we can only hope that their crews did the smart thing and sought cover on Fisherman's Cay, where they often camp overnight when they can't get home before dark.

Sanctuary

We got everyone out of town before the storm hit and set up temporary camp in the hillside rain forest a few miles away. The wind blew down a few tents and the rain soaked just about everyone, but no one has been hurt and we're all safe, if not comfortable. But we can see Landing Site from where we are, with Lindy's module stack towering above the cabins and shacks we left behind, and no sooner did the brunt of the storm hit us than we heard a loud, awful groan like [a] wounded giant, and everyone who happened to be looking in that direction saw the stack come crashing down.

Never before has any of us seen anything like this, but I always thought this would happen. The stack was the height of a skyscraper, but it had been listing to one side ever since it touched down. None of my engineers could figure out a way to either dismantle the modules or gradually lower the stack to the ground, or at least not with the limited resources we now have. So I can't say I'm totally surprised. But it was horrible to see that colossal thing topple over. Several people screamed and some of us cried, myself included. The ground shook when it hit, and although the wind picked up the displaced sand and created a cloud that obscured our vision for a minute or two, when it settled the remains of our starship now rested upon its side.

We'd long since salvaged everything we could from <u>Lindy</u>, and I'm glad I had the foresight to make everyone move our original camp away from it. We haven't yet returned to town, but it doesn't appear as if any of our dwellings were crushed (if anything was lost, it was because of the storm itself). But seeing <u>Lindy</u> come down was like watching a friend die. And even though none of us believed it would ever fly again—an impossibility, really, and none of us fool ourselves with such magical thinking—it really drove home the fact, once again, that we're permanently marooned on Tau Ceti-e and will never leave.

Sanctuary now has a new mountain: the wreckage of our ship. I imagine our descendants, if we have any, will look upon it and wonder just what it was.

[The entries for Earth dates 2/17/2267 through 3/1/2267 mainly concern the efforts to rebuild the original Landencyte settlement, and therefore have been omitted.]

* * *

3/2/'67

The Cetans have returned. This time, they came in numbers.

Our new watchtower became useful this morning. The sun was barely up when Wu Chang began beating on the salvaged conduit pipes we've hung up there until we can make a proper bell. Like everyone else, Grey and I were awakened by the racket. We got dressed quickly and ran out to see what was going on. I knew it wouldn't be another storm because Katie hadn't given us any advance warning; ever since Typhoon Alice, our resident meteorologist has been given a lot of respect, so when she says that the first week of Summermonth (as we're now calling the second four-week period of Tau Ceti-e's sidereal year) will be clear and calm, I tend to trust her.

Sure enough, it wasn't another typhoon. But when Grey and I scrambled up the tower to the top deck and saw what Chang had spotted, we saw something just as awesome as an oncoming storm, and maybe worse.

Stretched across the western horizon was a row of sails; six ships in all, each the size of the original Cetan vessel to find us. These Cetan vessels looked a little different, though, with larger sails and a broader beam while lacking the catamaran outrigger of the first ship. When they got close enough for me to use the makeshift telescope we'd put up there, I saw the reason why. Along the sides of their hulls protruded what first appeared to be small black sticks. The moment I spotted them, I knew what they were: deck guns. These weren't vessels of exploration or trade, but rather warships.

We were being invaded. Or so it seemed.

The armada was still in the distance when the Council of Stewards and I convened in the half-rebuilt town hall. If any of them had still been asleep when Chang sounded the alarm, they damned sure were awake now. Awake and scared. Everyone was talking at once, and when it got to the point where they were trying to outshout each other, I whistled and clapped my hands as loudly as I could and told them to sit down, shut up, and don't panic.

Until then, I'd been the "cap" as some people now call me. Just then, though, the Council and I subconsciously reverted to our former roles; I returned to being Captain Greer, and they went back to being <u>Lindy</u>'s command crew. So I treated this as if it was a shipboard emergency, with me getting status reports from my bridge officers. The top priority on everyone's mind, of course, was the state of our defenses… and it isn't good.

Ted and Luanne Gillespie—whom I put in charge of manufacturing firearms because of Ted's previous experience as an antique gun hobbyist—told us that, while they've managed to fashion a couple of makeshift flintlocks from wood, flint, and pieces of scrap metal from the ship, they're still trying to concoct gunpowder volatile enough to be useful. They've found sulfur and charcoal, but saltpeter is hard to come by; as it stands now, all they'd be able to give us are stink bombs.

Susan Kim and Floyd McGee have successfully rebuilt the archery works, and their people have fashioned plenty of long-bows and arrows along with a handful of crossbows. Susan's experience as an Olympic archer on the Korean team (she was a bronze medalist way back when) has been invaluable in training our hunting parties, and she has a few talented sharpshooters. However, these guys are only good at hunting game; none of them have ever shot at anything on two legs, human or Cetan, besides the occasional loper (and they're too damn fast anyway; Floyd swears he once saw one of those things outrun an arrow he shot at it). So even if we had enough bows to arm everyone—and we don't—using them as defensive weapons is questionable at best.

Knives are plentiful, both ones brought from Earth and those made from salvaged metal, and various individuals have been fashioning swords as well. But the knives are meant as tools and the swords are little more than novelties; in any case, there's simply not enough of either.

Finally, as Julius Fletcher has pointed out, even though we have nearly a thousand people here (not counting the handful of babies that Dr. Wolfe informs us are on the way, a reminder that our little colony already has a few pregnant women), there may be as much as half as many Cetans aboard those ships. If the Cetans are heavily armed and come ashore with the intent of slaughtering or enslaving us, there's little we can do about it. Even if we were able to beat them back somehow—and it's a good bet that our people will fight to the death rather than be taken away in chains—it's us against the whole goddamn planet.

Tonya van Pelt has advocated that we evacuate Landing Site and head for the highlands, the way we did a few weeks ago during Typhoon Alice. Julius and Jill pointed out that we simply don't have enough time for that, and even if we tried, the Cetans would simply follow us. And this is an island, after all. There is a limit to how far we can run or hide.

Paul Johnson seemed to want to circle the wagons and fight to the last man, but I shot that down as hard and fast as I could: that sort of action would only guarantee our massacre, and I have no desire to be General Custer at another Little Bighorn.

So it seems that we have little choice but try to stay calm and wait to see what the Cetans mean to do.

As I write, their ships have parked themselves off our coat. They've dropped anchor within our harbor, a little less than a quarter of a mile away, and although no one has come ashore yet, we can see figures moving along their decks. There are a lot of Cetans on those ships, enough to overrun us. Fae, my tentative friend, may be among them, but I don't know for certain. I hope so; she and I developed a good relationship, however cautious it may be, and even though she belongs to another race, nonetheless I consider her to be a woman of peace. I hope I haven't misjudged her, for we need someone like her now.

Grey has just come in to tell me that a small boat is being lowered from the starboard side of one of the ships. A landing party is coming ashore. Time to put down my pen and see what's what.

I'm praying this won't be a bad development, but I'm afraid that it will.

3/3/'67

My worst suspicions have turned out to be true. The Cetans have come to take control, and they're here to stay.

Fae was aboard the boat that came over yesterday morning, but any lingering hopes I may have had for a happy reunion disappeared the first minute she set foot on Sanctuary again. The Cetans have facial expressions that are similar to humans, even though they don't always show them; they can smile, too, when they want to. And Fae didn't smile when she saw me. We'd become friends the last time she was here, or at least that's what I thought, but it soon became obvious that her duty and obligations came first. And if I doubted this, all I had to do was look past her at all those Cetan warships anchored in our waters.

We exchanged cordial bows while I did my best to overlook the Cetan males in leather body armor flanking her on either side. They carried workas in scabbards slung over their backs, and I knew how deadly those sabers could be from watching a Cetan use one to put an old, sick gorsch out of its misery. I'd told my own people to keep what few weapons we've made out of sight, but in retrospect I wish I'd told them otherwise. It might have let the dogmen know that humans aren't pushovers (and yes, I know I shouldn't call them that). This may be their planet, but they ought to leave us alone.

It appears, though, that leaving us alone is no longer an option they're willing to accept. Once Fae and I greeted each other (I think she was just as uncomfortable as I was), she asked if she could speak with me in private. When I asked if I could convene the Council so that they, too, could hear what she had to say, she declined… or, more accurately, she refused. No, what she had to say to me was for my ears only, and that was final.

So I led her to my cabin, which had recently been rebuilt. The first time Fae was here, we hadn't yet begun erecting permanent dwellings, so she was a little surprised to see the number of log structures that had been constructed during her absence. She paused outside my cabin to look it over, and at one point she asked just how big we could build log structures like it. I told her that, because we'd learned how to cut and carry timber from the nearby highlands, our only limitation was how far a gorsch could drag a blackthorn my people had chopped down. I'm still wondering why she was so interested in this. I don't know why, but it seems like this was important to her.

Her bodyguards (that's what they were, really) remained outside while we went in. I offered her a seat, which she accepted, and a mug of cold inkberry tea, which she declined. There was no small talk; Fae went straight to the point. And as it turned out, my suspicions were correct. It was the decision of Princess Iko and her court advisors (I'm using approximate terms) that, although the human colonists would be allowed to remain on Mahha (i.e. Sanctuary), henceforth we were to be quarantined here. The rest of Bakkah (i.e. Tau Ceti-e) was now off-limits to us. We could sail no farther than our immediate coastal waters, and then only for the purpose of fishing; the tiny island we called Fisherman's Cay, which our people been using for overnight stays, was the sole exception, although she made it clear to me that this small privilege would be rescinded if anyone abused it, such as to use the cay as a jumping-off point to explore the rest of the archipelago.

Second: while Sanctuary was to be our home, by no means were we to consider the island to be ours. We were tenants, not owners. A set of laws would be established to guide our conduct, and failure to abide by them would have consequences. When I tried to ask what those consequences might be, Fae didn't respond, which was chilling, because Cetans don't answer questions when they think the answer is obvious. Her silence meant that the armed Cetans standing outside my door was the only reply I deserved.

Third: to assure our cooperation, a large number of Cetans will be permanently garrisoned on our island. Those are the people aboard the ships in our bay. Some will be here to help us adjust to our new world, but quite a few will be "Guardians," native police stationed here to make sure that the human colonists obey the Cetan laws. Resistance is unwise; the Guardians are authorized to use deadly force if necessary. They will have their own settlement—Fae told me something we've already figured out, that some of our ways are baffling or even repugnant to her people, and vice-versa—and so they'll live apart from us while offering their assistance. We should never forget, though, that while we may outnumber them, nevertheless we are their guests, and therefore are expected to behave as such.

The fourth condition is puzzling: for some reason, they want us to erect a wall around the Lindbergh and make certain the ship is never again entered.

I don't know why, and Fae won't explain, but they want us to take measures to hide the remains of our ship. It's actually a wise thing to do. We've salvaged just about everything useful from the modules, and now that the stack has fallen over, Lindy is unsafe to enter. With children on the way, I'm also leery of having something that might tempt curious kids to explore. And the modules are already half-buried anyway; the typhoon dumped a lot of mud, sand, and vegetation on top of them, and in time I imagine nature will take its course and eventually hide the rest of the ship. So building palisades around the Lindbergh and declaring it off-limits isn't such a bad idea. I just don't understand why the Cetans insist that we do so.

Fae's demeanor wasn't hostile, but nonetheless she was much cooler to me than she'd been the last time I saw her. I had a feeling she didn't like being the bearer of bad news. I told her that I'd relay everything to my people, and after she left to return to her ship, I called another emergency session of the Council.

Not surprisingly, their response was angry (to say the least). Paul even went so far as to accuse me of conceding too much to the "aliens," but Julius reminded him that it's we who are the aliens, not them, and therefore we should expect to abide by their terms if we're going to live in peace on their world. Others wondered if we were being groomed for slavery, or even fattened for dinner. I scolded them for being hysterical; there was nothing in the Cetans' conduct that hinted at either of these extremes. I think they simply want to keep us apart from the rest of the planet's population, and confining us to Sanctuary is the best way to go about this.

It took a lot of talking, and I have little doubt that most of the Stewards are still suspicious of the Cetans' motives, but I managed to keep the council members from panicking. Now we'll just have to see how everyone else reacts.

There's one more thing that baffles me. During our conversation, Fae asked me about the <u>Santos-Dumont</u>. Was I sure that our sister ship was destroyed? I told her that, yes, I'm positive that it was: I watched with my own two eyes as the other ship broke up and disintegrated in Tau Ceti-e's upper atmosphere. Was everyone aboard killed? Yes, I was positively certain that they were, and tried to explain as best as I could how such an uncontrolled atmospheric entry would be fatal to the crew.

I think she understood, but I clearly remember telling her this before, the first time she was here. So why did she ask again?

Part Four:
The Palace of Dancing Dogs

I

The ocean was calm the morning we reached Gruhar.

A rippling blue-green mirror, its cold waters parted effortlessly on either side of our vessel, a three-masted Cetan argosy. The rigging creaked quietly in the salt-flavored breeze; the sun, still low on the horizon behind us, promised warmth later in the day. Only yesterday we'd been caught in a violent storm that rocked the vessel back and forth on its outriggers, soaking the fur of the sailors clinging to the sail-lines and railings, and making seasick the four human passengers huddled belowdecks. But the storm finally subsided; now the sky was clear and, at last, we were nearing the end of our long journey.

Over the past six weeks, the vessel had sailed westward upon what our kind called the Western Ocean, following a parabolic route that took us south of the equator to take advantage of trade winds blowing from the east. It wasn't the most direct way of getting there, but the Cetan sailors knew the sea and the wind better than we did. Besides, it was their ship; far be it from us to criticize.

Like Cetans themselves, the argosy's name was unpronounceable by humans, a sibilant sequence of hisses, growls, grunts, and barks. We were told, though, that it roughly translated to *My Ship Is Big and Fast and Will Never Sink*. Whatever else might be said about them, Cetans could never be accused of modesty. We needed something close enough in meaning to call it in our own language, though, so Galileo decided to rename it the *Titanic*: some sort of private joke based on old Earth folklore that he didn't explain to the rest of us.

When the *Titanic* departed Smuggler's Cove, it was still Autumnmonth. We'd spent almost all Wintermonth on the ocean, the transition from *anno humanitis* 772 to 773 unremarked and uncelebrated by the sailors aboard. The Cetans didn't care about the change of the human calendar; for them, all that mattered was the change of season. Our passage had been long, cold, and often uncomfortable. This was the first time humans had been aboard a Cetan argosy, or so we believed. And although the captain (whom we called Jack; like his ship, his real name was unpronounceable) had done his best to be hospitable to us, there were times when Galileo, Philip, Pilot, and I had no one to turn to but ourselves. The crew seemed to prefer that we remained apart from them; they were incurious about their human passengers, and clearly wished that Captain Jack hadn't agreed to carry us back to their home.

Humans have always been aliens on Tawcety, but at least in Landencyte humankind has been in the majority. Aboard the *Titanic*, the four of us were the minority, and the differences between Cetan and human culture couldn't have been more obvious. Our skin itched from sleeping on straw beds, our clothes were filthy from seldom being washed, and we'd lost weight from a diet of raw fish and little else.

On this morning, though, all that was in the past.

Philip, Pilot, and I stood on the f'castle and watched as the coast of Gruhar came into view. We were now in the straits separating the continent from a large island, Ouwu, whose coastal reefs had threatened the *Titanic* during last night's storm. During a brief visit topside to empty our chamber pot overboard, I'd spotted lights on the island. Ouwu was obviously inhabited, small comfort in case the ship foundered. At least we'd have a direction in which to swim, provided that we got off the ship and didn't drown; the Cetans were such strong swimmers that they never bothered to invent lifejackets, and their launches were not big enough to accommodate everyone aboard.

Nonetheless, Ouwu was also the first sign of civilization, Cetan or human, we'd seen since leaving the Southern Archipelago. As we sailed up the straits, we spotted a pair of small white triangles off the starboard bow.

"Fishing boats," Philip surmised. "Must be close to port. I can't imagine any of them being on the water last night."

"Makes sense," Pilot said. She stood in front of her husband, his arms wrapped around her waist. She turned her head to peer back the way we'd come. "Can't see that settlement on Ouwu anymore," she added, speaking softly. Of the crew, only Captain Jack understood Anglis, but nonetheless we felt compelled to keep our voices low. "If those are fishing boats, they might have gone out earlier this morning from somewhere else, fairly close."

Philip nodded as he pulled her a little closer. They looked warm and content together, and not for the first time I found myself envying him. Over the last few weeks, I'd tried to overcome my dislike for Pilot. She could be selfish and manipulative, and I still resented the fact that she'd purposefully withheld vital information when she and Philip had hired me. Yet she wasn't entirely the privileged brat I originally thought she was, even if she seemed to consider me to be little more than another servant. Seeing her and Philip almost made me miss my ex-wife. Almost.

Putting my back against the f'castle rail, I gazed at the ship. It was a big vessel, about sixty feet long and fifteen wide amidships, with two decks above and two below, not including the massive holds where cargo was stored. There were a half-dozen gunports on both the port and starboard sides, but the cast-iron cannons seemed to be rarely used; their maws didn't smell of gunpowder, and the cannonballs racked beside them were gathering rust. Captain Jack told us that the guns were aboard in the event that the *Titanic* was mustered into service as a warship, but that hadn't happened in many years, or at least not while he'd been in command.

When I asked him why his ship would go to war, though, he'd done what Cetans usually do when they don't want to answer a question: he turned his back to me and walked away. But the presence of cannons aboard a merchant vessel told me enough: the Cetans, or at least the ones from Gruhar, had enemies. I doubted any humans before me had ever learned this in all the years my people have been on Tawcety.

Hearing footsteps on the companionway behind us, I turned to see who was coming up from below. It was Jack, and right behind him was Galileo. The old man had made friends with the captain over the past several weeks; it was Galileo who'd talked him into taking us aboard, no small favor considering the fact that humans had been contained on Landencyte for generations. But I think Jack was as curious about Galileo as Galileo was about Jack, and their mutual interest had been our ticket aboard.

Or so it seemed. As always, the Cetans didn't share everything they knew with humans. I believed there was another reason why Jack had agreed to this, and so did Galileo. We just didn't know what it was… yet.

Seeing Philip, Pilot, and me, Galileo smiled. "Oh, there you are. Good morning. The captain tells me we should soon be within sight of Ha-Faha."

"C-c-c-c-i'y there." Captain Jack raised a hand to point toward the coastline passing by off the port side. "S-s-s-see s-s-s-soon."

Jack didn't speak our language as well as other Cetans I've known. On the other hand, he didn't live on Sanctuary, so his contact with humans was only as frequent as when the *Titanic* visited Landencyte, its usual port of call before sailing south to Freeman Cay. But he and Galileo were both senior citizens—Jack's snout and head crest were streaked with grey, and he walked hunched over, the way Cetans do when they reach a certain age—and this made for an emerging friendship. They were both old dogs, to use a human expression that most Cetans find offensive… dogs, I mean.

"Did you talk to him about what we're going to do when we get in?" Philip asked.

"Or what to expect when we do?" Pilot added.

"I have indeed," Galileo replied. "In fact, we had a good chat about that over breakfast."

Most of the crew were still belowdecks in the galley. Although we shared meals with them, we'd eat as fast as we could. There's few things that can kill your appetite faster than watching hungry Cetans consume fish; they don't clean or cook them first, but simply eat them whole: head, tail, and everything in between. Yet this didn't seem to bother Galileo; when we'd seen him earlier in the galley, he was having a breakfast conversation with Jack. Galileo was the only guy I've ever met who could manage a few Cetan words and expressions without sounding silly or offending his listeners, a talent that had been useful to us over the past few weeks.

"When we reach Ha-Faha," Galileo went on, "we'll be met at the pier by what we'd call customs officers. That is, government officials responsible for inspecting the ship's manifest and determining the tariffs they'll levy."

"No 'alk genera'ors-s-s-s." Jack stared at us. "No gener-r-ra'ors-s-s-s, 'alk you."

"Yes, of course." Galileo raised a placating hand before turning to us again. "He means we're not to mention anything about the electrical generators he and his crew transported to Freeman Cay. He and his crew could get in a lot of trouble if the inspectors find out they've been selling them to us."

The three of us nodded even though we didn't need reminding. Indeed, the last thing I'd expected to learn was that the small, vegetable oil-fueled generators that had been popping up here and there on

Sanctuary were made by Cetans on Gruhar and brought to Freeman Cay aboard the *Titanic*. The fact that Cetan authorities were unaware that Gruharan generators were finding their way to humans on Sanctuary was just another piece of the puzzle the four of us were trying to put together.

"All right, fine," I said. "Mum's the word. But what happens then? Does the captain mean to claim us as cargo, too?"

I was only kidding—slavery wasn't something the Cetans practiced, or at least so far as anyone knew—but Pilot turned pale and hugged Philip a little tighter. I hate to admit it, but I enjoyed her reaction. Philip didn't say anything, but he glared at me for scaring his wife.

"No, he won't." Galileo's smile faded. "We're not merchandise, and Jack's an honorable man." It was almost as amusing to hear him refer to the Cetan as a man. "Once we reach the pier and the customs officials come aboard," he went on, "the captain will present us as paying passengers who wish to meet with higher Gruharan authority. If all goes well, the customs inspectors will understand and take us into custody until such a meeting can be arranged."

This much was true. After the *Titanic* dropped anchor off Freeman Cay, we'd met Jack and his crew after they came ashore. It had taken a lot of talking and every bit of gold we had to buy passage aboard their ship, and I kissed goodbye to the drawstring purse of Cetan gold that had been my down-payment and expenses for this job. Philip promised to reimburse me once we got home—*if* we got home—but that was what it took for Galileo to persuade Jack to carry us across the ocean to Gruhar.

"With whom are we supposed to meet?" Philip asked.

Jack understood him and replied without needing Galileo to interpret what Philip had said. "Iko," he replied.

"Iko?" I vaguely recalled having heard that name before. "Who's that?"

The captain growled something I didn't understand but Galileo did. "It's difficult to translate," the old man said, "but it seems that this Iko—that's an abbreviation of her name; the rest is about eight syllables long—is their leader, what we'd call a 'princess.' All major decisions are mainly made by her, it seems."

"If she's a princess," Pilot asked, "isn't there a queen?" The Cetans were largely a matriarchal society. Indeed, it was rare to see a Cetan sailing ship whose captain was male.

"Not a queen, an empress, and her name is Saikka. But the captain won't explain to me why Princess Iko wields more authority than her mother. I gather that, in their culture, it's disrespectful to discuss the Gruharan royal family with outsiders. That's why we've never been told anything about either of them. In any case, that's not important just now. Once we disembark, we'll—"

"Ha-Faha," Jack said, pointing toward the Gruharan coast.

I saw nothing at first but what appeared to be stone bluffs towering above the shoreline. Then I looked more closely and realized my mistake. It wasn't a natural rock formation, it was…

"I'll be damned," Philip murmured, awestruck. "Is that a *wall*?"

It was indeed a wall, but like none we'd ever seen before. From the distance, it appeared to be about thirty feet tall. The off-white color of quarried limestone, it stretched northward across the coast for as far as the eye could see; to the south—the direction from which we were sailing—it appeared to turn inland, rising upon a low hill before disappearing over the western horizon. Watchtowers were periodically spaced along its battlements, which were crenellated with archer's loops.

I looked at Galileo; he shook his head. "I wasn't anticipating this either," he said softly. "It's a surprise to me, too."

"It's *huge*." Letting go of Pilot, Philip leaned against the railing to stare at the vast edifice. "Why would anyone build something like this?"

Galileo didn't respond, and if Jack understood, he wasn't bothering to reply. Neither of them needed to do so; the answer was obvious. Why would anyone build a wall like this? To keep someone out… namely, an enemy.

Realizing this, I felt a chill that didn't come from the ocean breeze. Suddenly, talking our way aboard the *Titanic* no longer seemed like such a good idea.

II

My forebodings, deep as they were, faded as our ship reached Ha-Faha and sailed into its harbor. It was larger than Landencyte's Miracle Bay, its wharf and stone quays all but hidden behind a forest of ship masts. I tried to count the sailing vessels anchored in its waters, but gave up after fifty. The waterfront lay outside the wall, seemingly unprotected, yet it didn't seem as if the city was on a war footing. Although I spotted a number of vessels like the *Titanic*, argosies and galleons that could be converted to warships, their gunports were closed and it appeared as if the deck guns had been removed from some. Like the city wall, the presence of military craft hinted at some past conflict. Yet that time was over, and now Ha-Faha was at peace.

Titanic's decks swarmed with Cetan sailors making ready to come into port. Instead of dropping anchor in the outer harbor, the ship picked its way through the crowded harbor, heading for the quay where its cargo would be offloaded. Everyone aboard had a job that needed to be done. Everyone, that is, save for my traveling companions and I, who stood behind Captain Jack on the bridge while he barked orders at his crew.

None of us knew what to expect. As the first humans from Sanctuary to cross the Western Ocean, we had no idea what was in store for us. Even Galileo, who was on good terms with Jack and accustomed to dealing with his people, was quietly nervous. When he tried to question the captain, though, Jack pointedly ignored him, and when Galileo persisted, a deep-throated growl was the only answer we got: *I'm busy, now shut up and leave me alone.*

With the helmsman at the wheel, the big ship maneuvered through the inner harbor. As it glided toward the waterfront's longest quay, we saw Cetan longshoremen awaiting our arrival. They caught the mooring lines thrown from the ship and lashed them to the pilings. The captain ordered the anchor dropped, then tugged a bell rope beside him. The ship's bell rang six times, signaling that the *Titanic* was safe at port.

Jack turned to us. "Come," he said, cocking his head toward the quay. A couple of crewmen had already lowered the gangplank.

"Where are we going?" Galileo asked.

"'Ake you 'o—" Jack fumbled for the right word to mispronounce "—'eader," he finished, meaning *leader*. "One who 'akes 'axes."

"One who what?" Pilot raised an eyebrow, not understanding what he'd said.

"'One who takes taxes,'" I repeated. "A customs official, I think."

"That would make sense," Galileo said, nodding in agreement. "I don't think they'd have much need for immigration officers, seeing how we're the first humans here."

A customs official was among the longshoremen, waiting for the ship to be tied off and the captain to come ashore. Like Jack, he was an older Cetan, his authority asserted by the gold rings braided through the long fur crest atop his head. He accepted the scroll containing the ship's manifest from Jack and was about to open it when he saw the ship's passengers come trooping down the gangway.

His crest stood up straight and a querulous growl rose in his throat. He wasn't only Cetan to have that reaction. Just about everyone stopped what they were doing. The longshoremen, the drivers of the gorsch wagons lined up along the quay to receive the *Titanic*'s cargo, sailors from other vessels, all turned to stare at the four humans disembarking from the ship. I thought it was because we were the first of our kind they'd ever seen. But if that were so, their curiosity didn't last very long. A quick look, a few muttered comments to one another, and then everyone went back to what they'd been doing.

Philip noticed this, too. "If we're aliens," he said quietly, "then we're not the first ones here."

"We *should* be," Pilot said. "No human has ever sailed to Gruhar before."

"No one from Sanctuary, you mean."

"Hush, you two, I can't hear what they're saying." Galileo was trying to listen to the conversation going on between Jack and the customs officer. The old man was far from being fluent in their language, but he knew a few words and phrases. He listened for a minute or so, then turned to us again. "The official is surprised to see us," he murmured, "but he doesn't appear to be particularly upset. However, I think he's told Jack that we're not to go any farther until someone else gets here."

"Who?" I asked.

"I don't know, or at least I'm not sure. He... wait." Galileo fell quiet again as he listened to the yips, growls, and whines of the Cetan conversation. A concerned look appeared on his face. "I might be mistaken... I *must* be mistaken... but I think he just said something about Guardians on the way."

"Guardians?" Philip scowled. "I sure hope not. I've seen enough jail cells, thank you."

He hadn't forgotten the cell he and I had shared back in Castaway Point. Neither had I. And this time, there would be no highwaymen to facilitate our escape. I never thought I'd find myself hoping for Guido's Raiders to show up, but that wasn't going to happen; they were on the other side of the ocean.

Jack turned to us. "'You s-s-s'ay here. Come s-s-s-soon, ge' you."

"Who's coming to get us?" Galileo asked, but Jack was already walking away to oversee the cargo being offloaded from his ship. The customs officer followed him, paying more attention now to the manifest than to us. He didn't understand our language, so it was pointless to try and get answers from him.

"This doesn't look good," Philip muttered.

Pilot turned to me. "Well, aren't you going to *do* something?"

"What would you have me do?" I patted the hilt of my saber, sheathed and dangling from my belt along with my holstered flintlock. "Draw my sword? Who would I fight, everyone in the city? We're strangers here, kiddo. That means we play by their rules."

Pilot glared at me but let it drop. Over the past several weeks, she'd gradually come to realize—if not totally accept—that she and Philip were no longer in a place where it mattered that they were scions of wealthy Steward families. Perhaps for the first time in her life, she couldn't make demands or expect deferential treatment. And while I might still technically be in her employ, I wasn't about to draw my sword or gun on her account. Not while we were outnumbered and in a strange land.

So the four of us took seats on crates and barrels being unloaded from our ship. The dock workers were nearly done when two more gorsch wagons arrived. Both were passenger coaches, but the one in front was larger, with barred windows along its sides. I immediately recognized it for what it was: a paddy wagon, just like the one that Bart had used to transport us from Castaway Point to Landencyte... or tried to, at least.

The wagons came to a halt near the moored ship. The paddy wagon's rear door opened, and four Cetans wearing the capes and leather armor of Guardians climbed out. Swords drawn, they marched over to where the four of us were sitting.

"Easy, everybody." I kept my hands in sight, on my knees where they could be seen. "Stay calm. I'm sure they—"

Then I stopped. Beside me, I heard Pilot give an incredulous gasp, and for once I couldn't have agreed with her more. From the second carriage —smaller and more elegant, with a gilded emblem upon its passenger door—someone else had climbed down, a slight figure dressed in full-length white robes brocaded with elaborate Cetan designs, a matching skullcap covering his shaven head. Hands clasped together within the robe's bell sleeves, he strolled toward us. When he passed between the Guardians, they respectfully stepped aside to let him pass. Stopping in front of us, he raised his left hand in greeting.

"Hello," he said, speaking our own language. "Welcome to Ha-Faha. It's an honor to meet you."

He was human.

III

His name was Huang Chen, and once we were alone with him in the back of his carriage—when they saw him, the Guardians went away; we'd soon find out why—he told us that he was descended from one of the scientists who'd been aboard the *Santos-Dumont*.

As soon he said that, Galileo, Philip, and Pilot recognized his surname. His ancestor, David Chen, had been the crew member whose voice we'd heard on the mysterious recording device Philip and I had stolen from the wall safe in the House Van Pelt library.

The others were excited to learn this, and as the carriage passed through the massive waterfront gates in the city wall, were hitting him with questions so fast that he became tongue-tied. Yet I was more interested in the gates themselves. At least twenty feet tall and made of iron-bound wood several feet thick, they looked sturdy enough to resist a battering ram. They dwarfed the steady progression of native Cetans entering and leaving the city. On the other side of the gates was a tunnel leading through the city wall; it was now clear that the wall was nearly as thick as it was tall, twenty feet or more. Obviously it had been in existence for some time, and yet there was little sign of wear, an indication that the inhabitants had made an effort to maintain it.

Sometime not so long ago, the wall had been built around Ha-Faha to fend off invaders, and determined ones at that. Another clue that the Citizens of Ha-Faha had enemies, in the past if not necessarily in the present.

My traveling companions barely noticed this. They were consumed with questions about Huang Chen and his ancestors from the *Santos-Dumont*. "Wait, please, just wait." Smiling with faint amusement, Chen raised his hands in surrender. "I realize there are many things you wish to know—"

"That goes without saying." Sitting across from him, Galileo bent forward to hear him better over the clatter of carriage wheels on paving stones.

"And I promise you, Citizen Galileo, all will be explained." Chen's smile never faltered; although he projected a calm demeanor, he seemed to be just as excited to meet us as we were to meet him. "But I think it would be wise if we waited until we're—" a meaningful nod toward the Cetan driver seated on the buckboard, out of sight but not earshot "—in more private circumstances."

Galileo nodded and so did Philip; they understood his unspoken inference. Pilot was impatient, but she nodded anyway, albeit reluctantly. I was listening with only half an ear, though. I was paying more attention to what was passing outside the carriage windows.

We'd passed through the tunnel and were now on the other side of the wall, and the city of Ha-Faha was opening before us.

Until then, the biggest city I'd ever seen was Landencyte. It quickly became evident that Ha-Faha was larger, much larger. Buildings of stone and wood, some as tall as six stories, rose above broad avenues paved with cobblestones worn smooth by countless feet and wheels over countless years. This was surprising; most Cetans I knew had a fear of heights. But here I saw plenty of balconies, with building residents casually lounging or hanging out laundry upon them. Apparently the inhabitants of Ha-Faha were more sophisticated about such things than the Cetans who lived on Sanctuary.

This wasn't the only difference. Cetan villages were usually chaotic, their streets branching off at random or suddenly ending in cul-de-sacs, with no signage at all. Here, the streets were neatly arranged in blocks that were spaced evenly apart from one another, with signposts in the Cetan language at each intersection. The streets were crowded with delivery wagons and passenger carriages, but they stayed on their proper sides of the street; pedestrians used sidewalks and marked crosswalks, and didn't carelessly step out in front of moving vehicles.

Along the streets, I noticed slender cast-iron posts topped with glass globes. They faintly resembled the oil lamps back home, but these were different; if these were streetlights, then where were their wicks? It also occurred to me that, although I could smell the faint aroma of vegetable oil, signifying the presence of generators and engines, absent was the fecal stench pervasive of Cetan villages. The Gruharans of Ha-Faha appeared to have moved their public toilets indoors, out of view. Definitely a relief, but when had they done this?

I was still pondering this when my train of thought was interrupted by a loud mechanical noise the likes of which I'd never heard before. "Hey!" Philip exclaimed. "What's that?"

On the other side of the carriage, Philip was staring at something coming toward us from up the street. Leaning across him, I peered out the window beside him and saw… what the hell was that thing? At first it appeared to be a carriage much like ours, yet no gorsch, loper, or any other kind of animal was harnessed to it. Instead, it moved on its own accord, the Cetan seated on the open seat up front maneuvering it with some sort of wheel-and-lever contrivance, an engine of some sort in the rear belching vegetable-oil fumes. It rolled past us, heading in the opposite direction, followed by Cetan children running after it.

"It's called a geecee." Huang Chen was mildly amused by our reaction. "Gee, cee… g.c., get it? Short for 'gorschless carriage'."

"I got it," Galileo said, "but that doesn't tell me what it is."

"A recent invention." Chen was as proud of the geecee as if he'd invented it himself. "Runs off an engine that consumes vegetable oil. It can travel as fast as twenty miles per hour."

"Twenty miles?" Galileo was as astounded as I was. "In just an hour?"

"Yes, but that's only if the driver isn't on a crowded street like this. That one was—"

"*Look!*" Pilot shouted, pointing at something on our side of the carriage. Startled, I looked away from the geecee and spotted what she'd seen on the sidewalk:

A woman. A *human* woman.

She wore a long, ankle-length dress and an elaborately embroidered cape, but wasn't much taller than the Cetan female she walked alongside. Her hair, dark red, was piled up on top of her head in an elaborate coif; there was a simple yet pretty gold necklace around her throat, but no marriage tiara. Nor was there a leash around her neck, but the way she carried herself—silently, eyes down, hands at her sides—intimated servitude. Even if she wasn't a slave, she definitely was a servant; whatever her status was, though, her very presence was as amazing as Huang Chen's.

Pilot reached for the door handle, but Chen stopped her before she could jump out and run back. "No," he said quietly, "that would be unwise."

"Who is she?" Pilot demanded.

"She's a—" Chen growled something in Cetan; it was the first time I'd heard a human speak the native language as well as they did "—a serf, as we'd call her. Although it's possible she might be a—" another growled Cetan word, different this time "—a tutor, as many of us are."

"Is that what you are?" Galileo asked. "A tutor?"

"Yes, I am." Straightening his shoulders, Chen drew himself up proudly. "Both my wife and I serve in the court of Her Imperial Majesty, Princess Iko, and her mother, Empress Saikka, in whose household we've lived our entire lives."

"You and your wife were born and raised there?" Philip asked.

"Yes, since childhood. Ours is an arranged marriage, as most human marriages are in Ha-Faha."

"I see." Galileo nodded. "And as their teacher, can you tell us how the empress and the princess intend to deal with us, seeing as how we're the first humans to come here from Sanctuary?"

"It's not my place to speak for Their Royal Majesties." His smile fading, Chen regarded Galileo evenly. "You'll have to wait until you meet them. Which you shall two days from now, when they'll hold their annual Royal Audience in observation of the first day of Springmonth."

"I see." Galileo nodded. "So we can't ask you anything until then?"

"You may ask anything you like, but my apologies if I may not be able to answer it."

As Chen spoke, I spotted another human on the street, an older man about Galileo's age. Dressed in loose-fitting white togs stained with paint, he stood beside a terra cotta wall, paintbrush and palate in hand as he worked on an elaborate abstract mural. An artist at work, he paid no attention to us as we went by.

Now I knew why none of the *Titanic*'s crew were curious about the humans in their midst. They'd seen our kind before on the streets of Ha-Faha. Those of us who lived entire our lives on Sanctuary didn't know there were humans elsewhere on Tawcety, but they did. And for generations, the Cetans had kept this knowledge from us… but why?

"All right," Galileo said, "then let's try finding questions you *can* answer. Where are you taking us?"

"The imperial palace," Chen said, "where you'll be the guests of Princess Iko until she and the empress have their audience with you two days from now. In our tongue, it's called the Palace of Wehakawa, after the Cetan general who's the most famous ancestor in their dynasty."

A furtive smile and a sly wink. "But we humans have our own name for it," he added quietly, his tone conspiratorial. "We call it the Palace of Dancing Dogs."

IV

Huang Chen said little else of consequence for the rest of the ride. Neither did we, though Pilot looked like she going to burst from all the questions she wanted to throw at him. Instead, we settled for letting Chen point out the sights: a sprawling open-air market, an elevated aqueduct built to bring fresh water in from the nearby highlands, windmills standing atop some of the taller buildings to generate electricity, the last causing Galileo to pound him with technical questions he couldn't answer.

Every so often, we'd spot another human. They weren't many, and almost always they were accompanied by a Cetan, yet none wore chains or manacles. And while it seemed as if they were always focused on one task or another, none seemed particularly miserable. I noticed a young woman seated by a fountain, scroll open in her lap, reading aloud to a handful of children, both Cetan and human, gathered at her feet. Through the carriage's open window I caught a snatch of her voice as we went by; she spoke the Cetan language as effortlessly as Chen. Until then, I'd always thought our kind was physically incapable of speaking their language. Perhaps that was true on Sanctuary, but not on Gruhar. Apparently, humans here had long ago learned to speak as the Cetans did, physiological differences notwithstanding.

There was something significant about this, but I couldn't quite put my finger on it. Philip noticed the same thing, though. Over the past several weeks, he and I had come to know each other well enough to anticipate what the other was thinking. So when he and I shared a quiet look, I knew that he probably had the same notion that I had. Everything about Ha-Faha suggested that the Cetans had a far more sophisticated civilization than anyone back home ever believed. Not only was their technology greater than our own, but their standard of living was higher, too. Or at least among their own kind. Ha-Faha had none of the chaotic squalor of Wa'Hag, the Cetan village outside Landencyte. Its streets were orderly and clean, the dwellings had windows, its sewage wasn't visible, and the air didn't smell like fish and shit.

Was it because humans were living among them, and had influenced their culture over time? One more question among many.

Ha-Faha sprawled as far as the eye could see, so it took a while for our carriage to reach the middle of the city. When we finally did, we emerged from the orderly network of streets and buildings to an open plaza so wide that it seemed as if every Cetan who lived in the city could stand on its perfectly laid cobblestones. On the other side, surrounded by high walls of its own, was a sprawling edifice, its gabled rooftops visible above the battlements.

"The Palace of Wehakawa," Chen said as our carriage travelled across the square; the pavement was so smooth, the wheels barely bounced at all. "The Springmonth celebration will commence here in two days' time, within the Imperial Courtyard." Again, a quiet smile. "I envy you," he added. "You'll be seeing this for the first time."

"I see." Galileo was only casually interested. His attention was drawn to the same thing mine was: the fountain we were passing just then. A statue stood at the center: a larger-than-life bronze figure of a female Cetan warrior, clad in battle armor with a worka in hand, standing defensively above two naked humans, a man and a woman, huddled at her side. She looked heroic, the humans cowering and helpless. General Wehakawa, I presumed.

I glanced first at him, then Phillip and Pilot. We all traded a significant look. No one said anything, but I could tell we all had the same thought. No one would erect a statue like that for no reason. It *meant* something.

The palace gates, nearly as large as those at the city wall, were topped by a bell tower. The driver paused long enough for one of the Cetan sentries to pull a thick rope dangling from the wall, ringing three times the ornate brass bell within the tower. The reverberations had barely faded when the gates swung open from inside. The guards posted out front stepped aside; they didn't bow as the carriage passed through, but neither did they unsheathe their workas. We were expected, but not necessarily respected.

Within the palace's outer perimeter lay a courtyard nearly as large as the plaza outside, featureless save globe-topped lampposts like those we'd spotted earlier. The palace itself was an immense edifice, its marble walls carved with intricately abstract bas-relief designs. Broad steps cut from polished granite led upward to a veranda surrounding the building; gilded doors, each three times the height of a Cetan, loomed above the veranda.

Sculpted gargoyles resembling fierce-looking warrior-males held firepots upon their muscular shoulders; the artisans who created them apparently saw no need for modesty, because each gargoyle had preposterously large genitalia dangling between their legs. Pilot blushed and laughed uncomfortably when she noticed this.

 The carriage didn't go straight to the palace, but instead veered right and headed for a row of two-story buildings built against the perimeter wall. The driver halted in front of the largest building. Two men, each dressed like Chen and also with shaved heads, came out to meet us. One carried a small stepladder over to the carriage while the other opened the door and chivalrously extended a hand to Pilot. Neither spoke to us as we climbed down; from their wide-eyed expressions, though, I could tell that they were just as curious about us as we were about them.

 Chen led the way to the front door, where another human in what I now realized was servant's livery opened it for us. We found ourselves in a vestibule, a staircase to the right. As Chen escorted us upstairs, I noticed more of the mysterious globes, smaller yet almost identical to those I'd seen earlier, positioned at intervals along the stairs. Galileo noticed the same thing; he paused to examine one of the globes. I stepped over to look more closely as well; it contained a thin wire loosely stretched between two tiny, fragile-looking posts.

 "Do you know what this is?" I asked quietly.

 "I believe I do." Galileo stared at the globe with the envious fascination of a genius admiring the work of another genius. "If it's what I think it is, I'll show you how it works… later."

 Chen had stopped at the top of the stairs; he, Pilot, and Philip were patiently waiting for us to catch up. He didn't ask Galileo and me what interested us so much, but instead led us down a second-floor corridor. The four of us followed him until we reached another door, faux oak and carved with a bas-relief of a loper.

 "This will be your quarters while you're here." Chen opened the door, and we followed him into a suite whose luxury was matched only by the Steward manors on Sanctuary. Three bedrooms were adjacent to a central sitting room furnished with beautifully carved tables and comfortable armchairs. The beds were a little small, meant for Cetans rather than humans, but they were comfortable enough for us to use; at least they weren't straw mats, just one more thing that made Ha-Faha different from

Wa'Hag. Although sunlight was coming in through an open door leading to a balcony overlooking the courtyard, it was still dark enough for none of us to see anything clearly.

I'd just noticed yet another globe, this one a hemisphere affixed to the ceiling, when I heard a soft click behind me. At the same instant, the globe flashed to life, glowing with light as bright as any oil lamp or torch I'd ever seen.

Startled, I clamped a hand against my eyes. Philip and Pilot were caught by surprise, too, because they did the same thing. The only ones not caught off-guard were Chen and Galileo. The old man stood by the door, hand still resting upon a small button he'd found on the wall.

"Just as I suspected," he said. "An incandescent electrical light, isn't it?"

"Yes, it is." Chen smiled. "I'm surprised you recognize it. I've been told that your people haven't rediscovered this yet."

I wasn't sure I'd heard him correctly. "What do you mean, 'rediscovered'?"

"Just what he said, Jeremy. This is an old form of human technology." Squinting a little, Galileo gazed up at the ceiling fixture. "Long ago, lights like this—powered by electricity, which in turn is created by massive generators—were quite common. Not here on Tawcety, though. When plastic became unavailable to us—that is, when our ancestors discovered that the Rot caused plastic to quickly disintegrate—it meant that they could no longer insulate the wires necessary for conducting electrical current." He turned to Chen. "I've dabbled with this for years, but never devised an adequate solution. How did you do it?"

"I couldn't tell you. I'm not an electrician." Chen walked over to the door. He poked his head outside, checking to make sure no one was eavesdropping. Finding the hallway vacant, he shut the door and returned to us.

"Make yourselves comfortable, please." Chen gestured to the chairs and couch arranged around the fireplace. Someone had obviously prepared the suite for occupancy, because a warm fire hissed and snapped at the logs. "There is much we need to talk about before you meet the princess. This way, you'll be able discuss certain matters without the burden of ignorance."

"Ignorant of what?" Pilot glared at him, offended.

"History, of course. Much has been hidden from you, and by that, I mean everyone who has lived on Sanctuary since the time of the original *Lindbergh* colonists."

"That's why we've come here," Galileo said. "What we don't know is the reason why our knowledge of history has been suppressed."

Chen walked over to the fireplace. Clasping his hands behind his back, he waited for us to take seats before going on. "The reason is simple. It was to make sure your people remained ignorant of the past… because ignorance was the only way our ancestors were permitted to live."

V

Before he could go on, there was a knock at the door. Chen started to walk to it, but I was closer and got there first. I was expecting to find a Cetan, but instead I found another human: a slender woman about my age and Chen's, dressed in a feminine version of servants' livery, her black hair highlighted with the first hint of middle-aged gray and woven into a thick braid that fell almost to her waist.

She nodded, smiled, and tilted her head forward in a quick bow. "My wife Sasha," Chen said as she came in. "Like myself, a tutor in the royal household."

"Really?" Galileo was immediately interested. "That's what I am, too, not to mention an armchair historian as well."

"Oh yes, we know," Chen replied. "We know of you, sir, as does Princess Iko. Your reputation has travelled far, which is why you're our honored guest."

This obviously startled Galileo. In fact, it was one of the few times I saw him speechless. His mouth moved silently for a moment or two, making him look like a gray-bearded fish gasping in the air. Pilot couldn't help herself; she laughed behind her hand at his embarrassment.

"Breathe, sensei, breathe!" she chortled. "It's okay, you can—"

"Aw, stuff it," Galileo growled, red-faced. The rest of us finally broke down, and he had to endure some good-natured laughter at his expense. He let it go for a few seconds, then shook his head and turned to Chen and Sasha again. "I don't understand. How could have you heard of me? And how would the princess know?"

Chen and Sasha glanced at one another, the sort of silent exchange you see when a long-married couple tries to decide who's going to go first. Sasha won. "Perhaps it's best if you first told us about yourselves," she said. "We know more about our situation than you do, of course, but it might save time if we find out first what you *don't* know and go from there."

"Makes sense," Galileo said, and the rest of us nodded in agreement. He did most of the talking, with Pilot and Philip filling in details every now and then. I added a comment or two, but so far as I was concerned, this was history best told by historians.

It took a while to get through everything, but Chen and Sasha listened closely, occasionally asking questions, but mainly taking everything in. It seemed that, although Galileo startled them now and then—his invention of a flying machine caught them by surprise—much of what he said merely confirmed what they already knew. When he was done, the two were quiet for a bit, Sasha gazing out the window and Chen meditatively letting it all soak in.

"So I see," Chen said at last. He looked at his wife. "It all fits, doesn't it?" Sasha nodded. She seemed satisfied by what she'd just heard. "Thank you," Chen said to Galileo. "For your candor, and also for—" he paused to take a deep breath "—the astounding efforts you've gone through to come all this way and tell us this."

Galileo started to reply, but I cut him off. "I'm glad you're happy," I said, "and we're grateful for the hospitality, but my clients didn't travel this distance just to tell you a story. They came—*we* came—because we want to know—"

"Why the knowledge of your existence has been deliberately kept from us," Philip said, interrupting me. "And why we've never been allowed to leave Sanctuary."

"And those are just the big questions," Pilot added. "There's a lot more."

"Yes, of course," Chen said. "Very well, then. Now it's our turn."

VI

When the *Lindbergh*'s first sortie to Tawcety—or rather, Tau Ceti-e—returned to the mother ship unwittingly carrying the Rot, the plastic-destroying microbes spread through the vessel so quickly that it was all Captain Greer and her crew could do just to deal with the crisis. They had little idea of what was going on aboard the *Santos-Dumont*.

Because the *Santos-Dumont* was circling Tawcety at a lower altitude than the *Lindbergh*, it was also traveling at a higher orbital velocity. Galileo had to ask Chen to stop for a moment so that he could explain the physics of this to Philip and me—as his student, Pilot knew this stuff already—but the upshot was that it meant the two ships were periodically on opposite sides of Tawcety, and therefore were unable to communicate with one another via something called *radio*.

"I've heard of radio," I said, "but I always figured it was magic trick." Every kid in Landencyte has seen the gag played by street mages, where they'd speak to a small magic box called a radio, then have a ghostly voice reply from the box. A ventriloquist act, and a simple one at that. Only small children and superstitious fools fall for it anymore.

"Radio is really technology," Chen said, just a trifle condescendingly. "No magic at all." He looked at Sasha, who was seated beside him. "See? It's as we expected. In their culture, science has been suppressed for so long, belief in the supernatural has taken its place. We'll have to cope with that."

I didn't appreciate his patronizing tone. "What do you mean by—?"

"Don't get him sidetracked," Galileo said. "Let him finish. Go on, Chen."

A grateful nod, then Chen continued. "Because the two ships soon fell out of radio contact with each other during the crisis, the *Lindbergh*'s crew, your ancestors, were largely unaware what was happening to the *Santos-Dumont*'s crew, our ancestors."

"The logbooks that were hidden in the House Greer library tell of Yvonne Greer witnessing the destruction of the *Santos-Dumont* from space," Galileo said. "Until recently, it's always been assumed by my people—that is, the few of us who've been able to read the logs—that the ship was lost with all hands."

"But we know different," Philip added, "now that we've found that... that object in the House van Pelt library. Is that a radio, too?"

"No, it's not. It's called a recorder. That one was salvaged from scientific equipment brought down to Tawcety's surface by the *Santos-Dumont* landing team. It's fortunate that its outer case isn't made of plastic but rather of graphene, a material impervious to the Rot. And since the interior electronics were made of copper, silicon, and other industrial—" He noticed the puzzled looks on our faces and stopped himself. "Anyway, it's not magic."

"I didn't think it was." Now it was Galileo's turn to be annoyed. "Not everyone on Sanctuary believes in magic, I'll have you know."

"I didn't say you did. But when a culture loses its history, myth takes its place. Likewise, when a culture loses its understanding of science, magic and superstition fill the void. Belief in magic is a form of denying reality. From what we understand has happened on Mahha—"

"Sanctuary. We call our home Sanctuary. Not Mahha."

"Forgive me." Chen raised a placating hand. "I apologize if anything I've said has offended you. I'm afraid it has. Please believe me, I'm only trying to describe your situation... *our* situation, that is."

He cast his wife a meaningful look, and Sasha picked up the thread. "What the *Lindbergh* crew didn't know was that quite a few members of the *Santos-Dumont* crew didn't perish with their ship. Captain Cortez had let most of the landing party to remain on Bakkah—Tawcety, I mean—when their shuttle returned to the mothership. He did this without informing the *Lindbergh* because his landing team thought the expedition's chief scientist, who was aboard the other ship, was being overcautious, even though they were certain that Tawcety was habitable. Besides, they were tired of being cooped up aboard ship. And when the Rot set in, Captain Cortez acted more quickly than Captain Greer, and managed to transport down about three dozen more members of the flight crew aboard an unaffected shuttle."

"So there were more survivors of the disaster than the *Lindbergh* crew believed," Chen said, "but because the two groups were on opposite sides of the planet, with no means of communicating with one another, each group believed that they were the sole survivors and everyone who'd been aboard the other ship was dead."

"I see." Galileo had gotten over his irritation. "And where did the *Santos-Dumont* survivors land? Here?"

"No," Sasha said, "they landed in same place the first party did: the highlands of Hak-ka, a small land mass in the northern latitudes of the western hemisphere. Not as temperate as Sanctuary, I'm afraid, which made survival even more precarious when the Rot destroyed their clothing and much of their equipment. But they weren't alone for very long. Like the *Lindbergh*'s survey team, their landing on Hak-ka was observed by Cetans. In this case, the inhabitants of Horraf, a large continent to the southeast.

"At this time," she continued, "the Horrafans were at war with the Gruharans, the inhabitants of this continent. They'd been fighting for many years when the *Lindbergh* and the *Santos-Dumont* arrived, mainly over disputed territory straddling the eastern and western hemispheres. As it so happened, the *Santos-Dumont* shuttles were spotted by a Gruharan ship that happened to be scouting the Ohah-Wah archipelago south of Hak-ka. Realizing that they'd seen something significant, its captain immediately sailed back to Gruhar, where she delivered a report to the Empress Hasah."

The fire was getting low by then, and although none of us were particularly cold, Chen got up from his chair to tend to it. "By then, another Gruharan vessel had been dispatched to Mahha—Sanctuary, sorry—to investigate the landing there. They discovered the *Lindbergh*'s survivors, who were more in number but just as helpless. Yet the first contact between Cetans and humans went well, and for a while the Cetan captain—I believe your people called her Fae—believed that the two races could peacefully coexist."

"What changed her mind?" I asked.

"It was obvious from the start that humans came from a technologically superior race." As he spoke, Chen selected a log from the small stack of firewood beside the hearth. "Although the *Lindbergh*'s survivors were just as helpless as those from the *Santos-Dumont*, the remains of the *Lindbergh*—that is, the hibernation modules jettisoned from the ship before it was destroyed—were clear evidence that our people possessed knowledge and tools far beyond that of Cetan civilization of that period."

"But that's not all," Sasha said. "It wasn't long before Cetans became aware of something even more alarming: that they bore a strong resemblance to the animals back on Earth called 'dogs.' And although these creatures were little more than domesticated pets, the Cetans mistakenly believed that they were intelligent creatures much like themselves and that humans had enslaved them."

"No wonder they've always taken offense to us calling them dogs," Philip said.

"That's correct." Chen fed the log to the fire, then picked up an iron poker and used it to stir the coals. "It didn't help when they heard one of the *Lindbergh* scientists theorize that Cetans may have evolved from a similar dog-like species, just as humans evolved from a lesser species back on Earth. But the Cetans hadn't yet discovered evolution. The spiritual beliefs of their principal religion, Dagghan, held that their race was formed in the image of their divine creator. So—"

"There were misunderstandings," Galileo said, finishing Chen's thought for him, "and those misunderstandings made them fearful of humans."

"Right." Brushing bits of bark from his hands, Chen returned to his seat. "And this put the Cetans—that is, those on Gruhar, including the Empress—in an uncomfortable position. Dagghan obliges its followers to render aid and comfort to those who are helpless and in need, even if you don't necessarily like them. So they couldn't kill the *Lindbergh* survivors, because such a massacre would have been a major sin. But they were also fearful that, if we were allowed to perpetuate our race around the world or regain our technological superiority, in time we'd become a serious menace to them, maybe even enslave them just as we'd enslaved the dogs of Earth… or so they believed."

"In the meantime," Sasha said, "Hasha dispatched a military expedition to Hak-ka with the mission of locating the other group of humans that her advisors rightfully believed to be there. By then, the *Santos-Dumont* survivors had been discovered by the Horrafans. They'd sought shelter within fortifications they'd hastily put up around their village, but the Horrafans were determined to kill them all, thinking them to be invaders from another world who had to be wiped out."

"I take it that the Horrafans aren't strong believers in Dagghan," Philip said.

"They weren't," Chen said, "but they are now, just as Horraf itself now belongs to the Gruharan Empire. Remember, all this happened centuries ago. Much has changed since then."

"At the time, though," Sasha went on, "the *Santos-Dumont* survivors were in serious peril, and might well have been slaughtered if the Gruharans hadn't come to their rescue. A military leader by name of Wehakawa led the liberation of the humans—"

"We saw her statue outside the palace," I said.

"Yes. Wehakawa is a legendary hero, and not only because she rescued our ancestors. Anyway, once the Horrafans were defeated on Hakka, the humans were brought here to Ha-Faha—"

"And became slaves," Pilot said, her voice bitter.

"No," Sasha sternly replied as both she and Chen shook their heads. "Nothing of the kind. Dagghan teaches that slavery, too, is a mortal sin."

"Once Wehakawa's forces overcame the Horrafans and rescued the *Santos-Dumont* survivors," Chen said, "she brought them back here, to Ha-Faha, where they were presented to the empress. By this time, the expedition sent to Mahha had also returned, and Fae had reported to Hasha what she'd discovered. So the empress and her advisors had not only an account of the Mahha expedition, but also a large group of humans brought back from Hak-ka. And while the outlook for peace didn't appear good, it wasn't the worst thing that could have happened."

Galileo raised an eyebrow. "Explain."

"On one hand, it was clear to everyone that the humans belonged to an advanced race, one whose technological superiority made the Cetans seem primitive by comparison. Yet for reasons the Cetans didn't understand, our people no longer possessed that advantage. The Rot had destroyed nearly everything they'd brought with them from Earth, down to the clothes on their backs. And although it was feared at first that our ancestors were the vanguard of an invasion, the Empress soon learned that what they'd told both Fae and Wehakakwa was true: there were only two ships, and both had been destroyed, with no more likely to come. So the Cetans had little to fear from us. The aliens who'd come to their world were shipwrecked, helpless, and desperately in need of help if they were to survive."

"And as a devout follower of Dagghan," Sasha said, "Hasha knew that it was her responsibility, along with that of her people, to be merciful to the strangers that fate had deposited upon her world."

With the fire going, the room had become quite warm. Removing his skullcap, Chen produced a handkerchief and used it to mop the sweat beading his shaved scalp. "So she met with her advisors, and together they arrived at a solution."

As solutions go, the one devised by the Empress Hasha was both elegant and complex.

First, the *Santos-Dumont* survivors were temporarily taken in by the imperial family. Placed under the protection of the empress herself, they were brought to the palace—the original one, which had stood on the site of the present palace; a few years later, it was destroyed in the catastrophic fire that devastated most of Ha-Faha—where they were taught to understand and communicate in the native language and educated in the Cetan way. Once this was accomplished, the humans were allowed to leave the palace and placed in the care of Cetan households willing to sponsor them, not as slaves, but as tutors, artisans, inventors, and other roles in which they could be useful. Eventually, the humans were allowed to live by themselves, in a quarter of the city set aside for them after Ha-Faha was rebuilt.

It was a wise decision, for the humans taught the Cetans a great deal about science and technology, bringing their knowledge to a race that, after many years of war, was on the verge of social stagnation. When they inevitably came up against the Rot's effects upon the development of advanced technology, humans and Cetans worked together to develop substitutes for plastic, like silicon and industrial ceramics, alternative materials the humans knew about but the Cetans were unlikely to have discovered on their own.

As things turned out, this arrangement was fortuitous in ways no one expected. Despite the advantages the Gruharans now had, the war with Horraf continued drag on. Finally, in an act of desperation, the Horrafans sent their war fleet to Ha-Faha, where they used trebuchets aboard their ships to catapult gorakas—bundles of dried gorsch manure that had been set ablaze; the word meant, literally, "flaming gorsch shit"—over the city wall. The assault succeeded in destroying most of the city, including Hasha's palace, before Wehakawa's naval forces attacked and sank the Horrafan fleet. This counterassault left Horraf largely defenseless, forcing them to surrender. With the war over, the humans assisted their hosts in rebuilding Ha-Faha. Only this time, they did it the human way, with orderly streets, underground water and sewage systems, and eventually electrical power, the last utterly amazing a race that, until then, had used only candles and oil lamps to light their homes.

Yet this renaissance didn't occur on Sanctuary as well.

Because there were so many more humans on Mahha, Hasha decreed that they were to remain isolated from the rest of the world. Just as the human inhabitants of Ha-Faha were not allowed to leave Gruhar, the humans on the island they called Sanctuary weren't permitted to venture any farther than its coastal waters, and an off-shore quarantine zone was put in place to assure this. A garrison of Cetan soldiers, posing as civilians, were brought to Sanctuary, where they took up permanent residence among the humans. If there was ever an uprising, these Cetans were to drop everything they were doing to take up arms and quell the revolt. A wide-reaching set of rules, codified as Cetan law, was devised to control human conduct on the island, with the Guardians appointed to ensure that these laws were obeyed.

"But the science and technology your ancestors brought to their people," Pilot asked, "why wasn't it brought to us, too?"

"Because," Sasha said, "it was feared that, if the humans on Sanctuary ever regained the technology they once had, they might try to conquer the Cetans."

"It was never forgotten that our ancestors on Earth kept as household pets a race of creatures resembling Cetans," Chen said. "They learned this when a human picked up a stick and threw it, telling a Cetan to go and fetch it. Even though it was meant as a joke, it was demeaning to be treated in such fashion."

Again, Sasha picked up where her husband left off. "So the laws Cetans imposed upon the humans on Sanctuary were meant, in large part, to keep their descendants from learning about their past. The stockade wall around the remains of the *Lindbergh*, for example. It was erected to keep everyone away from the technology the Cetans believed was still inside, and over time your ancestors came to believe that the ship was both mythical and magical. Same for plastic. It became known as 'plastik,' and everyone thought it was magical, too."

"That explains a lot," I said.

"Yes, it does," Galileo said, "but it doesn't explain everything. If it was their intent to keep people on Sanctuary from ever acquiring advanced technology, or even learning about it, then why allow generators to be smuggled into Sanctuary? Or didn't they know what their own merchantmen were doing?"

"Oh, they knew about that, all right." Chen smiled. "In fact, it was our idea, Sasha's and mine."

"And the Cetans haven't stopped you?"

His smile grew wider. "No. In fact, this has been done with Princess Iko's approval."

Galileo stared at him. "What? I don't—"

"Let me explain. As I said, advanced technology—that is, any form of powered machinery more sophisticated than, say, a waterwheel—has been embargoed from Sanctuary for centuries now. It's not even permitted in Wa'hag, the Cetan settlement there. Its inhabitants have agreed to continue living as their ancestors did, and a surprising number are willing to have that simpler lifestyle." He shrugged. "Some Cetans are still uncomfortable with the innovations perpetrated by humans."

"However," Sasha said, "in recent years a number of Cetans have wondered if it's really necessary to continue the effort to retard the development of human technology on Sanctuary. Reports from scholars who've discreetly visited the island to study the indigenous human population have shown this to have long-term consequences no one anticipated, namely, the rise of superstitious beliefs and practices, some of them quite detrimental."

"Yeah, well, you can blame your friends for that," I said. "Cetan law protects bogus magicians from legal prosecution." I was thinking of the small boy who'd fallen to his death from a rooftop while trying to imitate a street illusionist's levitation act.

"Some Cetans have come to realize that, yes, they have themselves to blame." Chen frowned. "But your people share some of that blame. This kind of magical thinking was your own doing. No one taught you to put your trust in spells and incantations; you did that yourselves."

"I'm afraid I have to agree," Galileo said. "Ignorance drives out rational thought, but only with the willing cooperation of the ignorant."

Chen nodded. "Princess Iko understands this, as do certain members of her court. She belongs to a younger generation of Cetans, who are no longer fearful of the human presence on Tawcety. And with her mother, the Empress Saikka, old and ailing, the power and authority of the throne has gradually been vested in her."

"And how does the empress feel about this?"

"Hard to say. We've tutored her as well, as did our predecessors, so she knows our history and even understands a little Anglis. But she has always been more reserved than her daughter, and it's difficult to know her mind."

"But Iko sees the need for change," Sasha said, "so several years ago, she agreed to a plan that my husband and I devised."

"You decided to covertly introduce vegetable-oil generators to Sanctuary," Philip said, and they nodded. "So why make a secret of it? Why not simply have them carried straight to Sanctuary and sell them openly?"

"Because Cetan Law, with its prohibitions against powered machinery, is so thoroughly engrained in your culture, it's thought that introducing such technology to a magic-based culture too quickly would cause social upheavals. That and the fact that quite a number of Cetans, mainly those living on Mahha—"

"Sanctuary," Philip said, pointedly.

"Apologies. I meant Sanctuary. Anyway, many Cetans there are opposed to humans ever regaining the science and technology knowledge they once possessed. They've taken measures meant to assure that your people never remember who they were or where they came from. They would've succeeded if the *Lindbergh*'s commander and senior officers, the ones who became the original Stewards, hadn't carefully hidden away Captain Greer's logbook and diary, along with other historical relics, rather than surrendering them to the Guardians to be destroyed."

"But one of those relics was the recording made by your own ancestor," Galileo said. "How did it get from here to House van Pelt?"

"We arranged for the recorder to be taken to Sanctuary. This was done for two reasons. First, we wanted to test the route we'd devised for smuggling the generators to the Southern Archipelago. And second, we wanted to find a way to lure someone like you from Sanctuary. So—"

"Wait a minute!" I said, sitting up straight. "You mean to tell us that we've been put through all that just to get our attention and persuade us to come here?"

"Well…" Chen looked embarrassed.

"I'm afraid to say it, but… yes, that was by design." Sasha appeared reluctant to admit this; I don't think she or Chen would have confessed the truth if Galileo and I hadn't forced it out of them. "We gave the recorder to a Cetan captain whom we knew to be trustworthy and asked him to make sure that it got into the hands of Steward van Pelt, whom we knew from field reports to be one of the more progressive members of the Council of Stewards. Those reports also informed us that the Steward employed a tutor whom we suspected of being a so-called Originalist, someone engaged in investigating the past and rediscovering the true history of humankind on this world… namely you, Citizen Galileo."

"Well, I'll be damned." Stunned, Galileo fell back in his chair. "Well played, madam, well played."

"So, you've succeeded in luring us here," Pilot said. It was the first time she'd spoken in a while; now she leaned forward in her seat. "Now what? What happens next?"

"Two days from now," Chen said, "there will be the annual Springmonth ritual here at the palace: the Public Dance, followed by the Royal Audience. Both the Empress Saikka and Princess Iko will be present, along with the rest of the royal court. It's then that Citizens of the Gruharan Empire are allowed to publicly petition the empress and the princess, stating their grievances and requesting relief. We've already taken up the matter with Princess Iko, and she has agreed to let a human representative from Sanctuary address the court."

Sasha turned to Galileo. "We feel that person should be you. The Cetans respect and revere senior Citizens, so the choice is obvious."

"I see… I see." Galileo pensively stroked his beard. "And what am I supposed to be requesting?"

"For humans on Sanctuary to be allowed to travel off the island," Chen said, "and to possess the technology we've re-invented here. And most importantly, freedom for both the human inhabitants of Gruhar and Sanctuary."

"Particularly for those of us in Ha-Faha," Sasha added. "We may not be slaves, but serfdom is only a little better. But your freedom matters as well."

"All right… and if I fail?"

"Then you will never be allowed to go home and tell anyone what you've learned, and nothing will change for humans either here or on Sanctuary."

Galileo didn't respond. He was silent for a moment, as were the rest of us. We'd never expected to become responsible for the future of humankind on Tawcety. It certainly wasn't the job I'd been hired to do, that's for damn sure.

Yet it didn't appear that we had any choice. Like or not, it was up to us to prove that humans were worthy not only of freedom, but also respect. I looked at Galileo. "I sure hope you're as smart as I think you are," I said.

He said nothing, but I had little doubt that he was thinking much the same thing.

VII

Chen and Sasha left shortly afterwards, giving us a chance to do what we desperately needed to do: rest, bathe, and have something to eat besides raw fish. Our suite had its own bathroom that included a shower stall, another example of human influence on Gruharan culture. I won the straw-vote for who got to use it first, and I think I would have stood under its solar-heated spray for hours if Philip hadn't yelled through the door that I was using up all the hot water.

When I finally got out, I discovered that Chen had returned with gifts: a change of clothes for all four of us and a couple of baskets of food suitable for human consumption: granola, fruit, and fresh-baked bread, the human diet on Gruhar being mainly vegetarian. The clothing was identical to the outfits Chen and Sasha wore, and while none of us were happy about being dressed like palace servants, our own clothes were so filthy and worn-out, they were fit only to be burned. We disposed of the stinking rags and put on the trousers, smocks, and moccasins. One size fit all, and at least they were comfortable.

We didn't leave the suite again until next morning; it was a pleasure to sleep on a bed instead of a straw mat and not to be kept awake by rough seas. Our hosts returned the following morning and together we figured out what we needed to do. Although Galileo was tempted by their offer to show us around, he decided instead to spend the day preparing for the Royal Audience.

"We're only going to get one shot at this," he said. "If we don't get it right, we'll have plenty of time to see the city… we'll be living here for now on."

Pilot elected to stay with him—as his student, she knew that her place was at her teacher's side—and Sasha volunteered to help as well. Philip wanted to stay, too, but Pilot insisted that he go away for a while: too many cooks and all that. So, he joined me on a carriage tour of the city, with Chen as our guide. His wife pushed us out the door with the command not to return until dinnertime, and we set out to explore the city.

Before we left, Chen made sure that Philip and I weren't carrying our swords and that I didn't have my pistol. Bladed weapons were commonplace on Sanctuary, but it was against the law in Ha-Faha for humans to possess arms of any sort. We'd not known this, of course, when we stepped off the boat; luckily, Chen had spirited us away before the Guardians noticed the scabbards on our backs or the gun on my belt. But we couldn't leave the suite with our weapons, so we hid them under our beds.

The palace grounds were being prepared for the festivities. As we walked across the vast courtyard, we observed dozens of palace servants, Cetan and human alike, working side by side: sweeping the cobblestones, draping the walls with symbolic tapestries, unrolling a purple carpet down the marble steps leading up to the veranda where two identical thrones had been placed beneath the awning. On the far side of the courtyard, a long row of tables and benches was being set up; a feast would be served late in the day for those who'd been honored with invitations, with the empress, the princess, and their respective courtiers seated at either end.

This was the one day of the year, Chen explained, when the Gruharan royalty mingled with the commoners. But this year, it would be more than that. Many suspected that this would be the last time the Empress Saikka would be seen in public. She was very old, her health was frail, and it was only a matter of time before Princess Iko was coronated and formally assumed the throne. She'd already assumed most of her mother's duties, although the empress still had the last word.

"I've thought that the Cetans have little to do with their offspring after they're born," Philip said.

"They don't," Chen replied, "but this is one of the few exceptions. Although male children are adopted by other families in the usual fashion, the daughters of empresses have always remained with their mother to assure an unbroken lineage. The Empress Saikka is directly descended from Oushaka, the first empress of her dynasty, who was born over a thousand years ago."

"And Iko's father?" I asked. "Who was he?"

Chen shrugged. "A soldier. An officer in the Royal Army selected on the basis of physical fitness and intelligence. He did his duty and was excused. I don't even remember his name, and Chen and I have been with the princess since the day she was born."

"Doesn't seem fair, knowing that your daughter belongs to the royal family but never again having anything to do with her."

Chen shrugged. "He was given a good meal and bumped up a little in rank. What more can you ask for?"

A gorsch-drawn carriage with the imperial seal on the door was waiting for us at the courtyard gate. We climbed aboard, and after Chen spoke to the Cetan driver—it was amazing to hear a human bark and growl just like one of them—the carriage trundled through the gates and away from the palace.

Outside, more servants were busy preparing the plaza. Wehakawa's statue was being festooned with garlands of fresh-cut flowers, but the two humans by her side were not being adorned. When I pointed this out to Chen, though, he responded in a characteristic Cetan manner by turning his head and pretending not to hear. Yet the message was clear. Humans had been accepted into Gruharan society, but we'd never be their equals.

The carriage left the plaza and joined the vehicle traffic crowding Ha-Faha's streets, and soon Philip and I had other things to see, many amazing.

In the center of one of the wider avenues, long strings of copper wire were suspended horizontally about ten feet above the pavement, where steel rails were imbedded within the pavement. I was still wondering what purpose they served when a bell clanged from just ahead. The carriage driver pulled over to the right, making room for another vehicle to pass: a double-decker streetcar similar to those in Landencyte, yet not drawn by an animal but instead seemingly moving by its own accord, its wheels following the tracks and a metal prong dragging along the overhead wires, sparking and humming faintly as it went along.

"An electric tram." Chen was amused by our astonishment. "It receives current from the wires above. The city has several routes like this, mainly to carry citizens to their workplaces and home again at the end of the day."

All very progressive, but for something I noticed as the tram went by. There were humans aboard, yet they were all crammed together in the back, with some standing in the aisle, although there appeared to be vacant seats up front among the Cetan passengers. Again, Chen didn't respond when I asked about this. Philip and I looked at each other. Here was another sign that, although humans and Cetans coexisted in Ha-Faha, they did not live as equals.

The more Chen showed off the city's wonders, the more Philip and I realized that they weren't shared equitably by both races. There were electric fans in the windows of shops, offices, and cafés, but only those occupied mainly by Cetans; the places where humans worked and dined were not furnished with these inventions, and in the morning warmth they sweltered without them. Clean public restrooms had replaced the foul squatties where Cetans still relieved themselves on Sanctuary, yet Anglis signs next to the door prohibited them from being used by humans; men and women alike were forced to share reeking single-sex outhouses in the alleys between buildings. Chen showed us a factory where generators and engines were manufactured; humans had taught Cetans how to make these things, yet it was primarily humans who labored on the assembly lines, and Chen informed us that they weren't permitted to buy the machines themselves.

Never once did Chen criticize his masters. In public, we were almost always within earshot of Cetans, and everyone knew how sharp their hearing was. After a while, though, I realized what Chen was doing. Instead of *telling* us about the inequality of humans and Cetans in Gruhar, he was *showing* us. Although his people weren't slaves, neither were they free, and they'd remain that way unless things changed. And although humans on Sanctuary enjoyed greater personal liberty, that freedom came at a price: it was limited to the island we'd never be permitted to leave.

Tomorrow would be our best chance for change… and it might be our only chance.

It was getting close to siesta, the midday hour when Cetans and humans alike customarily took time off for lunch and a nap. At least that was the way things were done on Sanctuary; when Philip mentioned this to Chen, he informed us that the tradition was on its way out in Ha-Faha. This was a city too busy to sleep; with the invention of ways of keeping cool during the hottest part of the day, many Cetans and humans no longer felt it necessary to drop everything just to snooze for a while. However, since there was an errand he needed to run down by the harbor, he suggested that Philip and I might have lunch in a waterfront bistro while he did this. He knew of a good place, an eatery where there wasn't a "No Humans" sign outside the door.

The carriage returned to the same gate through which we'd entered Ha-Faha the previous day. Upon passing through the city's massive wall, the carriage made its way along the busy waterfront until it reached an open-air bistro on the wharf. Chen handed us a couple of gold coins to pay for lunch, then the driver shook the reins and the gorsch-carriage pulled away. Chen's business lay elsewhere, at one of the wholesale fishmongers supplying food for the imperial feast. He told us that the driver would come back in an hour or so to pick us up.

The bistro was small but pleasant, about a half-dozen tables scattered around a shaded veranda. No Cetans here, and a glance at the menu board told us why: nearly every item listed was cooked food. I wondered if this was deliberate. The customers all appeared to be longshoremen or sailors; a few glanced at Philip and me as a waiter led us to a table, but without much curiosity. We were dressed the same way as Chen was, so they probably assumed that we were just two more palace servants, humans with a slightly higher station in life but not much.

We inspected the printed menu on the table and ordered food familiar to us—pasta soup, fresh-baked bread, cold tea—then sat back to observe the loud, crowded waterfront. As it so happened, the café was within sight of the quay where the *Titanic* had docked yesterday morning. Our ship was still there, but it didn't look like much was going on aboard save for a couple of dock workers, human and Cetan, making minor repairs to the hull above the waterline. On the other side of the quay, another vessel had just arrived, a twin-masted schooner of the kind that carried passengers instead of freight. They were coming down the gangway; all were Cetans, with not a human among them.

I'd looked away for a moment, distracted by a minor quarrel between two Cetan sailors outside the café, when Philip suddenly grabbed my wrist. "Look!" he whispered urgently. "Over there, coming off the ship... is that who I think it is?"

He didn't point, nor did he need to. Another Cetan had just disembarked from the schooner, this one wearing the dark blue cape of a Guardian. He didn't need the uniform, though. Humans recognize Cetans by the colors and patterns of their fur, each of which is unique to that individual, and I knew that face all too well.

Bart.

My enemy Bart, the Guardian with whom I shared a long-standing grudge. I thought Philip and I had left him behind on Sanctuary. Yet here he was, and all of a sudden, I wished I hadn't left my sword and pistol behind.

"Look away," I muttered. Philip was half out of his chair; I took hold of his elbow and forced him to sit down again. "Don't run, you'll only attract attention to yourself. Just turn around and don't let him see your face."

Philip reluctantly resumed his seat, and we quickly turned our chairs about so that we weren't facing the quay. Fortunately, there were a lot of Cetans and humans between us and Bart. With any luck, the crowd would hide us from sight.

"This can't be a coincidence," Philip said quietly. His face had gone pale.

A chill swept down my spine. No, this wasn't a coincidence. Somehow, Bart had learned where we'd gone. And he'd followed us here.

VIII

Early that evening, I was sitting on the suite's balcony. I'd come out to have a glass of wine and watch night settle on the courtyard. The sun had set some time ago, but just as it was beginning to get too dark to see, I'd witnessed a small miracle: seemingly all by themselves, the lamp posts arranged around the palace grounds gleamed to life, a bright and steady luminescence like none I'd ever seen.

I called for the others and they came out to see. Philip and Pilot were just as nonplussed by this as I was, but Galileo wasn't surprised; he had seen the very same thing the night before, after the rest of us had gone to bed. It wasn't magic; once again, it was a miracle of science. Somewhere inside the palace, he explained, someone had simply thrown a switch, and with no fuss or bother, the lights had come on.

While some technological miracles are welcome, some aren't. After Philip and I spotted Bart, we waited impatiently for Chen to return while making sure that the Guardian didn't spot us. We managed to lie low until we were sure he was gone; about twenty minutes later, Chen returned, and once we located our carriage, we had the driver take us straight back to the palace.

Along the way, Philip and I quietly told Chen that we'd seen and who Bart was. Chen already knew that we'd been pursued by a Guardian while we were still on Sanctuary, and how we'd been rescued by highwaymen when that same Guardian was taking us back to Landencyte. Until then, though, I hadn't told either of them about the longstanding enmity Bart and I shared for each other. His hatred for me was enough to make him cross an ocean to recapture us, of that I had little doubt. It was *how* he got here so soon after we did, not to mention how he'd correctly deduced where we'd gone, that puzzled us.

Galileo figured it out. Once we returned to the palace, we reiterated everything to him, Pilot, and Sasha. Galileo surmised that the only way that Bart could've learned where we'd gone after we disappeared on Sanctuary was if he'd been told by someone who knew all this, and that person could only be Michael Gillespie. Although we'd left him in the custody of the inhabitants of Freeman Cay, it was possible that he might have found a way to free himself and steal a boat to travel back to Sanctuary, where he would've found Bart and told him what he knew.

That was bad news; the Guardians could use that knowledge to raid the island and shut down the covert smuggling operation. But that wasn't the only thing; our mission to Ha-Faha was in jeopardy now that Bart was here.

Galileo had an explanation for how Bart had manage to reach Gruhar so quickly. The same human technology that allowed the Cetans to reinvent electric lights and motor vehicles had also recently given them the ways and means to build faster seagoing vessels. In recent years, a few Gruharan ships had been constructed with internal combustion engines. Cetan vessels equipped with such engines weren't yet efficient enough to do away with sails entirely, and Cetan sailors were prohibited from using them within Sanctuary's coastal waters where they might be spotted by humans, but if one such craft was anchored off Castaway Point or Landencyte to intercept Michael when he returned to Sanctuary, Bart could've commandeered that ship and used it to make the crossing in record time to catch up with the four of us.

The four of us? No, it was *me* whom Bart was after. He probably couldn't care less about Galileo, Philip, or Pilot, and I doubted he gave a gorsch's ass about preventing them from learning why humans on Sanctuary had been denied knowledge of their history. His grudge was personal, against me and me alone.

Nonetheless, Chen wasn't alarmed. "While you're in the palace, you're under the protection of Princess Iko," he said. "The Guardians can't take you into custody unless she says they can. And I promise, the Princess will never turn you over to them."

His assurances mollified the others, but not me. Galileo, Philip, and Pilot didn't know Bart the way I did. The only thing that restrained him in Landencyte was the very same Cetan Law he was sworn to uphold. But those laws were primarily intended for Sanctuary; they had no jurisdiction here in Gruhar. We were no longer in a place where humans were the majority. We were now in a world we'd never made, at the mercy of inhabitants who'd shown our people mercy yet nonetheless feared us.

All these thoughts went through my mind after the others went back inside and I sat alone out on the balcony again. Chen and Sasha had left our quarters a short time ago; I'd seen them cross the courtyard to the palace. Over dinner, we'd discussed our options. Chen had persuaded us that he and his wife should visit Princess Iko at once and let her know about Guardian Bart. If she heard about this from two palace tutors whom she'd trusted her entire life, the princess would be better prepared to defend us, particularly if Bart demanded that we be arrested and turned over to him.

It might work. Maybe.

The tolling of the bell above the palace gate heralded an arriving visitor. I watched as the enormous doors were pulled open across the courtyard and a gorsch-drawn carriage with the imperial seal came through. Preparations for tomorrow's festivities had been completed late that afternoon, so the courtyard was deserted save for the sentries patrolling the palace grounds.

As I watched, the carriage moved across the courtyard to the palace, where it came to a halt before the marble steps leading up to the veranda. The footman, a human dressed in palace livery, came over to open the door and put a stepladder in place, but someone inside the tonneau impatiently slammed the door open just as he got there. Startled, the footman hastily dropped the stepladder in place under the door and stepped back, bowing to the Guardian who stepped out.

As I expected, it was Bart. It simply had to be him, the one person in the world who wanted me dead.

Ignoring the footman, Bart started toward the palace steps. Then, all at once, he stopped. The Guardian was far enough away that I couldn't see his snout wrinkle the way Cetans do when they catch a whiff of a familiar body odor; when I'd spotted him earlier, there was a steady salt wind coming off the ocean to keep him from picking up my scent and Philip's he hadn't detected us. But the clean, gentle breeze drifting across the palace that evening was traveling in the right direction, and this time I was upwind of him.

He caught my scent.

I sat still, not daring to move, but it was too late for that. His head slowly turned toward me, his eyes catching the lamplight and reflecting it with a malicious amber hue. Although we were far apart, our eyes locked and held.

For nearly a full minute, Bart and I silently regarded one another, a conversation that was without words but profound nonetheless. Then he abruptly turned away. His stride was unhurried as his booted feet carried him up the marble steps. He marched past the two empty thrones on the veranda and through the palace's front door, patiently held open for him by another palace servant, a Cetan who shrank away as Bart marched past him; I didn't need to hear him growl to know that Bart had just muttered something hostile. Bart's hatred for me was extended to all humans as contempt for our face.

It wasn't until Bart vanished through the palace doors that I realized I'd been holding my breath the entire time. It came out of me as a sudden rush of expelled air, and it was only then that I felt the hammering of my heart, the trembling of my hands.

My enemy was here, and he'd come to take my life.

IX

A light rain fell overnight, rinsing the courtyard and adding freshness to the dawn. By late morning the sky was deep blue and cloudless, a warm breeze fluttering the pennants atop the palace walls. When I stepped out on the balcony again after breakfast, the courtyard was no longer empty. Ha-Faha's citizens were already arriving, along with outlanders who'd made the pilgrimage from the Gruharan Empire's colonies elsewhere on Tawcety.

Chen told us that we'd be the first humans to attend the Royal Audience as Citizens of the Empire… or would be, if the Empress accepted and approved our petition. Chen, Galileo, and Pilot had decided amongst themselves that our goal should be just that: full Citizenship for the human inhabitants of Sanctuary, Gruhar, and any other places in the empire where our kind might live on the planet the Cetans called Bak-ka, with all privileges and rights that come with it. We'd been on Tawcety long enough: the time had come for its inhabitants to stop treating us as invaders or uninvited guests and give us our freedom.

I read the open letter Galileo, Pilot, and Chen had written. Six pages of calm and well-reasoned argument, nothing incendiary or defiant, but rather a polite yet firm statement of principles. A manifesto, Galileo called it; I'd never heard that word before, and he had to define it for me.

I gave it my blessings, but I didn't tell them what I was thinking. I didn't think it had a crawp's chance in hell. The Cetans had held us in captivity for so long that no one remembered a time when we were free, not even we ourselves. Princess Iko might be on our side, but so far as we knew, she was the only member of the imperial government who was. Not even Chen or Sasha knew how the Empress Saikka stood on this issue; she seldom spoke to anyone but her daughter anymore. Sasha suspected that she might even have become senile, or at least on the verge of dementia.

But I kept my opinion to myself. No sense in expressing my doubts about the efficacy of what the others planned to do. I could only hope that, after I became a permanent resident of Ha-Faha—it went without saying that I'd never see Sanctuary again—I'd find a job that didn't require heavy lifting. I wasn't getting any younger, and it was unlikely that the Cetans had much use for a dick like me.

Sasha presented us with a fresh change of clothes, and Chen insisted that we all bathe again even if we didn't feel like we needed it. With so many Cetans present, we couldn't afford to let body odor make a bad impression. On the other hand, the only traveler from Sanctuary who'd present himself to the empress and princess during the Royal Audience would be Galileo; Sasha would be there as well to act as his interpreter. No more than two Citizens were ever allowed to petition the royals at a time, and since Sasha was a woman and this was a female-dominant society, her voice ought to be the one heard by those who didn't understand Anglis, even though we'd been assured that the empress and princess had both been educated in our language.

As honored guests of Princess Iko, Galileo and Sasha would be seated on the veranda along with the princess—again, something that had never been done before—while Philip, Pilot, and I would watch from our balcony, with Chen as our translator. He firmly told us to sit still and keep our mouths shut. All eyes would be on us even if we weren't on stage, and because we were from Sanctuary, many Cetans believed that we were barbarians whose ancestors enslaved a primitive people much like their own. We needed to avoid saying or doing anything that might reinforce that misunderstanding.

"Whatever you do," Chen told Philip, Pilot, and me as we stepped out onto the balcony together, "don't applaud by clapping your hands—"

"Yeah, we know," I said. "The Cetans interpret that as an invitation for sex." Everyone on Sanctuary was taught this at an early age. The Cetans didn't take seriously anyone who forgot this—our respective races had never found anything sexually attractive about each other, except for the occasional pervert—but they seemed to think it was the funniest thing when they saw a human clapping their hands for one of their kind.

"Good," he said, "and don't try howling like them either."

I wasn't about to do that either, so I tuned out the rest of what he was telling us. By then, we'd come to realize, because we weren't born and raised in Ha-Faha, Chen and Sasha tended to believe that we knew nothing about Cetans. They also seemed to think that Cetans were superior in every way to humans. I wasn't inclined to argue with them, so let that pass. One day, though, if our efforts today were successful and humans were allowed to travel freely, I'd have to bring Chen and Sasha to Landencyte. I'd love to see them in a society where humans weren't second-class non-citizens.

By late morning, the courtyard was completely full. It appeared as if the entire city had turned out for this; there was no more room in the courtyard, and even more were out in the plaza beyond the palace walls, waiting and hoping to be allowed in if someone left. Thousands were there, maybe even as many as ten thousand. Everyone had come dressed in costumes of endless variety: puffy, loose-fitting pants, togas, hoop skirts, long capes and hoods, top hats with towering crowns, sashes, kerchiefs, robes, on and on, in so many colors that it almost hurt the eyes to look about.

A cacophony of barking, growling, snuffling, whining, and howling voices made it seem as if the whole palace courtyard was on the verge of rioting, even though every ear was perked up in a happy, fun-loving way. Chen offered us wax earplugs, along with the warning that things would get even louder with this many Cetans crammed together. Pilot wore hers but Philip and I did not. We both knew that we needed to be on our toes, and that included hearing everything that was said even if we couldn't understand most of it.

And one more thing. After Galileo and Sasha left, while Chen was occupied elsewhere, Philip and I took our swords out of hiding and put them where we could get them in a hurry, against the wall behind the balcony drapes. I also loaded my pistol and placed it in the drawer of an end table near the door, along with my powder bag, wadding, and ammo balls.

We hoped our precautions were unnecessary. But we weren't taking any chances.

The four of us had been seated for a while on the balcony when a Cetan in an iridescent robe marched out onto the veranda. Chen had just identified him as the master of ceremonies when he raised an instrument that looked like a trumpet and let forth with a loud, discordant bleat that echoed off the courtyard walls. At once, every Cetan rocked back their heads and, as one, howled at the tops of their lungs, so loud that Philip, Pilot, and I covered our ears. As they did, a Cetan musician in the twenty-piece orchestra set up in front of the veranda swung a mallet against an enormous brass gong. Its reverberations rippled across the crowd, and once again everyone who wasn't a human responded with a great, harmonious howl.

As this happened, a pair of smoke-pots on either end of the veranda exploded. A thick, reddish-brown cloud filled the stage, a dense veil that hid the twin thrones from sight. There was movement within the cloud, though, and when it finally dissipated, it left behind two figures standing side-by-side before the thrones: Empress Saikka and Princess Iko. Chen silently gestured for Pilot, Philip, and me to stand up. As we rose, the Empress slowly raised her left hand, palm out, and barked something. Everyone responded the same way, and the Empress acknowledged them with a stiff bow, before allowing two courtiers to come forward and gently lower her into her seat.

As we watched, the Cetans started forming orderly rows that stretched across the vast courtyard. For a race that seemed to thrive on chaos, this was something of a miracle; I wouldn't have believed that they were capable of doing so if I hadn't seen it with my own eyes. And they managed to do this in near silence; the only sound we heard from the balcony was the shuffling of their feet and the occasional subdued growl.

I started to say something about that, but Chen hastily reached over to put a hand across my mouth. He shook his head, his unspoken message clear: *shut up, don't talk.* Apparently it was a sacrilege to speak during this part of the ceremonies. I nodded quietly and he withdrew his hand.

Within minutes, everyone in the courtyard had lined up so precisely that you could see the diagonal lines they formed from one row to the next. They left one space vacant, a semi-circular spot directly in front the place of the veranda where the royals were seated.

While this was going on, servants quickly carried more chairs out onto the veranda, and soon the empress and the princess were joined by the royal court and their invited guests. Galileo and Sasha came out last; in silence, they walked out together to sit behind Princess Iko. Although silence reigned, every eye turned toward them.

When we'd come out on the balcony, Chen had handed me a small brass spy-glass. I extended its barrel and held it to my eye. Through its polished lenses, I could see the empress and princess more clearly. Even among their own kind, Saikka and Iko stood out. While most Cetans have whorls, streaks, and irregular blotches in their fur that distinguish them from one another, both mother and daughter were solid black, with just the faintest dark-brown highlights in their ruff and crests. The fur of the empress's face had become white with age, though, and her eyes were dull and unfocused. When she opened her mouth to yawn, I noticed that her teeth were yellow and snaggled, with one fang missing. Cetans live to a ripe old age if nothing kills them or they don't come down with one disease or another; making a guess, I figured that the Empress Saikka was around 150 years old, perhaps even more.

The multitude in the courtyard stood quietly at attention, hands at their sides, eyes straight ahead. The silence was broken by the percussionist once again swinging his mallet against the gong. On that signal, everyone bowed. Chen did, too, and Philip, Pilot, and I did so as well.

And then the orchestra commenced to play and the Royal Dance began.

Until then, I wouldn't have thought that anyone could dance to Cetan music, not even Cetans. To human ears, it's harsh and discordant, with stringed instruments, drums, and horns fighting for dominance within a rhythmless structure that seems chaotic and random. At the very least, it's the noisiest and most obnoxious music in the universe, and nearly impossible for humans to listen to without clamping their hands over their ears. I started to, but Chen quickly shook his head. Not wanting to offend anyone, I folded my hands in my lap; from the corner of my eye, I saw Philip and Pilot do the same. Only Chen wasn't wincing. In fact, he actually seemed to enjoy it. Me, I didn't know which was going to go first: my hearing or my sanity.

But in the next instant, I forgot about the cacophony, because before our eyes something both amazing and beautiful happened: every Cetan in the courtyard began to dance.

In perfect unison, as if they'd spent their entire lives practicing for this moment, their bodies swung into choreographed action. Arms outstretched until their fingertips were nearly touching their neighbors', they took three steps to the right, then stopped, twirled clockwise until their backs were turned to the veranda. Then it was three steps to the left, twirl counter-clockwise, and three steps to the right again.

They repeated this twice, then things started getting fancy. They pirouetted, they crouched low and stretched their arms high, they leaped and landed, they windmilled their arms and hands and high-kicked their legs and feet. Every move they made as individuals was repeated by everyone around them. Watching closely, I perceived how this was done: everyone kept a sharp eye on the person directly in front of them, and copied what they did when they did it, with the dancers in the first row, all of whom were female, leading everyone behind them. Simple to describe, but much harder to do; these people must have spent months in practice and reheasal.

As they danced, something else was going on. From the first row behind the vacant semi-circle, individual Cetans stepped forward, by themselves or in pairs, into the circle. Each wore a white headband and sash inscribed with Cetan characters. Once in the semi-circle, they paused briefly to respectfully bow to the empress and princess, then commenced to perform a brief dance different from the one being done by their fellow Citizens around them. Each solo performance lasted no more than a minute or so and was unique, or at least an attempt at uniqueness; few succeeded, but even the failures were spectacular.

Apparently we were allowed to speak again, because Chen leaned over to Philip and me and spoke in a whisper. "The ones who are dancing in the Circle of Honor are petitioners who'll be addressing the empress and the princess during the Royal Audience," he said, his voice all but drowned out by the blaring orchestra. "They make up their dances themselves or hire a choreographer to do it for them if they're wealthy. It's hoped that Saikka and Iko will be pleased enough by their performance to grant their wishes, whatever they may be."

Philip and I glanced at each other in alarm. We hadn't heard about this until just then. I was about to ask why we hadn't been told when Pilot turned to us. "Sorry, forgot to mention it to you," she said softly. "We were informed that Princess Iko agreed to let us forgo that requirement. She's aware that their people simply dance better than us, and she didn't want Galileo and Sasha to embarrass themselves before the empress."

Philip sighed in relief. I could've slapped her for scaring me like that. If we'd come all this way just to fail because... I didn't want to think about it. I looked over at the empress and the princess. Perhaps this was custom, but Saikka seemed unmoved by the performances in her honor. Slumped in her oversized chair, gazing straight ahead with heavy-lidded eyes, she looked like what she was, a monarch who'd seen this countless times and expected nothing new or different. By contrast, Iko was paying close attention to each petitioner, sitting up straight with her ears cocked forward.

The Royal Dance lasted for another half-hour or so, long enough for every petitioner to get their chance to perform their obligatory solo. Finally, it came to an end. Tired and footsore, some panting heavily, the Cetans collectively twirled to a halt. Princess Iko gave everyone a few moments to catch their breath, then she stood up, threw back her head, and let go with a long, high-pitched howl that Chen told us signaled her satisfaction. Every Cetan in the palace courtyard answered her by doing the same, except for Empress Saikka, who continued to gaze at nothing in particular, eyes dull and ears limp.

"Doesn't look like the Empress is very much impressed," I murmured.

Chen responded with a tight, worried frown. "The Royal Audience is next," he said after a moment. "Princess Iko has already granted Galileo permission to speak first."

"I hope—" Pilot began, then stopped herself. It was obvious what she'd been about to say, though, and I was glad she didn't say it out loud. I'm not superstitious, but all the same, this was a bad time to jinx things by talking out your luck.

Iko turned to the Cetan master of ceremonies and said something to him. He responded by stepping forward to produce a scroll from within his cape. Unrolling it, he read aloud from it in a stentorian, barking voice that carried across the courtyard.

"He is proclaiming this to be the first day of Springmonth," Chen said softly, translating for our benefit. "In celebration of the change of season, the Empress Saikka and the Princess Iko have graciously extended an invitation to the Citizens of the Empire to come forth and make personal requests of the throne, without fear of persecution or reprisal for anything they may have to say."

The MC paused to allow for brief, high-pitched yips and howls, the Cetan version of applause, to pass through the courtyard. Then he spoke again, this time directing his remarks to Galileo and Sasha. "He's introducing your teacher and my wife to the royal court," Chen said.

"Okay," I murmured, "here we go." From the corner of my eye, I saw Philip reach over to take Pilot's hand. Neither of them had anything to add. We all knew what the stakes were.

Galileo rose and walked forward, Sasha a step behind him. Stopping before the thrones, they turned first toward the courtyard and bowed to the Cetans gathered there, many of whom were growling at the appearance of two humans on this stage. Chen had already explained that, although this wasn't the first time humans had been allowed to address the empress during Royal Audience, the last time had been so long ago, no one remembered who had spoken or what had been said. Probably one of the *Santos-Dumont* survivors, and if that were so, we could only hope that Galileo was more persuasive than they'd been.

Galileo and Sasha turned toward the thrones and bowed again, a little longer this time. Then Galileo opened the scroll in his hands. Unrolling it a few inches at a time, he began to read aloud the speech he, Pilot, and Sasha had worked so long and hard to write. Because he was speaking in Anglis, he took it slow, pausing after each line to give Sasha a chance to translate his words.

They'd rehearsed the night before, doing final revisions as they went along, so the rest of us already knew what he was going to say. I won't bore you by quoting him verbatim. Essentially, it was a plea for the rights granted to the Cetan Citizens of the Gruharan Empire to be extended to its human Citizens as well. Specifically, the right of humans to travel freely, the right to the same treatment and standing enjoyed by other Citizens, and the right to learn and preserve our history and bring an end to centuries of enforced ignorance.

Galileo told the empress and the princess—indeed, every Cetan in the courtyard—that they had nothing to fear from humans. Our ancestors had never intended to conquer Bakkah (he was careful to use the Cetan name) and vanquish its people. He reminded them that it was only by accident that humans had been shipwrecked on this world in the first place. Despite their misfortunes, though, they and their descendants had sought nothing more than to live in peace. On Sanctuary, they'd become fishermen and craftsmen, exporting food and materials to Gruhar. Here in Ha-Faha, they'd become household servants, artisans, and teachers, the last most important of all because they'd taught the Cetans the secrets of science and technology that otherwise they might have never learned for themselves. The original *Santos-Dumont* survivors had even helped the Gruharan Empire defeat its enemies once and for all, and then aided in the rebuilding of Ha-Faha once the war was over.

By Cetan reckoning it had been nearly eight centuries since humans had come to this world. Almost eight hundred times our people watched the cycle of the seasons, which we now knew to be so much more rapid here than on Earth. The people of Bakkah had been generous and kind to our people, Galileo said, but the time had come for us to ask for more: our freedom. So it was with humility and gratitude that we'd come from Sanctuary to petition their highnesses for that which the Cetans took for granted. We were Citizens, too. All we wanted was to be treated as such.

Great words, great thoughts. Yet as Galileo spoke and Sasha translated, I watched the empress and the princess. What I saw didn't give me much confidence. Although Iko paid close attention, leaning forward a little with her ears fully erect and tilted in his direction, Saikka seemed to be barely listening at all. Her ears lay flat against her head and her eyes seemed to gaze past Galileo and Sasha. She looked as if she was about to doze off right then and there; her eyes closed for a few seconds and didn't open again until Iko reached over to prod her awake.

I didn't ask Philip, Pilot, and Chen if they'd noticed the same thing. I didn't have to; the grim expressions on their faces told me that they had. Princess Iko was on our side, yes, but it was Empress Saikka who'd have the final word, and it appeared that a heartfelt plea for freedom and equality was doing nothing more than boring her to death.

Galileo finally finished. Again, he bowed before the empress and the princess. No howls of approval this time; the courtyard was dead silent. Galileo stood in silence, head bowed, Sasha quietly waiting for either Saikka or Iko to say something.

"So what comes now?" Philip whispered to Chen.

"At this point, we wait for—"

A sudden, angry bark interrupted him. It came from the other side of the courtyard, loud enough to be heard by everyone on the veranda. "I was afraid of this," Chen said, worry in his voice. "After a petition is made by a Citizen, a moment is given to allow another Citizen to voice opposition, or issue a formal challenge, if they so desire."

I couldn't see who'd called out, but I had a bad feeling that I knew who it was.

The master of ceremonies turned to look expectantly at Princess Iko. She growled something in response, and the MC turned in the direction from which the protest had come and silently gestured for the individual who'd made it to come closer.

"Sounds like someone out there has something to say," Pilot said softly.

"Yeah," I replied, "and I think I know who."

A familiar figure detached itself from the crowd to march into the circle used by the solo dancers. Bart was wearing his full uniform today, but the cape couldn't conceal the worka sheathed behind his back.

Standing before the thrones, he bowed respectfully to Saikka and Iko, then pointed to Galileo and began to growl and bark as loudly as he could. I didn't have to know the Cetan language to pick up the anger in his voice. Chen's translation was almost unnecessary, but he told us what Bart was saying anyway.

"He says that Galileo is a liar and a criminal who travels with other liars and criminals," Chen murmured. "He says that we broke Cetan Law to come here by using proscribed technology, that the four of you belong to a criminal conspiracy to undermine Gruharan authority on Mahha, and that one of you is known to be a violent offender."

"I think that means you," Philip whispered. Like I needed to be reminded.

More barking, this time even more agitated. Chen listened, and as he did, his face paled. "I was afraid of this," he said after a moment. "He's requesting that the matter be settled here and now in the Cetan fashion: single combat, what we'd call a duel."

And then Bart did just what I figured he was about to do. Turning toward the balcony where he knew I would be, he raised a hand and pointed straight at me.

X

A few minutes later, I was standing in the courtyard, saber in hand and surrounded by Cetans, all of whom seemed to be barking and growling at once. No one was dancing anymore. Everyone was here to see a fight.

I had no choice. If I'd tried to make a run for it, I would have been stopped by the Guardians who'd been sent to the suite to collect me. In this culture, there was no backing down from a duel; once challenged, you had to accept, or else the person who'd issued the challenge had the right to hunt you down and kill you, no questions asked. But even if I'd been able to decline, I wouldn't have done so.

My feud with Bart had festered long enough. Now the stakes had become unimaginably high. Time to settle things with him, once and for all.

On the other side of the semi-circle used only minutes ago for dancing, Bart stood but a few feet away, worka drawn and ready to spill blood, mouth pulled back in an ugly grimace. He'd removed everything from the waist up and now wore only his loincloth, in keeping with Cetan dueling custom to fight with the bare minimum of clothing. I was allowed only my trousers; I could wear nothing that might conceal a short sword or dagger, not even my boots.

Behind me were my companions, along with Chen and Sasha. Chen was by my side; as well as acting as my translator, he was quickly and quietly informing me of the rules. I'd been called out before, but the Cetans have rules and customs for dueling that are different from those of humans. Galileo and Philip were grim, while Pilot was pale with terror; when she'd briefly hugged and kissed me for good luck, I'd felt her trembling. She didn't say so loud, but I could tell she wasn't expecting me to survive. I almost liked her then.

Once we were ready, Princess Iko stood up and walked to the edge of the veranda, leaving Empress Saikka silently watching from her throne. She was no longer looking bored. A hush fell across the courtyard as Iko raised a hand for silence, then she turned and spoke to us. Chen listened until she was quiet, but before he could translate what she'd said, Bart growled something to her. I didn't know what he said, but it didn't sound good.

Yet he hadn't finished before Iko cut him off. She responded with a few curt, growled words of her own. Bart's ears fell flat, and I thought for a second that he was going to disagree, but instead he lowered his head for a few seconds, the Cetan sign of agreement under protest.

"What's going on?" I whispered to Chen.

"Princess Iko has set the rules for the engagement," he said quietly. "You two will fight until one of you is too wounded to carry on or has had enough, at which point that person will signal surrender by dropping his sword and raising his hands. Once that happens, his opponent will be declared the winner and the Empress will grant his request... or at least agree to take it under advisement."

"Sounds reasonable. So what's Bart upset about?"

"He wants this to be a duel to the death, with no allowance for surrender. She told him that your offense, even if true, doesn't warrant this." Chen hesitated. "But don't let your guard down," he added. "He may still try to kill you and accept the consequences later."

Not much comfort there. I glanced at the others. They were tense and silent, anxious to see what was going to happen next. Philip gave me a thumbs-up; he'd offered to be my stand-in, which Chen had told me was allowed, but I don't let others do my fighting for me, particularly not my clients. I nodded back to them, then gave Bart my full and undivided attention.

"All right," I said, "let's get on with this."

Chen said something to the princess in her language, formally bowed to her and the empress, then stepped away from me. Now it was just Bart and me. A few short barks from the closest bystanders that I took to mean *Get him, dude! Kick his ass!*, but otherwise an expectant silence prevailed.

Then the master of ceremonies raised his mallet and struck the big ceremonial gong, and even before it echoed off the courtyard walls, Bart came at me.

If I'd thought that he'd circle me warily the way a human would, patiently waiting for me to make a mistake, then he might have taken me by surprise. But he wasn't the first Cetan I'd fought, and I knew that wasn't their way. Bart lunged at me hard and fast, and I had just enough time to parry with my sword while sidestepping to the right. Our metal clashed, an angry sound all but drowned out by the roar of the crowd around us, and the fight was on.

Humans and Cetans seldom dueled, mainly because Cetan Law made few allowances for our people to use single combat to settle their differences with this way. A common mistake humans have often made fighting Cetans is believing our taller height and higher strength gives us an inherent advantage. They do not. Cetans are ferocious and determined, and a Cetan well-trained in sword arts is more than an even match for a human. And whoever trained Bart had taught him well.

I don't know how long we fought. Time lost meaning. Again and again, he came at me, thrusting and slashing, forcing me to either parry and riposte or dodge and lunge a half-second later. I wasn't always on the defensive; whenever possible, I came at him just as hard as he came at me. But he was fast, very fast; he knew when to get out of my way and when to counter-attack, and it was all I could do just to anticipate his next move, or at least try to.

Once his worka came close enough for its wicked blade to draw blood, a shallow cut on the right side of my rib cage when I didn't parry fast enough. I responded by trying for his sword arm, hoping I'd wound him sufficiently to make him switch hands, always a disadvantage. I missed, but he didn't get away in time to keep me from nicking his left ear, severing its tip. Snarling at me, he fell back, clapping his free hand against his mutilated ear. He barked at me; I had no idea what he said to me, but it was probably obscene. Despite myself, I smiled. No matter how this came out, he'd be reminded of this fight for the rest of his life, every time he saw his reflection in a mirror.

I was getting tired, though, and so was he. Although our wounds were minor, we were both losing blood, and that would sap our strength. My body was slick with sweat. Bart was panting hard. I had no idea how much longer I could keep this up, and no doubt the same thought was crossing his mind. So we circled each other warily, keeping to the outer edges of the circle, trying to ignore the Cetans around us, barking like mad and barely being kept back by the Guardians. Philip, Pilot, and Galileo were shouting words of encouragement, but I was barely aware of them. All that mattered were Bart's eyes, narrow and mean, and the cunning way he studied me.

If I were you, I thought, *I'd change my strategy.* And that's what he did, all right… just not the way I expected.

When he came at me again, it was with a broadside swing from the right. Easy to dodge, the kind of careless move a novice would make. I thought that perhaps he'd simply committed a mistake, but when I tried to attack, I missed him by less than an inch and he barely got out of my way. I tried again and this time he parried and riposted, but not quite fast enough; he should have been able to stick his blade through my ribs, yet all he managed to do was give my elbow a little scratch.

What was going on here? He was exhausted and so was I, but I wasn't getting sloppy the way he was. Maybe he was feinting, pretending to make minor errors in order to seed overconfidence in me so that I'd do something stupid like rush him, thus giving him a moment of opportunity to end the fight quickly and decisively. But that was a trick that every experienced swordsman knew, human or Cetan; Bart would know that I'd never fall for such an old gag, which can also backfire and open yourself to counterattack.

Not once had he spoken to me since I'd come down from the balcony, yet there was a certain look in his eye. Bart was taunting me, playing with me, but to what end? What was he trying to accomplish? If he was trying to entice me into attacking and even defeating him, then what was the purpose of…?

Suddenly, I *knew*.

And I stopped fighting.

XI

Stepping back, I retreated out of reach of Bart's sword. Then I let my arms fall to my sides while being careful not to drop my sword. Never once, though, did I take my gaze from him. My eyes were locked on his, and although the Cetans around us continued to roar, I refused to let myself be distracted by their blood lust.

"I'm not fighting you anymore, Guardian," I said, forcing calm into my tone of voice. The perplexed look on Bart's face told me that my words had been lost in the uproar; I repeated what I'd said, more loudly this time. "I'm done fighting you. This fight is over."

His eyes widened. "You s-s-s-sure-r-r-render?"

"No." I shook my head. "I'm not surrendering. I just refuse to fight you anymore."

From the corner of my eye, I could see Galileo, Pilot, and Philip staring at me as if I'd lost my mind. Galileo and Philip were astonished, but Pilot was furious. "You idiot!" she screamed. "Get in there and kill him!"

So much for the idea that humans were more civilized than Cetans. But maybe that was the point.

"Figh'!" Bart snapped, his muzzle pulling back from his teeth again. He took a step closer, raising his sword.

"No." I remained motionless, sword still in hand. Until I deliberately dropped it on the ground between us, I wasn't surrendering. But I didn't lift it either, which would have signaled my intent to return to combat. Those were the rules of engagement.

"*F-f-f-figh'!*" Bart wasn't playing with me anymore. His eyes were black, narrow holes and his ears were pulled back against his skull, the one I'd nicked dripping blood upon his cheek and neck.

"*No!*" I yelled back at him, staring him straight in the eye. "I'm not fighting any longer! This duel is—!"

Snarling, Bart hurled himself at me. His worka came up, then swept down toward my head. It took all my willpower to keep from raising my sword to parry the blow. Instead, I closed my eyes and waited for death.

It didn't come. I waited and waited, and the seconds that passed seemed much longer. Something cool and smooth lightly touched the left side of his neck. I opened my eyes to see what it was: the leading edge of Bart's worka, hovering less than a half-inch from the place where he would've decapitated me if he hadn't stopped himself.

I looked past the blade. Bart stood only a couple of feet away, so close that I could smell on his breath the fish he'd had for breakfast. Yet his eyes no longer squinted with anger but were wide with astonishment.

"Why won' you—?" he started to say.

"*S'op!*"

The voice belonged to Princess Iko. Unnoticed by either Bart or me, she'd risen from her throne and walked to the edge of the veranda. It was the first time she'd spoken Anglis since the festival had begun.

"S'op figh'ing now-w-w!" she shouted, arms above her head. "Drop your-r-r sw-words!" Her voice was very low, almost stentorian; it must have carried, because all other sound in the courtyard suddenly ceased.

Bart stepped back, reluctantly tossing his worka on the ground between us. I held out my hand, opened my fingers, and let my rapier fall beside it. The clatter our weapons made when they hit the pavement was the only sound in the courtyard. The Cetans had stopped yelling, and when I looked around, I saw that every eye was upon the Princess, Bart, and me.

"W-w-why you no' figh'?" Princess Iko asked, looking at me. "He w-w-will k-k-kill you if he can."

"I know," I said, "and I could kill him if *I* wanted to. But I don't and I won't, because that won't settle the differences between Cetans and humans. It'll only make them worse."

As I spoke, Sasha quietly walked up the veranda steps. She approached the Empress Haikka, bowed, then began translating what I'd said. Seeing what his wife was doing, Chen turned to the crowd around us and also began translating my words. It was a little hard to make myself understood over the sound of two humans barking in the Cetan tongue, but I was glad they were doing this; what I was saying needed to be heard by everyone.

"What Galileo said is true." I was addressing the princess, but I meant for my words to be understood by every Cetan within earshot; I had to assume that those who had human servants would understand at least a little of what I said. "It was never the intent of my people to conquer your people or do harm to them in any way. Yes, my friends and I broke the law in many ways to get here, but it was necessary, for there was no other way to discover for us whether more our kind lived elsewhere on Bakkah than Mahha." I was careful to use the Cetan names for Tawcety and Sanctuary.

"W-w-why w-w-won' you figh' me?" Bart had calmed down, but he still wanted to know the answer to that question.

"If I defeat you," I said, turning away from the Princess to speak to him, "then it would prove that my people are capable of harming your people. That's not why we came here. All we want is for our people on Mahha and in Gruhar to be reunited and live in peace with your kind. Our ancestors never meant for us to do anything else, and your people have nothing to fear from us."

Bart listened quietly to what I had to say. When I was done, he nodded, then turned to Princess Iko again. A deep, respectful bow, and then he spoke to her in the Cetan tongue. I glanced at Chen, expecting a translation, but he shook his head. For some reason, he felt it was more important just then to listen rather than speak.

When Bart was finished, he bowed again, first to the Princess and then —much to my surprise—to me. He bent down, picked up his sword, and walked away, leaving me alone in the circle.

The duel was over. What next?

Princess Iko thoughtfully regarded me for a moment, then turned about and walked back across the veranda. She stopped before her mother and, in a subdued voice, spoke to her for a couple of minutes. Saikka listened quietly, and when her daughter was done, she gazed contemplatively at the pennants fluttering in the breeze atop the courtyard walls.

Something was going through her mind; I knew not what. Nor did anyone else, although an expectant hush had fallen across the palace grounds. The Cetans knew that their empress was about to speak; breathlessly, they awaited her words.

Finally, the Empress Saikka rose to her feet. With the assistance of her courtiers, she unsteadily walked to the edge of the veranda, where she stopped to look down at the small band of humans gathered before her.

She raised her hand, pointed to us, and said, "Y-y-ou... fr-r-r-ee."

And in that instant, centuries of isolation for those on Sanctuary and servitude for those in Gruhar came to an end. At long last, the humans of Tawcety were liberated.

XII

Four days later, I was back at the waterfront. This time, I was there to board a passenger schooner bound for Sanctuary.

I no longer wore the livery of a palace servant, but instead a new outfit—tunic, leggings, boots, cape, and wide-brimmed hat—made specially for me by the best human tailor in Ha-Faha. My sword and pistol were on my belt again, and in my cape pocket was a gorsch-skin purse stuffed with Cetan gold: payment for services rendered, presented to me by the Princess Iko just before I boarded the carriage that brought me here.

I was going home, but I wasn't traveling alone, and neither was I leaving Gruhar with the same people who'd been with me when I sailed here. Chen and Sasha were coming with me, while Philip and Pilot were staying behind. And there would be one more, whom we were waiting to join us.

"I know the princess has insisted on paying you," Philip said, "but Pilot and I were the ones who hired you, so it's only fair that I do so as well." Reaching into a trouser pocket, he pulled out a folded sheet of paper. "A promissory note, drawn on my bank account," he said, handing it to me. "It's not a cheque—sorry, I didn't think to bring my book with me—but any senior official there will recognize my signature and honor it just as if it was."

I unfolded the note and glanced at the amount. It was for nearly as much gold as the princess had given me. I wasn't going home a rich man, but neither would I have to lurk in the shadows spying on cheating spouses, or at least not for a while.

"Thank you." I folded the note again and tucked it in my pocket next to the purse, then extended my hand. "And thanks for standing with me when I needed it. You can watch my back any time."

Philip bowed and we shook on it. He was no longer my client, but I'd always consider him my friend. Pilot said nothing, but instead offered a tentative nod and a smile. We'd never be friends, and I think she still disliked me as much as I disliked her, but Philip was her husband so… well, if we ever saw each other again, we'd just have to be cordial.

Chen and Sasha were there, too. Their bags had already been loaded aboard the schooner along with mine. Just as Philip and Pilot were remaining in Ha-Faha to act as emissaries from Sanctuary, Chen and Sasha were making the journey to Sanctuary to be Princess Iko's emissaries—her human emissaries, that is—from Gruhar. Empress Saikka's proclamation had caught everyone by surprise, her own court most of all. Although the humans on Tawcety were now free by imperial decree, everyone knew that the transition would be long and not without trouble. Nothing changes overnight, particularly not when it comes to cultural adaptation.

But change was coming all the same. Soon, we'd all be living in a different world.

I stepped aside to let both couples say farewell to one another. In the short time that they'd been together, they'd become close. Soon, they'd be sharing the responsibilities that come with being envoys. Just as Philip and Pilot would continue to live in the palace, Chen and Sasha would be guests of House Greer. It was an exchange that both hoped would work out. They were still doing the handshake and hug thing when another carriage came rolling down the quay. The remaining passenger who'd be accompanying us to Sanctuary had just arrived.

Bart stepped down from the carriage without looking at any of us. He carried only a small bag, and still wore the uniform of a Guardian, the hilt of his sheathed worka visible behind his back. His left ear was still bandaged, and when he caught sight of me both ears flattened in anger. But he walked over to us, and everyone went quiet.

"S-s-so… w-w-we're all r-r-ready?" His voice was a quiet growl, and he avoided looking at me.

"Ready when you are," I said. "Waiting for you."

Bart grunted and started to walk past us. Then he seemed to think better of it and stopped to turn to me again. "W-w-wan' 'o s-s-speak w-w-wi' you."

Obviously, whatever he wished to say, he wished to say to me alone. A brief nod to the others, then I let Bart lead me away. We stepped around a stack of barrels that the longshoremen were preparing to load aboard our ship.

I knew it wasn't going to be an apology, and for once I was right about him. But what he did say surprised me anyway.

"W-w-we're no' enemies-s-s," he said quietly, keeping his voice down so as not to be overheard by the Cetans working around us.

"No," I said. "We're not enemies anymore." I didn't have to explain myself, and neither did he. We'd worked out our differences in the palace courtyard. Once you've spilled the other guy's blood, there's not a lot else you can do short of taking his life. Bart apparently didn't want to do that anymore, nor did I.

Another grunt. "And we'r-r-re no' fr-r-riends-s-s."

"No, we're not friends either." I paused, then added something I never thought I'd say to him. "But that doesn't mean we can *never* be friends. We can be, if we work at it."

His right ear lifted; the left one tried to, but he winced a little when it twitched within its bandage. Bart looked straight at me then, his eyes searching mine. Then his hand raised, palm open and claws retracted, and after I got over a moment of surprise, I clasped it in a handshake, a human gesture few Cetans ever bothered to learn.

There were no more words between us, or at least not then. Yet as we turned to walk back to join the others, I knew that my former enemy and I would have a lot to talk about on the long journey back to Sanctuary.

Change was coming. And change is good.

Epilogue

From the Memoirs of Jeremy Crowe

It's been ten years since the events of the narrative I've just told, which is to say about three years by Earth's calendar, if you're someone from humankind's home world who happens to be reading this. Galileo tells me that may be possible one day, if he and other members of the Landencyte Institute for Science and Invention are ever successful in their efforts to reinvent radio and manage to build one powerful enough to transmit a message across space. Even if they are, they believe it may take more than ten years (by Earth reckoning) for such a signal to get there.

I'm not holding my breath. Instead, I've written a book. Words on paper last longer than words spoken aloud, and this time, no one will hide them away in a locked safe.

Because I was involved in the affairs that led to the Great Awakening, the Landencyte Historical Society asked me to write an account of what happened. I'm not a historian, though, so three previous attempts to write this book as a definitive account ended in frustration, not to mention countless wads of half-finished paper, before Philip made an excellent suggestion: write this work as if it was a novel, a work of fiction. I still don't think I'm much of a writer, but since Sasha has volunteered to be my editor and unsigned collaborator, I'll have someone to come along behind me and turn this into a narrative that, hopefully, will not bore the socks off anyone reading it. So if you've reached the end of the book and haven't tossed it on a woodpile, you have Philip and Sasha to thank for this.

To describe in detail everything that occurred after Chen, Sasha, Bart, and I left Gruhar to sail back to Sanctuary would take another book, and I'm not interested in writing a sequel (unless someone pays me well). But you may want to know, so in brief:

Things changed. As I said before, it didn't happen overnight, nor did it come easily, but nothing was the same afterwards. For the inhabitants of Sanctuary, both human and Cetan, even daily life was altered, sometimes in very dramatic ways. For humans, it began with the revelation that they were not alone on Tawcety and that they had distant cousins on the other side of the hemisphere, descendants of another starship that came to Tau Ceti-e by non-magical means. For Cetans, this meant that their collective role as sentinels was coming to an end and they were no longer expected to enforce Cetan Law. But if anyone believed this would result in vengeful humans descending upon Cetan captors with swords and daggers—Bart was afraid this might happen, and he wasn't alone—then they were wrong.

Our two peoples had lived together in peace for so long, no one had ever really thought of themselves as oppressors or the oppressed. Even the average Guardian was no more disliked or disrespected by civilians than the average badge. Little changed in that regard except that the old, Cetan-imposed laws meant to suppress human technological development while protecting superstition and so-called magicians fell by the wayside, just as humans were now allowed to learn the true story of their origins, beginning with the Rot and the subsequent destruction of the *Lindbergh* and the *Santos-Dumont*.

Some people still practice magic, of course, or at least try to. Old ways die hard, especially since science takes an effort to learn while magic promises easy short-cuts. But there aren't as many mages as there used to be—I spotted Magus Woodstock just the other day; he has a new occupation as a bricklayer, and seems to be good at it, too—and when someone comes to me to ask if I'll investigate something having to do with spells or spirits, I tell them to go read a book.

To be sure, many Cetans were perturbed by the changes that came as a result of Empress Saikka's proclamation of freedom for humans. For the citizens of Ha-Faha in particular, it meant the elimination of a social class that they'd come to depend upon for hard labor and menial tasks. Some even tried to claim that the empress had become so senile that she had no idea what she was doing when she'd surprised everyone during the Royal Audience by issuing what came to be known as the Liberty Proclamation. Yet they were still arguing about this when the old empress passed away, peacefully in her sleep, and her daughter ascended to the throne. As her first official act following her coronation, the Empress Iko affirmed the Liberty Proclamation and even added to it such items as making it legal for generators and engines to be sold to and operated by humans. Within a few weeks, the first shop in Landencyte to legally sell vegetable oil-powered machinery was opened. The name above the door is Galileo's Machines, but my friend doesn't run the place himself; he's still working as a tutor, mainly because he sees teaching as a sacred task that he'll never give up. Good for him.

We now have electricity in Landencyte, with lights that come to life with the flick of a switch and street cars that are quickly replacing gorsch-drawn carriages. We even have electric fans for those day in Springmonth and Summermonth when the heat is miserable. The Squat is still the same, though, and probably forever will be. For some reason, I take comfort in that. Eventually this part of the city may come to resemble the Heights, but I rather hope not. Let the Stewards have their manors and the walls that surround them. I like it down here and never want to move up there.

As for me: yes, I'm still a dick, and always will be. I still shadow husbands who fool around with women they didn't marry, and track down kids who ran away from home and didn't come back, and locate deadbeats who ran up a line of credit and made lame excuses for not paying. And every so often, I have to draw my sword, if only to teach some fool a lesson in manners.

Someone is coming up to my office. I know this because the loose riser on the stairs has just creaked, telling me that they're on the way.

One story ends and another one begins.

So be it.

The End

Acknowledgments

A number of people helped bring this novel to reality, no small feat considering that the author was dancing on the thin edge every step of the way. They are:

My former agent, Martha Millard at Sterling Lord Literistic, who pressed me to write again even though I didn't feel like I was ready to tackle another novel, and my new agent, Eleanor Wood at the Spectrum Literary Agency, who unhesitatingly took me on as a client when Martha decided to retire. And finally, my friend and publisher Ian Randal Strock, who said yes when just about everyone said no; ageism has become a problem in publishing, and it's only because guys like Ian are in business that older writers like myself are still able to publish the books we've written.

Jonathan Strahan, who commissioned the prologue as a stand-alone short story for an anthology he was editing, then took it to Tor.com when the anthology fell through, and Sheila Williams at *Asimov's Science Fiction*, who published the subsequent chapters as a series of novellas.

Rob Caswell and Steve Berg for feedback on the story and plot, Les Johnson and my nephew Nicholas Steele for information about alternatives to plastic, James Benford for reading the manuscript and checking my science (if there are any mistakes, they're my fault, not his) and my dogs Jack and Iko for insights on canine behavior (yes, that's them in this book, somewhat evolved).

And, as always, my wife Linda, who took care of me when I doubted whether I'd live to see this through. This book was written under very trying circumstances, and she made it possible for me to write these words. Really.

—Whately, Massachusetts

CPSIA information can be obtained
at www.ICGtesting.com
Printed in the USA
LVHW110815121022
730513LV00001B/82